FISTS OF JUSTICE

HEROES AND VILLAINS

by Zachary Coleman

Published by Portobello Studios
www.portobello-studios.co.uk
ZacColeman@Portobello-Studios.co.uk
E-book published via Amazon Kindle
Printed by Book Empire
www.bookempire.co.uk
Unit 7, Lotherton Way, Garforth, Leeds, LS25 2JY
Printed in Great Britain

Although every precaution has been taken in the
preparation of this book, the publisher and author
assume no responsibility for errors or omissions.
Neither is any liability assumed for damages
resulting from the use of information contained
herein.

THIS BOOK IS DEDICATED TO ALL THE VICTIMS WHO HAVE LOST THEIR LIVES BECAUSE OF THE VILLAINS OF THIS WORLD, AND TO ALL THE HEROES WHO STAND UP TO STOP SUCH INJUSTICES FROM HAPPENING AGAIN.

CONTENT WARNING

Although this is a fantasy book in the superhero genre, it deals with real-world themes. As a result, some of the content may be upsetting to some readers.
This book contains references to sexual assault, racism, islamaphobia, homophobia, transphobia, and the murder of innocent people of colour by the police. It is my belief that this book should not be read by anyone below the age of 15. Proceed with caution if you are sensitive to any of these topics.

Special thanks to:

Spencer Anderson

&

Peter Hamilton

Thanks also to Kate Arnold, Rob Cotterill, Tim McDonald, Joe Betteridge, Jack Segal, Tom Westbury, Sajjaad Gareeboo

Contents

INTRODUCTION

We live in a world of normalcy and mediocrity, when compared with the vast possibilities of the human imagination. And yet we are surrounded constantly by stories of heroes fighting evil: people with great powers, defending us from otherworldly threats. Superheroes. And each time it seems we become obsessed with where these people got their powers and how they were forged into the heroes they became: just a normal scientist caught up in a terrible accident, or an average school kid struck by lightning. And yet, ultimately, what is really important is not where they got their powers, but the content of their character: *why* they choose to do what they do. Our world, the real world, is full of heroes too. Not people with great power but people with great *resolve*: people who risk life and limb to do the right thing, even when the rest of their society is against them. In the stories and the legends, in the movies and in the comics, often there is a very clear line between good and evil, and we know that we should be rooting for the hero to beat the villain. Yet in the real world we don't just blur the line, we abandon it completely, and what might seem right to some becomes fundamentally wrong to others. Those who some see as victims, others see as villains. One man's terrorist is another man's freedom fighter. And sometimes, when we're lining up to watch the next superhero team-up movie, or sitting in a cafe or a pub debating which stories were good and which were bad, maybe we should also take a moment to consider who are the heroes in our world, and who are the villains.

***

In another world, the same as ours in almost every way, where superheroes and supervillains were, as of yet, fiction, a single rubber boat filled with refugees attempted to cross the channel between France and England. Overhead, a furious storm whipped the boat this way and that, churning the sea into a raging torrent. The men and women struggled to stay on board, silently praying that their perilous journey would soon come to an end.

In the middle of the crowded boat, a nineteen-year-old woman, still seen as a girl to most, hugged her knees tightly to her chest, her eyes fixed on the coastline, just out of reach. Zakirah had been travelling for months. Each time she found a place to settle, she was quickly displaced and forced to move on. But ahead, Great Britain, a place she had only heard about in stories, a place so beloved by its people that they travelled the world telling all they met how **great** their home was. Surely, a place with such a name must be a paradise, with refuge for all, with the space and resources to keep her and those around her safe? This thought was all that had kept her going, and now she was so close.

Thunder roared. Lightning flashed. The boat was thrown sideways, and several people were sent tumbling into the water. The remainder cried out, a few reaching to try and pull them back into the boat, but they were snatched up by the winds and thrown further away. Another toss of the waves and another man fell off the back, crying out as he plunged into the icy depths.

Zakirah's eyes widened with horror as she reached her hand towards her uncle, who scrambled towards the edge of the boat to grab hold of the man. Too late, and now he too was thrown overboard. His hand grabbed a rope dangling from the rubber boat, and for a moment he was able to stay there, dragged behind the boat as it was thrown about like a ragdoll. But only for a moment, then he was gone.

Zakirah clenched her eyes shut and hugged her knees tight, praying to whatever god may be out there that when she opened them again, she'd be safe, and warm, and alive.

But the wind still snatched at her, the rain still pelted down from above, and when Zakirah opened her eyes, she was alone. The boat was empty, and every other passenger had been thrown into the water. Zakirah cried out, rushing to the side of the boat, her eyes searching the waves for even just one of her fellow refugees.

Gone.

A giant wave snatched the boat up and for a split second, she was airborne… But then, as fast as the boat had gone up, it came crashing down, and Zakirah was thrown from the craft, plunging beneath the waves.

Everything went quiet. All that Zakirah could see were grey blurs. Her arms flailed, grappling for anything to hold onto. For a moment, she was thrown above the waves again, and she tried to snatch a breath of air, but instead got only water. Spluttering, she was dragged beneath again, the boat just out of reach.

Zakirah prayed again, wishing with all her might that she might be granted one glimmer of hope, one moment of respite from the torment the sea was inflicting upon her.

Then, a miracle. For just a moment, the water parted, and a bubble of calm formed around Zakirah, where the waves could not touch her, and she had a moment to think, and to breathe. If anyone had been around to see it, they would have seen a young woman in the middle of a storm in the sea, floating several feet above the water, bathed in light. And though Zakirah would not remember that moment, it was what saved her life.

And the moment ended, and Zakirah was provided one glimmer of hope, as her hands wrapped around one of the ropes dangling from the boat. She clasped it tightly, wrapping it around her arm, and pulled…

The rest was a blur. Zakirah did not remember the storm passing. She did not remember scrambling onto the upturned boat. But she did remember the speedboat that rushed out from shore, and the kindly face of the bearded Asian man who smiled down at her as she was pulled from the water.

"You're safe now." the man said. "We've got you. We'll take care of you."

And Zakirah was carried inside, shivering and weak.

And everything sunk into darkness.

CHAPTER ONE: ORIGINS

The National Science and Engineering Convention was a big deal for any young scientist or inventor across the UK, or indeed across the world. The competition drew funding from eight major corporations and from the government, and offered fully funded scholarships at a PhD level to young people between the ages of eighteen and thirty. The event drew in an audience of several hundred scientific researchers, business owners and professors, all looking for new ideas, inspiration, and often even new hires, and that was just the core of the audience: many more people from the scientific community came just to watch and learn. The competition was judged by some brilliant minds: previous years had been judged by the likes of Stephen Hawking, Tim Berners-Lee, Brian Cox and many more. Winning the competition could set you up for a life of success. The three judges sat at the front of a great hall, staring with blank, emotionless faces at the stage as they waited for the first young mind to come and attempt to dazzle them. Over half the seats laid out behind were filled by people in suits, chattering quietly in small groups. Outside, in the foyer, various companies had stands advertising their products: everything from the newest breakthroughs in medical technology, to new mobile phones and smart devices, pieces of useful tech, and so many other interesting inventions. Representatives from all the big companies, from Apple to Tesla, were among them, and some from smaller companies that were making waves in the world of tech, like Bionic Ltd. Backstage, a small cluster of young people paced nervously as they awaited their turn to present their invention, and be told whether it was the next big breakthrough, or just junk.

In the corner, a twenty-two year old man with shaggy black hair sat in a wheelchair, fidgeting and staring at the floor. He was dressed a lot less smartly than the others, with a wrinkled shirt buttoned most of the way up, creases in his trousers, and his hair flopping awkwardly over his pale, white face. Next to him, in complete contrast, a smartly dressed black woman named Iona, approximately the same age, in a dress-suit and blazer, placed a hand on the disabled lad's shoulder. Her suit was neatly pressed, every wrinkle ironed out of her shirt. Her black hair flopped down over her face, but not in a tangled mess like the man in the wheelchair, but instead in loose curls. She smiled down comfortingly, the warmth in her eyes seemingly amplified by her glasses.

The man in the wheelchair fiddled with a giant pair of metal gauntlets that sat in his lap. The gauntlets had wires sticking out of them, and lights shining out of the fingertips. They looked like they had been torn off a futuristic space suit, or stolen from the set of a sci-fi film.

"You've got this, man. Trust me, your invention is good." Iona said, her tone soft.

"Good." the man in the wheelchair replied. "Sure, but not g-great. They're l-looking for b-b-b." He sighed as he stumbled over his words, taking a moment to compose himself. "They're looking for the k-k-kinds of breakthroughs that everyone will be t-talking about. Like yours."

"Look, my work is fantastic, **if** it works. And that's a big if. But you have a genuine, proven invention. It works. You know it works. You can prove it works. Just believe in yourself, Jason. Once we get through this, you have all summer to relax before you start your Masters... Your sister is coming to watch, right?"

"She should be." Jason replied, fiddling with the joystick that controlled his wheelchair. "I haven't h-h-heard from her since last night. Sh-she was out drinking with her uni friends."

"I'm sure she'll be here."

The first speaker was called to the stage: a young designer who had built a new weapon for law enforcement agents across the country. As the inventor began to talk, the other young creators stood back stage, flicking through their notes.

"You're up next, Jason." Iona said.

As she touched him on the shoulder to comfort him again, Jason's phone rang. He pulled it out, his hands trembling as he answered.

"Sarah?" he said, putting the phone to his ear.

"*Jason! This is Claire, Sarah's flatmate. We're at the police station. How quick can you get here?*"

"The police station?" Jason frowned. "What's going on? Is Sarah okay?"

"*She's not hurt, but she's not okay. She's shaken up, I'll explain everything when you get here.*"

"Ok. I'll b-b-b-be there soon." Jason said.

He hung up and swivelled around to Iona.

"M-m-my sister's at the p-police station." he stammered.

"What?" Iona frowned. "What happened?"

"I don't know. I need to get there now."

"Can't it wait?" Iona said, indicating to the stage. "You won't get another chance at this until next year, and they won't look fondly on an application from someone who bailed the previous year."

Jason fixed Iona with an intense stare.

"Nothing is more important than my sister." he said.

Iona needed no more convincing than that. They turned and headed out the back exit, as the first speaker left the stage.

"Now, please welcome to the stage: Mr Jason Fox, an engineer and bright young mind, and his friend, Dr Iona Page."

The crowd began to applaud, but it was in vain. Jason and Iona were already gone.

Jason and his sister Sarah had a troubled upbringing. To say they had lost their parents wouldn't be accurate: they never really had parents. Biologically, they had a mother and a father, of course. But parents in the sense of carers, not so much. They were deadbeats: an abusive mother and an absentee father. Jason had not had to endure much of their mother's abuse, but his older sister had. For six years she tolerated the constant abuse and neglect, until Jason came into the picture. Sarah had never felt such a strong bond before in her life, and suddenly there was this little baby who she cared for more than she cared about her own life. So she did the only thing a six-year-old could do in that situation: she told. Child services swept in and quickly took the two of them away, and they were placed in foster care.

Their foster-parents did their best, but abuse can change children all too easily. Sarah was distrustful and disobedient. Jason grew up completely antisocial, uncommunicative and socially awkward. He was non-verbal for a long time, and when he finally did talk, he had an awful stammer. Jason's diagnoses could fill a small book: along with the spina bifida he was born with, which had led to asthma, developed from his poor physical fitness, he was left with a host of psychological differences and disorders: social anxiety, autism, attachment disorder, and opposition to all authority figures (a condition labelled ODD, or oppositional defiant disorder). But he was smart, and Sarah had dedicated most of her teenage years to pushing him to succeed: even when she dropped out of school, she pushed him to keep working hard. Sarah was the only person that Jason had ever listened to, until he met Iona. Somehow, she could press all the right buttons in the same way Sarah did, to motivate and inspire him.

Sarah was twenty-eight this year, and last year, having seen Jason succeed at getting a placement at university, achieve his degree, and offers for a Masters degree, Sarah had finally begun to focus on herself, applying to go to university to study psychology. Sarah meant the world to Jason: the thought that something could have happened to her now that she was finally living her life tore a hole in his heart.

As Jason wheeled in through the doors of the police station, a short, twenty-year-old woman ran up to him. She was wearing trainers and a jacket, but underneath it looked like she hadn't changed out of the sparkly dress she had worn clubbing the night before, and her messy hair and tired expression told Jason she hadn't slept.

"Jason, you're here!" she exclaimed, leaning down to hug Jason. Jason awkwardly wrapped a hand around her for a moment, then pulled away.

"Claire, are you okay?" Jason asked, a look of concern shadowing his face.

"I'm fine, it's Sarah." Claire replied, her tone hushed. "Jason…

She was assaulted last night. Some guy from our uni… We were all drunk, I didn't see what happened. No one did. She's in there with the police now but she can barely get a word out. Rachel and I found her in the toilet."

"Take me to her." Jason said.

"You've got to sign in at the front desk." She indicated to the reception area behind them, where a friendly woman sat, watching them.

Jason wheeled over and impatiently scrawled his name into the visitor book, and Claire led him past the desks of police officers and community support officers, along with the odd office clerk, all typing at computers or filing paperwork. Mostly they didn't pay Jason any heed. At the back, an office with a big glass window filled the back wall. Through the window, Jason could see the back of his sister's head, and across the table a sympathetic officer in full uniform sat: mid-thirties, with ginger hair, slim build, average height. The officer stood and went to the door as she saw Jason approaching.

"You must be Jason." she said, extending a hand. "I'm Officer Parker, but you can call me Sabrina. We're trying to get a statement from your sister, but she's struggling to talk, we were hoping that maybe you could talk to her?"

Jason nodded, ignoring the extended hand and wheeling straight past the officer. Sarah was staring at her lap, lines of mascara dried onto her cheeks. She had her leather jacket wrapped tightly around her, one hand gripping the jacket, the other scratching repetitively at her upper arm.

"Sarah!" Jason exclaimed. She didn't react.

"**Are you okay?**" he signed, his hands motioning the words in British Sign Language, which he and Sarah had learned when he was a child and still non-verbal. "**What happened?**"

No response.

"**Please talk to me. Then we can get out of here, we can do whatever you want. Get milkshakes. Watch TV. Not talk for the rest of the day. You just need to tell them what happened.**"

Sarah looked up at her brother, her lip quivering.

"We went clubbing." she began to silently sign, slowly at first. **"Just a few people from uni. I was trying to get out more. Meet new people. I only knew Claire and Dan, from my course. The rest were new people. There was this guy. He seemed nice. He wanted to buy me drinks. I never turn down free drinks, you know?"**

"Did he… hurt you?" Jason signed.

Sarah shook her head.

"He kept trying it on, I wasn't feeling okay. Dan told him to take a hike. Claire, her friend Rachel, her boyfriend Mark, and Dan, all agreed to go back to the uni halls with us. We had some drinks in the kitchen, we played board games until everyone passed out. Except me and Dan. Then he…"

Sarah stopped.

"Go on." Jason signed. **"What did he do?"**

"He tried to kiss me, but I said I wasn't feeling well. I went to the toilet to throw up, and I passed out. I woke up to Dan asking if I was okay, saying he should get me to bed. He helped me get to bed, but then he didn't leave. He tried to kiss me again. I could barely speak. I could barely think."

Sarah stopped signing, the tears now rolling down her face again. Jason felt the hole in his heart tear even wider, and rage began to boil his blood. He turned and beckoned Officer Parker back in, and relayed to her everything that Sarah had said.

"Okay." Officer Parker replied. "Obviously this is a difficult experience, and I'm really sorry you had to go through this." She addressed Sarah directly, her tone soft and warm. "We have some services that help victims such as yourself. We will be calling your classmate, Dan, into the station to answer some questions, and we have the statements from your friends. Unfortunately, I feel like I have to warn you, in cases such as this, with no witnesses, when there is alcohol involved, it's very unlikely that we'll be able to make an arrest."

"You're kidding me?!" Jason blurted out. "My sister has b-been assaulted! You're telling me you're not going to arrest the g-guy who did it?"

"I'm telling you that we'll do our best, but we cannot arrest

13

someone without evidence of a crime."

"You've g-g-got the evidence, she's told you what h-happened!" Jason snapped back, his face growing red with anger.

"And it's her word against his, unfortunately." the officer replied, her tone still soft. "I understand that this is a difficult situation, but we'll do the best that we can, and in the meantime, I highly recommend that your sister checks out this support group."

She slid a leaflet across the table to Sarah.

"Ridiculous." Jason scoffed. "Honestly."

Iona gave Sarah and Jason a lift back to Jason's place, where Jason escorted his sister inside. Jason lived in a bedsit connected to an incredibly old pub and hotel, in a room so small even the hotel workers rejected it, but he found he had little need for space. What would have put anyone else off, worked to his advantage: from his bed, he could reach the lightswitch and the desk, and if he sat up he could reach the kitchen counter and the cupboards. He was only two steps away from what was essentially a closet, in which could be found a toilet and shower. He had very little in the way of physical possessions. His books and all his work were on his laptop, but he did have a small bookcase filled with comic books.

"I'm sorry, sis." he said. "The system always fails us. Our p-parents failed us. I guess the only ones we can t-trust are each other. What do you want? Want to watch TV? Want to have a d-d-drink?"

"TV. Ice cream. Blanket." she signed.

"Okay." he replied.

He awkwardly maneuvered his wheelchair around the tiny bedsit, setting up his laptop so they could watch TV, and reaching into the tiny freezer for a tub of chocolate ice cream. He then pulled himself awkwardly from his wheelchair, plopping himself down on the bed next to his sister, pulling out his blanket to wrap around her, and the two settled in silently, spending the next few hours letting ice cream melt in their mouths while they watched TV and forgot about the world.

But Jason didn't forget about the world.

He sat and brooded.

And when Sarah fell asleep, he found himself on his phone, scrolling through the social media page for Daniel McDonald, staring at his smug face, that anger bubbling inside his veins yet again.

It was one thing in particular that set everything into motion for Jason.

Dan was out again tonight. He'd posted pictures just ten minutes ago at a bar, just five minute's walk from Jason's bedsit…

If asked, Jason wouldn't have known what possessed him to do this, but for some reason he slipped on the gauntlets he had been waiting to present to the panel at the competition and snuck out of the bedsit, rolling down the street in his electric wheelchair, heading towards the sports bar where Dan and his friends were drinking.

And he waited outside for what must have been at least an hour.

And finally, Dan and his friends stumbled out of the pub. Jason followed at a distance as the group of drunk lads wandered home, boisterously laughing to one another as one after the other split off to their different houses, flats and student halls… Until it was just Dan, heading to his apartment building.

Jason accelerated as Dan headed for the entrance, but he couldn't quite catch him before he reached the door.

"Hey!" Jason called out, his voice shaking as he did so.

"HEY!"

Dan stopped, and Jason's heartbeat quickened.

"Who are you?" Dan frowned, his eyes settling on Jason. "Can I help you?"

Jason lifted himself from his wheelchair, his legs wobbling and he stepped towards Dan, fists clenched within the gauntlets.

"You assaulted my sister." Jason said, through gritted teeth. "B-big mistake."

"I don't know who you think you are, but you better back off." Dan said, pointing a finger at Jason. "I don't want to hit a disabled guy."

Jason let out a growl and took a swing for Dan, who easily dodged the punch, and Jason was sent sprawling across the ground, pain shooting through his back.

Dan loomed over Jason, and Jason instinctively raised his hands above his head, unclenching his fist and sprawling out his fingers.

Light.

A beam of bright light shot from the palm of his gauntlet, striking Dan directly in the face, dazzling him, as his eyes had become accustomed to the darkness of night. Dan let out a cry, stumbling backwards, momentarily blinded. Thinking fast, Jason moved his hands again, giving the gauntlets their second command. He held one hand, outstretched, towards Dan, and a sudden pulse of energy burst from the gauntlets, knocking Dan off-balance and causing him to stumble and fall backwards.

The gauntlets fizzed and sparked, and Jason felt the circuits rapidly heating. He looked down at his hands just in time to see the gauntlets catch fire. With a yelp, he pulled them off, ripping off his jacket and throwing it on them to suffocate the flames.

"What happened?" Dan moaned, rolling over on the sidewalk. "What the hell just happened?"

Sirens blared behind him, and the sound of a police car pulling up on the curb stopped Jason in his tracks.

"Crap." he groaned, grabbing the bundled up, broken gauntlets and tossing them in the storage space beneath his wheelchair.

***

Zakirah awoke to whiteness surrounding her. She was lying in a bed covered in plain, white sheets, with white paint flaking off the walls, a white cabinet in the corner, even a white bedside table.

At the end of the bed, a pale, mixed-raced man with light brown skin dressed in a smart shirt, with glasses sliding down his nose, was organising a first aid kit.

Zakirah groaned, her entire body aching, and the man's head snapped towards her, and he pushed his glasses up his nose and gave her a smile.

16

"Imam, our patient is awake!" he called out, and the door swung open.

The man on the other side looked familiar: he bore a resemblance to the man who had rescued Zakirah from the storm, but there were some differences. His beard was longer, his nose shorter, his eyes perhaps a different shade, and his face more worn with wrinkles. He was dressed in a thobe, with a white skullcap placed on the top of his head.

"Hello, it is good to see you awake and well." the man said, approaching Zakirah.

Behind him, a middle-aged woman hovered in the doorway, her hijab emphasising her kindly face, her awkward smile, and her sensitive eyes.

"Do you speak English?" the man asked, and Zakirah nodded, sitting herself up in the bed.

"What is your name?" he asked.

"Zakirah." The word was croaky, her voice hoarse.

"My name is Asim Abad, I am the leader of the local mosque." the man continued. "This is my wife, Saabira. My brother, Hammad, brought you here after he found you in the channel. He works with a Refugee Action charity, and when he saw the state you were in, he brought you here to recover."

"Where am I?" Zakirah asked.

"You are in Downtown City, the capital." the imam replied.

"England?" Zakirah asked, her heart racing. Had she made it?

"Indeed." Asim smiled.

"Did any others make it?"

The imam's face dropped, and he shook his head solemnly.

"I am afraid you are the only one that my brother found." he said.

"It's a miracle that you even survived." the pale man with the first aid kit spoke up. "In the mosque, they're calling you the Miracle Girl."

"This is Dr Ian Arbour." Asim said, indicating to the man. "He's the one who has been looking after you."

"Or, trying." Dr Arbour said, adjusting his glasses again. "I was convinced we would lose you to hypothermia. But it seems Allah has different plans for you."

"Do you believe in Allah, Zakirah?" Asim asked, his smile still

17

warm but his eyes staring pointedly.

"It is hard to believe in anything when you have been through what I have been through." Zakirah replied.

"Well, let's see if we can't restore your faith in the world." Asim said, his kindly words washing over her like warm water. "Are you hungry?"

"Starving." Zakirah admitted. She couldn't remember being this hungry in a long time, but she felt a pit in her stomach that needed filling.

"My love, get our guest something to eat and drink."

The woman in the doorway nodded silently and disappeared into the hallway, in search of food and drink. Zakirah slumped back onto the pillow, exhausted, her mind cast back to all the people who had been with her when they had started their journey.

And now it was just her.

But she made it. And now she didn't know how to feel.

CHAPTER TWO: SOCIAL JUSTICE

"Leave me alone, Alex!"

The evening had settled in, and just a few streets away, a couple fought through the window of an apartment building. A man clad in military cargo trousers and jacket coloured with green and brown camouflage and carrying a plain green duffel bag stood in the streets, staring up at a second storey window, where another man was leaning out over the street and shouting down. Both men must have been in their mid-twenties, but there was a significant contrast between them: the one in the street was tall and pale, with his fair hair cropped so short he might have appeared bald from a distance, with less than a millimeter left on his head, and thick arms and a broad torso, like an action man doll brought to life. He wore a stern look on his face, like he was trying his hardest not to display any signs of emotion, frozen to the spot. In contrast, the other man was short and slender, mixed race, with long, dark hair, and a pierced lip and nose, his clothes alternative and colourful, straight out of a thrift shop, his face streaked with tears as he hurled abuse down at the man in the street. It was fiery passion versus icy silence.

"You can't just turn up here after everything!" the man in the window screamed down, his voice very well-spoken, but trembling with each word. "Just go away! You're a jerk, I don't want you here!"

"Babe, please, I can't hear you properly! Just let me in so we can talk, I've had a long day." The man on the street spoke calmly, his voice carrying without the need to yell. His voice betrayed very little trace of emotion, and overall he just seemed tired.

"You're not getting in!" his ex-partner yelled back. "You're out of my life, out of my flat, just… out, Alex!"

"You're being childish, Blake!" Alex let out an infuriated sigh. "Come on, just let me in so we can talk about this properly!"

"GO AWAY!"

"Is there a problem here?"

In all the commotion, Alex had not noticed two police officers come around the corner. One was a short, hairy man in glasses, who barely seemed to be paying attention and was dawdling a couple of paces behind the other. The other officer was a black woman, late twenties, with a tired look that said "I'm done with today."

"No, everything's fine, it's a personal matter." Alex replied, gruffly. "We're fine."

"Well, we've had a few noise complaints, and some of the neighbours are concerned." the officer said. "We are going to have to ask that you please take this inside."

"He's not coming in here!" Blake yelled down from the window.

"Sir, do you live here?" the officer asked Alex.

"Yes." Alex said.

"No!" Blake snapped back.

"I'm in the army, I've just returned from active duty." Alex explained. "I used to be a tenant here."

"This is my apartment, and you're not staying here!" Blake yelled, and with that he slammed the window.

"Blake! BLAKE!" Alex's voice cracked and suddenly his face betrayed him, a flash of anger in his eyes.

"Sir, we're going to have to ask you to calm down." the officer said. "Is there somewhere else you can stay?"

Alex looked from the window, to the officer, scowled, and stormed away without another word.

The night was well underway when Alex found his way to the little mechanics shop a few miles out from the centre of the city. The buff man stood, awkwardly fiddling with his hearing aid, his duffel bag cast over his shoulder. Though his hair, his clothing, even his bag were all that of a soldier, he had the slightest spread of stubble sprouting across his face, as much

20

of a shadow as the hair on his head. He looked tired: not just physically but mentally drained. In his mind, he forced back memories of the torment he had been through in the armed forces, but images and sounds occasionally broke through.

"*FIRE YOUR WEAPON, PRIVATE, THAT'S AN ORDER!*"

Alex winced, forcing up the mental barrier that kept those memories at bay, and wandered into the mechanics shop.

The mechanics was almost completely empty, with the shutters pulled nearly all the way down, but inside a single mechanic could be heard, clattering about with his tools.

"Robby." Alex called out, poking his head under the great garage door. The warmth of the garage hit him, and he stooped to get in, the smell of petrol and sweat suddenly surrounding him.

The mechanic poked his head out from behind a car. He looked to be early-forties, with dark skin and patches of white and grey peppered throughout his hair. When he saw Alex, he let out a sigh.

"You're back." he said. "Well, this is going to be trouble."

"I hoped I might find you here. How's it going?" Alex asked, approaching the mechanic.

"Was going fine until you showed up. Now I'm not so sure." Robby said. "What happened?"

"Discharged. I'll tell you all about it. Look, Blake kicked me out. Can I stay with you?"

Robby let out a hesitant sigh.

"Just for tonight?" he asked.

"Just for tonight, until I find somewhere to stay." Alex said. Robby nodded.

"Fine. You can crash on the sofa." he said. "Head to the off-licence, get some beers, then you can meet me at mine and we'll have a catch-up. But don't let anyone know you're staying with me. I don't want to get on the wrong side of Big Tuna."

"Christ, is that what he's calling himself now?" Alex snorted.

"Don't get cocky, Alex." Robby warned. "Tony's not the same kid you remember. He's gotten a lot more dangerous since you left, and if I recall things didn't work out too well for you last time you clashed."

21

"Well, he's not the only one that's changed." Alex said.
And with that, he turned and wandered out of the workshop.
Though it was summer, it was a British summer, and the
evening chill cut. The city air wasn't exactly much of an
improvement from the musk of the garage, but the 24-hour off-
licence was only round the corner. It was a tiny corner store
which mostly only sold essentials. Behind the counter, a young
Asian woman, maybe nineteen years old, was flicking through
a magazine. Her hair and makeup were done perfectly, with
colourful nails and subtle eyeshadow, her hair neatly tied back
in a ponytail, and though she was dressed casually, she still
looked incredibly neat and presentable, considering she was
working the dead nightshift and unlikely to see many
customers.

"Alright mate." she said as Alex walked in, her eyes barely
flicking up. Then, it was like a switch went on in her head, and
she did a double-take. "Hey, it's you! I thought you'd run off
to join the army!"

"Yea, I did." Alex replied, picking up a small crate of beer and
two family-sized bags of crisps. "I'm back."

"How was it?" she asked, as Alex put the beer and crisps on
the counter.

Alex shrugged.

"A job's a job. There's not much to tell."

The woman seemed disappointed, tutting slightly at the reply.
Alex handed over a twenty pound note and she clicked the till
open.

"Ah well." she said, handing over his change. "See you round,
I guess."

The door swung open as Alex headed for it, and a man barged
in, staring at his phone, almost knocking Alex's crate of beer
out of his hands.

"Watch it." Alex grumbled.

The man looked up, grunting in apology, and Alex slipped
past. As he exited, the newcomer's eyes burned into the back
of his head, and he quickly tapped on the screen of his phone,
dialling and raising it to his ear.

"Blud!" he exclaimed. "Is Big Tuna there? You'll never guess
who I just saw! Alex Axton. Yeah mate, he's back in

22

Downtown. I swear down it was him…. Init!... Yo, we still on for D&D later? I got mad snacks, bruv… Cool. Later."

***

Iona jumped out of her car and rushed into the police station. It was almost completely empty this time, the reception manned by a tired-looking bearded man, and most of the desks empty. Her eyes fell on Jason, who was sitting in the corner, staring at his shoes. Officer Parker stood a few feet away, talking quietly to a disgruntled-looking student. He was maybe six feet tall, average looking, with a mop of brown hair. As Iona entered, the man nodded to Officer Parker and turned to leave. The officer's eyes fell on Iona, and she walked over to her.

"What happened?" Iona asked.

"He was caught trying to start a fight with the guy who his sister said assaulted her." Officer Parker said. "I managed to convince Mr McDonald not to press charges… It didn't take much convincing. He wasn't hurt, he didn't even seem entirely sure what had happened, and I convinced him no one was really going to buy that a man in a wheelchair posed any threat to someone like him. But listen, I can't cover for him if this happens again. Can you have a talk to your friend?"

"Thank you." Iona replied. "Is Jason free to go?"

Officer Parker hesitated, then nodded. Iona indicated to Jason, and he silently followed her out, wheeling after her in his wheelchair. Iona headed straight to the car, opening the passenger-side door and wordlessly helping Jason into the passenger seat, before folding up his wheelchair and putting it in the back. Something crunched in the storage space beneath the seat as the wheelchair folded, and she frowned and poked it, but decided to leave it. She walked round to the driver's side and got in, turning to face her friend.

"What the hell got into you?" she exclaimed. "You should be at home, looking after your sister!"

"The system f-f-f-failed her, I was g-getting justice." Jason replied.

"You were going to get yourself hurt! It's a good thing the police showed up!" Iona snapped back.

Jason snorted.

"Sure, good on them. Always there when you d-d-don't need them, never when you do." he stammered.

"What were you going to do?" Iona asked. "Overpower him with your massive muscles? Come on Jason! Think before you act!"

"Someone had to d-do something, he was going to get away with it!"

"And he still will!" Iona replied. "Look, I'm sorry, I know this is a crappy situation. But there are ways of dealing with these things. There's a system."

"The system sucks." Jason interrupted. "It's broken."

"Well, you're not going to fix it by getting yourself beaten up." Iona replied. "Come on, let's get you back to your sister."

They spent the journey back in silence, and Iona helped Jason inside. Once in, she gave him a quick hug and left, maintaining the silence. Sarah was sitting on the bed, clutching her knees, dressed in one of Jason's t-shirts and his dressing gown.

"Where were you?" she asked, her voice croaky, her throat dry. Jason didn't reply for a moment, then took a breath, wheeling his wheelchair fully into the room.

"I went to confront Dan." he admitted.

"Jason!" Sarah exclaimed, her face as pale as a ghost. "What! Why?"

"I was just so angry!" Jason replied, the feeling of rage still festering inside him as he fidgeted with the joystick on his wheelchair. "I... I... I just... He was g-going to get away with it!"

"Jason, you can't do things like that. I don't know what I'd do if something happened to you!" Sarah said, staring at her brother. Jason forced himself to meet her gaze.

"You've looked after me for so long, I j-just wanted to look after you." he said, beginning to tear up.

Sarah got up and went to hug her brother, planting a soft kiss on the top of his head.

"I've called a friend in Edinburgh." Sarah said. "I'm going to go and stay with her for a bit. I can't stay in this city, it's too painful. But I need to know you're going to be okay while I'm gone."

Jason nodded.

"Focus on your studies, Jason." Sarah said. "Promise me that."

Jason hesitated, then nodded again.

"You can do great things, Jason." she said sitting on the bed again. "But you can't let your emotions control you. Use your head, and you'll be fine. I know you will. You're the smartest person I know. I'm trying my best to move on, you need to do the same… Now come on, come watch trashy TV with me."

Jason smiled an awkward smile, and shifted from his wheelchair onto the bed. For the rest of the night, the two siblings cuddled up under the blanket, watching TV until their eyes got sore and they drifted to sleep.

***

Monday morning. 8AM. Officer Sabrina Parker had been in the police station for an hour already, finishing off paperwork and preparing for the day, and she was sitting in the meeting room with a pen and paper, waiting eagerly for the staff meeting to start. She sat, sipping on her coffee, as the other staff trickled in and took their seats.

Sabrina's sergeant, Sergeant Burns, walked in and took his seat next to her. He was a white man in his mid-forties, who looked like he was probably quite intimidating in his prime, but now his broad shoulders and upright demeanour were discounted by his pot belly and tired expression.

"You know you don't need to attend all of these staff meetings, Constable Parker." he said, with an emphasis on the word 'constable'. "You'll be filled in on any major updates."

"I like to take part, hear it all first hand." Sabrina replied, sipping on her coffee. The sergeant only grunted in response.

A short, round-faced man walked into the room and took his seat at the head of the table.

"Good morning all." he said, and the room of mostly white, middle-aged faces chimed back "morning" in chorus. "I'm Inspector Warren, I'll be chairing this meeting for Superintendent Huntley, who is at a conference. First order on the agenda: We have increasing reports of friction between two rivalling gangs in the inner city area. Sergeant Burns, an update on that situation, please."

The Sergeant sat forward in his chair and cleared his throat.
"My information tells me that the Bridge Boys are back. Their former leader, Ronnie Smith, is still serving out a life sentence in Downtown City Prison, so-"
"Please use the correct terminology, there was a memo about this last month." Inspector Warren interrupted.
"Of course." Sergeant Burns took in a sharp intake of breath. "Downtown City Correctional Facility."
Inspector Warren nodded in approval, and the sergeant continued.
"We aren't sure who is running the gang now. All we've been able to get is the alias 'Big Tuna', which seems to be the street name of their new leader. But we have picked up one or two of the old dealers on minor possession charges, which will hopefully stick. Maybe we'll be able to get one of them to talk. Word on the street is that they seem to be expanding their territory, and we could be looking at a gang war between them and the Bovver Boys, but until we can work out where they are operating from and who is leading them, who this Big Tuna is, we can't do much."
"Okay." Inspector Warren replied. "I'll talk to the Superintendent, and we'll get you some more manpow-" the inspector stopped himself, correcting his own terminology. "Some more officers to aid with your investigations. Have you been coordinating with the drug squad?"
"We've been involved." one of the other men at the table spoke up. "But we could do with a few more detectives. We're stretched thin at the moment, what with running out School Safety programmes, half of our officers are busy giving speeches, and working with teachers across the city."
"Noted." said the inspector. "Let me know if you make any additional progress. Oh, additionally, we've had a call from Interpol about a missing girl: her name is Anna Sarkissan, but she goes by Anna Sanders. She's the daughter of Armenian-American politician Andy Sanders, who was killed last month by a terrorist who goes by the name of Grey Hat. Anna Sanders has gone on the run, but they have reason to believe she might be coming here. They don't know when, but they want us on high alert, looking out for her. She may be

travelling under an alias, so I want you to memorise her face. She's not guilty of anything, but she is in incredible danger and it's vital that she be found." He picked up a headshot from his pile of papers, showing a passport style photo of a young, dark haired girl. " Meeting adjourned."

As the officers filed out and back to their desks, Sabrina turned to her sergeant as he collected his papers.

"Sir, I wondered if I might have more time to work on the Sarah Fox case? I feel like there must be some way to catch the guy."

"Officer Parker, that case is only still open because we legally have to keep it open for the mandated amount of time, as per policy. There is no evidence: leave it until we can legally close it, then send out confirmation that the case has been closed." He collected his papers and stood up, neatening them into one pile by tapping the pile on the desk to straighten them.

"I know, I just feel like we owe it to the victim to try." Sabrina replied.

Sergeant Burns let out a tired sigh.

"Look, I get it. You want to do the right thing, for everyone, but you know how these assault cases go: even when they make it to trial, they usually don't go the victim's way. It's a waste of resources. Anyway, I've got a lot to do. Seems a bunch of civil rights activists have chained themselves up outside parliament in protest against the decision to not allow the recent boatload of refugees to remain in the UK. Everyone's a bit tense, as the media somehow got wind that there was a second boat three days prior that never made it. Tragedy always lights a few sparks with the protest groups. I need to go sort it out, and I need you to go check out the abandoned warehouses on the dockside. We've got reports of squatters there, we need to move them on."

Sabrina nodded reluctantly.

"Whatever you say, sir." she replied.

***

The gentle morning breeze floated by the houses of parliament, carrying the stench of city pollution. Commuters rushed by on their way to work. Businessmen and women in suits sipped on their morning coffee and chattered away with their idle smalltalk. A line of young activists lined up along the gates that stood at the end of the driveway leading up to the houses of parliament, chaining themselves to the railings using bike locks.

At the front, a short woman with braided hair stood with a megaphone. She was curvy, with hair that went down to the small of her back, and dark black skin that matched her dark brown eyes. She wore little to no makeup, and her t-shirt was large and baggy, but her nails were a work of art, each one painted with a slightly different pattern.

"People of Downtown!" she said into the megaphone. "We are here to protest the injustice of the decision our government has made, to not allow innocent people fleeing a war-torn hell that we helped create to take sanctuary behind our borders. The way our country has treated refugees is shameful, and we will not stay silent!"

As she was speaking, a giant of a man, around six feet and seven inches tall rushed over to her, tapping her on the shoulder.

"Rhiannon, babe." he said. "The police are on their way."

"Alright, I'll deal with them." she said, handing him the megaphone. "You keep this going."

The big man took the megaphone and continued to speak, and Rhiannon looked over in the direction he had come from, where a police car had just pulled up, and an old, tired-looking white man stepped out.

"Good morning miss." the officer said. "I'm Sargeant Burns. Mind telling me what you folks are doing here?"

"We are exercising our right to peaceful protest." Rhiannon responded curtly.

"Well, that's all very well and good…" the sergeant responded. "But you can't chain yourself to these gates, cars need to get through here."

"Well, we're not budging until parliament agrees to budge on their position on allowing refugees into our country." Rhiannon said, her words pointed, but calm.

The sergeant sighed.

"Do you really want to go down this road?" he said.

28

"I don't want to do anything." Rhiannon responded. "I want to be at home, in bed. But until the government starts treating people like people, we have a duty to stand up and make a difference. Social justice is all that matters to me, sir. If you want to get in the way of that, then fine, but you're going to have to drag us away."

The police officer stared intently into Rhiannon's eyes, and she stared unwaveringly back. It was clear there was only one way to end this. The sergeant put his hands on his handcuffs. Rhiannon knew where this was going. She had danced this dance before. But if she backed down now, nothing would change.

She looked back at her boyfriend, who stood with the megaphone in his hands, looking nervous. He made eye-contact with her and nodded. Rhiannon turned back to the officer.

"You do what you gotta do."

CHAPTER THREE: BRIGHT SPARKS

Zakirah's legs felt wobbly and uncertain as she stepped down the stairs. Through the hallway she could see Asim with a small group of people, sitting around the coffee table, talking softly. There was an older man with a long beard sitting next to a much younger man in jeans and a neat shirt, with gelled hair and a close shave. Across from them, a woman in her forties sat, her phone in her lap, every so often glancing down to check her texts. Saabira was pouring them all cucumber water from a jug, and she was the first to catch sight of Zakirah at the doorway.

"We have received almost a hundred letters just this week." the younger man said. "Perhaps it's just not worth it."

"These hate letters and threats are exactly why it is worth it." Asim replied. "We need a new place of worship. After our last mosque was burned down, we have been forced to meet in public halls and theatres, even in the park. We can't let them intimidate us like this, we have every right to have a place to worship."

"The community centre is just as adequate a place as any." the woman suggested. "I'm sure people won't mind."

"But it's the principle of the thing." Asim argued.

"I am beginning to think the fire was not an accident, Asim." one of the older men said. "Someone is targeting our community. The new mosque will become a target."

Saabira tapped Asim on the shoulder and pointed at Zakirah, and Asim stood up and walked over to the doorway.

"It is good to see you up and about." he said. "Do you need something?"

"Is this the Miracle Girl you have told us so much about?" the older man asked. "Mashallah."

Mashallah. An expression of joy and thankfulness. Zakirah shifted uncomfortably. She didn't feel her situation was one to be joyful or thankful over. She had lost her uncle, she had no family left, and she had nearly been killed just trying to find refuge. She turned her attention to Asim.

"Thank you so much for your care." Zakirah said, speaking slowly as she stumbled over the language that was not her native tongue. "My strength is returning, though I feel hungrier than I have ever felt."

"Saabira, take our guest through to the kitchen and get her some food." Asim said.

Saabira ushered Zakirah into the next room, and the sounds of the mosque committee talking became muffled by the wall.

"It is good to see you on your feet."

Zakirah jumped a little. It was the first time she had heard Saabira speak.

"What are they talking about in there?" Zakirah asked.

"There is a new mosque under construction on the outskirts of the city." Saabira explained, busying herself with some pots and pans. "Many people do not like it. Many people here fear our faith, they fear our god, and they fear us."

"Why?" Zakirah asked, frowning.

"They believe that the more of our culture that is brought to their city, the less room there will be for their culture, until their culture will be gone entirely."

Zakirah snorted. Back home, she and her family had spent their lives in fear that western armies and western wars would tear their home to pieces. And here, in the western world, they were scared of a building?

"Truly, this place must be a paradise, if their worries are so small." Zakirah said.

"It is best not to belittle them, but instead to meet them with the kindness and compassion we wish to receive from them." Saabira replied, softly. "Many of the men from around here were factory workers, many years ago, before the old mosque was even built. The company they worked for decided to outsource their production to Pakistan, because it was cheaper. The old factory was torn down, and it just so happened that the building that ended up taking its place was the old mosque. Many of them resented that."

"Then they should be angry at the company, not at the Muslim community." Zakirah pointed out.

Saabira let out a sad sigh.

"I agree, but hate and anger do not always follow sense." she said.

"I would like to see the city soon, I'm tired of being stuck inside." Zakirah said, changing the topic.

"Are you sure you're ready?" Saabira asked. "You still seem weak."

"I think some distractions could help me regain my strength." Zakirah replied. "Perhaps you could show me the new mosque?"

Saabira's eyes lit up.

"I am sure we can arrange that. It is not quite finished, it still needs to be decorated and furnished, but we can go inside and have a look around."

Zakirah smiled.

"I'd like that." she said.

In truth, Zakirah had no interest in visiting a place of worship, but she wanted to get outside, and seeing the mosque seemed as good a reason as any. Besides, these people had looked after her. It seemed only right to be respectful of their faith and take an interest in their lives.

Saabira finished reheating some leftover coconut and lentil dahl and spooned a healthy portion into a bowl for Zakirah, who wolfed it down in no time at all, and was left feeling slightly satisfied, but also still slightly hungry.

"More?" Saabira asked.

Zakirah nodded shyly, and Saabira laughed.

"Never feel embarrassed to ask for more." she said. "You have a healthy appetite."

Zakirah smiled as Saabira spooned out another serving of dahl, grabbing a bowl for herself and sitting down to join her.

***

Iona sat in her lab, bags under her eyes. A half-drunk smoothie sat on the table in front of her, thick and green and not

32

particularly appetising. She pushed her glasses up her nose as she attempted to focus on her computer screen.

Behind her, a research assistant was examining a petri-dish through a microscope, taking notes on a tablet. Her hair was tied neatly back in a ponytail, and she was wearing a clean lab coat, buttoned up all the way to the top.

"Are you sure you don't want a coffee?" she said, looking over at Iona. "You look like you could use one."

"No thanks." Iona replied. "I don't drink coffee."

The door to the lab opened, and a second research assistant entered: this one a slightly older woman.

"We have a visitor." she said, and stood aside to allow a woman to enter.

The woman was maybe late thirties, white, with short, dark hair. She was dressed in a suit, and wore minimal jewelry and make-up. Iona recognised her immediately.

"Dr Wood!" she exclaimed. "What a pleasant surprise! What… What brings you to our lab?"

"Dr Page, nice to meet you again." Dr Wood extended her hand. "As you may know, I have been invited as a guest speaker to give some lectures at this university, and one of your lecturers recommended I take a look at your research. I have to say, your work intrigues me. I simply had to come and see it for myself. Would you like to show me around?"

"Absolutely!" Iona exclaimed, slightly flustered. "Yes! You may know if you've looked at my research that I spent my PhD researching the medical applications of nanotechnology, and whether viruses can be manipulated to work for us, rather than against us. The university has given me the funding to bring my theory into practice, and we have been able to prove that viruses can be manipulated, using nanotechnology, to carry out tasks, such as targeting cancerous cells, aiding in tissue regeneration, and so much more."

Iona indicated to her computer screen, loading up a series of computer graphics that showed the breakdown of her nanotechnology and how it worked, with detailed diagrams and blueprints.

"We have been working with Nanix Inc., a Japanese company specialising in microscopic technology, to bring my designs to

33

life, and we recently entered our initial testing phase."
Iona ushered Dr Wood over to where her lab assistant was
working at the microscope.

"Here, we've programmed prototype 17 to repair damaged
tissue. So, if you look through the microscope."

Dr Wood placed her eyes up against the microscope, staring
down at the petri-dish, which contained a strip of what looked
like raw chicken flesh. Iona delicately took a scalpel from the
desk and ran it across the strip, cutting it in half. Dr Wood
watched as a string of what even from her view, amplified
through the microscope, looked like incredibly tiny blue dots
crawled towards the strip and pushed the two halves back
together, repairing it like a needle sewing thread.

"My god." Dr Wood breathed. "Impressive. So what's the next
step?"

"Well, ideally, animal testing and further computer trials." Iona
replied. "But this project has already been more expensive than
anticipated, and we're low on funding."

"Well, it's a good thing I visited." Dr Wood smirked. "I would
very much be interested in funding your research further, and
lending my expertise to this project."

"That would be amazing!" Iona beamed. "I would be very
grateful!"

"I do have one concern. I am informed you have had some
health complications. Can you be certain you will be fit and
able to continue your research?"

Iona was taken aback for a moment, but quickly regained her
composure.

"I've undertaken chemotherapy." she said. "No signs of cancer
for six months, but I'm still getting regular checkups."

"That's good, I'm happy for you." Dr Wood said. "I know it's
a delicate topic, but if I am going to be helping to fund this
project, I would need assurances. Would you be willing to sign
a contract granting me full control of the project if your health
conditions prevent you from working further?"

"I… I suppose… Would I be able to think about it?" Iona
asked, her brow furrowing.

"Certainly, though my funding may be contingent on this. I
don't like uncertainties." Dr Wood replied. "Here is my

proposed contract. The work you are doing is very much revolutionary, Dr Page: it could change medical science as we know it. With my help, this might be Nobel Prize-worthy."

She pulled a punched poly-pocket containing several pages of A4 paper and slid it over to Iona.

"Give me a call when you've thought it through, or if you have any questions or concerns. I look forward to working with you, Dr Page."

Iona took in a deep breath, staring at the contract. If they were able to get the additional funding required, she could potentially become known not only as the woman who cured cancer, but also the person who laid the foundations for the next steps in human evolution.

***

Jason sat in his wheelchair, at the train station, just before the barriers. Crowds of people rushed to and fro, heading off on their morning commute.

"Are you sure about this?" Jason said. "You know you can call me if you need anything, or if you want to come back."

"I'm sure. Thank you, Jason." Sarah said. "Look after yourself."

Jason forced himself out of his wheelchair so that he could hug his sister goodbye properly. It was a long hug, and Jason wasn't much of a hugger, but it was nice. Then she was gone, and he sat back down, sighed, and steered his wheelchair back out of the train station.

The Railway Tavern was just round the corner from the train station, and it was the hotel where Jason's little bedsit was situated. It was a decent place: traditional British pub, with overpriced food, and pretty standard hotel rooms upstairs. But it's closeness to the noisy train station, and the two clubs just up the street that played music until the early hours of the morning, brought the prices down, and with his disability allowance, Jason had no trouble affording the bedsit, and no stairs meant no hassle getting in and out of the wheelchair. The 24-hour hotel staff meant that there was always someone Jason could call in an emergency. And with the extra money Jason was saving, he was able to rent out a workspace… If you could

35

call it that.

The bedsit was behind the hotel and pub, accessed through the back door in the car park. Along the side of the car park were three garages. The one closest to the hotel was what Jason called his workshop. The garages were really just big enough to fit a car inside, but since Jason didn't have a car, he turned it into a workspace. He turned his motor towards the first of the garages lined along the back wall, leaning forward out of his chair to where the lock was. He had to all but step out of the wheelchair to slide his key into the lock, and the garage door came sliding upwards. Inside, there were a set of workbenches like you would see in a carpenter's or mechanic's workshop, covered with various pieces of circuitry, metal and other mechanical bits. At the back of the garage, a set of car batteries powered his workplace. He rolled over to them and flipped a switch, and the garage filled with light.

Jason used a hooked pole to pull the garage door closed, then rolled over to his desk. On Jason's work table, a prototype of his gauntlets sat, this set much more bulky than the pair he had meant to showcase at the convention. They were huge, like the fists on a suit of armour for a giant, with touchscreen pads on the wrists. Each knuckle was the size of a child's fists, and each fist had various panels that looked like they opened up. Jason pulled his laptop out of the satchel on his wheelchair and opened it up, going straight to Google. First, he looked up the closest Army Surplus store. Then, hunting supplies. Then sports gear. All shops Jason never had any reason to go to in the past. He scribbled down the addresses, and then he was off.

It was a twenty minute walk to the Army Surplus store, though it took Jason nearly twice that, navigating the streets in his wheelchair. When he got there, there was a step to get in the door. Jason sighed, pushing himself shakily to his feet and stepping inside. The store was cluttered with stock, and the only occupant was the sullen-looking forty-something-year-old man sat at the till, staring at his phone. He looked up, frowning as Jason entered, then caught sight of the wheelchair blocking the doorway.

"Oh!" he exclaimed. "Sorry! We don't get many customers…

like you… in here…"

He stumbled awkwardly over his words.

"Sorry, I don't mean to be rude!" he said. "Here, let me help you."

He rushed forwards and lifted the wheelchair over the step.

"Thank you." Jason muttered, awkwardly.

"Is there anything in particular I can help you with today?" the man asked.

"Um, yes, actually." Jason said. "I'm looking for a taser."

The man frowned.

"What do you want a taser for, lad?"

"M-my sister was attacked the other night, I'd l-like her to have something for protection." Jason lied.

"Tasers are illegal in the UK, lad. We can't sell them. We've got pepper spray, though."

Jason nodded.

"I'll take it." He looked up. "And how much are those armoured vests?"

"Armoured vest, that's overkill isn't it lad? Can't expect her to wear it everywhere?"

"No that's… a prop, for a short film. I'm a film student."

"That one is eighty quid, though I'm sure you could find a fake one at a costume shop, far cheaper."

"Looking for authenticity." Jason said. "I'll t-t-take that too."

The man shrugged.

"Fair enough."

"And do you have any smoke grenades? Like you'd use in paintball? Also for the film."

The man rummaged around behind the till and pulled out a pack and added them to the tally. Once Jason had paid, the man helped him back over the step.

"Have a nice day." he called out, then once Jason had rolled out of earshot, he muttered. "Weird kid."

***

Robby and his wife lived in one of the burrows further out from the city centre. Robby was a senior mechanic, and his wife was a primary school teacher, and between them they could afford a modest house for them and their two children. It wasn't big, and it was a bit of a tip, due to the children's toys being constantly strewn about the floor, but it was a nice place.

Alex was awoken early in the morning by the two children bouncing across the room as their mum tried to dress them and get them ready for school.

"Good to see you again, Alex." she said, as she rushed the children towards the door. "Did you sleep well?"

"Yes, thanks." Alex replied, shaking his head in the hopes that he could shake away his hangover.

"Got to go!" she said, and just like that she was gone.

Robby appeared, lingering by the door, staring down at where Alex lay on the sofa in the main room, half of which was a kitchen, the other half a living area with a TV and sofa.

"What are your plans for the day, then, Alex?"

"I need to find some work." Alex replied. "I guess I'll give Joey a call."

Robby nodded.

"I'd give you work if I could, but…" he sighed. "The Bridge Boys have gotten a lot worse since you left. As you know, Antonio took over after Ronnie got locked up, but I don't think anyone expected it to get this much worse. Antonio seems to think he's got something to prove. Got some real anger problems, that guy. They're no longer just doing drugs-"

"Yeah, I heard. He's got a protection racket going." Alex said. "Someone needs to put him back in his place."

"He's a real weasel. He's got dirt on half the people this side of Downtown City, no one will snitch on him. And his boys are loyal. Why not? He's good to them, and they're all a lot richer now that he's in charge. But the other gangs… They're not liking that he's been expanding his territory. If someone doesn't sort him out soon, there's going to be a gang war…" Robby shook his head. "Anyway, I've gotta go. You need to get yourself some work. And stay out of trouble. I love you like a son, I cared for your dad, but I can't have any trouble coming back to me. I left that life a long time ago."

Alex rolled his eyes.

"Don't be so dramatic. You talk about dad like he's dead. He moved to Florida, not six feet under."

"With the amount he writes, he may as well be dead." Robby snorted. "Don't worry about finding somewhere else to stay just yet, you can stay here until you find your feet. Just not too long, okay? See you tonight, mate. Here's the spare key."

He tossed Alex a key and headed out the door.

Alex took some time to freshen up and get dressed, then headed outside. It was a cloudy day, a little windy. Alex closed the door and pulled out his phone, dialling as he walked. After a few rings, he was through to an answer phone.

"Hey, Joey, it's Alex. I'm back. Look, I could really do with some work, something casual until I can get back on my feet. Give me a call back, yeah? We'll go for a drink."

Alex turned a corner that took him into a park. He stopped, and stooped to tie his shoelace. As he came back up, he found himself face to face with two guys, both about his age. One of them was black, with small dreadlocks, the other was white, with tattoos poking out from beneath his suit. They looked like typical Downtown city lads, except that they were dressed in tailored suits, with smart shoes, wearing ties, carrying briefcases instead of sports bags. Alex scoffed.

"Wow, he's gone proper 1940s gangster." he muttered. "Got you all dressed up and all."

"Alright, Axton." the white one said. "Big Tuna wants a word with you."

"Tell Antonio to piss off." Alex replied, shoving past them. "I'm not working for him. That's the whole reason I left."

"Well, a little birdie told us you got kicked out of the army. Dishonourable discharge. Seems to me you could do with the cash."

Alex felt a twinge of anger at the reference to his discharge, and winced as he tried to contain the emotion.

"Come on Alex." the black Bridge Boy chimed in. "He just wants to talk. Could be good, getting the old gang back together! It's not the same as when you left. Big T isn't like Ronnie."

"Not interested." Alex said. "And you can tell the fish that if he wants to talk, he can come talk to me himself. You should consider leaving too, Jeb. You're better than this."

39

And with that, he strode confidently away, leaving the two men staring at each other in awkward silence.

***

Jason wheeled back to his garage, his heart and mind racing: his brain planning and scheming, his heartbeat matching the frantic chaos of his thoughts. His bag hung off the back handles of his wheelchair, now heavy and wobbling precariously with the weight of all the supplies he had gathered.

Jason went over a dip in the asphalt, and the bag spilled open, tipping the contents over the ground. He cursed, wheeling the chair around to try and gather his belongings.

"Here, let me help you."

He saw the man's feet first, as they came into view amongst his scattered belongings. The shoes were ancient and battered, and one of them had a hole so big that the man's toes could be seen. Jason looked up to see an older man, rugged and tanned, with dirty jeans with holes in the knees and a hoodie tainted with various food stains. A few of his teeth were black, but he still had a warm smile, and a certain kindness in his eyes.

Jason had seen the same homeless man camping out at the end of the carpark a few times. He'd given him change, but due to his social awkwardness, he'd never actually spoken to him.

The man stooped to retrieve the contents of the bag, putting it back into the bag and hanging it properly off the wheelchair again.

"Th-th-thanks." Jason stammered.

"No problem." the man said. "I don't suppose you've got any change?"

Jason reached awkwardly into his pocket, pulling out his wallet. A few pitiful coppers fell out, but that was all the coins he had, though the edge of a five pound note caught his eye. He looked at the note, then back to the man, then back to the wallet. He pulled out the note, offering it to the man.

"Really?" the man asked. "That's kind of you mate."

"You n-need it more than I do." Jason said.

40

The man took the note, and extended his hand again.

"I'm Jack, but my friends call me J." he said.

"Jason." Jason replied, shaking the man's hand.

"I'm going to go get myself some lunch, I'll see you round, Jason."

Jason nodded, and Jack returned to his corner of the car park, where a blanket was strewn across the ground.

Jason headed to his garage, closing the door behind him and rolling up to the desk. He emptied his bag of all the supplies he had gathered over the desk: Smoke grenades, a spool of nylon wire, a penknife, a padded chest protector jacket and trousers for motorcyclists, the kevlar vest, a laser pointer, and all sorts of other bits and pieces. He popped in his headphones, turned up the classic rock, and got to work. He began dismantling the bulkier, prototype gauntlets, soldering and rewiring.

Jason spent the bulk of his afternoon working on the gauntlets, and as evening approached he was finally ready to try them out. He popped the gauntlets on, and the lines along the fingers lit up. The gauntlets were controlled with different gestures, an idea he'd had when practising his sign language. He motioned the sign for '**electric shock**'. The fingertips of the gauntlets sparked with electricity, and Jason recoiled.

'**Push.**'

A sudden burst of energy shot from the gauntlets, with enough force to roll his wheelchair backwards, and knocked over his coat rack, even denting one of the big metal cabinets in the corner.

"Cool." Jason breathed.

He had his weapon. Now, to track down his target.

***

"Come on, man. I just need some temporary work. Something to keep me occupied while I get back on my feet."

Alex stood in the carpark of an office building. It was approximately midday, and for England, it was pretty warm. The building looked like a normal city office, stretching high into the sky, with big glass windows stretching all around each floor of the building. A man stood in the entrance of the building, sweating in his suit under the midday sun. He was shorter than Alex, but incredibly muscular, with slick hair and a slim-fitting suit. He wore a look of impatience, glancing at his expensive Rolex every few seconds.

"I'm perfect for security work, Joe, you know that!" Alex pleaded.

"You're a hothead." Joe replied. "And you haven't even told me why you were discharged."

"It's a long story, mate, we can get into that later. I just…" Alex took a deep breath. "I need something to keep me busy. I can't be doing nothing right now. Please?"

Joe rolled his eyes.

"Look, if you just want something to do, I'll give you a trial shift tonight." he said. "Cash in hand, you're not going on the books, mate, but we could do with an extra pair of hands. Got an important client. But you're not security, okay? You're just… an extra pair of eyes and ears, keeping an eye out for trouble, at a distance. Okay? And get something nicer to wear. A suit or something."

Alex grinned.

"Thank you so much Joey." he said, beaming. "I really owe you one."

"Meet me at the airport at 7PM."

***

Afternoon trundled on, and Sabrina and three other officers pulled into the section of abandoned warehouses near the docks. The riverside was mostly a thriving part of the city: along both banks in the centre it was full of shops and restaurants and tourist attractions. But as you got further out from the city centre, the northside was filled with apartment buildings, and southbank was a string of abandoned warehouses and rundown cark-parks. The warehouses were in disrepair, many of them unsafe or riddled with damp and mould, some filled with asbestos. The other three officers were men: one was a short, stocky man with glasses who Sabrina often found herself partnered with, named Danny Jones. He was nice enough, but a bit quiet. The other two were typical tough lads: joined the force for action, and were constantly hoping to find it. Sam Andrews and Arthur Weston were their

42

names. Andrews was handsome, but had a mean look in his eye. Weston was a typical Downtown lad: average looks, always going on about football. They took the lead, heading to the first warehouse and pushing the door open.

Sabrina followed, and Officer Jones dawdled behind, hanging close to the two police cars.

The warehouse door didn't even have a lock on it, and all the windows were broken. Inside, various bits of immovable factory equipment, rusted and broken, was strewn about, and old shopping carts filled with junk had been rolled in. There were blankets all over the place, and even a big bin piled to the point of overflowing with trash. A small cluster of men and women were sitting in a circle playing cards when the officers entered.

"Afternoon folks." Officer Weston said, ambling over to them. "Mind telling me what's going on here?"

"Squatters rights." one of the women said, without looking up from the game.

Weston looked back at Sabrina and Andrews.

"Unfortunately, you are trespassing here." Officer Andrews said. "Under the Criminal Justice and Public Order Act of 1994, section 9, we are going to have to ask you to leave."

Sabrina frowned. She couldn't remember that act in full, but she was pretty sure he was misquoting it.

"Bull." the woman replied. "Squatters rights."

"Looked to me like that door was forced open. This land is council property, and that's breaking and entering." Weston said. "Could I get all of your names?"

The others in the group were starting to look a bit more hesitant now, and some were muttering to one another about leaving and finding somewhere else, but the woman who spoke was stubborn. She looked to be mid-forties, and had probably been on the streets for a long time. She was used to dealing with the police.

"Just because I'm homeless, doesn't mean I don't know my rights." she said, stubbornly remaining in the card game.

"These buildings are abandoned, no one is using them, we haven't damaged anything. You cannot arrest us for squatting."

43

"Guys, she's right." Sabrina said to Weston, keeping her voice low. "Let's just move on here, we've got better things to be doing."

Weston opened his mouth to speak, but his partner spoke first. "Go and radio for back-up." he said. "I'll deal with this."

He reached for his handcuffs.

"If you do not move on, I am going to have to arrest you for breaking and entering and aggravated trespass." he said.

The others in the group were convinced, and started gathering their belongings and making for the exit, grumbling as they did so. The woman didn't move.

"Ma'am, I'm going to need your name." Officer Andrews said.

The woman spat on the ground.

"Pig." she growled.

"That's it."

The officer pulled out his handcuffs and grabbed the woman's wrist.

"You're under arrest for aggravated trespass and damage to council property. You do not have to say anything. But, it may harm your defence if you do not mention when questioned something which you later rely on in court. Anything you do say may be given in evidence."

"Get off me!" the woman wailed, struggling against the handcuffs, and Officer Weston rushed forward to help his partner.

"Hang on!" Sabrina exclaimed. "I'm sure we can handle this peacefully!"

"Go back to the car!" Andrews growled, as he successfully managed to cuff the woman's other wrist, and the two officers dragged the struggling woman to their car as she hissed and spat.

Sabrina watched, her jaw agape, as the officers dragged the woman out. The other homeless people grumbled as the police passed them, and one of the men stepped forwards.

"You should be ashamed of yourselves!" he called out as they passed, pulling up his sleeve to reveal the letters 'ACAB' tattooed on his shoulder. "Bloody cops."

Sabrina got a sickly taste in her mouth. She knew what had happened wasn't right, and yet she had been unable to stop it. This was not why she had become a cop at all.

**

Alex arrived at Downtown City International Airport at 6:45PM, his heart racing. He had found a cheap, second-hand suit that seemed to just about fit, though having worn it for a good hour now it was starting to feel tight and restrictive. No tie, and an old shirt that had a couple of stains on it, but other than that, a lot smarter than he had appeared before. And he had finally gone through the effort of shaving.

He got himself a coffee from the airport deli and sat in the entrance, fidgeting uncomfortably. It only took a few minutes for Joe to pull up in a black limousine with tinted windows. He stepped out of the front, wearing the same neat, black suit and tie, with a black shirt. Out of the back of the car, two women and two men, all dressed in matching suits, stepped out. Alex stood eagerly and walked over to them.

"What's the deal then, boss?" he asked.

"We've got a client meeting us here in twenty minutes." Joe said. "She's the paranoid rich type, doesn't want anyone to know she's flying in, is convinced everyone is stalking her. We're going to meet her at the gate and escort her to her hotel. I just need you to keep a distance, look for anyone suspicious. There's a motorbike in the carpark: a Yamaha YS125, in section C5. Here are the keys." Joe passed Alex the keys without making eye contact. "Follow us. Let me know if you see anything suspicious. That's all I need from you, okay? If anything is wrong, we'll handle it."

He pulled an earpiece out of his breast pocket and handed it to Alex.

"Will you be able to hear through this, what with your...." Joe indicated to his own ear, in the same place where on Alex's ear, a hearing aid rested.

"Yeah, it's all good." Alex replied.

"Good." Joe said. "Remember: Anything seems wrong, you let me know, okay? Do a check of the perimeter."

Alex nodded, and Joe and his colleagues walked past, towards the Arrivals section of the airport. Alex stood at a distance and finished his coffee, watching the people that went past. It was mostly normal tourists, or airport workers. The time dripped on by, and soon enough a line of people began building up behind the double doors into the baggage claim, and exited through passport control. For the most part it seemed to be businessmen and families of tourists, but for some reason Alex's eyes were drawn to a young woman travelling alone: she looked to be maybe Armenian or Greek, though Alex couldn't quite tell from a distance. She had frizzy, black hair, and couldn't have been more than five and a half feet tall, with a slightly curvy figure. She looked young, at a guess only twenty. She was wearing a cheap leather jacket that Alex would have guessed was probably fake, ripped jeans, off-brand trainers, and was clutching a laptop bag to her chest. Her eyes flickered about nervously with every uncertain step. As she passed through the Arrivals hall, Joe raised his hand to gain her attention, and she rushed over to him. The two of them exchanged quiet words, and then Joe indicated to the two women in his team, who approached and ushered the young woman away.

Alex dropped his coffee cup in the trash and waited until they had exited, then rushed to the carpark, looking above to where signs indicated the sections of the parking structure. He rushed straight to C, then followed parallel until he reached section 5. The section was mostly empty, and Alex saw the motorbike immediately. He hadn't ridden in a while, but hey, you know what they say.... It's like riding a bike.

The helmet was placed on the seat, on top of a satchel that contained a jacket and trousers. Alex slipped them on as quickly as possible, popped the helmet on his head, and jumped onto the bike. He slid the keys in and brought the engine revving to life. The limo was already heading out the exit by the time Alex got moving, but it wasn't difficult to keep them in view as they headed back towards the city.

***

Jason pulled his wheelchair into an alleyway, his heart beating rapid-fire. The sun was setting, the cover of darkness had settled over the city, and Jason was just round the corner from the halls of residence for Downtown University: where many of the students lived. Where Dan lived.

Jason tucked his wheelchair away behind a set of giant bins. Hung off the back of the wheelchair was a rucksack, which Jason opened, his hands shaking.

"W-w-what am I d-doing…" he stammered to himself.

Inside, a reinforced, armoured, black motorcycle jumpsuit, with pads on the chest, elbows and knees, was folded as much as it could be considering the un-foldable pads. Jason took off his jacket, revealing the armoured vest he had gotten from the army surplus store, and stood from his wheelchair, his legs shaking. He slipped awkwardly into the motorcycle overalls. Then, from the bottom of the bag, he pulled out a black eye-mask fashioned out of fabric, like a scarf, which tied at the back of his head, like something Zorro would have worn, and a bandanna. He put the bandanna around his neck, covering his mouth, and tied the eye-mask over his eyes. Then, the final piece of the ensemble: the gauntlets.

Jason slipped the gauntlets on, took a deep breath, and took a few steps forwards.

His back began to ache. His legs wobbled. He groaned. Reaching back into his bag, Jason pulled out a little bottle of pills and took two. He slipped the bottle back into his bag. His eyes fell on the smoke grenades and the pepper spray, and he slipped one into each pocket on the motorcycle suit, along with the pepper spray, and then began walking again.

He slipped into the building through the fire escape at the back, heading directly for the elevator, thanking his luck that people like Dan were far too open on social media. He'd been able to figure out exactly what floor and what room Dan lived in.

Jason pressed the button for the fourth floor. The elevator carried him up two floors, then opened, and Jason found himself face to face with two girls. They stopped in their tracks, frowning, then one of them grinned.

"Neat costume, who are you supposed to be?" she asked,

slurring her words. "Zorro or something?"

Jason hesitated.

"Nightwing." he replied, after a moment's thought. "H-he's from Batman."

"Nice!" the girls got into the elevator.

They pressed the button for the fifth floor, and the elevator went up again. Ding. Fourth floor.

Jason stepped out and strolled wordlessly down the empty hallway. Room 403.

Jason stopped outside the door. His heart was racing like crazy, and he was sweating more than he realised he was capable of sweating. He closed his eyes, steadying himself. Then, he knocked.

There was a moment's silence, then the door handle wobbled. A moment passed. The door opened.

In front of Jason stood Dan, dressed in a baggy t-shirt and joggers, looking exhausted.

"What the-"

'**Push.**' Jason signed, and quickly placed both hands on Dan's chest and shoved him backwards.

A wave of kinetic energy burst from the gloves and Dan was sent flying backwards, landing on the floor of his room.

Jason stepped in and slammed the door shut behind him. This time, Dan had a look of fear on his face as he scrambled to his feet.

"What do you want? Who are you? Please!" he stammered, pulling himself up using the desk for support.

Jason gave another signed instruction to the gauntlets, and his fingertips sparked with electricity.

Dan saw this, and immediately clenched his fist and took a swing for Jason. Jason moved to block him, but Dan was a lot faster, and his fist connected with Jason's face, knocking him backwards. Jason's hands grabbed for Dan in defence, and sent a shock running through Dan's arm. Dan yelped in pain and fell backwards again, and Jason steadied himself, shocking Dan again. Dan's eyes widened, and when he tried to pull himself up, his entire body weight seemed to pull him right back down, his body spasming. His head flopped backwards, and his eyes closed.

Jason stood over the limp body of the man who had assaulted his sister, and that feeling of rage bubbled inside him once again. He caught sight of a can of spray paint on Dan's desk, and picked it up. Leaning over Dan, he pressed the nozzle, and red paint sprayed out the end. He wrote one word across Dan's chest.

Jason looked through the peep-hole into the hallway. The other residents of that floor had begun to gather in the hallway, murmuring to each other, drawn out by the noise of the struggle.

He reached into the pockets of his motorcycle suit, pulling out both smoke grenades. He released the pins one by one, opened the door a crack, and threw each one a different direction down the hallway. He quickly closed the door, waiting for the smoke to fill the hallway. As he counted to ten, his eyes fell on an open shoebox on top of a chest of drawers, with a brand new pair of trainers. Barely even thinking about it, Jason snatched up the box and headed out into the hallway, which was now filled with a haze of coloured smoke. Quickly, Jason looked up and down the hallway, then turned and wrote the same word across the door in bold, red paint, then discarded the can of spray paint.

RAPIST.

He headed for the stairs and rushed down, leaving the students coughing in the haze of artificial smoke.

Jason took a moment to compose himself in the stairwell, his legs shaking like crazy. He steadied himself on the bannister, his breath ragged, and stumbled down the stairs as quickly as he could manage. Even despite the painkillers he had taken, his back was aching. The quicker he could get back to the wheelchair, the better.

***

Alex had forgotten how much he liked to ride, and was caught up in the thrill of it within minutes, almost forgetting what he was there to do. The city became a blur in his peripheral vision, and all that mattered was the road. There was a serenity to it, that Alex seldom found in any other aspect of his life. The ride was relatively uneventful, and soon enough they were in the city. Alex began to relax a little, following loosely behind the limo.

They were in the heart of the city at this point, and each corner the limo turned, Alex followed thirty seconds later, trying his best to follow while keeping a distance.

The limousine turned a corner, just passing through an amber traffic light, and Alex was caught by the red. He came to a stop.

There was a deafening crash, and the screeching of tyres.

"Crap." Alex murmured, revving the bike to life and speeding round the corner.

He was greeted by absolute chaos. A white van had t-boned the limousine at the next corner, and a smaller car had blocked their exit. Joe and his people had jumped out of the limousine and rushed to detain the driver and passengers in the white van, who were struggling back against them. The driver of the van was a bald man in his forties, but out of the back of the van had jumped four figures in balaclavas, who immediately began fighting with Joe and his colleagues. Meanwhile, the driver of the car had stepped out and was walking towards the limousine.

Spooked, the client jumped out of the car and began to sprint in the opposite direction, clutching her laptop bag.

The driver of the car quickly broke into a run to follow. The client ran right past Alex, and as the driver followed, Alex stuck out his foot and tripped the man, jumped off his motorbike, whipped off the helmet, and slammed the helmet into the man's head, knocking him out.

The client was still running, but up ahead three more men in hoodies appeared out of a side-alley to cut her off. She skidded to a halt and turned and ran the other way. Alex gave pursuit, as did the men in hoodies.

The client was barrelling down an alleyway, the three men in hoodies close behind. She turned her head to see them, and ran straight into a wheelchair, sending herself and the wheelchair toppling to the ground, the laptop bag flying from her grasp.

One of the men went for the laptop bag, the other two went for the woman. She let out a shriek, kicking and scratching at them as they grabbed her.

50

Then, something really weird happened.

Out of a fire door stepped a man, dressed in an armour-padded motorcycle jumpsuit, with a mask over his eyes and a bandanna over his mouth. His hands were clad by two giant, metal gauntlets, lit up with lines of LED-style light along the fingers, and he had a shoebox cradled under one arm.

"HELP ME!" the woman cried out, her accent strongly American, with a hint of Armenian.

"Hey, w-what's going on?" the masked man called out. "Leave her alone!"

Without so much as a word, the man with the laptop bag struck the masked man with a right hook, sending him crumpling to the ground. Alex moved quickly, bursting down the alley and grabbing one of the attackers, throwing him across the alley. The second of the two men released the client and took a swing at Alex, but he easily dodged, grabbed the man's wrist, and pinned his arm behind his back. Now behind him, Alex rammed his foot into the back of the man's knee, and his leg folded underneath him. Alex threw him to the ground with force, stamping again on the back of his knee. The man let out a cry, and Alex turned on the second, who was now on his feet again, and immediately turned and lurched towards Alex. Alex dodged the first punch, blocked the second, then gave the man a swift jab to the nose, followed by a second to the stomach. The man reeled over, clutching his now broken nose, and Alex slammed both of his fists into the back of the man's head. The last attacker pulled a switch-blade out of his pocket and rounded on Alex.

"Wait!" cried out the masked man, still lying on the ground. He wobbled both of his fists near each other, then reached his hand towards the man with the knife. The knife shot from his hand and the masked man caught it.

"What-" the final opponent frowned, turning on the masked man again.

The masked man made another movement with his hands, and a small burst of energy shot from the gauntlets, narrowly missing his assailant. The gauntlets fizzed and sparked, and the LED lights dimmed. The masked man cursed, and his attacker let out a growl and stooped to grab the masked man by his

51

collar, clenching a fist to strike him again. The masked man grabbed his attacker by the upper arm, and an electric shock ran through his gloves. His attacker let out a cry and stumbled back, and Alex surged forwards, grabbing his head and ramming it into the wall. The man fell limp to the ground. Alex turned to look for the client, but she was long gone. He extended a hand to the masked man, who took it, but Alex had to practically pull him to his feet, and he almost immediately slumped onto Alex, putting all his weight on him.

"W-w-wheelchair." he wheezed.

Alex frowned.

"That's yours?" he asked.

The masked man nodded, and Alex turned the wheelchair upright and helped the guy slump into it.

"Do you need an ambulance?" Alex asked.

The masked man shook his head, pulling an inhaler from his bag, pulling down his bandanna, and took a couple of puffs.

"I need to get out of here." he breathed.

Alex suddenly heard a voice through his earpiece.

"*Alex, this is Joe! Have you got eyes on the client?*"

Alex pressed the button to activate the earpiece.

"No." he replied. "She escaped, I think. I detained the assailants."

"*Crap. Everyone fan out, search for the client.*"

Alex turned back to the masked man in the wheelchair, who was already heading off down the alley. Police sirens could be heard in the distance.

"Wait, who are you?" Alex called after him. "Where are you going?!"

The mysterious man didn't reply. He seemed to be in a rush to get away. And Alex still had a job to do.

"Copy that Joe." he said, touching his earpiece. "I'm on it."

CHAPTER FOUR: BRITISH PRIDE OR RACIST LIES

The police station looked ominous in the night, just far enough back from the road that the streetlights didn't illuminate it in the way they did the other buildings, but instead it became a dark monolith in the cityscape. The public car park that sat in front of it only served to distance it from the street, and Rhiannon couldn't help but think of how that distance seemed the perfect metaphor for the distance the Downtown City police put between themselves and regular civilisation, as they toed the line between their duty to the people to protect and serve, and their duty to a corrupt government to oppress and control.

The bulk of Rhiannon's activists had been released earlier that day, but as the ringleader, she had been kept in the station for extra questioning. She was released late that evening, and her giant, hulk of a boyfriend sat on a wall on the other side of the street, waiting for her. Though big in stature, Louis could be a quiet and gentle soul, and when out in public alone, particularly at night, he always seemed to make an effort to seem smaller, retreating into himself, so as not to seem like a threat to anyone. Louis wanted so badly to break the stereotypes around black men, but Rhiannon also knew it was partially for his own protection too: too easily police would look at him and see a threat, and every step he made was made with consideration and caution, knowing that any move that an officer in that station perceived as wrong or threatening could put him in serious trouble.

"There's my beautiful boyfriend!" Rhiannon exclaimed, grabbing him by the waist and pulling him in for a hug.

"We did good today." Louis said.

"We did alright." Rhiannon said. "Not as much media focus as I'd have liked, but change takes time."

"You're my hero." Louis said, kissing her on the forehead.

"Come on, let's go home. I'm knackered."

The two of them marched away from the police station, arm in arm, disappearing into the night. Rhiannon felt Louis relax, his stiff shoulders slumping as they distanced themselves from the police station. She pulled herself close to him as they walked, and found herself picturing a future where they didn't have to be constantly on guard.

*****

Jason slumped in his wheelchair, tucked away in his garage workshop, and tried his best to steady his breathing. His heart was pounding like a drum, the whole room spinning around him. He felt as though he had just stepped off a rollercoaster, his stomach still doing summersaults.

He closed his eyes and sat, breathing deeply. In. Out. In. Out. His heart began to settle.

The room stopped spinning.

He sat in peaceful silence for a few minutes, then took off the gauntlets and the face covering, and removed the motorcycle suit and armoured vest.

His whole body ached and he sunk back into his wheelchair. "I need a break." he muttered.

He switched the power off in his garage and headed round to the front of the hotel, sliding smoothly up the ramp and into the lobby. Inside, the young, blonde receptionist was talking quietly to an old man in a suit. She smiled politely at Jason as he wheeled in, heading directly for the bar.

Behind the bar, a friendly face awaited him. The short, slender barman, with his cropped black beard and hair styled like a model on an aftershave advert, his ears pierced, the edges of his tattoos showing beneath his sleeves, perked up as soon as Jason entered the room. He was dressed smartly, in a shirt with braces attached to his belt, running over his shoulders.

"Ah, Jasey, Jasey!" he grinned, his voice the silky smooth Italian accent Jason had become so used to every time he came into the bar. "Come, have a table by the bar. You will be my VIP tonight, my friend. How are you?"

Jason smiled, and for a second his woes washed away.

"Hey Will." he said, wheeling over to the far end of the bar, where Will removed the chair from a small corner table so that he could slot in. "It's been a r-rough day, how are you?"

"I am always good, you know this!" Will beamed back. "It is quiet, I don't mind it. What can I get for you?"

His English, though good, was strange, his sentences grammatically accurate but unusual, sometimes formal and somes informal, as he switched between what he had been taught by teachers, and what he had been taught by friends.

"G-gin and lemonade, thanks Will. M-make it a d-double."

Jason settled into his seat as the friendly Italian barman made his drink. The hotel bar was basically empty. At the back, a group of very boisterous lads were a few pints in, but they seemed to be keeping to themselves. Every so often one of them would let out a boisterous laugh, or a cheer and slap one of his friends on the back.

Will leant over the bar to place Jason's drink on the table, winked at him, then saw the bruise on his face.

"You were in a fight?" he asked.

"Yes." Jason said, without thinking. "Some guy… did something to my sister. Something bad. So I g-gave him a taste of his own medicine."

"Good man!" Will exclaimed, impressed. "You protect your sister. Men like that deserve to be put down. Did you win?"

Jason smiled, blushing.

"I guess I did." he said.

"Well, anyone who comes looking for you, you tell them you were here all night, my friend." Will said, grinning. "Friends look out for friends, yes?"

Jason smiled and nodded, and Will went back to cleaning and tidying.

The lads downed their pints, let out a cheer, and stood to leave.

"Don't wait up for us!" one of them yelled as they headed out. "Except maybe you!" He pointed at the young receptionist, who smiled politely. The lads cheered and headed out into the street. Jason felt a little pang of relief. He preferred an empty bar. As silence resumed, he found himself collecting his thoughts.

What was he thinking?

He was definitely going to be arrested.

And yet he felt a weird sensation, warming his chest and lifting his chin.

Pride.

***

Alex rushed back to the scene of the car crash, where Joe and his colleagues were regrouping. A police car had just pulled up, and two of them were talking to the officers.

"What's going on?" Alex called over to Joe on approach. Joe quickly jogged towards Alex.

"I called the client, she's safe, but she was spooked." Joe said. "You should get out of here, we're giving statements to the police, there's going to be a lot of paperwork, and I don't want to have to explain why someone not officially under our employment was helping us here. I'll call you later, okay?"

"You don't need anything else from me?" Alex asked.

"Just go." Joe said. "We're all good here."

Alex shrugged, handing Joe the motorbike keys and the earpiece, and turned and headed off round the corner.

As his heart-rate began to slow, and he was away from the chaos, he found himself wandering through the city, aimlessly. And just like that, the images and the voices were back. A flash of the desert. The sounds of gunfire. That voice, again, that haunted his dreams.

"*FIRE YOUR WEAPON, PRIVATE, THAT'S AN ORDER!*"

And the faces: a young boy, maybe fourteen, running frightened. An older boy with a gun, his arms shaking. And Alex's comrades, cowering behind their vehicle as gunfire rained over them.

Alex growled, shaking his head as if to shake away the memories. At the end of the road, he could see the train station, and just parallel to it, a pub. Suddenly, he realised how much he was itching for a pint.

It was a traditional British pub, with a hotel attached. The front door was a wooden framework with glass panels, and inside was a cosy reception area with massive, ornate armchairs. The bar was just up a short ramp and through an archway, and once through the fancy reception area, it looked much more like a regular pub. The receptionist smiled politely as Alex entered. She said something, her voice quiet.

"What was that?" Alex asked, indicating to his hearing aid.

"Do you have a booking?" she asked, louder this time.

"No, I'd just like to have a drink." he replied.

"Certainly, sir. Feel free to head through to the bar."

Alex nodded and wandered into the bar. A bartender in braces and a plain, white shirt was waiting. He had a cropped beard and tattoos along his arms, which were revealed only by the fact that his sleeves were both rolled up.

"Evening, my friend." he said, in a thick, Italian accent. "Can I get you a drink?"

Alex took a seat at the bar.

"Just a pint, whatever lager you have on tap."

"Certainly." the barman said, pouring a pint from the nearest tap. "That would be four quid, mate."

Alex exhaled, pulling out a fiver from his wallet and slapping it down on the bar. He was sure he could find a cheaper place, but he couldn't be bothered.

It was then that he noticed they were not alone in the bar. A young man, probably a little younger than Alex, was sitting at the other end of the bar, tucked away behind a table. Alex caught the man staring at him. He was slim, with a mop of messy black hair. He was pretty average looking: slightly handsome, but not stereotypically handsome. Definitely the intellectual type, but his gaze was intense. He was dressed in a creased, blue shirt, but something else struck Alex as oddly familiar about this man. As he looked at him, the stranger brushed his hair out of his face, revealing a nasty bruise developing on the upper part of his cheek. And then it hit Alex. The man wasn't in a seat, he was in a wheelchair. The same wheelchair he had seen in the alleyway earlier.

And that bruise on the man's face was from a fist fight.

Alex snatched up his drink and went to sit at the table with the man, who shifted uncomfortably and averted his eyes as Alex sat down.

57

"What's a disabled guy like you doing dressed like a knock-off superhero, hanging out in alleys?" Alex asked.

"E-excuse me?" the man in the wheelchair frowned.

"That's the same wheelchair, a bruise in the same place on your chin, you're even wearing the same shoes." Alex said. "So what's the deal, are you some sort of vigilante? Did you make those magic gloves yourself?"

The man fell into silence, taking a sip from his drink, then looked over at Alex, not quite meeting his gaze.

"What about you?" he asked. "What was going on with that w-woman, being attacked by those m-m-men?"

"She was a client." Alex replied. "I was working for a private security company."

"Was?" the now unmasked vigilante raised an eyebrow.

"Well, I don't really work for them." Alex said. "It's my friend's company, I was just helping out. Anyway, you never answered what you were doing there. Were you there to help our client?"

The man shook his head.

"I was in the w-w-wrong p-place at the wrong t-time." he replied.

"Oh come on!" Alex exclaimed in a hushed tone. "There's no way. What were you doing there?"

The man remained silent, taking another sip from his drink.

"I could just go to the police, I'm pretty sure they'd have a thing or two to say about those gloves." Alex said. "They definitely electrocuted that guy."

The man downed his drink.

"Sure, tell the police a d-disabled man in an alley tasered a man with magic gloves." he said. He changed the topic. "Where did you learn to fight like t-that?"

"Martial arts since I was twelve, then I enrolled in the army at nineteen." Alex replied. "I'm Alex, by the way."

Alex extended his hand.

"Jason." the man in the wheelchair replied, quickly shaking his hand.

Alex turned his head to check for the barman, who was at the other end of the bar, talking to a couple that had just walked in.

"I'm not going to report you to the police." Alex said. "But I am interested in what you were doing. Are you some sort of wannabe-superhero?"

Jason thought for a second.

"What if I am?" he replied.

Alex shrugged.

"Well, the gloves are impressive, but I'd say you're insane. You're going to get yourself hurt. Clearly you can walk, but how easy is it for you?"

"It takes effort." Jason replied. "I h-have spina bifida. It's a spinal condition. It was corrected with surgery. On a good day, I walk with a stick. But mostly I use the chair."

"And the stutter, is that related?" Alex asked.

Jason shook his head.

"T-that's psychological." he replied, mumbling. He mumbled something else, but it was too quiet.

"What was that?" Alex asked, pointing to his hearing aid. "Sorry, I struggle when people mumble."

Jason looked at the hearing aid, and realisation settled in.

"**Do you sign?**" he said, both verbally and in sign language.

"**I do! I don't meet very many other people who know sign language.**" Alex replied, also signing.

"**I was non-verbal for most of my childhood.**" Jason signed. "**Then when I did start speaking, I had this stammer. Without sign language, I could barely communicate.**"

He stopped, staring intently at Alex for a moment, then seemed to make a decision.

"**Finish your drink, I've got something to show you.**"

The door to Jason's garage slid open, and he flicked on the light, revealing the musky workshop. In the corner, the motorcycle overalls and armoured vest were hung on a coat stand, and the gauntlets were on the table, the plastic panelling on the back pulled open to reveal the inner workings: circuit boards and clusters of wires, with cogs and springs and all sorts.

"Woah." said Alex, walking in behind Jason.

"Pull the door down." Jason said, and he reached into a little cupboard beneath his work table, pulling out a bottle of spiced rum and two glasses.

"So you are some sort of crime-fighting vigilante?" Alex said, as Jason handed him a glass of rum.

Jason quickly downed his own glass, and poured a second. He found a drink or two helped his speech impediment: not a healthy coping mechanism, but sometimes it came in handy.

"Not really." Jason replied. "I'm an engineer. An inventor. B-but the other night my sister was assaulted. The police said they didn't have enough evidence to arrest the guy. So I took matters into my own hands. He lived in that building."

"You killed him?" Alex asked.

"No, just roughed him up." Jason replied. "Tried to scare him straight."

"So these gloves…" Alex picked up one of the gauntlets and inspected it. "They're really something."

"I made them in the hopes that they would help people like me function more like ordinary people. They help me reach things that are just out of reach. They help me lift things I wouldn't otherwise be able to lift, give me stronger grip, they steady my hands." Jason took the gauntlet from Alex and placed it back down on the table. "It didn't take much adjustment to turn them into a weapon.."

"You could sell these." Alex said.

"Or I could use them to do good." Jason countered. "The way I felt when I gave that jerk a taste of his own medicine… I've never felt anything l-like it." He took another sip of rum, and placed the glass down so that he could sign again. **"My parents were deadbeats. They abused me and my sister. We got taken away from them, but my mum never ended up in prison for what she did.** Got off scott-free. Then all through school **I was bullied, picked on because I was weak, and the school never did anything about it. Then this happens: my sister gets assaulted by this creep, and the police sit there and twiddle their thumbs and say they can't do anything. The system is broken. There is no justice for the little people. But tonight I made my own justice. I guess you must know how that feels: you're a soldier**, a martial artist, a real action man. **I bet you know exactly what it feels like to stick up for yourself, to put a bully in their place."**

Alex finished off his rum, and Jason picked up the bottle and poured him another shot.

"I suppose so." Alex mumbled. "I joined the army to run away from my problems, to tell you the truth. I was involved with all the wrong sorts of people: drugs, organised crime. Everything just seemed to be going wrong in my life. Then my partner…" he stopped himself. "Anyway, I just sort of ran off, joined the army, never looked back."

"**What made you leave the army?**" Jason asked.

"I was discharged." Alex replied. "I was stationed in Syria. There was a combat situation: suspected ISIL forces caught in a standoff with our troops. We couldn't be sure if they were enemy combatants, or civilians. I disobeyed orders, and was discharged for it. It was the right thing to do. Our commander wanted us to butcher them. No survivors. I just couldn't bring myself to do it."

"**Doesn't that make you angry? You got punished for trying to do the right thing.**" Jason said, his hands still emphatically moving along with the words.

Alex shrugged, taking another sip of rum.

"**So what now?**" Jason asked. "Private security?"

"I don't know." Alex admitted. "I just need to do something. I need to keep busy."

Jason thought for a second, inspecting his gauntlets.

"Why not work with me?" he asked.

"What?" Alex asked.

"**Why not work with me?**"

"Doing what?"

"**Making the world a better place. Giving people justice.**" Jason said. "**I couldn't do it alone. But together? With your strength and skills, and my gadgets, we could give this city a hero, who will take a stand when the law fails.**"

"I don't know about that, mate." Alex said, taking a seat on the end of the desk.

"Did you know that less than one percent of sexual assaults in this country lead to a conviction?" Jason said, rolling closer to Alex. "So many people are being failed by the system, and we have a chance to do something about it."

"Look, man, I understand why you did what you did, but you

think two guys running around dressed as vigilantes can solve societal problems? Beating up one or two pervs isn't going to stop assaults happening."

"But we can make people think twice. And not just assaults, other injustices too! You must have causes you care about. We can really make a difference. You and me, as a team: it's like fate brought us together. Do you know how m-my gauntlets are c-controlled?" Jason slipped on the gauntlets and they sprung to life. He clipped the plastic panels back into place, and put one hand up just above his head in a fist, and sprayed out the fingers: the BSL sign for **light**.

"They're controlled by sign language. That's a hell of a coincidence: us running into each other. How many people in this city, with our skill sets, speak sign language? And we just happened to run into each other. We have a chance to do something good here, shouldn't we at least try?"

Alex sighed.

"Thanks for the drinks, but I don't know, mate. I don't think you've thought this through."

"At least think about it." Jason said. "Here's my number."

He grabbed a notebook and a pen from his desk and scribbled down his number, tearing the page out and handing it to Alex.

"Give me a call, even if it's just to try out the gauntlets, see what they can do." Jason urged. "Sooner or later, you'll face some kind of injustice, and you'll see what I mean."

Alex nodded.

"I'll think about it." he said.

And with that, he finished his drink and placed the glass down, and headed for the exit.

"It was nice to meet you, Jason. You've got a great mind. What you've created is impressive."

"Thanks." Jason replied. "Take care."

And with that, Alex pulled open the garage door, and the cool evening air spilled into the garage. And Alex was gone.

When Alex left the garage, he found himself wandering absent-mindedly through the city, his head lost in fantasies of doing exactly what Jason had suggested: becoming a vigilante, bringing some justice to the city. It was just a dream, he knew that. Superheroes belonged in comic books.

And yet, it did seem like a convenient coincidence that he, an ex-soldier with a hearing impairment, would happen to run into a man who designed technology specifically designed for someone who uses sign language.

As he passed the train station, a hooded figure spotted him from across the road and immediately pulled out his phone. Alex continued to amble aimlessly, taking no note of the hooded figure now following him. One city block later, and the figure was joined by two more.

Now Alex took notice, catching them out of the corner of his vision. As he turned to look at them, a woman in a matching tracksuit and trainers stepped out in front of him. She wasn't bad looking, but her resting face was solemn and unimpressed.

"Axton. We've been looking for you." she said, in a thick cockney accent, and Alex turned to face her, stumbling as he whipped his head round, the alcohol slowing his reflexes.

"No." Alex said. "I told the others to tell Tony I don't want to work with him."

"Well he wants to hear it from you in person." the woman replied. "You gonna come quietly?"

Alex sighed.

"Might as well get this over with." he said. "Lead the way."

Alex was taken down to the dockside, where a string of storage containers and abandoned warehouses were dotted along the polluted riverside. There were no streetlights at this point, and the area was littered with discarded construction equipment. The woman in the tracksuit ushered Alex towards a warehouse with blacked-out windows, covered with cardboard or wooden planks. They went in through a metal side-door.

Inside, the warehouse had been cleared and was mostly empty. In one corner there were three sofas and a table, all positioned around a TV. In another corner, there was a long table with a toaster, a microwave, a hot plate, and a fridge next to it. There was a man making cups of tea, and three other men lounging about on the sofas, with two women in-between them. They were all dressed in suits, though the men had all loosened or removed their ties, and had undone buttons on their shirts.

In the corner of the room, there was a portable toilet cubicle, and as Alex entered the room he heard a flush, and the cubicle opened, and out of it stepped a man in a grey three-piece suit, wearing a trilby hat. He had smartly polished shoes and was wearing a multitude of rings. He looked about twenty-two, though Alex knew for sure that he was twenty-eight, with a severe case of baby face. He had slick black hair and a slight tan. He was of stocky build, and quite a bit shorter than Alex.

"Tony." Alex said. "What's up?"

"Come on guys!" the wannabe 1940s gangster exclaimed, his accent not matching the look at all: very much a working class Brit. "Where are your suits?"

"Sorry, we were off the clock." the woman said. "J.J. just happened to see Axton walking past the train station and called us."

"I'm trying to bring some class to the organisation." He finally addressed Alex directly. "It's Big Tuna now, by the way, show a little respect."

"The organisation!" Alex scoffed. "You're drug dealers. You're not American gangsters, and it's 2022."

"We're not just dealers any more, Alex." Big Tuna said, heading over to the sofa and indicating to those lounging about to clear off so that he and Alex could sit down. They cleared the sofas, and Alex went and sat adjacent to the gang leader.

"I changed things when I took control. We do personal protection, we're more organised now. I've made a lot of changes since I took over from Uncle Ronnie. Which you'd know if you stuck around to support me."

"I had to get out, Tony." Alex said, pointedly. "I didn't like the way my life was going. I didn't want to be a thug. I wanted to make something of myself."

"And look at us now: I've made something of myself, and you're an army reject." Big Tuna said. "Funny, that."

Big Tuna leant forwards, placing his elbows on his knees and interlocking his fingers in front of his face, to rest his chin on. "I need you, Alex. The Bovver Boys are getting more and more rowdy by the day. Word on the street is that the Gov is back. Whatever you think of me, we're better than those racist, neo-

64

nazi nationalists." he said, a note of genuine concern in his voice. "I tell you what, Alex. Tonight, we forget about all this, share a drink with me, just chill. Tomorrow morning, come and see what I do, then make your decision. I miss you, man. You were always supposed to be my right-hand man. I want that back. You'll see, we're not just crooks. We're actually trying to make a positive difference in this corrupt, capitalist hellhole. So just, hear me out, for old time's sake?"

"And if I'm still not convinced, I can walk?" Alex asked.

"Sure." Big Tuna replied, extending a hand. "We can shake on it."

***

A grey morning dawned over the city, and Iona stood in her lab, sipping from a lemon, tumeric and ginger detoxifying smoothie, sweetened with a touch of maple. Her lab assistants were darting to and fro, packing everything into boxes.

At the entrance, Dr Wood stood in her slim fit suit and waistcoat, smiling.

"I'm glad you decided to take me up on my offer." Dr Wood said. "You will have all the resources you could possibly need at my laboratories."

"Thank you, doctor." Iona said. "To tell you the truth, it'll be refreshing to get out of the uni labs."

"I would like you to start animal testing as soon as possible." Dr Wood instructed. "I will be overseeing the project, but I want to get fully caught up on all your research, so I will be reading all your notes and analysing them as thoroughly as possible. Would you like to get breakfast, and we can discuss your work? I find there's no better way to start a day than a Full English."

"I haven't had one in two years." Iona admitted. "I went on a strict diet during my recovery. Straight-edge: no alcohol, no caffeine. And plant-based: I haven't eaten meat or dairy in a long time."

"Well, there's a lovely vegan cafe near my office building." Dr Wood said. "I'm not averse to a veggie sausage, though I must admit, tofu scramble is a poor substitute for egg. Come on, I'll show you the place. I'll have my assistant help your people move the rest of your stuff."

"I'm a pretty hands-on team leader." Iona replied. "Would you mind if I stayed to help?"

Dr Wood nodded absently.

"Lunch, then. Have my P.A. show you to my office once you're done."

Without waiting for a response, Dr Wood exited, leaving Iona and the small handful of assistants to pack up the lab.

***

Jason didn't sleep that night. He spent the entire night tinkering with his gauntlets, his mind a mess of possibilities of the good his gauntlets could do, with the subtle undertone of paranoia: surely Dan knew it was him that attacked him? What if he came looking for revenge? The possibility haunted Jason. As morning dawned, he found himself in need of fresh air and a clear head. There was one place Jason tended to find himself when he needed to clear his head and distract himself from the real world:

The comic book store.

Jason headed out into the carpark, zipping his coat up as the cool morning breeze hit him. Jack was just leaving his corner of the car park to head out, probably to beg on the high street, and he waved at Jason as he passed.

"How are you?" he called over to him.

"Oh, I've got something for you!" Jason suddenly remembered. "Wait here."

He rolled back towards his little garage and slid the key into the lock, pulling the garage door up. Inside, the shoebox he had taken from Dan's room was tucked under the table. Jason groaned as he stooped to retrieve it, and rolled back out of the garage, locking it up behind him.

"These aren't m-my size, I thought they might f-fit you." Jason said.

"Jeez, that's thoughtful!" Jack beamed, opening the shoebox and pulling out the trainers. "These are nice, man!"

He pulled off his batted old shoes and slipped the trainers on. "Half a size too big, but hey, maybe I'll grow into them!" the man joked, tapping Jason on the shoulder.

66

Jason smiled awkwardly, giving a polite chuckle.

"That means a lot, mate." Jack said. "Thanks for thinking of me. I'll see you later, alright?"

Jason nodded, and watched as Jack headed out of the car park, whistling cheerily to himself. Jason smiled, a warm feeling filling his chest, and rolled away towards the comic book store.

The store was in the Covered Market. It didn't have its own building: in truth it was little more than a room, on the second floor, on the balcony, overlooking the indoor market stalls. The building only had one lift, and it was ancient, and made all sorts of groaning and screeching noises. Every time Jason used it, he felt sure it was going to break down and leave him stranded, though it never had.

The building was made out of stone rather than brick, and looked almost like a church from the outside, though not nearly so elegant. Inside, there were various market stalls and pop-up cubicles with small-business owners peddling their wares. The second floor was a balcony that ran around the market and looked down on the market stalls, and was occupied by more permanent, stable businesses. As Jason rode the elevator up, he found himself scrolling local news websites for any mention of last night's events. So far, one local paper had put up a photo of Dan that looked like it was a passport photo or stock image, with the headline '*Downtown University student assaulted last night*', though the article had very little details. But on social media, it was a different story: two posts had been shared by multiple friends of Sarah's, both ending in '#metoo'. Two other women, talking about Dan's behaviour towards them. Jason scrolled down to the comments, his heart pumping. The top rated comment: '*did you hear what happened to him? Talk about karma!*'

The elevator doors slid open and Jason put the phone away and headed towards the comic book shop, eager to get lost in a fantastical world of caped crusaders and maniacal supervillains. There was only one person in the store when he arrived: a stocky Pakistani man with a shaved head and long beard and a batman t-shirt that looked at least a size too big for him.

"Yo, Jason!" the man grinned a toothy grin as Jason rolled into the store, his accent a thick Downtown accent, with only the lightest hint of his South-Asian heritage. "How's it hanging!"

"Naveed." Jason nodded awkwardly.

Naveed was not exactly what you pictured when you thought of comic book nerds and gamer geeks. He was a typical, working class city lad living on the council estate. Nevertheless, Naveed knew everything there was to know about geek culture, and his little comic store was the best place in the city for games, comics, cosplay costumes, collectibles, and even some DVDs. How he was able to keep his prices so low and still make a profit, Jason could easily guess: his sources for stock must have been less than legitimate. But it was hard not to like Naveed. He supported local artists, he gave heavy discounts to those less fortunate, and even helped run the local food bank. Jason sometimes spent hours in his store flicking through comics, and was never pushed to make a purchase.

"Mate, we got the new Earthraiser comics in. No one's got them yet!" Naveed grinned. "You want a look?"

"Go on then." Jason rolled up to the till as Naveed pulled a comic off the stand next to the till.

"Vegan superhero, who'd have thought, eh?" Naveed said, sliding the comic over to Jason. "It's pretty good though, not gonna lie, not gonna lie. Eh!"

Naveed let out a loud, singular laugh.

"What would you do if you got superpowers?" Jason asked, as he flicked through the comic.

"What powers we talkin', mate? That makes a lot of difference, don't it?" Naveed asked, leaning in.

"I don't know." Jason shrugged. "Like superman, I guess."

"Forreal? The whole lot? Proper blessed, man! I'd get all the ladies, mate, no lies!" Naveed let out another singular laugh.

"I'm being serious." Jason said. "In the comics, the heroes always vow to use their p-powers for good, but in the real world, everyone has a d-d-different idea of what good is, don't we? Like, this guy is a vegan, so he's all about freeing animals. But like, some hardcore right wing guy would genuinely think he was d-doing good by getting rid of immigrants. And an

68

antifascist might think they were doing good by taking d-down all the world leaders. A hardcore feminist might take on creeps at the club, a civil rights protester might take on corrupt cops. What would you do?"

"That's deep, man." Naveed's face changed, and he was suddenly thoughtful. "I reckon I'd get all the world's richest geezers into a room together, force them to sort out all the shit in the world. Like, there's so many billionaires, I don't believe that they can't solve world hunger, if they worked together. And global warming and all that stuff. I'd just smash capitalism, make them sort it all out, you know?"

Jason nodded.

"I like it." he replied.

"I mean, if you think about it, it's proper messed up that Batman and Superman use their skills to beat up the average crook on the street rather than actually fixing the stuff that was wrong with society that caused those people to become so desperate. You got a proper rich dude and the most powerful man on the planet, they could really fix some societal problems, I reckon. You got me thinking now. But I guess that's not as entertaining. No one wants to watch two hours of Batman and Superman in a boardroom, talking about taxes with some rich tossers. "

Naveed's phone buzzed, and as his eyes fell on the screen his expression soured.

"What's wrong?" Jason asked.

"It's nothing mate. Look, you know me, I'm always happy for you to chill in the store, but you might want to make yourself scarce for a bit, you get me?"

Jason frowned.

"What's g-going on?" he asked.

"It's just some business stuff, it's nothing to worry about, confidential though. My supplier might be dropping by and he's not the nicest chap, you know? Come back in a bit, yeah? We can chat some more."

"Alright." Jason agreed, reluctantly. "If you insist."

He rolled his wheelchair around and out of the store. As he came out onto the balcony overlooking the market, his eyes caught sight of a small squad of people, dressed in suits, entering the market. In the middle, a short, dark-haired man in a trilby hat and long coat was chatting to a man Jason recognised: Alex, still in the same clothes as last night, looking a little worse-for-wear, with bags under the eyes and a shadow of stubble across his face.

Jason watched as Alex and the finely-dressed group worked their way through the market stalls, stopping at one or two to exchange words with the owners. Some handed over wads of cash, some simply chatted for a few minutes. In the group, there were three men and two women, all dressed in very similar suits and ties. The men stayed close to their obvious leader, but the women spread out and mingled amongst the market stalls.

Eventually they found their way to the stairs, and Jason tucked himself into an alcove behind a pillar near the comic book store and peered round the corner. He watched as Alex and the men entered the comic book store, slowly creeping his wheelchair closer so as to hear what was going on inside…

"Listen here, Alex. I want you to see that this isn't just a gang of crooks and bullies. I'm running a business here, it just so happens not to be a particularly legal one."

Big Tuna indicated toward the entrance to the market, and his men led the way in.

"I know how a protection racket works, Antonio." Alex said, rolling his eyes. "You're a working-class Brit, not a 1940s gangster, you didn't invent organised crime. You can give yourself a fancy mobster name and dress yourself up however you want, you're still just running a gang."

"See if you still think that at the end of the day." Big Tuna replied, placing a hand on Alex's shoulder and steering him into the market.

The atmosphere inside seemed to change immediately as the group entered, with the stall owners all awkwardly eyeing up the wannabe-gangster as he made the rounds of the stalls. He headed straight for an old woman selling bottles of home-brewed gin. She was wrapped in a knitted scarf that was almost definitely home-made, and had a tattered grey jacket, stained and discoloured from what looked to have been its

70

original blue hue.

"Irene." Big Tuna beamed. "How's business?"

"It's been alright, can't complain." the woman replied.

"And that liquor licence I acquired for you?" Big Tuna asked, lowering his voice.

"Ah yes." The woman reached into her little cash box and pulled out a few twenty pound notes. "Here's the final payment for that. Thank you."

One of Big Tuna's men accepted the payment, and Big Tuna began to slowly amble towards the next stall.

"Without my help, Irene would've been closed down by the council weeks ago. Luckily, I was able to acquire a legitimate-looking licence so she could keep selling booze, the council is happy, Irene is happy, we get paid, no one gets hurt."

The next stall was run by a thirty-year-old blonde woman with striking blue eyes and a crooked smile. She was sporting a tie-dye dress, and wearing a ridiculous number of bracelets and necklaces. The market tables around her were filled with everything hemp-related: hemp bags, hemp socks, hemp jackets; everything made of hemp, and a whole shelf full of CBD oils, CBD-infused food and drink, and so much more.

"Hey there boss!" she said, as the group approached.

"Sandra, I trust your shipment arrived on time?" Big Tuna asked.

Sandra reached into her till and pulled out a small wad of notes. Again, one of the men collected the money.

"Sandy here is the finest purveyor of CBD oils and products." Big Tuna said. "She also happens to sell a different part of the same plant, on the side. We supply, she sells, and in turn supports her family. It should be legal anyway, but since she can't sell it in her shop, we help her out."

They headed out of the main area of the market, making a turn for the stairs up to the balcony.

"We help people when the law is working against them." Big Tuna said. "What's wrong with that?"

"And then if you want anything from them: more money, for example… You have just the information you need to hold over their heads, is that right?" Alex said. "What you're showing me may all sound great, but I've heard what's been

71

going on, Tony. I'm not an idiot."

Big Tuna rolled his eyes.

"Come on, let's head upstairs. We still have another shop to visit."

They headed up the stairs and straight towards a little comic book shop, currently devoid of any customers and only occupied by a stocky Pakistani man.

"Naveed!" Big Tuna exclaimed, spreading his arms wide as he entered.

"What's up, big man?" the shopkeeper said. "You got some more stock for me?"

"No, actually, not this time. I'm here to collect on a payment." The man let out a sigh.

"Come on man." he said. "I'm all paid up. I'm doing my best to make ends meet, I've given all I can give."

"We've been making extra effort to keep you stocked." Big Tuna said, approaching the counter and leaning against it. "And last week we made sure the police hit a dead-end when tracking those collectibles you made such a profit on."

"Collectibles I would have turned down if I'd known where you got them!" Naveed interrupted.

"You know how this works, Naveed." Big Tuna responded. "We get you what you need, no questions asked, and the more work we have to do, the more risks we take, the more you pay. You don't ask where it comes from, you don't question the price. That is how it is."

"Well, maybe I don't like how it is." Naveed replied, his voice taking on an attitude. "Maybe I want to go legit."

"I'm sorry you feel that way." Big Tuna sighed. "Unfortunately, that's not your call to make. Unless you want the police to find out? See, we only cover the tracks of those who are with us… And it sounds like you don't want to be with us." Big Tuna indicated to one of his men. "We'll be taking what's in your till."

"Like hell you are!" Naveed exclaimed.

"Come on Tony." Alex said, stepping between his old friend and the comic store owner.

"It's Big Tuna!" the young gangster snapped, a flash of anger in his eyes. "You're going to have to learn to respect me,

72

Alex." He turned to his men. "Take the money."

"Back up!" Naveed yelled, rushing over to the till as one of the men walked over to it. The man turned as Naveed rushed at him, pushing Naveed back. One of the other men stepped in, tripping Naveed from behind and throwing him to the ground. "Enough, Tony!" Alex exclaimed. "I've seen enough. You're done here, I'm not working for you, get out of here."

"It's Big Tuna!" came the screamed reply, and the mobster's fist came soaring through the air towards Alex. He went wide, in haymaker fashion, and Alex was easily able to dodge out of the way and, having thrown all his weight behind the punch, Big Tuna stumbled forwards. Alex noticed that his old friend had slipped on a pair of brass knuckles before taking the swing, and anger flared up inside him. Big Tuna's thugs were all advancing on him now, and two came at him from either side in unison. Alex stepped into the first one, grabbing him by the collar and swinging him quickly round into the other. Another one of the men tried to grab him from behind, but Alex caught his reflection in the window and elbowed him in the stomach, spinning around and bringing his knee up hard into the man's chest. The man let out a groan and collapsed. Big Tuna took another swing at Alex, coming much quicker than he expected, and the brass knuckles hit home in the lower part of Alex's back. Pain shuddered through his spine, but it had been a weak punch and Alex ignored the pain, spinning round and aiming a jab at where Big Tuna's head had been. Big Tuna ducked, bringing his unarmed fist into Alex's chest. Alex reeled back with a grunt, and one of the other thugs pushed a shelf over onto him, knocking him to the ground. Face red with rage, Big Tuna took the chance, kicking Alex in the chest, once, twice, three times, roaring a wordless cry on the third kick. He stopped for a moment, catching his breath, and then stooped down next to Alex, who was wheezing and clutching his chest.

"I told you, Alex. You're with us or you're against us." Big Tuna said. "I want you by my side, I miss you, but that doesn't mean I'll tolerate your disrespect. I can make you rich, or I can make your life miserable. Choose wisely."

He clenched his fist, baring the brass knuckles, and raised it above Alex's face, hesitating. After a moment of contemplation, he lowered the fist, stood up, brushed off his coat, and turned to leave.

"The price of our services is going up, Naveed. If you want out, that's fine, but you're going to need to buy your way out. If you can get me something I want, I'll consider cutting you loose."

"What do you want?" Naveed asked, picking himself up off the ground.

Big Tuna shrugged.

"Figure it out. Something valuable. See you next week."

He headed for the door, and his men followed.

"No hard feelings, Naveed. Just business." one of the men said on his way out.

"Don't turn up to D&D again, got that? Prick." Naveed replied.

"Get out of my shop."

The Bridge Boys headed back down the stairs, and Naveed looked over at Alex.

"You alright, mate?" he asked.

"I'm fine." Alex grumbled, pulling himself up.

"Best not to get involved with that lot." Naveed said. "Antonio used to be an alright geezer but he's lost it. Drunk on power or something."

Alex grunted and headed for the door.

"Alright, well nice speaking to you mate." Naveed called after him. "Drop by anytime."

Alex took a few deep breaths as he looked out over the market, waiting for his heart-rate to drop.

"Don't y-you wish you c-could have done something ab-bout that." the familiar, stuttering voice came from behind him.

"Jason." Alex said, turning his head. "Are you following me?"

"No." Jason said. "Coincidence, but I'm g-g-glad. Imagine if you'd had my gloves. That would have been an easy fight. It's not just pervs we could deal with, it's people like that."

"So I'd have won the fight." Alex said. "Big Tuna would still have the Bridge Boys, and he'd come down even harder in revenge. And even if we dealt with him, someone else would take his place."

74

"Which is exactly why there n-needs to be someone to keep p-people like him in check. And not just people like him. There are far worse c-c-crooks than him in this city. Just come b-back to mine with me, s-s-see what my technology can do."

"I already told you I'm not interested!" Alex snapped, his face red with anger. "Just leave it, okay?"

He turned and stormed away, clenching and unclenching his fists as his anger flared up inside him.

Jason shook his head, letting out a long sigh. He knew he couldn't do this alone, but now that he'd had the idea, he felt he couldn't let it go. He needed someone like Alex.

***

"Officer Parker, could I speak to you in the meeting room for a moment?"

Sabrina looked up as the sergeant stood over her desk, staring down at her.

"Sure, sir." she said, and followed the sergeant into the room. He closed the door.

"Take a seat."

Officer Parker obliged.

"I've read your report of the arrest made last night. The homeless woman at the dockside. Your report differs greatly from the others." Sergeant Burns said, pushing his reading glasses up his nose. "You mind recounting to me what happened?"

"They were squatting." Sabrina replied. "They quoted squatters rights, but Officers Weston and Andrews arrested one of the women anyway. She didn't do anything wrong, the arrest was unlawful."

"Weston and Andrews say that she spat at them and verbally assaulted them." Sergeant Burns said, shuffling through the papers in front of him.

"She may have gotten a little heated, but nothing criminal." Sabrina replied. "She spat on the floor, not at them."

The sergeant sighed.

"You need to have your colleagues backs in situations like this. It reflects badly on the force as a whole if there is in-fighting. Any disagreements should be handled by me, you shouldn't be voicing your thoughts during an arrest, it just encourages the offenders. Constable Weston tells me that the woman was a lot of trouble on the ride back to the station, and he believes you encouraged her."

"I simply voiced my opinion that we didn't need to make an arrest." Sabrina replied.

"And you should have saved that opinion until you were back at the station. Now, the language used in your report is… Unsatisfactory. I believe you have made several errors. I would like you to amend your report."

"With all due respect, sir, my report is accurate." Sabrina replied.

The sergeant rolled his eyes.

"You are one of our best constables, and you're likely to rise through the ranks, what with our diversity quotas. Don't screw it up by making enemies out of colleagues." he said.

"Sir, if I rise through the ranks, it will have nothing to do with sodding diversity quotas. It will be because I am good at my job. Am I being written up?"

The sergeant hesitated, then sighed.

"Not this time, but be careful. I don't want to hear of another incident like this."

Sabrina stood up to leave. She stopped.

"What happened to the woman?" she asked.

"She was released, no charges." Sergeant Burns replied.

Sabrina nodded and headed back out. As she walked into the main area of the station again, she saw the same young man from the night before: same overly styled, gelled hair, even dressed in similar skinny jeans and v-neck. Daniel McDonald, the one who had assaulted Sarah Fox. He was covered in bruises, looking rather pale, and was giving a statement to Officer Jones.

"And have you any idea who it was?" the officer asked.

"I don't have a clue!" Dan exclaimed. "Maybe that psycho disabled guy, Sarah's brother!"

"Who is Sarah? And who is this disabled fellow?"

"Sarah is-" Danny stopped himself. "Sarah is the girl who was telling all those lies about me. Sarah Fox. And her brother… I don't remember his name. He attacked me once already."

76

"You didn't say anything about the attacker being disabled. How disabled is he? Was he in a wheelchair?"

"No, the guy who attacked me wasn't in a wheelchair. But I think her brother can walk sometimes? I don't know. She said he struggles, but he can walk, if he really tries. I don't know! The guy was wearing a mask but I bet you it was that little freak."

The Sergeant came out of the meeting room and Officer Jones beckoned him over. They exchanged a few words, then Sergeant Burns headed back to Sabrina's desk.

"I need you to go and take Jason Fox in for questioning." he said. "Take Officer Briggs, I'm going to be partnering you with him for a bit. He's more experienced, hopefully some of his professionalism will rub off on you."

"Jason? Why?" Sabrina frowned.

"Daniel McDonald was assaulted, he's our main suspect."

"So we're arresting him? What evidence do we have?"

"Just do your job, officer." the sergeant said.

"So we're arresting Jason on no evidence, but we can't arrest that little creep for assaulting his sister?"

Sabrina kept her voice low, but the words cut through the air, and Daniel McDonald turned his head to frown at her, as if trying to listen in.

"We're not arresting him. He's assaulted him once before. We're just bringing him in for questioning." the sergeant said. "Either you go, or I'm sending Weston."

Sabrina took a deep breath and let out an exasperated sigh. "Yes sir." she said.

***

From outside, the mosque looked complete. It was a building mostly constructed of brick, but interwoven elegantly to form arched patterns in slightly differing shades of brown and beige. The entranceway was formed out of archways of brick over a set of wooden double doors, and on each end, at the roof, was a slender minaret, towering into the sky, though still humble amongst the other city buildings.

Saabira had provided Zakirah with a full-length brown gown, otherwise known as an abaya, that fit her, though she felt awkward in it, and as they walked through the Downtown streets she longed for some local clothing to wear: Zakirah had no wish to stand out. She wanted to become one with Downtown City, and forget her past. She wanted jeans, she wanted hoodies. She was sick of white people looking at her all the time.

Asim held the door open for Zakirah and Saabira as they entered the mosque. Inside, the entranceway was bare and empty, and the hall it led into was equally so, with no decoration and no furniture. Just the hollow husk of what the building would soon be.

"Imam!" a man rushed over as Asim entered. "It is good to see you. We have received more threats. Many are afraid that the mosque is going to be attacked."

"We must meet this hostility with calm serenity, my friend." Asim replied. "Allah will protect us, but only if we stay true to him. We must not raise our fists in anger, but open our hearts with love."

"With all due respect, uncle, screw that." A slightly overweight man in a Star Wars t-shirt wandered over. "I'm sorry, Asim, I know I don't have the faith that you have, but I do love my community, man. And if some racist douchebags want to target my community, you can be damn sure I'm going to stand up and try and stop them, you get me?"

"Language, young man, you are in a house of god!" Asim chided the younger man. "Mobeen, control your friend."

"I am sorry." the first man said. "My cousin isn't used to being in a place of worship."

He turned to the other man with a glare.

"Naveed." he said. "Let's talk outside."

Zakirah watched as the two men left.

"The young have much to learn about faith." Asim said, shaking his head.

"He makes some good points." Zakirah said. "I am used to doing nothing, and I've watched my home be taken from me, and been thrown from place to place, slowly losing all the people in my life. Many of my family are dead, the rest I do not know where they are or what has happened to them. Sometimes I feel like you have to take a stand."

"I admire your passion." Asim said. "But if you had taken a stand, you might not be here today. And I for one am glad to have met you, and am happy you are alive… There is not much more to see here, but we are not far from the shops. Saabira, perhaps you should take our guest to choose some clothes of her own."

Zakirah smiled, and she found herself feeling just the faintest pang of happiness.

"That would mean a lot to me." she said.

***

Rhiannon and Louis approached a large, old building that looked to have been built in the highpoint of Gothic Architecture. The building had tall towers and spires, like a church, but was actually more of an events venue, with a great hall for speeches and conferences.

Louis sniffed, then inhaled deeply through his nose.

"Do I smell…" he muttered.

Rhiannon grinned, reaching into her rucksack and pulling out a brown paper bag.

"You're like a bloodhound for these things, I swear." she said, opening the bag and pulling out two raspberry croissants, handing one to her boyfriend. "Your nose practically has super-powers."

"Just when it comes to raspberry croissants." Louis grinned, taking a huge bite.

Behind them, the other activists sauntered along, following their leaders.

"Did you see the story about that guy who broke into the uni halls and beat the crap out of some creep for taking advantage of a bunch of different women?" one of the activists was saying to the others.

"Who, the masked guy with the metal fists?" Louis said, turning his head to respond. "I saw that! Respect, honestly." Rhiannon snorted.

"Such a man-move. I bet he was related to one of the women." she said. "See, that's the problem with men. It's not a problem, until it happens to someone they care about, then suddenly it's the worst thing in the world. Maybe if men acted like it was a

79

problem regardless of who the woman was, we'd be better at handling it as a society."

"I don't know, how do you know he knew the victims?" Louis said. "Maybe he was just standing up for what's right?"

"Why that guy, then?" Rhiannon asked. "Why specifically him? Nah, he knew the victim. Otherwise he'd have beaten up hundreds of other creeps, and he wouldn't stop there. I'm not saying he's a bad guy. If some creep ever tries something with me, I fully expect you to tear him in half... But it's a sad state our society has gotten into when it takes an angry friend or relative in a mask to break in and assault the creep for any justice to be served."

Louis nodded in agreement.

"Right, let's get this started then."

There were a few people milling about outside the hall, with two older men guarding the door. They were both in their forties, with clean-shaven heads, wearing football shirts that may have fit them back in the day, but were growing tight around the belly.

Rhiannon marched with purpose towards the entrance of the hall, and the few onlookers gathered outside started to murmur as her and her activists barged past. The two men moved to block the door.

"You can't go in there." one of them said, in a gruff voice.

"We can, and we will." Rhiannon replied. "We are not moving until you let us in."

Inside the building, a handful of middle-aged men and women (all white, not so coincidentally) were setting up chairs. A few of them looked over to the entrance, scowling as they saw Rhiannon and her activists crowding around the door.

At the front of the hall, a man in a suit was pacing up and down, talking to himself. He was about six feet tall, but his bulky shoulders and massive arms made him seem bigger. His chest looked like a barrel, practically bursting out of his shirt, and he was unable to do the buttons of his shirt up to the top, as his neck was twice as thick as a regular person's. He had a classic short-back-and-sides haircut and just the shadow of facial hair covering his face, and an intensity in his eyes that could scare even the toughest of men.

"Johnny!" one of the men at the door called, and the man stopped his pacing and looked over.

His eyes immediately locked onto Rhiannon, and he marched over to the door.

"I was wondering if any of your lot would show up." he grinned. "I'd suggest you walk away now, before I call the coppers."

"Johnny Johnson." Rhiannon forced a smile in response. "Unlike you to call the pigs. Aren't you usually running from them?"

"Those days are behind me now, love." Johnny replied. "I'm a man of the people now. Or haven't you heard? I'm a politician now."

"Still a crook, just a different kind of crook." Rhiannon fired back. "We don't want racist scum like you giving talks in our city."

Johnny stepped in closer, placing his hands up in a shrugging motion.

"Freedom of speech, love." he said. "The people want to hear me speak, who am I to say no?"

"Move out the way, snowflakes!" a shout came from behind the activists.

"Go back to where you came from!" came another shout. "We don't want you here! Britain for the British!"

"It's not your lot we have a problem with, leave us alone!" one woman called out.

"The people have spoken!" Johnny Johnson's grin spread even wider, practically splitting his face in half. "I can either have the coppers deal with you, or I can have my boys haul you out, your choice."

"You wouldn't dare." Rhiannon said.

Johnny leaned in close.

"You know what they call me, love?" he said, breathing directly into Rhiannon's ear. His breath stank of beer. "They call me the Gov. Because I'm the boss, and those boys will do anything for me. Believe it or not, I'm not just in it for me any more. Half of these lads lost their jobs when the factory closed, and now they're at risk of losing their jobs again to immigrants and illegals. I'm here to make a stand, and I'm not backing

81

down. Neither of us want this to kick off, but I'm willing to let it if I have to. Are you?"

"Back off." Louis growled, pushing Johnny back and stepping between him and Rhiannon. "Don't touch her!"

The two men guarding the door grabbed Louis and threw him against the wall. They were big guys, but Louis was bigger, and it took both of them to restrain him. Behind Rhiannon, a bunch of red-faced, gammon-like men, each indistinguishable from the one next to him, were pushing and shoving with Rhiannon's civil rights group.

"OOH. AHH." A chant rose up from the back of the crowd. "WHO. ARE. YA!"

"OOH. AHH. WHO. ARE. YA!" the men all began to join in, becoming more and more aggressive with their shoving.

"OOH AH. WHOAREYA! OOH. AH. BOVVER BOYS!"

Rhiannon saw one of the men throw a punch, and one of her activists dropped to the ground.

Louis broke free of the men holding him back, pushing his way back to Rhiannon.

"We need to get out of here, babe." he said. "It's not safe."

Rhiannon turned and glanced back at Johnny Johnson just in time to see a shorter, slightly chubbier man with glasses place a hand on Johnny's shoulder and guide him back into the hall.

"Alright, move out!" Rhiannon said.

The activists pushed and shoved their way away from the hall, to the cheers from the crowd of nationalists. Louis bent down to help up the activist who had been punched, and the group rushed away. Rhiannon lingered by the doorway, and the crowd pushed past her into the hall, some of them shoving forcefully against her on their way past. Rhiannon took a few steps backwards, watching through the doorway as Johnny Johnson approached the podium to begin his speech. One of the bulky men in a football shirt slammed the door in Rhiannon's face, but through it she could hear Johnny begin his speech.

"They will always try and silence us!" he roared out to his small crowd. "But we will not be silenced! People like them want to take away our voice, but they will just make us louder!"

A few of the men cheered.

"Just a few streets away from here, they've built a new mosque!"

This was met with a chorus of boos and hisses, like a children's pantomime.

"If we stand by and do nothing, they are going to bring their Shariah Law to our city! We're overrun with refugees and illegals, and our British culture is being taken away from us! They take our jobs! The government gives them free housing while Brits are on the street! They scrounge off benefits! We need to make a stand! We will make a stand! Tonight, we will show them!"

"Bloody hell…" Rhiannon muttered, turning and rushing down the path after her group as the crowd cheered. "Tonight…"

The Bovver Boys were a gang of racist thugs that had caused havoc across Downtown City for generations. Most of the members were affiliated with far right parties such as the UK Defence League and the British Independence Party, many of them were even neo-nazis. They had started out as a gang of football hooligans, but in the 1990s had become involved in organised crime, after their leader, Johnny Johnson, and a small group of his most loyal followers had carried out a series of bank robberies. He had served a life sentence, but the gang had continued with their illegal activities, and upon release, Johnny Johnson had become a prominent member of the UK Defence League, still rubbing shoulders with the new leaders of the Bovver Boys. He'd even published a book about British pride entitled 'GOD SAVE GREAT BRITAIN'. Johnny's rise to popularity could almost certainly be traced back to the closing down of the old factory: that's when the attitudes of many of the locals started to sour.

There was one thing Rhiannon knew for sure: if Johnny Johnson and the Bovver Boys made a threat, you took it seriously.

CHAPTER FIVE: THE MIRACLE GIRL

As the hall cleared out, Johnny Johnson stood near the stage, giving friendly greetings and firm handshakes to some of his supporters. As the last exited the hall, leaving only a few Bovver Boys chatting in the corner, Johnny's right hand man pushed his glasses up his nose and let out a sigh.

"You're not really going to march on the mosque, are you?" he asked.

"Come on, Huey." Johnny said. "We gotta take a stand, have you not been listening to any of what I've said?"

"Listening?" Johnny's brother rolled his eyes. "I wrote half of it. Practically all of it, actually, despite the last minute changes you always slip in. Look, Josiah, you're good at this, and you've got a real future ahead of you. People listen to you, people like you. You can really spread the cause, get people back on Britain's side again... But not if you allow people to keep seeing you as the violent thug the media tells them you are."

"Don't call me Josiah, Huey." Johnny snapped back. "It's Johnny, or Gov."

"Don't be so sensitive, brother." Huey replied. "Listen, going after the mosque is a bad call. Fight with words, not with aggression. Prove that we are in the right, don't let them paint us as terrorists."

Johnny sighed, placing a hand on Huey's shoulder.

"Don't worry about it, bruv. We're not actually going to do anything. Just want to make our presence known, get them a little riled up. Give the boys something to take their aggression out on."

He turned and started walking towards the Bovver Boys, who now stood waiting for him.

"I made you, Johnny." Huey said. "Don't forget, those words that made everyone fall in love with you: your book… Those are my words, Johnny. That's my book."

Johnny turned his head.

"And you got paid, didn't you? You were the one who didn't want to risk having your name on the cover if it went badly. That was your idea."

"You know I'm on your side, but I just think there are smarter ways to go about it. You'll see, soon enough. You can win the people over, then you won't need to keep acting like brutes."

"Maybe I like being a brute."

Johnny joined the Bovver Boys and they exited the hall, leaving Huey rubbing his temple firmly, with stress building up inside him.

***

Jason slunk back to the hotel with a heavy heart, not sure what to do for the rest of his day. The midday sun was now high in the sky, and the rays of light had banished the cutting morning chill, replacing it with a summer breeze. It wasn't particularly warm, but it was a pleasant enough day. As Jason rolled into the carpark of the hotel, a police car pulled into the entrance. Officer Parker stepped out, followed by a middle-aged white officer with glasses and a stern expression.

"Jason, can we talk to you for a second?" Officer Parker asked.

"W-w-whats up?" Jason stammered.

"Would you be willing to come down to the station, for a quick chat?" Officer Parker asked.

"A chat about what? Is t-there an update on my sister's case?" Jason asked, fiddling with the controls of his wheelchair.

"It's related to the case." the other officer said.

"Has something happened?" Jason asked.

"Daniel McDonald was assaulted last night, we just want to be sure that you weren't involved." Officer Parker replied.

"Where were you between the hours of seven and ten last night?" the other officer asked.

Jason frowned. Perfect timing, the bartender from last night was just arriving at work, walking through the car park to the

85

back entrance of the hotel.

"Jason!" Will exclaimed, beaming and walking over. "What is going on? Is something wrong? Still recovering from last night?"

"You were with Jason last night?" Sabrina turned her attention to Will.

"Yes, he came in for drinks at the hotel bar. He spent most of the evening drinking with another man." Will said.

"Who are you?" the officer turned to Will and frowned.

"I am the bartender." Will said. "My name is William Ricci."

"What time did Jason enter the bar?" Officer Parker asked.

Will frowned and shrugged, looking from Jason, back to the officers. His eyes met Jason's and there seemed to be a non-verbal exchange between the two of them.

"I don't know, around 6:30, 7ish." he said. "I forget exactly. It was early evening."

"And can anyone else vouch for this?"

"Maybe the friend he was drinking with." Will shrugged. "Anyway, I must get to work."

He tapped Jason on the shoulder and winked at him, walking away.

"Well, unless you think a disabled man was able to transport himself quickly backwards and forwards between a bar and wherever Dan was attacked, it seems I have an alibi." Jason said.

"I'm sorry." Officer Parker said. "Could you possibly give us the name and contact details for the friend you were drinking with."

"His name is Alex Axton." Jason said. "I don't have his contact details... Except his Facebook page."

Jason held up his phone and showed the Facebook profile for Alex, which he had found earlier that day.

"When I attacked Dan on the night of my sister's attack, it was a spur of the m-m-moment mistake." Jason said. "It didn't go well for me. I was driven by passion, and it was stupid. I definitely wouldn't d-do it again. But I'm sure plenty of others would. Have you seen the social media p-posts about Dan?"

"What posts?" Officer Parker asked.

"Two other girls have come forward on social media. I guess

they heard what happened to my sister. There are a lot of h-h-hateful c-comments towards Dan. He's not popular right now."

The officers exchanged a look.

"Can you show us?" Officer Parker asked.

Jason shrugged and pulled back his phone, opening to the page he had seen earlier. Officer Parker angled the phone to show her partner, then handed it back.

"Don't leave town." the other officer said. "We'll let you know once we've determined whether your alibi checks out, or if we need you to come in for further questioning."

With that, the officers returned to their car.

Jason made a mental note to thank Will later. They weren't close friends, but it was nice to know people had his back.

***

"Beginning animal trials."

Iona stood, syringe in hand, with Dr Wood hovering above her, watching intently. In front of her, a lab assistant had pulled a mouse out of a cage and was inspecting the rodent thoroughly.

"Subject one has a tumour between its amygdala and its entorhinal cortex." Iona said. "Our patented NanoVirus has been programmed to target the tumour, remove it, repair the brain tissue and aid in recovery."

Iona injected the mouse, and allowed it to scamper back into the cage.

"Subject two has a heart condition. The NanoVirus has been programmed to repair the heart and improve its capacity." Iona said, as the assistant reached for a second mouse. Dr Wood continued to make notes. Iona picked up a second syringe and injected the second mouse.

"Subject three has lost a leg. The NanoVirus has been programmed to rebuild the lost limb and aid in recovery."

Iona leaned forwards as the assistant offered up the third mouse. Her hand began to tremble, and she dropped the syringe.

"Is everything okay, doctor?" one of the assistants asked.

"I'm just feeling a little faint." Iona replied. "Can you take over?"

She stepped away and allowed her assistants to continue the

trial. Dr Wood followed her over to her desk, where she took a seat. The room started to spin gently, like she was on a boat, and she steadied herself against the desk, closing her eyes and taking a few deep breaths.

"Is it a relapse?" Dr Wood asked.

"No, I'm fine." Iona replied. "Just… Exhausted."

"Take a break." Dr Wood said, placing a hand on her shoulder. "Go and get one of those smoothies you love. You've done good work here today."

"Thank you." Iona smiled. "I'll do that."

Dr Wood returned to the experiment, and Iona placed her head in her hands. Her vision grew blurry, and she focused on her breathing.

"You're okay." she murmured, under her breath. "It's okay." It took her a moment to regain her composure, and even then her knees felt weak and she had trouble focusing. Internally, she cursed her ill health. It was the most horrible irony: her work could mean an end to terminal illnesses forever, but she was being prevented from properly carrying it out due to her own terminal illness.

***

The general hustle and bustle of the police station made for a momentary distraction as Sabrina and her new partner entered the station empty-handed, and the sergeant took a couple of minutes to notice.

"Where's Mr Fox?" he asked, power-walking straight over to her as she sat at her desk and busied herself with her paperwork.

"He has an alibi." she said. "And it turns out Mr McDonald has a lot more enemies than we first thought, he-"

"I told you to bring him in for questioning." Sergeant Burns interrupted.

"He has an alibi." Sabrina repeated. "Anyway, as I was saying-"

"Officer Briggs?" Sergeant Burns turned to her partner.

"It's true." the older man said. "He was drinking with a friend last night, there was a barman who confirmed. And Mr McDonald does seem to have a lot of enemies. There are people all over social media wishing harm on him. It seems two other young women have come forward with similar statements to Sarah Fox."

"Can you try and contact the friend to get a statement?" the sergeant said. Officer Briggs nodded and walked away.

"Shouldn't we be getting statements from the two girls, so that we can use them as evidence for Sarah Fox's case?"

"I told you that case is closed." the sergeant snapped.

"It's not closed!" Sabrina exclaimed. "You know as well as I do, we can't close it!"

"A technicality."

"And what happened to innocent until proven guilty?" Sabrina asked. "There's less evidence against Jason than there is Mr McDonald, but you seem all too eager to spend time and resources going after him."

Sergeant Burns snapped his head round, his face starting to grow red, his jaw clenched in frustration.

"Officer, I will bust you down to traffic control if you don't watch your tone. You can go home early today, you are dismissed."

He let out a "hmmpfh" noise, and marched away, leaving Sabrina feeling frustrated and disheartened. There was nothing to do but turn and leave, and as she did she was painfully aware of the eyes burning into the back of her head as everyone else watched her go.

Sabrina hated this. She just wanted to do her job, but it seemed her and her boss disagreed on what that job really was.

***

Alex headed back to Robby's place in the suburbs, walking the whole way to clear his head. It took a good hour and a half, and by the time he got there, his thoughts had passed on from Jason and his dreams and onto Blake, and how much he missed him. He thought about texting or calling, but just ended up staring at his number in the phone. He found himself walking whilst staring at his phone, and before he knew it he was in the more blissful suburban part of the city where Robby and his family lived. Their humble house was just across the park, and though it wasn't a large place, Alex found it to be a pleasant respite from the stress of the rest of his life.

Alex sighed, and headed for Robby's door, ringing the bell.

It was his wife that answered, and she had a stressed look. She sighed when she saw him.

"Hi, Alex." she said. "He's in the kitchen, you better go talk to him."

"Cynthia. Did something happen?" Alex frowned.

"Did you not get my text? Well, it's best you let him tell it anyway."

Alex walked into the house, kicking his shoes off and heading for the kitchen. Robby was there, in his overalls, an ice pack clutched to his head. He had the beginnings of a bruise forming on the side of his cheek, and his face was scrunched up in pain.

"What happened to you?!" Alex exclaimed.

"Bridge Boys." Robby replied, gruffly. "Tony came by the garage an hour or so ago, we… exchanged words. Don't get involved with that lot, Alex. I know he was your friend, back in the day, but I warned you he'd gotten worse."

"That twat." Alex growled. "He tried to recruit me last night, but I told him no."

"I wondered why you didn't come back here." Robby said.

"Good on you for telling him no, but I may need you to find somewhere else to stay. I'm sorry mate, but I can't have any of this coming back to me at home."

Alex felt that familiar rage bubble up inside him again, thrashing like crazy to break free and take over.

"Of course." Alex replied, clenching and unclenching his fists. "He's out of order."

"Someone needs to shut that boy down." Cynthia said. "We should call the police."

"Calling the police would be more trouble than it's worth, honey." Robby said. "That boy has got more dirt on me than I've got on my overalls."

"I'll get us all some beer, order takeout and we can forget about Antonio for the night." Alex said. "I'll find somewhere else to stay tomorrow, and make sure he knows you're off-limits. I'll sort it out."

90

"Be careful, Alex." Cynthia said. "I don't want to have to call your father to tell him something has happened to you."
She placed a hand on his shoulder, then headed out of the room.
Alex pulled out his phone and opened up the messenger app. All he needed was two sentences, sent to Jason:
'I'm in. We start with the Bridge Boys.'
It only took a minute or two for the response to come through.
'When?'
'Tomorrow.' Alex replied. *'But we need to do this properly. We'll meet at yours to plan it out.'*

***

Zakirah sat down to dinner with her gracious hosts, feeling a little more comfortable now in clothes that actually belonged to her, though feeling slightly guilty that Asim and Saabira were still paying for everything for her. She'd found herself a pair of jeans and a slick, green jacket, and was feeling pleased with her new style. Compared to the very traditional Muslim house, decorated with Middle-Eastern and South Asian ornaments and a few pieces of artwork, her new clothing was probably the only western thing in sight, but she liked it. She felt like a new person.
Asim led the three of them in silent prayer, their heads bowed, and for a minute Zakirah just listened to the clock ticking, wondering if it was impolite not to pray with them, even though the prayer was silent and they couldn't actually tell the difference. Then the moment was over, and Saabira began serving out the food.
On the wall, the phone rang, and Asim rushed over to answer it. He still had an old, corded phone mounted on the wall, though to Zakirah that wouldn't have even seemed an odd thing. Most of the houses she'd stayed in before she reached England, while she was on move, completely without a home, hadn't had modern phones, and some of them didn't have a phone at all. And that was when she'd been lucky enough to stay in a house.
"Hello, yes, this is Imam Abad." Asim said, putting the phone to his ear.

There was a moment of quiet as he listened to the voice on the other end.

"I see." Asim said, his face betraying very little emotion.

"Thank you for telling me."

He put the phone down.

"What is it?" Zakirah asked.

"The mosque." he said. "Someone is going to try and burn it down. Tonight. Some of the local community want to try to stop them. I must go, and make sure no one is hurt."

Zakirah burst to her feet.

"Let me help." she said.

"Absolutely not." Asim replied. "I need you both to stay here, where it is safe. I cannot allow you to put yourself in harm's way."

"But you've done so much for me!" Zakirah argued. "Let me do something to help you!"

"The answer is no, but I thank you for offering." Asim raised a hand in dismissal. "Now, I must go."

He rushed out of the door, grabbing his keys and slipping his shoes on as he exited the house, barely breaking stride as he did so.

Zakirah said nothing, but rushed up to the guest room. She grabbed the flip phone that Asim had got her for emergencies, slipped on her trainers, and rushed out the door. Asim wasn't going to stop her: these people had taken her in. She was taking a stand.

***

Rhiannon, Louis and a small cluster of activists were waiting when the Bovver Boys showed up. The mosque was not far from the city centre, and was situated on a side street. Before the mosque, every building was an office building, and after the mosque there was a road. Across the road, the houses started. The new mosque had taken the place of what used to be a car park, and was actually quite small compared to the buildings surrounding it. Evening had settled in, and the sun had set, and Rhiannon and her activists linked arms and blocked the entrance to the mosque, as ten to fifteen middle-aged men in football shirts, with bandannas over the bottom

92

half of their faces, made their way to the mosque. Some were carrying bats, others were simply clenching their fists, trying their best to look imposing. In any other circumstance, Rhiannon would have been tempted to mock them. But they outnumbered the activists.

"Out of the way!" The butch man at the front of the group stepped forwards to address the activists. Even with the bandanna covering his face, there was no mistaking him for anyone but Johnny Johnson. He was wearing a jacket over his Downtown City Football Club t-shirt, and though he was unarmed he somehow looked the most menacing of all of them. "This building is an affront to our culture! We will not have their muslamic ways forced into our city!"

"Back off, you racist ballbag!" one of the activists, a bearded man with glasses named Ricardo, shouted back.

The doors to the mosque opened, and behind the line of activists, a handful of Muslim men exited the mosque. They all had a frightened look in their eyes, but seemed to be trying their best to stand tall.

"We do not wish to harm your culture." one of the men said. "We just wish to worship in peace."

"You should have thought about that before you tore down our factory to build your mosque! You took our livelihoods!"

"The old mosque was built long after the factory closed!" one of the Muslim men tried to reason with them, but it was hopeless. "We had nothing to do with the closure!"

"Go home!" another of the Bovver Boys yelled. "Terrorist!"

From down the street, the imam of the mosque appeared, with another group of muslim men. They walked with purpose, the other men clustering behind the imam and quietly muttering to one another.

"Please!" the imam called. "We do not wish for this to descend into violence. We mean you no harm!"

"Your country stole our jobs, then your people come over here and build mosques on our land and erode away our culture!" Johnny snarled back. "You started the violence! We are just defending our heritage!"

He marched towards the imam, and Rhiannon rushed in to block his path.

"Stop!" she said. "We're not going to let you do this!"

"You again." Johnny replied. "And here I thought you was a Christian."

Rhiannon frowned, taken aback.

"How did you-"

"That's right, I know who you are." Though his lips were not visible, Rhiannon could tell he was smirking. "You've got no idea who you're messing with, Rhiannon. You should be more careful what you post on the internet, little girl."

"Who I am is irrelevant." Rhiannon replied. "And a good Christian looks out for their neighbour."

"They are not your neighbours. WE are your neighbours, born and bred."

"Our lord and saviour was more similar to them than he was to you." Rhiannon shot back.

Johnny rolled his eyes and pushed past Rhiannon, heading straight for the leader of the mosque.

"Oi! Don't touch her!" Louis yelled, not breaking the line, but looking like he wanted to tackle Johnny Johnson and smash his head against the curb.

Johnny ignored him, grabbing the imam by the scruff of his robes.

"How about you get your people to run away, or someone's going to get hurt!"

Zakirah watched from the alley as the racist thug grabbed Asim by his tunic and pulled him in close. Rage bubbled up inside her, and she sprinted from the alleyway next to the mosque, slamming hard into Johnny Johnson. She caught the man off-balance and by surprise, and even though she was much smaller than him, she still managed to send him tumbling to the ground. Unfortunately, this was all the gang of hooligans needed to set them off.

"OOH AHH!" two of them screamed, launching themselves towards Zakirah. One of them swung a bat straight for her head, but he tripped at just the last second and fell flat on his face. The other made a wild grab for her, only to trip over the bat from the first one.

Zakirah thanked her streak of good luck, and turned towards

94

the rest of the gang of thugs, her eyes filled with passion and rage.

"Bloody hell, that was lucky!" Rhiannon muttered, watching as this mysterious woman faced off against the angry mob. But what happened next, not even a streak of good luck could explain. To Zakirah, time seemed to slow down.

The gang ran towards her one by one taking a swing at her. She took a side-step, and the first man's fist completely missed her, and with all his weight thrown behind the punch, he tumbled to the ground. Another took a swing at her with a bat, but his grip on the bat wasn't tight enough and it flew from his grasp, smashing into the head of the man next to him. Each movement seemed punctuated by a subtle wisp of light, darting backwards and forwards between her attackers.

Rhiannon watched as one by one the men took their own swing at Zakirah, and one by one they topped to the ground. Zakirah barely moved, and yet still, somehow, every single blow missed.

"Miracle Girl." Asim breathed.

Johnny Johnson pushed himself to his feet, his face red with rage, and sprinted towards Zakirah from behind. He barrelled into her with full force, knocking her to the ground, but Louis and Ricardo were on him in seconds, pulling him off.

Rhiannon and Asim rushed over, and Asim helped Zakirah up, ushering her away inside the mosque.

"I guess her luck ran out…" Rhiannon muttered, then her eyes caught sight of Johnny Johnson's hands. Clasped in one hand was the handle of a switchblade. The blade part lay broken on the ground, where he had stood facing off against Rhiannon. He must have pulled it out as he made a run for the woman, but as he flicked the blade out, it had broken off, and instead of stabbing the woman with an actual blade, he'd poked her harmlessly with the handle.

"That's just impossible…" Rhiannon muttered.

Johnny Johnson broke free of Ricardo and Louis' grip and turned and ran. Most of his men followed him, though one or two still lay on the ground, recovering from their falls.

"Alright everyone, break it up, break it up!"

Two police officers stood at the end of the street, marching with purpose towards the mosque.

"They attacked us!" one of the Muslim men called out. "They wanted to burn down the mosque!"

"We'll take statements in a moment." the first police officer said. "If everyone could please calm down, take a seat on the curb. We're going to call for back-up and sort this whole mess out."

Rhiannon walked over to the officer.

"It's true." she said. "We saw it all. They came here looking to attack the mosque. They were led by Johnny Johnson, but he ran away."

"Johnny Johnson the author?" the police officer said.

"Yes, and the former bank robber, weird that you focus on the author part." Rhiannon said.

The police officer rolled his eyes.

"Can you prove it?" he asked.

"I recognised him." Rhiannon said.

"Well, alright." the other officer said. "Settle down, miss, and we'll take your statement in a moment."

Rhiannon let out a frustrated sigh.

"What's the point?" she muttered. "Not like you lot are going to do anything about it. Pigs."

She turned and walked away.

"What did you say?" the first officer called after her.

"You heard me!" Rhiannon called back, still walking away.

Zakirah sat in the back of the mosque, perched on a bucket, as the doctor, Ian, checked her over.

"Good thing I happened to be here." he muttered. "Looks like you're okay, aside from a nasty bruise on the back of your head from when you fell."

"It could have been a lot worse." Asim said. "You should not have come, it was foolish."

"I make my own decisions." Zakirah said. "I wasn't about to let you face danger alone. I only took the same risks as you."

"But you are a woman." Asim pointed out.

"Yes, I am a capable woman who faced months of hardship in far more dangerous places than this and survived." Zakirah said. "I appreciate everything you've done for me, but please don't underestimate me because I am a woman. Asim, I care about you and Saabira greatly, but you need to understand that you are not my parents and that I am not a child, and if I want to do something, I am going to do it. My life has been far too difficult and filled with far too much grief for me to waste it by not seizing the day, every day."

Asim sighed, taking a moment of solemn contemplation.

"Clearly, Allah has a plan for you." he said. "And he was watching over you today. Whether I like it or not, Allah clearly meant for you to be here."

"I saw what happened outside, and it was nothing short of a miracle." the doctor added.

"It was strange." Zakirah admitted. "Surely that couldn't just have been luck?"

"If it were just luck, then you have perhaps gone from being one of the unluckiest people to one of the luckiest people." Ian replied.

"It is Allah, for sure." Asim said. "Allah has given you a great gift. Use it well."

CHAPTER SIX: THE BATTLE FOR COVERED MARKET

"The Bridge Boys have their main hangout at an abandoned warehouse by the dockside, not far from the main bridge. There are probably usually between five and ten people there at any one time." Alex said. "We need to make sure we get the right warehouse: there are a few, and some of them are just shelters the homeless use."

The two men sat in Jason's garage, looking at a map on Jason's laptop. Alex pointed to the docklands area of Downtown city on the map.

"We can take them by surprise pretty easily, but we need to have a big impact, make sure the point is heard, otherwise we'll just be starting a war."

"And we need to make sure we send a m-message that other gangs hear." Jason added.

"We want Antonio to come out of this still in power." Alex said. "I know him, so we have leverage there, but we wouldn't have that advantage if someone new took his place."

"How do you know Big Tuna, anyway?" Jason asked. "He's pretty n-notorious, but you seem to really know him?"

"We grew up together." Alex replied, rubbing the back of his head and leaning against the table. "We're loosely related, by law, I suppose. My uncle was his step-dad for a while. His actual dad was a petty crook, he always idolised him. We actually got involved with the Bridge Boys together, years back. I had some real anger problems, and I took that anger out in really unhealthy ways... but I decided I wanted out pretty quickly, and joined the army. Good thing I did: there was a major sting right after I enlisted, and a whole load of gang members served time. Most of them are still in prison now. That was when Tony took his chance to seize power, and he's been in charge of the gang ever since."

"So you and Big Tuna were friends?" Jason asked.

"We used to be." Alex replied.

"We should use your knowledge to our advantage, b-b-but we need to be c-careful. We don't want them figuring out it's you." Jason said. "And remember: this isn't a personal feud. We're doing this to p-protect the p-p-people they've been extorting. We want to shut down their protection racket."

Alex nodded.

"Well how do we do that?" he asked. "How do we make it clear that this is about shutting them down, not starting a gang war?"

Jason thought for a second, then smiled.

"What if we don't do this on their turf? What if we do this at the Covered Market? Lure them there, and make a p-public statement."

"Alright... What are you thinking?"

***

Big Tuna sat with his feet propped up against the table, staring at the TV, which was half-way through showing Scarface. He mouthed along to every single line, having watched it countless times. Those closest to him knew it wasn't the only movie he could recite by heart: the Godfather, Goodfellas, Pulp Fiction, and a handful of others he insisted were classics everyone had to watch. Around him, the members of his gang, the Bridge Boys, lounged around playing cards and drinking, each of them wearing their suits, some with the top buttons undone and the sleeves rolled up.

The back door to the warehouse flew open and a woman came sprinting in, tie torn from her suit, sweating profusely.

"Someone's snatched up our guys." she panted, stumbling to a stand-still in front of Big Tuna.

"The cops?" Big Tuna asked. "Who did they take?"

The woman shook her head.

"Nah. Not the cops. Some guy with a bandanna covering his face, with big goggles on. I saw him drop from a fire escape

99

and beat the crap out of Brainy." she said, coughing as she struggled to catch her breath. "I went to find K and Winston, but they were gone too. I called Winston's phone, and some weird voice on the other end just said to tell you that you're going down."

On the table, a flip phone vibrated dramatically. Big Tuna leaned in and picked it up.

"*Big Tuna*." the distorted voice on the other end of the line came. "*Covered Market is no longer your turf. End your protection racket, leave it alone.*"

Big Tuna scoffed, and the men and women around him turned their heads to look at him, hushing so that they might hear the voice on the other end of the phone.

"I don't know who you think you are, but if you know who I am, you know you don't just take turf from me. I'd advise you to apologise, and hang up."

"*I'm not taking your turf. Covered Market is free, it belongs to no one. You don't like it? Come find me. I'm at the market. I have your men.*"

"Big joker, aren't you?" Big Tuna grinned. "Okay, I'll play your game. But I'd recommend you let my men go and get running, because when I get there, you're a dead man."

He slammed the phone shut and pulled a pair of leather gloves out of his pockets, slipping them on. The Bridge Boys jumped up and started grabbing their weapons: an assortment of bats and knives. One of them opened a cupboard in the corner and pulled out a short-barrelled shotgun.

"Jeb." Big Tuna said, extending his hand, and the man tossed the gun to him. He caught it and turned to the woman who had just run in.

"Take Smithy and go to the other end of the city: Kirby Road, or somewhere in that area. Not far enough away to be in the territory of the next police station over. Make a distraction, something that'll lure the cops there for a bit. Stay safe."

He turned to the rest of his men.

"Let's go." he said. "Covered Market."

***

"You cut the power, right?"

"Of course I cut the power, help me up these stairs."

Jason was struggling to climb the stairs, leaning on a set of crutches for support. Alex stood behind him, glancing towards the entrance of the market awkwardly. It was pitch black, and there was no one around at the moment, but it was the city, and no street was ever empty for long. Alex was wearing a big pair of goggles, equipped with night vision, and a bandanna over the bottom half of his face, with the protective vest and motorcycle outfit. Jason had a big coat pulled around him and a fabric eye mask tied around his face, his hood pulled as far forward as it would go.

"Where's your wheelchair?" Alex asked, putting an arm around Jason and helping him up the stairs.

"In the back alley." Jason replied.

As they got to the top of the stairs, Jason stopped to catch his breath.

"We've got to move quickly." Alex said. "They'll be here any minute."

Big Tuna and his men pulled up to the Covered Market in three separate cars. Big Tuna stayed back with the same group that he had taken to the Covered Market previously, and indicated for the rest of his men to enter the market. He handed the one called Jeb a radio.

"Let me know what you find." he said.

They approached the gate, pushing it. The chain that held it shut fell easily away, the padlock already broken. The inner door had been forced open.

As the men walked inside, they were greeted by the sight of the three dealers that had been taken, tied up and gagged in a circle in the entrance-way. One of them went straight for the lightswitches, flicking a couple of them on and off several times, but nothing happened. The entire Covered Market was bathed in darkness, and all any of them could see were shadows moving against the walls.

Two of them pulled out torches. Another turned on the torch function on his smartphone.

As soon as they did this, there was a distinct clatter as two objects flew from either side of the balcony and landed on the ground. Smoke poured from the objects, filling the general vicinity, and the objects were closely followed by two more: smoke grenades, pouring out coloured smoke.

Two of the Bridge Boys headed straight for the stairs, and as they did a figure dropped himself from the balcony, bending his knees and rolling as he hit the ground. He was clad in a padded motorcycle outfit: lycra, with a kevlar lining, his face covered with a bandanna and massive goggles that seemed to be lit up: perhaps night-vision goggles. His fists were three times the size of normal fists, and looked like they were made of metal.

Alex was on his feet in seconds, pointing his fists and the closest two Bridge Boys: a taller woman and a shorter man. A pulse of energy shot from the gloves, sending the two gangsters flying across the Covered Market. They hit the wall at the far end and slid down, unconscious.

Jeb pulled a gun from a holster hidden in his suit jacket and aimed at the figure, firing two shots at Alex. Luckily, Alex's reflexes were good, and the moment the gun came out, he dropped to the ground, and the shots flew harmlessly past him. It was dark enough that it took Jeb far too long to focus on where Alex had moved to, and he was on his feet and moving swiftly towards the next thug before Jeb even knew where to look. Alex electrified his gauntlet, grabbing the thug by the arm and sending an electric shock through his body. The man let out a cry and dropped to the ground, and Alex quickly sprinted towards Jeb, who fired another shot as he heard Alex coming, this time grazing Alex's upper arm. He grunted in pain, reaching towards the gun, which shot from Jeb's hand and into Alex's grip, clanging against the now magnetised gauntlet. One of the other Bridge Boys caught Alex from behind with a bat, swinging it hard into his back. He stumbled forwards, dropping the gun, which slid across the floor and under a market stall. Luckily, he was protected from the brunt of the blow by his padded vest, but still felt pain ripple through his spine. He spun round, kicking his attacker square in the chest, then grabbed him by the shoulder, electrifying the gauntlets once more and sending him tumbling to the ground,

102

spasming as he landed.

Two more men attacked Alex from either side, swinging their knives wildly. He caught one arm mid-swing, breaking the attacker's wrist in one swift jerk and throwing him into the other. He then punched the second man in the nose and kneed the first in the rear and they collapsed.

The ring-leader had now taken a bat from one of the others and let out a loud cry as he swung for Alex. Alex dodged the bat and jabbed the man twice: once in the stomach, the second in the chest. He dropped the bat, taking a swing for Alex with his fist. Alex pushed with both of his gauntlets, and a wave of kinetic energy sent the man flying across the market, smashing into the wall with a satisfying thud.

Bang!

Alex dropped instinctively to the ground as an explosion rang through the market, and the sound of Big Tuna's shotgun being cocked quickly followed.

The gun hadn't been aimed at Alex: if it had, it would have wounded both him and Big Tuna's right-hand man, who had still been in front of Alex when Big Tuna entered and aimed. Instead, it was aimed at the air, the market too dark for Big Tuna to take the risk of aiming.

"Do I have your attention?" Big Tuna roared, as he reloaded. "Good!"

This time he aimed the gun in the vague direction of Alex. Just in time, a brick dropped from the balcony, landing directly on Big Tuna's head. He grunted, collapsing to the ground. Alex brought the gauntlets together in front of himself and clapped, hard. This time, the wave of energy that shot out from him was enough to throw him backwards. The remaining Bridge Boys were sent flying with tremendous speed, skidding across the stone floor. They scrambled to their feet and fled quickly which was lucky, because Alex noticed the lights on the gauntlets start to fade.

He looked up to the balcony, but Jason was already hobbling to the fire escape.

None of the Bridge Boys were still standing. Outside, sirens could be heard.

Alex turned and ran up the stairs, heading all the way to the back, where a second staircase led to the roof. He pushed through the door and ran to the edge of the roof, where a banner was already waiting to be unfurled. In the alley below, he could see Jason in his chair, already rolling in the opposite direction to the front of the market, heading out onto the back street. On the main street, in front of the market, he saw the Bridge Boys scattering, some limping, some helping injured comrades. Two police cars and two police vans pulled up in front of the market, and police officers in riot gear poured out of the vans.

Alex unfurled the banner and turned and ran towards the fire escape, sliding down the ladder and disappearing into the shadows. As he did so, Big Tuna exited the market, immediately greeted by a line of police officers screaming at him to put his hands in the air. The gang leader slowly raised his hands, turning to see if any of his men were behind him. A few of them were there, and his eyes finally caught sight of the newly unfurled banner.

'ANTONIO ADKINS: THIS MARKET IS PROTECTED. PLAY NICE.'

With all the police focused on Big Tuna and his men, Alex and Jason were able to slip away and regroup at Jason's garage, and within half an hour were sat, enjoying a celebratory glass of whiskey, and congratulating each other. Alex had patched up his own wound from the fight, seemingly completely unconcerned about it.

"Well, it didn't entirely go according to p-plan." Jason said. "Big Tuna got caught."

"He'll be out by tomorrow." Alex replied. "They haven't got any charges to stick to him. But he'll have the police breathing down his neck now, and he'll be severely crippled… Sorry, no offence intended."

"None taken." Jason replied. "We need a better plan of action for the future though. My b-b-back is killing me, climbing down that fire escape nearly killed me."

Alex took a sip from his whiskey.

"I'm not even sure if this was a one-time thing yet." he muttered.

"Oh, come on! Didn't you enjoy d-doing some good?" Jason exclaimed.

"Easy for you to say, you stayed pretty far away from the danger." Alex pointed out.

"My gauntlets didn't fail you though, did they?" Jason asked.

"I suppose not." Alex admitted. "Come on, fill me up again." He pushed his empty glass towards Jason.

"Slow down!" Jason muttered "This is a good whiskey."

Alex rolled his eyes.

"Booze is for getting drunk. No one's drinking it for the taste."

"Something t-tells me you get d-drunk a little too often." Jason replied.

"Just fill me up." Alex said, a smirk crossing his face.

The two lads laughed as they refilled their whiskey glasses and continued their celebration. Neither one of them were thinking of the consequences of their actions yet: they were just happy that they had won the battle for Covered Market.

***

Asim sat in the front room of his modest house, head in his hands. His expression was tired, and let out a heavy sigh. The man had a sad look in his eyes that Zakirah had seldom seen in anyone since she arrived in the UK, but was all too familiar back home: it was the kind of look people wore at funerals or in hospital waiting rooms.

"What's happened?" Zakirah asked, entering the room and sitting down on the sofa next to him.

"The police took some of the men from the mosque in for questioning after the attack, but two of them were never released." he said.

Zakirah frowned.

"But they didn't do anything." she said. "Surely they haven't been arrested?"

"I don't know." Asim said. "But I just got off the phone with the receptionist at the police station and she said she would ask around, but she was sure all of the people brought in for questioning had been released."

"That doesn't make any sense." Zakirah said. "Perhaps we should go down to the police station and see for ourselves."

Asim gave a slow, tired nod.

"I was considering doing that tomorrow." he said. "But I would rather those boys not spend the whole night in a jail cell when they have done nothing wrong."

Zakirah stood up and zipped up her jacket.

"Well, let's go." she replied.

She offered a hand to Asim, helping him up. The older man hobbled over to the door to fetch his shoes, and they headed out together.

When they reached the police station, the place was in chaos. It was not at all what they expected to find there in the middle of the night. Several police cars were in the car park with their lights on, and at least ten police officers were clustered around outside the station, hauling several men in suits into the station. Inside the station, the receptionist was rushing about, collecting paperwork from the officers, and multiple men were sitting at the desks giving statements to various tired-looking officers.

"You can't be here." one officer said to Asim as the two of them approached. "What do you want?"

"We're here to inquire after two men who were taken in for questioning after the attack on the mosque the other evening." Asim said.

"Everyone taken in for questioning was released." the officer said, sighing impatiently. "You need to go. We are very busy. Come back tomorrow morning."

He turned and rushed away.

"This is not normal." Asim muttered. "Not normal at all. Come on, let's get some sleep. We will deal with this tomorrow, they are clearly very busy here."

Zakirah shook her head.

"No, those men didn't do anything wrong, we need to push harder." she said.

"Zakirah, think." Asim whispered, grabbing her arm. "You are an illegal immigrant. Do you really want to be drawing attention to yourself in a police station?"

Zakirah stopped in her tracks and hung her head.

"You're right." she muttered. "Let's go."

"We'll come back tomorrow." Asim promised. "We'll find out what happened."

CHAPTER SEVEN: CONSEQUENCES

Officer Parker arrived early the next morning, as always, but this time the station was already buzzing with energy, and half her colleagues were already in. As she entered, she walked past Officer Jones: a younger, black woman, her hair a mess, her eyes sunken with dark rings around them from lack of sleep.

"Tanya!" Sabrina exclaimed. "I thought you had the night shift!"

"I did." she replied. "I'm just getting off now, had to give a statement. Last night was wild."

"What happened?" Sabrina asked.

"I'm sure they'll fill you in, I'm heading off, I need rest!"

She waved Sabrina goodbye, heading round back to the staff car park. Sabrina headed into the station, where Inspector Warren and Sergeant Burns were heading towards the interrogation room with purpose. Sabrina headed straight for the observation room, where a handful of officers were already gathered, watching through the one-way mirror.

Inside, a well-dressed young man was sat, head in his handcuffed hands, hat on the table in front of him. He was plain-looking: short, with slick black hair, and a prominent nose and ears. Next to him, a man in his mid-thirties, with a neat suit and slim tie, a swanky haircut and an expensive watch, was grinning emphatically at the sergeant and inspector.

"Mr Adkins, now that your lawyer is here, would you care to give a statement as to why you broke into the Covered Market last night?" Inspector Warren asked.

"My client didn't break into the market. Why would he break

in? He has a key." the grinning man said.

"Excuse me?" Sergeant Burns asked.

"Mr Adkins has shares in several of the businesses that occupy space in the market." the lawyer said. "He's a close, personal friend of the landlord, Thomas Martin. Ask Mr Martin yourself, I have his number if you need it."

"So why were you there?" Inspector Warren addressed his question to the cuffed man. "And why did you have a gun?"

"Me and my colleagues heard a commotion at the market, and went to see what was happening. When we arrived, we were attacked by a man in a mask." the man answered in a sullen tone, his voice croaky, as if tired and dehydrated. "He was the one with the guns, not us."

"So if we check the guns for prints, we won't find yours?" The man remained silent.

"And the six other people we arrested with you, three of whom were tied up?" the sergeant asked.

"Three of them were my colleagues." the man replied. "The other three, I don't know. They were tied up in the market when we got there."

"And the message above the market with your name on it. What was that about?" the inspector asked.

"I have no idea!" the cuffed man exclaimed.

"Why didn't you call the police, Mr Adkins?"

"We were going to, we just went in to see what all the commotion was about, everything happened so fast."

"If my client isn't being charged with anything, he would like to go home." the lawyer said. "He will happily give a written statement on his way out, but he is very tired, on account of being held here for no reason all night. Can we go, or are you going to list the reasons for his arrest?"

The inspector sighed, then shook his head.

"You can go." he said.

The lawyer grinned again. That smug grin that was enough to make anyone want to punch him. The sergeant uncuffed Antonio Adkins, allowing the two of them to leave.

"He's the new leader of the Bridge Boys, I can just tell." the sergeant said, once they had gone.

"I agree." the inspector said. "But we've got nothing on him

109

right now. Their stories all match. The three that were tied up all had drugs on them, but they're not talking. The other three are all clean. But at least we know who we're looking for now. We have leads. I'll contact the landlord of the Covered Market myself, see if that angle pans out. Send everything we have to be checked for prints, we might get lucky on that."

The two exited the room, and Sabrina rushed out of the observation room after them.

"Inspector Warren!" she called.

The inspector turned.

"I'm Constable Parker." she said. "I was wondering if I could accompany you to question the landlord. I'm up for promotion soon, if all goes well, and I figured I could learn something from observing you."

Inspector Warren shrugged.

"Check with your sergeant and meet me outside in ten minutes." he said.

Sergeant Burns, who was still standing a few feet away, nodded in approval.

"Great, I'll just get my kit on." Sabrina said.

Sabrina rushed through to the changing rooms, eager to get a start on the day and learn everything she could from shadowing Inspector Warren. Hopefully this would be a much more positive shift than the last few shifts she'd had.

***

In the entrance to the police station, Zakirah and Asim waited, the receptionist finishing off a phone call in front of them. After what Asim had said the night before, Zakirah felt increasingly nervous in this place, and fidgeted awkwardly as they waited, her eyes darting around the police station, watching all of the officers as they went about their day. As the receptionist put the phone down, he looked up and smiled.

"How can I help you?" he asked.

"We called last night." Asim said."We were wondering what happened to our friends. They were brought in for questioning after the attack on the mosque the other night and were never released."

"Oh really?" the receptionist frowned. "I thought everyone

brought in for questioning was released. What were their names?"

"Hussein Isa and Mobeen Muhammad." Asim replied.

The receptionist typed the names on the computer, and a look of realisation crossed his face.

"I'm sorry." he said. "I'm actually not authorised to discuss this case."

"What do you mean?" Zakirah frowned. "Are they being charged with something? They didn't do anything wrong."

"I'm really sorry." the receptionist replied. "But I can't discuss this."

"Those men have families." Asim said, placing a hand on the reception desk. "And they have rights. They have the right to an attorney, which their family will provide to them, but we need to know what they've been charged with."

"I'm sorry." the receptionist stood up, beckoning some of the officers over. "I'm going to have to ask you to leave."

Asim frowned, taking a step back. Zakirah's eyes fell on the officers, now walking slowly towards the reception. Her heart began to accelerate, and she placed a hand on Asim's arm.

"Come on." she muttered, quietly. "Let's go."

Asim looked over at the officers, then back at the receptionist, and reluctantly turned to leave, mumbling to himself under his breath as they went. As soon as they exited the station, Zakirah's heart began to steady and slow down, and she breathed in the fresh air, wondering why the police were keeping Asim's friends, and why they refused to even talk about it. She thought this was a free country, but more and more she was learning that there were so many conditions attached to that freedom, especially for people who looked like them.

***

"Antonio, good to see you again. I take it this is about last night."

Big Tuna sat in a large office, lined with bookcases. In front of him, a much older man, with very obviously dyed hair to remove the signs of grey and whitened teeth to remove the yellow stains, sat and poured from a pot of tea. He was dressed

111

in a tweed jacket, and his bookcases were filled with leatherbound books, his desk lined with very expensive pens and paper that looked more like parchment, and there were several stuffed animals mounted on the walls. Big Tuna reached forward and picked up a snowglobe from the desk, examining it, shaking it up, and placing it back down. The fake snow and glitter twirled and twisted into a little storm, which he watched for a few seconds, before turning his attention back to the man.

"Yes." Big Tuna replied. "It seems I've made a new enemy."

"With the way you do business, I'm not surprised." The older man smirked.

"Enough of that tone." Big Tuna growled. "The police will want a statement from you. I told them that I have a key, I told them that we are friends. When they arrive, you will reiterate this."

"And if I don't?"

"Well, all those emails between you and my predecessor about your dealings will end up in their hands." Big Tuna replied. "All of the people he helped you blackmail. All of the problems he made disappear... Oh, and everything I know about that young girl who interned with your company." Thomas Martin sighed, taking a sip from his tea.

"You've manipulated me with that same tired old threat for over a year now, but now I have something over you: If I don't corroborate your story, you end up in prison. Finally, I have leverage of my own."

"The charges won't stick, you and I both know that." Big Tuna said. "I have too many witnesses. And besides, my story is mostly true: I didn't break in."

"Well, I've gathered enough information about your other... business ventures, I'd warrant I could cause you a bit of trouble." Thomas Martin replied, curtly.

"Yes, but you have very little evidence, and it would be suicide. Now either we can both end up in court, or neither of us can." Big Tuna said. "If you've really been looking into how I do business, you'll know I'm a gambler. Are you?"

The older man sighed, making eye contact with Big Tuna.

"Say I corroborate your story... What's in it for me? Make an offer, Big Fish." the older man said.

"Fine." Big Tuna growled. "Corroborate my story, and I'll keep my hands out of your dealings with your tenants at Covered Market. I won't have any more business with any of the stall holders, and I won't protect them from you."

Thomas Martin nodded.

"I am happy with those terms." He extended his hand. "Shake on it."

Big Tuna shook the man's hand with haste, and turned and headed for the door. Two of his men stood there, waiting for him, and one of them was his right hand man, Jeb. As they exited, Jeb spoke up.

"We're giving up the market?" he asked.

They exited the room, which took them into a hallway lined with fine art, and down to a front door, out onto the city street.

"It doesn't matter." Big Tuna replied. "The police will be all over that place now, and we don't know anything about this new enemy of ours… The man with the metal fists... It's best we cut our losses with that place."

"People will think we're weak, losing territory." Jeb said, and they headed down the street, away from the terraced house. "If the Bovver Boys catch wind of it, they might make a move."

"Well, then we'll have to find a way to show them we're not." Big Tuna replied.

As they turned the corner, a police car pulled up to the house and a man and a woman got out. The woman stared down the street in the direction Big Tuna had gone, but he and his men were already out of view now.

"Everything alright, Officer Parker?" the man asked.

"That looked like Antonio Adkins." she said. "The man you were interrogating."

"It wouldn't surprise me." the inspector replied. "He's covering his tracks, making sure Mr Martin's story matches his. It's alright, sooner or later he'll slip up. He's young. The young ones don't last long when they're in charge."

They knocked on the door, and a young woman in an apron answered.

"We're here to talk to Mr Martin." the inspector said.

"Just in his office." the woman smiled, stepping aside to let

113

them in, and leading them down the hall and into the study. Thomas Martin smiled as they entered, standing from his armchair.

"Inspector Warren!" he said. "I believe we met briefly at the superintendent's barbecue last month. Good to see you again. Take a seat."

That comment did not go unnoticed by Sabrina, and it made her uneasy. She knew that these kinds of people always had connections, and that was to be expected, but Thomas Martin was far too confident and comfortable with the inspector, and it suddenly seemed a bit suspicious that the inspector had chosen to come here himself. And yet, Thomas Martin was not a suspect, so she supposed there was no real issue. Perhaps their personal connection would make him more likely to talk openly with the inspector.

Perhaps.

***

Iona sat in the half-empty waiting room at the hospital, anxiously tapping her heel against the ground, causing her leg to wobble. The waiting room in the oncology ward was not big: just an enclave in a corridor, filled with chairs, and a small coffee table full of magazines. Iona just stared at the wall, tracing shapes with her eyes as she waited for the doctor to call her name.

A door just a few metres away from the enclave opened and an Indian woman in a white coat stuck her head out. She smiled a warm smile and beckoned Iona with her hand. Iona stilled her leg, took a deep breath, and headed into the doctor's office. On the door, a tiny plaque engraved with '**Dr. Nisha Patel**' was neatly placed at eye level.

"Iona, how are you?" Dr Patel asked. "Please, take a seat."

"I'm okay." Iona said. "Doing my best."

"Are you still experiencing dizzy spells?" the doctor asked. Iona nodded.

"They're getting worse."

Dr Patel smiled a sympathetic smile.

"I feared as much." she said. "You remember I did some blood tests at your last check-up? Well I'm afraid to say that I did

114

find traces of abnormal blood cells, and pairing that with your other symptoms, it looks like there's a chance that the cancer has returned."

Iona's heart stopped for a moment, and she fell silent.

"Now, there's no reason to panic yet. We'll run some more tests to be certain. The good news is that you're still young, and fit and healthy aside from the cancer. First line treatments of chemotherapy are not always effective, but that doesn't mean a second round won't be."

Iona felt her concentration waver, her mind a mess of different thoughts.

"I did everything right." she muttered. "I ate healthy, I cut out all animal products, all alcohol, I didn't smoke or take any drugs. I exercised regularly, ate only whole foods, no junk food, no oils… I did everything right."

"This isn't an exact science." Dr Patel replied. "You can do everything right and still get sick. But that doesn't mean it wasn't worth it. Doing all those things has probably boosted your chances significantly. The survival rate for people in your age range is high. You've just gotta keep fighting."

"What's the point?" Ioan replied, her eyes beginning to water. "I've been miserable! I never have any fun, I'm always so careful, just in the hopes that it will be worth it in the long run, but now I'm sick again anyway?"

Dr Patel sighed and placed her hand on Iona's.

"Have you been to any of the support groups I suggested?" she asked.

Iona shook her head.

"I went to one session but I don't like sharing with strangers."

"It can help, being around other people going through the same thing." Dr Patel said. "But if you'd like, I can refer you to a therapist who might be able to help you to deal with the stress. Do you have any friends you can talk to?"

Iona shrugged.

"Just one, I guess. No one else really understands. Everyone else just pities me too much, I hate it."

"Well, I suggest talking to this friend of yours." Dr Patel said, pulling out a piece of paper and a pen. "And here is a number for a private therapist who takes referrals through the NHS.

She's very good, I'll let her know to expect your call. She's called Dr Blake. I really recommend you talk to her. What with your anxiety attacks, I don't want this all to become too much for you."

She scribbled down a number and tore off a strip from the paper, handing it to Iona.

"Head back to reception and tell them that I need you booked in for some follow-up tests, some time in the next few days." She handed Iona a box of tissues, and Iona tore one from the top. "You'll be okay. Trust me."

"Thank you, doctor." Iona stood and walked out of the room, closing the door softly behind her. There was an old man sitting in the waiting area, watching her, a look of pity in his eyes. Iona hurried round the corner, straight into the toilet, fumbling with the lock. Silence surrounded her, but for the buzzing of a faulty connection in the electrical circuit of the light, and she placed her back against the wall and let the tears flow silently down her face.

***

Alex stood on the doorstep to Robby's house, duffel bag full of all his possessions slung over his shoulder. In front of him, Cynthia and Robby stood, smiling sympathetically.

"We're sorry, we'd love to have you stay here longer, it's just-"

"No, no I get it." Alex cut Cynthia off, waving his hand dismissively. "Thanks for everything you've done for me. With my dad in Florida and my mum god knows where, I don't know what I'd have done without your help."

"Where will you go now?" Robby asked.

Alex shrugged.

"I'll check into a hotel for a day or two, see if I can get a more permanent place. I'll be alright."

"Let me know if you need to borrow any money, just keep it on the down-low." Robby said, extending his hand.

Alex took the hand and shook it, then turned and headed away. As he left, Cynthia planted a kiss on Robby's cheek, grabbed her handbag, and headed off to work.

Alex headed into the park, ambling with very little purpose, but he hadn't got more than a few hundred yards away from Robby's house before he saw a man in a long jacket and trilby hat, leant against a tree, waiting for him.

"You came yourself this time, I'm impressed." Alex said. "The answer is still no, especially after what you pulled with Robby. You should have known he was off limits."

"Listen, Alex, I'm sorry, you know how I get when I'm angry." Big Tuna said, jogging over to Alex's side and walking along with him.

"I do, it's one of the many reasons my answer is no." Alex replied. "I have anger issues too, that's no excuse."

"Look, I need you, Alex. I know you don't approve of all my methods, but I'm trying to do good things here! You'll see that, just let me show you!"

Alex turned and faced up to Big Tuna, his face growing red, towering over him, his fists clenched.

"Tony, it doesn't matter what you think you're doing." he growled. "You're a thug and a bully. You can dress up the Bridge Boys however you like, but we both know their history: it's a gang."

He turned away, calming himself down with a few deep breaths.

"I know you, Antonio." he said. "Sooner or later, you're going to pick on the wrong guy, and you think having me there, I'll be able to protect you, like I did in school, but you're playing in the big leagues now."

"What if I already have picked on the wrong guy?" Big Tuna asked. "It looks like I've made a new enemy. Some wannabe-batman-type in a bandanna with magnetic fists. I don't even know... Look, I need you, Alex. Like old times."

Alex shook his head and continued walking.

"I'm sorry, Antonio. I joined the army to get away from all that." he said.

"And look how that turned out." Big Tuna replied. "I made some calls, I did some digging, I found out why you were discharged, Alex."

Alex stopped in his tracks, his heart racing. That was the final straw, and the barrier that he had put up to contain the rage came crashing down.

"What did you say?" he asked.

"You never were good at following orders." Big Tuna said.

"And you tell me I have an anger problem."

He chuckled softly to himself.

Alex spun round, pinning Big Tuna to a tree with one hand. An elderly couple walking through the park let out a gasp, and Alex and Big Tuna turned to look at them. Alex loosened his grip, backing away, and Big Tuna brushed himself off.

"I will pay you a lot of money... Just for your protection." Big Tuna said. "You know where to find me, just please, think about it. I just want your help dealing with this one guy. My lads are all scared of him now. You name a price, it's yours."

He turned and walked away, hands shoved into his pockets.

Alex sighed, shaking his head, and continued walking. After a moment, the irony of Big Tuna looking for protection from the very guy he was scared of settled in, and that lifted his spirits ever so slightly.

***

Jason woke up late the next morning, his head pounding, his back aching. He groaned, reaching to his bedside table and popping three paracetamol into his mouth before even attempting to get up. He took his time, making himself some breakfast, sitting in his wheelchair, flipping through his comic book collection, before finally heading out to his garage workshop, where he spent most of the morning fiddling with his gauntlets and idly browsing through social media on his phone. After a while of scrolling, a headline caught his eye.

'**Breaking News**' the headline read. '**Downtown City vigilante strikes again**'.

The picture that went with the headline was a blurry photo taken through a window that looked to be from the building adjacent to the Covered Market. It showed the blurry police lights, the unfurled banner, and the silhouette of Alex stood on the roof, massive gauntlets over his hands.

Jason clicked on the article.

'Earlier this week, a Downtown City University Student named Daniel McDonald was assaulted in the university's halls of residence, with the word 'rapist' spray-painted across his

118

door. Witnesses reported seeing a man in a mask, with giant metal fists, fleeing the scene. Hours after the attack, three different women had come forward to allege that Mr McDonald had sexually assaulted them, and the heavy-fisted attacker was there to deal out justice.

Just last night, it appears this same vigilante made another appearance: this time at the Covered Market, breaking into the market to unfurl a banner over the side of the building. The banner read 'ANTONIO ADKINS: THIS MARKET IS PROTECTED. PLAY NICE.' No information could be found on Antonio Adkins, and the police declined to comment, as did most of the stall owners operating inside Covered Market, however it seems that three men were arrested for possession of illegal substances, and witnesses say that the men were already tied up in the market when the police arrived. People have taken to social media, labelling the masked criminal as 'Big Fists', 'Metal Fist', and even 'the Fist of Justice'. It is not clear whether there is a link between these two incidents, or even whether they are, in fact, the same person, however opinions seem to be divided as to whether he is a hero or a menace.'

The article went on to display different social media posts with the hashtags 'BigFists' and 'FistsOfJustice'.

'Good on him! If the police won't lock up rapists and stand up for the people, someone has to.'

'He's a criminal and a thug. He assaulted an innocent man based on social media rumours. He should be locked up.'

'Is this what call-out culture has come to? Can't even speak to a woman any more, or some weirdo might come and beat the crap out of you. Shame.'

'Beating up drug dealers? Does this guy have nothing better to do! #legaliseit'

'Men: take note. Be afraid: You should be. If it takes the threat of justice from a vigilante with medieval gauntlets on to stop you from being a creep to women, then shame on you. #FistsOfJustice.'

***

119

The lab was cool, calm and clean: a welcome change from the polluted, crowded, noisy streets outside. Iona sunk back into her work, typing up her results at her desk as behind her the lab assistants monitored the behaviour of their lab mice.

"Iona, come look at this!" one of them called over.

Iona turned and walked over to where the lab assistant was observing a mouse, running round and round on a little rotating hamster wheel in the cage.

"What is it? Are they showing signs of relapse?"

"No, the opposite actually. Healthier than ever. This is subject two. She's been at this for two hours, she's not slowing."

Iona frowned, peering in at the mouse.

"Are you sure?" she asked.

"I mean, I've stepped away for maybe a minute or two to check on other cages, but she can't have had more than thirty seconds of rest." the lab assistant replied.

"Put some treats in there." Iona instructed her.

The lab assistant pulled the hatch at the top of the cage open and dropped in a piece of cheese. The mouse dashed from the wheel, quick as a flash and snatched up the cheese before any of the other mice even had a chance to process that it had entered the cage, wolfing down the piece of cheese.

"Increased speed, increased reflexes." Iona breathed. "Take it out, run some tests."

The lab assistant reached in to retrieve the mouse, and Iona turned back to her desk. As she stepped towards the desk, her vision blurred. The room began to spin.

"Not now." she groaned, and her knees buckled underneath her.

The ground came rushing to meet her, and everything faded to black.

When Iona came to, she was lying on a sofa in the staff room with the company's first aider sitting next to her. Dr Wood towered over her, a concerned look on her face. Iona's body was tingling, and her legs still felt weak.

"She just fainted." the first aider was saying. "Probably dehydration."

"Okay, could you wait outside please?" Dr Wood said.

The first aider nodded and headed out the room, leaving Iona and Dr Wood alone. Dr Wood pulled a chair from the table up to the sofa and sat next to Iona.

"Dr Page." she said. "How are you feeling?"

"Not great." Iona said. "But a bit better now I'm lying down."

"Is this…" Dr Wood stopped in her tracks. The rest of the sentence was implied.

"They're not sure yet, the doctor is going to run some more tests." Iona replied. "But it looks like the cancer has returned."

"I'm sorry to hear that." Dr Wood said. "I want you to know that this project will still be yours, but I am advising that you step into a more secondary, observatory role at this stage. Your tests look promising, and I think we should be able to get approval to move into human trials, but I don't want the stress of the extra workload having an adverse effect on your health. I will take on the primary role on this project myself, and then you can return to that role once you get better."

"I'd prefer to keep working." Iona replied. "It helps to distract me from it."

"You can certainly keep working." Dr Wood said. "But I am not prepared to let you continue as the head of this project with your health deteriorating. I'm afraid, as per our contract, I feel obligated to take over."

Iona sighed, but nodded.

"It will still be my name on the project?" she asked.

"Of course." Dr Wood replied. "Now go home, get some rest. Take tomorrow off as well, come back when you feel a little better."

Dr Wood stood, giving Iona a sympathetic pat on the shoulder, and headed out of the room, leaving Iona alone with her thoughts.

***

As late afternoon settled in, Jason had completely lost track of the passing of time, and worked the day away, tinkering with his gauntlets, sketching ideas for new functions in his notepad, googling the latest in technological breakthroughs and brainstorming the ways he could incorporate them into his gauntlets.

5PM rolled around, and suddenly there was a banging at the garage door. Jason threw a blanket over his table, covering the gauntlets and other gear they had been using, and rolled over to the garage door, pulling it upwards. Iona immediately rushed in.

"Thank god." she said. "I'm sorry I didn't text, I just… I kinda just walked here. I didn't know where to go."

"Iona." Jason said. "W-what's up?"

"I really need a drink, can we go to the bar?" Iona asked. Jason nodded.

"Just let me lock up my workshop."

He shut off the power and closed up the garage, locking it behind him, and followed Iona round the front of the hotel and into the bar. The barman, Will, rushed over to greet them, pulling a chair away from a table by the window so that Jason could roll his wheelchair into the spot.

"Nice to see you again, my friend." Will said. "What can I get you?"

"J-j-just water for me." Jason said.

"Oh come on Jason, please drink with me!" Iona exclaimed, placing a hand on Jason's arm. "I really need this."

"I thought you weren't d-drinking?" Jason said.

"I wasn't, when I thought it was working." Iona replied. "I'll take a shot of vodka and a pint of lager."

"Just a l-light beer, Will." Jason said. "Oh, and thanks again for the other night."

"Don't mention it!" Will grinned, waving a hand dismissively as he walked away. "Any time, my friend, any time. You are a good man."

He hurried away behind the bar and started pouring drinks, and Jason turned his attention to Iona, trying his best to break through his social anxiety and look her in the eye. Concern rose up inside him, and he stared intensely at her face.

"W-w-what's wrong?" he asked.

"The cancer is back." Iona replied, her voice cracking as she spoke. "But I don't want to talk about that. I want to forget about that, I need you to distract me."

Jason nodded silently, thinking for a moment.

"How is the r-research g-g-going?" he asked.

122

"Not that, either." Iona replied. "Just… something else… the news!"

Jason shrugged.

"Okay." he said. "What about the n-n-news? Did you hear about that American politician that was killed? I think he was a senator. The government says it was a car crash but the conspiracy theorists have gone wild about it. The media says none of it adds up."

"Really, Jason!" Iona scoffed. "There's a legit superhero going about the city dispensing justice, and you want to talk about politicians across the sea?"

"Superhero?" Jason frowned.

"The Fist! Have you not seen? The guy running round the city beating up rapists and drug dealers?" Iona said. "It's crazy."

"Oh yea, I did see something about that." Jason replied.

"I'd have thought you'd be all over it." Iona said. "What with you being a comic geek and all."

Will brought their drinks over, and Iona immediately downed the shot of vodka, then chased it down with a long chug of lager.

"T-take it easy." Jason said. "You haven't had a proper d-drink in over a year."

"Well, tonight I'm getting wasted and talking about superheroes with my best friend." Iona said, and took another chug from her pint.

"Best friend?" Jason asked.

"Yeah." Iona replied, smiling. "Yeah, you're my best friend. You're the only one I can really talk to, you're the first person I thought to come to when I found out the cancer was back. You're the only one who… gets it. In some way, I think."

"I'm not terminal." Jason pointed out.

"Well, you know what it's like to be pitied by everyone, and treated like a fragile object rather than an actual person." Iona said. "And you don't look at me like a sick puppy."

Jason smiled, blushing slightly, and took a sip from his beer.

"How's your research going?" Iona asked. "Done any work since I last saw you?"

Jason shrugged.

"Not really." he said. "I've been l-looking for a n-new angle.

Some new way to apply my tech, make it m-m-more useful."

"Don't let that competition get you down." Iona said. "You can apply again next year."

Jason smiled.

"I know. I have a few ideas, I'm just… n-not ready to show them to the world yet."

The two continued drinking and chatting together, getting lost in pointless small talk for the better part of the evening. Iona drank twice as fast as Jason, with Jason still nursing his first beer as Iona polished off her third drink.

"I think you b-b-better slow down a b-bit." Jason stammered.

"I love you man." Iona slurred. "You're the best, you always look out for me."

She waved her finger emphatically in front of her face.

"Has anyone ever told you that you have a pretty nose?" she said.

Jason snorted.

"What are you on about?"

"You know, you know…" Iona lost her thought, her brow furrowing, her eyes darting about as if she was looking for the end of the sentence. "You know, you're a mighty fine gentleman. A real nice guy."

Jason rolled his eyes.

"You can't friendzone me." he said. "We're already friends."

"Why is that?" Iona asked.

"W-w-what do you mean?" Jason asked, stumbling over his words from nervousness as well as his stutter this time.

"Why did you never ask me out?" Iona's eyes met Jason's.

"We've been friends all the way through University, I thought at some point you might…"

"What?" Jason smiled awkwardly, averting his gaze. "What are you talking about?"

"Why did you never ask me out?" Iona asked again.

"I guess I didn't want to ruin the friendship." Jason said. "Besides, you never asked me out either!"

Iona stood up, wobbling slightly as she did so, walked around the table, and planted a kiss on Jason's cheek.

"Well, maybe I will!" she said. "Now, take me home, friendo! Let's get takeout and watch a movie and pass out like we're teenagers again!"

Jason snorted.

"We were such dorky teenagers." he replied. "Okay, let's go."
He followed Iona out into the street, disappearing together into
the night. Jason found himself wondering about what Iona had
said. In truth, he had considered asking her out before, but as
far as he was concerned, the guy in the wheelchair with the
speech impediment didn't get the girl. He didn't even think he
really knew how to ask someone out. No, he was happy just
being friends.

***

Alex took the scenic route into the city centre, walking along
the riverside path. Near to the suburbs, the riverside path was
actually quite pleasant: with flowers and trees lining one side
of the path, and the riverbank looking out across the nicer
areas of the city forming the view to the other side. The closer
to the city centre you got, the more industrialised it became,
until the trees and greenery faded away and were replaced by
walls covered in graffiti, and ridiculous numbers of bridges
going overhead, with a steady stream of traffic polluting the
previously passive and peaceful soundscape with a cacophony
of noise.

The memories were back, like a dark cloud over him, and he
found himself going to his phone, seeking any distraction he
could. He browsed hotel prices, but found himself idly
switching over to browse the various social media apps on his
phone, and on each one eventually ending up on the same
profile:

Blake.

The man Alex had been dating before he ran away to join the
army.

The man he had never told he was leaving.

The man he didn't call. The man who, when Alex eventually
wrote to him, never responded.

The man who told him to go away when he returned, out of the
blue, with no warning.

Alex felt his heart sink into his churning stomach, and regret
and self-loathing washed over him in waves. He perched

125

himself on the riverbank and reached into his bag, pulling out a four-pack of beers and cracking one of the cans open.

It didn't take Alex long to finish the first beer, his eyes glued to Blake's profile picture. He was slender, and very handsome, with fine cheekbones and prominent lips. His skin was chocolatey-brown, and he had a red streak dyed in his natural black hair, and several piercings in his ears. He stared at the camera with a certain intensity. Alex would always find himself getting lost in those eyes all too easily.

Alex cracked open a second can and began to wander down the path again, heading slowly into the city. He wasn't consciously aware of a direction or destination, but his feet carried him to Moore Street, and before long he found himself standing beneath that same apartment building, yet again, staring up at Blake's window.

He opened his mouth to yell up at the window, but as he did someone exited the apartment building. Alex instinctively stepped forward to catch the door before it closed and slipped in, heading directly to Blake's flat.

Inside, he heard speaking and fumbling. Alex's heart began to race. He saw the door handle begin to turn.

He darted quickly round the corner and listened as Blake exited his room, talking on the phone.

"Calm down!" he was saying. "It's just a date. You don't need to freak out, Rhi."

He paused for a response, then spoke again.

"Because if you freak out, I'll freak out. This is the first third date I've gone on since… well, you know."

Blake disappeared down the hall in the opposite direction, and Alex slid down to the floor, his eyes fixating on the ground. He let out a wordless yell, punching the wall a couple of times, then sunk into silence. He wasn't sure how long he sat there, but eventually the sound of the apartment building's elevator dinging and the doors opening, and two people walking into the hallway, snapped him out of his trance, and he rushed out of the building and back into the night.

His entire body felt numb, and he found himself wandering aimlessly once more, finishing off his can of beer and opening the third can. The night was underway, darkness had settled in, and Alex perched himself in the entranceway of a tailor shop, taking long gulps from his beer.

"*FIRE YOUR WEAPON PRIVATE, THAT'S AN ORDER!*"

"*I can't. I can't do it! I can't do it!*"

Suddenly, the images were back: his comrades, sheltering from a hail of gunfire. The chaos of figures running to and fro, the civilians nearly indistinguishable from the enemy forces. Blood, dust and sweat filled the air.

"Are you okay, mate?"

The voice in the real world saved him from his memories. Alex looked up to see a rugged homeless man with wrinkled, tanned skin and brown hair, streaked with grey. He seemed to be wearing a pair of brand new trainers, and was smiling warmly down at Alex. As Alex snapped out of his thoughts once more, he felt wetness on his cheeks, and reached up to wipe his face with a sleeve. Unbeknownst to him, his eyes had started to water, and tears were streaming down his face.

"I'm fine." he said, gruffly.

"Well, I'd move on if I were you." the homeless man advised. "The coppers don't much like it when people camp up in the doorways of fancy shops like this one. They can get a little nasty."

"I'm fine." Alex repeated again, gathering his bag and disappearing off down the street.

Alex must have had a lot more to drink, though he did not remember it. All he knew is that just after midnight, he was standing outside Jason's place, knocking on the garage door and calling out Jason's name. Every so often a hotel guest would park up in the carpark and give him a look, but he was too drunk to pay them any heed.

After a few minutes, one of the hotel staff poked their head out the front to look at him, frowned, and went back inside the hotel.

"I don't think he's in."

Alex turned. It was the same homeless man as before.

"Oh, hey, it's you again!" the man exclaimed, pointing at Alex. "I saw Jason leave earlier with some girl. I don't think he came back, the little stud!"

127

He grinned widely.

"Anyway." the homeless man continued. "You might want to stop, the hotel staff have noticed, and if they get upset with you, they might kick us both out. You want some water?" He offered him a bottle.

"You really should have a drink… not booze… and a sit down." the man said. "I'm Jack, but you can call me J." He led the stumbling Alex over towards the back of the car park, ushering him with an arm around his shoulder.

"You want to play cards?" he asked.

"Sure, why not." Alex muttered.

"Alrighty!" Jack beamed. "You cool with Blackjack?"

The two men perched themselves in the corner of the car park, on Jack's blanket. Jack had made a little spot for himself up against a wall, on a section of tarmac that was too small to be a parking space, with two brick walls forming a corner. Two of the bricks were loose, and Jack pulled one of them away, reaching in to pull out a bottle of water and a deck of cards. The two men played into the early hours of the morning, telling jokes in between games, and eventually, Alex stopped thinking about Blake, and the pit that his heart was sinking into closed up for a little while.

***

Jason woke up the next morning lying on top of the covers of Iona's double bed, still wearing his trousers and crumpled shirt from the night before. Iona was lying next to him, half under the covers but with one arm across Jason's chest, also fully clothed. As Jason sat up, Iona groaned, the movement pulling her unwillingly from her sleep.

"I feel like death." she croaked. "How much did I drink?"

Jason stooped down and picked up a bottle of rum from the floor. It was actually mostly full.

"Not m-much, apparently." he said.

"I'm such a lightweight." Iona groaned.

"Come on." Jason said. "Let's go get smoothies."

"Five more minutes." Iona mumbled.

Jason lifted himself from the bed into his wheelchair.

"Come on," he said. "You're not spending all day moping in bed."

"I'll get up if you walk today. You could do with the exercise. I've got a spare set of crutches in the closet, from when I broke my ankle. I'll push your chair."

Jason sighed and nodded.

"If it'll g-get you out of b-bed." he said.

Iona pulled herself up with a dramatic amount of effort.

"Give me five minutes to change." she said.

Jason smirked, knowing how unrealistic five minutes was for her, and half an hour later, after Iona had showered, brushed her teeth, and changed her clothes, the two of them headed out of the apartment, Iona pushing the wheelchair and Jason using a singular crutch as a walking stick, leaning heavily against it. Across the street from Iona, there was an incredibly colourful smoothie bar. It was probably one of the most hipster places in the city, but the smoothies were fantastic: all vegan, mostly local ingredients, no added sugar, entirely organic. The woman behind the counter had dreadlocks going half-way down her torso and a hawaiin shirt covered in colourful patterns. She had the most beautiful dark skin, and a crooked smile.

"What can I get you beautiful souls!" she beamed as the two walked in, Iona struggling to get the wheelchair over the lip in the doorway. "Good to see you again, Iona."

"I'll get the hangover helper green detox smoothie." Iona said.

"T-tropical b-blast." Jason said.

"Coming right up."

The woman made their smoothies, humming along to the gentle acoustic music playing over the store's speaker system. Iona paid for the smoothies, and her and Jason headed out into the street, sipping their drinks and ambling through the city centre. At the end of the road was the Covered Market, and all the police cars had gone and the market looked back to normal: no sign of the banner that had been hanging from the roof.

"I want to go to the comic book store." Jason said.

Iona let out a long groan.

"Urgh, fine." she replied.

"You love comics!" Jason snorted. "You've got a bigger collection than I do!"

"And you will never tell a single person." Iona said.

Something didn't feel quite right as they approached the market, but Jason couldn't put his finger on it. He limped through the entrance, leaning heavily on his crutch, and immediately was greeted with a 'CLOSING DOWN' sign on the first stall. He frowned, his eyes scanning the market. Half the stalls had 'CLOSING SALE' signs in front of them. Jason cast his eyes up to the balcony, and his heart sunk.

In the window of the comic store, in bright red letters: 'CLOSING DOWN: EVERYTHING MUST GO'.

Jason headed for the elevator, allowing Iona to wheel the chair in first, and the two headed up to the balcony, marching towards the comic book store. Inside, the store owner was putting new prices on the shelves, his face stern and solemn.

"Naveed!" Jason exclaimed. "What's going on?"

"Oh, hey Jasey." Naveed pulled himself up from the bottom shelf with a grunt. "Closing down, the landlord is raising the rent on us. It's way too high, half of us can't pay, looks like most of the market will be gone."

"Why?" Jason frowned. "He's losing all his clients."

"Rumour is he got an offer a long while back to sell the building to some big corporation, so it can be turned into a modern shopping centre filled with chain stores. Seems he's taken the deal."

"Why now?" Jason asked. "If he's kept it as a market for local businesses for so long, why change now?"

Naveed looked about, hesitating, then back at Jason.

"I trust you, man, you're one of my boys. You're a good friend, you get me?" he said. "You know who Big Tuna is?"

"The g-gang leader?" Jason frowned. "I know of him, everyone d-d-does, only by reput-tu-tation though."

"I'm not naming names, and you didn't hear it from me, but I reckon some of the stall owners had deals with him." Naveed said. "Pretty sure he was keeping Thomas Martin from raising the rent somehow, but he's pulled out. Wants nothing to do with the market since what happened the other night, with that metal-fisted vigilante. Don't get me wrong, respect to the guy for standing up, but you know, there's consequences for everything these days."

"That really sucks." Iona said. "Are you going to try and find somewhere else to set up shop?"

"Nah, I can't afford city prices, I was lucky to be able to rent here." Naveed replied. "I guess I'll set up an online shop, maybe? I don't know how I'll compete with online sellers though. If you guys want anything, I'm selling it all cheap, gotta move this stock as quickly as possible."

Naveed went back to changing all the prices, and Iona and Jason started browsing the store, Jason sinking into thought. Had he made things worse by meddling? He wanted to help Naveed and the other small business owners, but by getting rid of Big Tuna he'd simply made their problems worse.

He snatched up a handful of comics that he didn't own yet, more out of some sense of obligation than anything else, and walked up to the till. Naveed hurried over to serve him.

"Full price, I insist." Jason said.

"Nah man, it's okay." Naveed said. "I-"

"I insist." Jason interrupted, sliding over the money.

"Thanks, mate." Naveed said, handing over the comics in a little bag.

As they exited the comic book store, Iona finished her smoothie and binned the cup.

"I should really get some work done." she said. "I'm not going into the lab today, but I've got so many notes to type up." Jason nodded.

"I'm not feeling too g-great anyway." he said. "I'm g-going to h-head home."

They hugged, and Jason plopped himself down into the wheelchair and handed Iona the crutch.

"See you soon, don't be a stranger." Iona said.

"See you." Jason replied, and he rolled over to the elevator as she headed off down the stairs.

As the elevator doors closed in front of him, Jason found himself wondering if this whole vigilante thing was such a good idea after all. His life had been a whirlwind since he started this, but every action he took had a knock-on effect that caused a chain of events he couldn't predict or control, and not all of those events seemed to be good. How was he supposed to know what to do?

131

He didn't want to stop now. Finally, he felt like his life meant something. He was going to hold onto that for as long as possible.

CHAPTER EIGHT: HATE FUELS HATE

"Mate, you gotta move, we need to work here."

Alex opened his eyes to the sun blaring down from a bright blue sky. He groaned, squinting up at the two bald men in hard hats and high visibility jackets staring down at him.

"Come on, buddy, we've not got all day."

Alex scrambled to his feet, his hands going immediately to his duffel bag.

"Sorry." he mumbled, getting out of the way of the workmen.

"Right, we've got to drill all this up, put in the bollards, and then we can set the new tarmac around the bollards." one of the workmen said to the other.

Alex sat to one side, collecting his thoughts and waking himself up as the two workers began their work, hauling in their tools and shifting the already crumbling and broken tarmac away so that they could lay fresh tarmac.

"Ah no!" a croaky old voice exclaimed, and Alex saw Jack walking back across the carpark, a coffee cup in each hand.

"My spot!"

He walked over to Alex and handed him a cup.

"I went down to the shelter for some free coffee. It's just basic black instant coffee, but you look like you need it."

"Thanks." Alex muttered, taking the cup and taking a long sip.

Jack turned to the workers. Alex pulled out his phone to check the battery.

"What's going on here?" Jack asked.

"Filling in the cracked tarmac and putting in some bollards." one of the workers grumbled.

"Ah, shucks, this was my favourite spot." muttered Jack.

"Sorry, just doing our jobs." the other worker said.

133

"Are these two bothering you?"

Alex turned to see two police officers jogging across the carpark. They were both young men: one rather plain looking but the other quite handsome, with a chiseled jawline and brilliant blue eyes.

"It's fine." one of the workers said.

The police officers joined the group anyway, and one of them caught sight of Jack's new trainers.

"Those are awfully nice shoes for a homeless person." the handsome officer said. "Mind telling me where you got them?"

"They were a gift." Jack replied.

"Oh yea?" the officer seemed unconvinced. "From who?"

His eyes flickered over to Alex, scrolling through his texts. "And that smartphone… Where's a guy on the street get a phone like that?"

"Huh?" Alex frowned. "I'm not homeless."

"Right, you just sleep in a carpark for fun!" one of the workers snorted.

The other worker slapped him on the arm.

"Don't be a dick, Bob." he rebuked him, and the worker who had spoken shot Alex an apologetic look.

"Mind showing us what's in your bag?" the second officer said to Alex, reaching over for the duffel bag.

Alex pulled his bag in close, instinctively.

"Why?" he asked.

"Sir, hand over the bag." the first officer's tone hardened.

Behind the officers, Alex heard the familiar hum of the electric motor on Jason's wheelchair, and saw Jason rolling towards them.

"Hey Alex, what's g-going on?" he asked.

"Nothing to see here." the first officer said.

"You know this man?" the other asked.

"Just tell us where you got the shoes and the phone." The first officer addressed Alex and Jack.

"That's his phone." Jason said. "And I g-gave him those shoes as a gift, do you n-need to see the receipt?"

"Where would a homeless person get a smartphone?" the second officer asked.

"Homeless?" Jason asked. "He's not homeless. What's going

on?"

"He was sleeping on the pavement."

"I passed out drunk, okay!" Alex exclaimed. "Besides, why is it any of your business where I got the phone?"

"I'm out of here." Jack said, putting his hands up. "This is a waste of time. Just let me get my stuff."

He tried to reach past the workmen to get his cards and his blanket, which had been pushed to one side.

"What are you doing?" the first officer said.

"He's g-getting his stuff!" Jason exclaimed, his face growing red. "What is the matter with you two?"

"Please sir, do not raise your voice at us." the second officer said.

"Why, are you threatened by the man in a wheelchair?" Alex growled.

"Honestly, I've half a mind to report you." Jason said, looking at the officer's name badges. "Weston and Andrews. Do you work with Officer Parker?"

The officers seemed taken aback by the fact that Jason was able to name one of their colleagues.

"Come on, it looks like everything's fine here." Officer Andrews said.

"Alright, move along you lot." Officer Weston said, waving his hand dismissively and turning to walk back to his car.

"The spikes going up tonight will put an end to this sort of nonsense." he muttered to his partner as they walked away.

"I can't believe that." Jason said, looking at Jack. "Do you get that kind of treatment a lot?"

Jack shrugged.

"Just part of being on the street." he said. "There's good cops and bad cops. Course with my luck I always end up getting the bad ones."

One of the police officers shot them a look, still not quite out of earshot, but they didn't come back over.

"I'm off." Jack said, grabbing his stuff and disappearing in the other direction.

Jason turned to Alex.

"We need to talk about the other night. We may need to think some more about our strategy. Let's go into my garage."

"So Antonio was blackmailing the landlord?" Alex muttered, leaning against the garage wall. "Figures. That's how Antion gets anything done: blackmail and extortion. He's great at getting everyone's gossip: figuring out the skeletons in your closet."

"W-whatever he was d-doing, he kept the landlord from raising the rent." Jason said. "It looks like all the stall owners had fixed contracts: the landlord couldn't kick them out unless they broke the contract, but he could raise the rent on them. B-b-big Tuna was keeping him from doing that. But now Big Tuna has backed off, he's free to sell. We m-may have accidentally made it worse for them."

"This is why I didn't want to get involved." Alex said. "You never know what the consequences of this kind of thing will be."

"Well, it just means we need to be more careful in the future. But perhaps we can fix it. If we can work out what leverage Big Tuna had over Thomas Martin, the land owner, we might be able to restore things to how they were."

"I don't know." Alex said. "Taking on a criminal is one thing, but a rich landlord?"

"It's the right thing to do, to correct the mistake. Aren't we here to s-stand up for the little guy?" Jason reasoned.

"I guess." Alex replied. "But how are we going to find out what leverage Antonio had?"

"I d-don't know." Jason said. "And I want t-to look into the police treatment of the homeless in this city as well. If that behaviour isn't an isolated case, someone needs to do something."

"Sounds like we've got a lot of work to do." Alex said. "Where do we start?"

***

Iona wandered back into her lab, her laptop bag slung over her shoulder. Her lab assistants were hard at work, all three of them hurriedly jotting down notes on pieces of paper or tapping away at the keys of their laptops.

"Iona!" one of them exclaimed as she walked into the room. "We weren't expecting you today!"

"Just picking up some of my notes so that I can work from home, keep my brain busy." Iona smiled. "What's going on?"

"Dr Wood has asked us to consolidate all our research so that she can apply to set up clinical trials on human subjects."

Iona frowned, a cloud of confusion settling over her. Dr Wood had promised her that she was still a project lead, even if she wasn't going to be able to be overseeing in person. Surely she would consult her before taking a step like this?

"It's way too early for that, we're still in the first round of animal tests."

The lab assistant shrugged.

"That's what we thought." she replied. "We're just doing what we're told."

"Right." Iona said.

She collected up her notes, shoved them into her bag, and marched straight to Dr Wood's office. The short-haired woman was sitting behind her desk, tapping away at her keyboard. She smiled when Iona appeared at the door.

"Dr Page, I wasn't expecting you." she said.

"What's this about you applying for permission to begin human testing?" Iona asked. "We're way off that stage! Why didn't you consult me?"

"We're just applying to get ahead. The application can take a few months to process." Dr Wood replied. "I was going to call you and inform you, I only decided last night, due to the massive success of our animal tests."

"We haven't waited long enough to see if any negative side effects present themselves!" Iona said.

"Well, we'll have time. And our application won't be accepted if it's found to be dangerous. Trust me, we won't move on to clinical trials without consulting you. I'm sorry if you felt left out of the decision, I meant to call you."

Iona took a deep breath, calming herself down.

"It's okay." she sighed. "I'm just under a lot of stress... I should go home."

"Come on." Dr Wood said, standing and picking up her handbag. "Let's go get a cup of tea, then you can head home." Iona smiled.

"Okay." she said. "That would be nice."

The two women exited the room and headed down to the canteen, and all of the stress melted away for a moment, and it was no longer about the work, and just two women getting a cup of tea together.

***

Evening settled in, and Officer Parker arrived at the police station at the change of shifts. She entered the changing room just as the day shift was clocking out.

"You working the night shift, Parker?" one of the women called over to her. "Good luck. That defensive architecture is going up tonight, you'll be overseeing it. Weston and Andrews will be out there with you."

Sabrina groaned.

"I forgot about that." she mumbled. "No wonder no one wanted this shift."

"You working the weekend?" the woman asked.

"Sunday." Sabrina replied.

"See you then."

The woman turned and walked away.

Sabrina headed out into the main section of the police station, where the night shift crew were gathering round for a briefing. She stood next to Officer Briggs, who smiled in greeting. Officers Andrews and Weston avoided eye contact with her.

The sergeant gathered everyone round in a circle.

"Listen up. The council workers are putting up the spikes tonight." he said. "If anyone asks, it's defensive architecture, meant to stop loitering, public urination, skating, and deter break-ins. You are not, and I cannot stress this enough, at any point or in any way to state, imply or infer that it is in any way to stop people sleeping on the streets. The workers are starting on the outskirts and moving towards the city centre, they'll be doing the city centre late at night, when there's no one around. Officers Andrews, Weston, Briggs and Parker, you'll be patrolling the city centre, making sure there are no problems. Remember: this is not our choice, it's a government decision that the police had nothing to do with. We are simply overseeing the council workers. Briggs is in charge. Any questions?"

A string of grumbled "nos".

"Great. I'm off for the evening. See you all round, have a good, uneventful night."

The sergeant turned and left.

The four officers walked out of the station and began to wander into the city centre, Sabrina and Officer Briggs going ahead, with Andrews and Weston behind. The council workers mostly hadn't appeared yet, though there were a few around the train station, laying the first of the spikes.

The 'defensive architecture' as they were calling it, was really sets of bolts, spikes and bollards being placed along walls, shop doorsteps, alcoves in the pavement, and dividers being placed on benches to turn them into multiple seats with armrests. Despite the given purpose, it was clear that they were being installed to deter homeless people from sleeping in the city centre.

"I'm not sure what I think of this hostile architecture." Sabrina said to Officer Briggs.

"Defensive architecture." he corrected her.

"If you say so. What do you think of it?" she asked.

Officer Briggs shrugged, and for some reason she found some solace in his placid stare, as if someone else was as fed up of it all as she was, though in reality he was most likely just tired.

"Life on the street is already pretty tough, it's a shame to make it harder." he said. "But hey, if it stops public urination, prevents loitering and deters break-ins, who am I to question it?"

"Does it?" Sabrina asked.

Officer Briggs shrugged again, an action that seemed all too familiar to his weary shoulders.

"No idea." he replied.

Their walkie talkies buzzed.

"*Officer Briggs, do you read? Over.*"

"I'm listening, over." Briggs replied.

"*We've got a possible robbery in progress on Lee's Approach. Suspect is a black female, average height, aged eighteen to twenty-five, black top, blue jeans. Over.*"

"On our way. Out." Briggs said, curtly.

Behind them, Weston and Andrews had already turned and

started sprinting towards Lee's Approach.

Sabrina immediately started after them, followed a little more slowly by Officer Briggs, who was not nearly in as good shape as the other officers.

Andrews and Weston were far faster than Sabrina, and by the time she reached Lee's Approach, they already had the suspect pinned to a wall. The woman had long hair and a sports bag slung over her back, and was struggling against Weston's grip.

"What are you doing!" she screamed. "Get off me, I haven't done anything!"

"You are under arrest for armed robbery, where is the weapon?" Weston shouted, as Andrews pulled the bag off her back and tipped the contents onto the floor.

"It's just candy bars!" the woman was crying. "I'm sorry! It was a dare! It was a stupid dare!"

From round the corner, a cluster of teenagers appeared, drawn to the commotion.

"What's going on?" one of them shouted over. "Let her go!"

The woman struggled, and Weston pushed her harder into the wall, one arm on the back of her neck, one knee pressed into her back. She cried out.

"I don't have a weapon!" the woman sobbed. "It was just a stupid dare!"

"Where's the weapon?!" Andrews yelled, the contents of the bag now over the floor.

Sabrina was next to them now, panting.

"Guys, relax, it's just candy bars, it was shoplifting, not armed robbery, just book her so we can take her in." Sabrina said, throwing up her hand as she approached the commotion in an attempt to get the attention of Weston and Andrews.

The cluster of teenagers was close now.

"Chill out man!" one of the guys yelled over. "Don't hurt her! It's my fault, I'm the one who dared her!"

"We've got this, Parker." Andrews turned to Sabrina.

Weston turned his attention to the group of teenagers.

"Step away from us, please, we are just doing our job." he said, releasing his grip slightly on the suspect.

The girl broke free of Weston's grip and panicked, running off down the street in the direction that Sabrina had come from.

Officer Briggs emerged round the corner and the girl almost barrelled into him, pushing him to one side as she ran.

"Stop!" exclaimed Officer Briggs, his hands going to his belt and pulling out a taser.

"Wait, no!" Sabrina yelled out, but it was too late.

Officer Briggs fired.

The taser connected with the girl's back, sending fifty thousand volts flying out of the weapon and down the wires. The girl spasmed, dropping to the ground, her head smashing against the curb with a sickening crack.

"Oh crap." breathed Sabrina.

Officer Briggs looked at the woman, then back at the other officers, then at the crowd of teenagers, his expression dropping. The colour drained from his face.

"What the hell! Tammie!" one of the girls screamed.

Two of the teenagers were holding phones. The cameras were on, they had filmed everything.

Sabrina rushed over to the girl, on the radio in seconds.

"We need an ambulance to the corner of Lee's Approach, NOW!"

The girl was unconscious, bleeding from the back of the head where her skull had connected with the curb. The teenagers rushed over, and Andrews and Weston jumped into action, forming a barricade between Sabrina and the girl.

"Alright, calm down, our colleague has this under control, she'll be alright, we just need you to stand back." Officer Weston said.

"Is she okay?" one of the girls shouted. "Tammie!"

Officer Briggs was frozen to the spot, the taser on the ground next to him.

Sabrina pulled off her armoured vest and unbuttoned her shirt, revealing her fabric vest beneath, and used the shirt to try and stop the bleeding, pressing it over the wound.

"Briggs, I need you to go get a first aid kit, go see if that shop has one, now!"

Briggs broke free from his trance, turning and looking at the 24-hour convenience shop across the street. The blood had all drained from his face, and he seemed still half in a daze.

"NOW!" Sabrina yelled, and he nodded frantically, running

141

over the road to the shop. Moments later, he arrived with the shopkeeper: a man in a short-sleeved button shirt and glasses, carrying a green first aid kit.

"My god, what happened?!" he breathed.

"Are you the one who made the call?" Andrews asked. "The armed robbery?"

"Armed robbery?" the shopkeep frowned. "No, shoplifting! I saw her pocketing snacks, she wasn't armed! Good god, what happened?!"

"It was an accident." Weston replied.

"An accident?" one of the crowd yelled. "You shot her with a fucking taser!"

"I need the first aid kit!" Sabrina called, and the man handed over the kit.

She immediately pulled out the bandages and cotton padding: anything that could stop the flow of blood. Her hands trembled as she pulled the plastic wrapping away.

The girl on the ground groaned, finally coming back around to consciousness.

"What's happening?" she asked, her tone groggy, her eyelids barely opening.

"You've been hurt." Sabrina said. "You're going to be okay, the ambulance is on their way. I just need you to stay conscious, okay?"

The girl groaned, trying to sit up.

"Stay lying down, honey." Sabrina said. "You're going to be okay, but you're losing quite a bit of blood."

"It was just a dare." the girl muttered. "It was just a stupid dare."

Sirens. Sabrina silently thanked god. The ambulance was round the corner in seconds, and two paramedics pushed past and took over from Sabrina.

It was all just a blur from then. Andrews and Weston took over, Weston calming down the crowd, Andrews taking a statement from the shopkeeper. Before she knew it, Sabrina was back at the station with Officer Briggs, and a solemn calm finally settled in.

For a moment.

"Why the hell did you have a taser on you?" she said to Briggs, as he plopped himself down in his chair, white as a sheet, staring off into the middle distance.

"I always carry it." Briggs murmured, his voice barely audible. "Just in case."

"Jesus, Briggs!" Sabrina exclaimed. "She was just shoplifting! A stupid kid doing a stupid dare! I'm driving over to the hospital to check she's okay."

She rushed into the changing area, throwing down her vest and blood-stained shirt and switching back into her civilian clothes, and was out of the door and sat in her car in minutes.

She didn't turn the engine on.

Her hands were still covered in blood, now dried and discoloured. In the glove compartment of her car, she found a packet of wet wipes. There was only one left in the pack, and it was barely enough to clean her hands.

Tears rolled down her face.

This was not what she signed on for.

CHAPTER NINE: NO REST

Jason woke up in his workshop, slumped over in his wheelchair. In front of him, the gauntlet lay open on his workbench, his tools all around in. Next to him, Alex was passed out on the ground, next to Jason's laptop, with all sorts of websites open, searching for any information about Thomas Martin, the land owner who owned the Covered Market.
The 'low battery' sign on his wheelchair was flashing, and he groaned, rolling over to the car battery at the back of his workshop and plugging the wheelchair into a plug socket leading out of it.
Jason pulled out his phone as he waited for the wheelchair to charge up, looking out for any news alerts. Two caught his eye.
'BREAKING NEWS: ANTI-HOMELESS SPIKES PLACED ACROSS CITY OVERNIGHT'.
Jason skimmed through the article, taking in the highlights.
'The sudden appearance of hostile architecture across the city has many of Downtown's residents baffled. Spikes have been placed across fences and walls, bolts placed in the ground in the doorsteps and entrance ways of the shopping centres and many public buildings, and bollards have been erected in car parks and alleyways. We reached out to the office of the Prime Minister for comment this morning and have received no response yet, but a council official informed us that the purpose of this new architecture is to stop loitering, deter break-ins and prevent public urination. However, similar measures have been used in the past to prevent the homeless from sleeping in certain places, and the more astute observer may notice dividers placed in the benches across the parks and the city centre: how these prevent break-ins and public

urination is yet to be determined.'

"What on earth?" Jason frowned, limping over to the entrance of the garage and pulling the door up. The sound caused Alex to wake up, sitting up suddenly, and Jason wandered past him. Outside, Jason looked up and down the street. Ahead, he could see the train station, where tiny metal bolts had been placed all across each of the entrances, and even on the tiny walls surrounding the bits of greenery placed on the street edges for decoration. Jason looked at his phone, then back up at the street, hardly able to believe his eyes.

"How did we not hear them installing all this?" he muttered.

"What's going on?" Alex asked.

Jason handed him the phone, and he skimmed through the article.

"Well that's pointless." he snorted. "What a waste of money just to piss everyone off… Hey, have you seen this one?"

He opened the second headline and handed the phone back to Jason.

'POLICE BRUTALITY! Woman shot with taser over stolen confectionery.

A nineteen-year old girl named Tamara Johnson started last night playing drinking games with her friends, and ended the night in Downtown Central Hospital. Tamara, known to her friends as Tammie, was described by one friend as "a teacher's pet" who "never did anything wrong in her life". So it seemed like the perfect dare to try and get Tammie to live on the edge, take a risk… and shoplift. Tamara had no prior convictions, and was too nervous to take anything more than a few chocolate bars, but unfortunately that seemed to be enough.

The shopkeeper, Darren Brooks, 32, said he saw her shoving chocolate bars into her pockets and immediately called the police. "I said she was shoplifting. I didn't know what she'd taken. You call the police, it's just what you do. I didn't think they would do this. I feel terrible." Darren Brooks told our reporter. "I never thought anything like this would happen over shoplifting. I'm appalled. I feel so awful. Utterly awful". One officer, who would not confirm or deny whether he was at the scene, said the officer who fired the Conducted Energy

145

Device (colloquially known as a taser, which is actually a brand name) had reason to believe that the suspect was armed and posed a threat. No further comment has been given by the police as of yet'.

"What is this city c-coming to?" muttered Jason.

"I think we're going to have a busy couple of days ahead." Alex said. "You were right: the police can't protect us. They just make everything worse."

Jason saw Jack walking past the edge of the car park, and grabbed a walking stick from the entrance of the garage and hobbled over to him. The homeless man looked a lot less cheery than usual, with bags under his eyes, his shoulders slumped and his back hunched over.

"Jack, are you okay?" he asked.

Jack forced a smile.

"Didn't get any sleep." he said. "Couldn't find anywhere, the council kept moving me on."

"This is ridiculous." Jason said. "I'm r-r-really sorry, J-J-Jack. Aren't there any shelters?"

"There's two." Jack said. "But I don't like being around large crowds, and they're always so crowded. Makes me feel claustrophobic. Besides, there are others that need those beds more than I do."

Jason thought for a minute.

"How would you like a job for the day?" he asked.

Jack shrugged.

"What's in it for me?" he asked.

"Fifty quid." Jason suggested. "A hot meal, and you can use my shower and my bed this afternoon, get a good nap."

"What do you need?" asked Jack, the grin returning to his face.

Jason wheeled back to his workshop, opening the cupboard and pulling out a map of the city. He handed it to Jack, along with a pen.

"Make note of all the crap they put up last night, what it is, and where it is. Any bollards, spikes, anything like that." he said.

Jack shrugged, seeming to perk up a little at the offer.

"Okay." he said. "Happy to, do you mind if I ask why?"

"I'm... going to check it's all legal and properly approved, see if we can get any of it removed." Jason lied.

"Good luck." Jack said. "You get used to this kind of thing when you're on the street long enough. But good on you for trying. You're a good lad."

Jack set off to the corner of the carpark and started noting down on his map, scratching his head as he made an effort to remember what he had seen and where.

"What have you got planned?" Alex asked.

"Something…" Jason said. "Can you do the same? Make note of as much of this stuff as you can. Go south."

Alex shrugged.

"Do I get fifty quid and a hot meal?" he asked.

"Really?" Jason asked, raising an eyebrow.

"I'm messing with you, mate. I hope you've got something big planned. If there's one thing I can't stand, it's the government screwing over the public. I signed up to work for the government to protect our country, coming home to find it really needed protecting from our own leaders just sucks."

"I thought you signed up to run away?" Jason said.

"Whatever." Alex said. "You got another map?"

Jason shook his head, pulling out a ten pound note.

"Go buy one." he said. "Take pictures for me."

"Can I use your shower first?" Alex nodded.

Jason tossed him the key to his bedsit, and Alex took his duffel bag and headed inside. Jason headed back into his garage, pulling the door closed.

"I need supplies." he muttered.

As midday approached, Jason was hard at work in his workshop, the gauntlets set aside, and a massive device with a giant metal coil inside was open on his table, with a soldering iron and bits of circuit board all around it. His laptop was open, playing a live stream of a group of reporters interviewing the Prime Minister, who was standing on the steps of parliament, giving a statement. Prime Minister David Jones was a tall, chubby man, with slick brown hair and wrinkled, white skin. He was in his forties, very posh, very proper: a Conservative, centre-right politician who was always trying his best to appear politically correct, and yet somehow always failing. And yet, he was in charge.

147

"The measures that were put in place last night have been in the works for a good while now, they are not in any way intended to hinder the homeless, but are in fact to protect our lovely city and our high street. The homeless are encouraged to seek accommodation in our many shelters available across the city, some of which have been funded by our government: two thousand beds, funded under our 'Help the Homeless' initiative."

"Prime Minister Jones, our survey found that there were closer to two hundred beds made available under that scheme, the figure of two thousand seems to be the total beds available, whether under the government scheme or not." one of the reporters shouted over the crowd. *"Is that not correct, sir?"*

"Well, I, uh. I don't have the numbers in front of me now, but I am told that there are adequate facilities available to the homeless." the prime minister fumbled in response.

"But there are around one hundred and sixty thousand homeless people in Downtown City, and only a few thousand free beds available." the reporter responded.

"You're told?" another reporter chimed in. *"So you haven't seen the facilities for yourself?"*

"Are there any other questions?" the prime minister asked.

"Prime Minister, would you care to comment on the assault of Tamara Johnson, who was injured by police officers last night?" one reporter called from the back of the cluster.

"Well, yes, I, uh, I very much, was, uh, I was deeply saddened to hear of the incident last night involving the, uh, the girl, Tamara Jones, uh, Johnson, sorry. I am sure the staff at Downtown Hospital are doing their best, to, uh, make sure she pulls through, and I can assure you that a full investigation will be carried out into what happened, and, uh, whether anyone was at fault."

"Are you suggesting that anyone else could be at fault, other than the officer who hit Ms Johnson with the CED?" the reported asked.

"Mr Prime Minister, are you able and willing to reveal the identity of the police officer who fired the weapon at Tamara Johnson?"

"An investigation is currently being carried out, and we will let

you know all the facts as soon as we are able. Good day." The prime minister turned and waddled back into the building to a chorus of questions from the reporters, who were held back by a string of police officers.

A knock came at Jason's garage door, and he threw a blanket over his work table and went to answer. Jack stood outside, proudly holding his map.

"What are you working on?" Jack asked, peering into the garage.

"Oh, just a project, I'm a bit of an inventor." Jason said. "Follow me, let's go into my p-place and make some lunch."

"Thanks for this, mate." Jack said, as Jason locked up the garage and led Jack inside. "You're a good lad. Remind me of my brother."

"You have a brother?"

"Did have." Jack replied. "Died of cancer a few years back. He always saw the best in people, always did his best to help people out. Even let me crash on his sofa when I first fell on hard times, till his landlord found out."

"I'm sorry to hear that." Jason said, opening up the bedsit. "Come on, let's f-find something to eat."

Jason and Jack enjoyed a few toasted sandwiches, which was one of the few things Jason could easily make in his tiny kitchen, and Jack had a long shower and passed out in Jason's bed. Jason almost immediately returned to the garage, and that was where Alex found him later that evening, hard at work. Alex slid the garage door closed behind him. Jason spending all day working there had heated it up, leaving both Jason and Alex sweating through their t-shirts within minutes. In the middle of the workshop, Jason had set up a long work table with three objects on it. The first was a series of metal spikes atop a metal bar. The second was a series of metal bolts that had been embedded in a brick. The third was a divider, like had been placed on the park benches, attached to the table. Each was held firmly down by its own set of metal clamps. Jason lifted one of the gauntlets, which he had made even bulkier than before, and slipped it onto his hand.

"I've boosted the electromagnetic capabilities of the gauntlets.

149

Watch."

Jason aimed the gauntlet at the work table and slowly began to rotate his closed fist. The gauntlet began to hum, and the metal bolts in the brick began to wobble, one by one shooting from the brick with a crack and hovering in the air in front of the gauntlet. Jason unclenched his fist and the bolts dropped to the ground. He clenched his fist again, aiming at the metal spikes. A few screws and nails that were on the floor of the workshop shot the gauntlet, and the metal the spikes were merged to began to twist, breaking free of the clamps and spinning to the air towards the gauntlet, colliding with his fist with a thud that almost knocked Jason off-balance. He released, and the spikes dropped to the ground. Finally, he turned to aim at the bench divider and it immediately shot from its clamps, and he caught it in his outstretched hand.

"Impressive." Alex said, nodding approvingly. "What's the plan?"

"We're g-going to undo what the council has done. Then tomorrow, there's a civil rights protest outside parliament… We're going to b-be there." Jason said. "If we're going to stand up for the people, we should stand with them too."

***

Blake sat awkwardly at the corner table of an unfamiliar pub a twenty minute walk from the centre of Downtown City. He fidgeted awkwardly with his phone, checking every thirty seconds to see if he'd received a message. His phone remained open on his last message. At the top of the screen, the name 'Owen' sat, in big bold letters, and beneath it the message '*sorry, be there in a few mins*'.

The pub was a traditional, British pub, with flags sporting a red cross on a white background littered all across the bar. It was mostly empty, but for a few middle-aged couples finishing their meals, and a group of typical, working class white men at the bar, having a drink. They looked like the sort to be regulars of this kind of pub: and definitely not the sort that Blake would usually spend a lot of time around.

He clutched his leather jacket tightly around himself, blowing his hair out of his eyes.

The bell above the door jingled as someone entered the pub: a handsome guy in his early twenties, with short hair and a clean-shaven face. He was slim, but tall: towering above Blake's five feet and six inches. He cast his gaze around the bar, before his eyes settled on Blake and he smiled, walking over to him.

One of the men at the bar turned and watched him enter, staring at the two of them for a few seconds, then went back to his drink.

"Sorry I'm late." the newcomer said, taking a seat across from Blake. "Got caught up at work."

"It's okay." Blake replied. "Why did you pick this place?"

Owen shrugged.

"It's half-way between work and your place, I've only actually been in here once, but hey, a pub's a pub. Let's go get drinks."

Owen hung his jacket over his seat and jogged over to the bar. Blake followed, hesitantly.

"Alright." Owen said to the bartender with a cheery grin.

The bartender, a jolly woman whose orange foundation did not match her pale skin, and left an obvious line at the neck, turned away from her regulars and looked Owen up and down.

"Hey handsome." she said. "What can I get you?"

"Pint of cider, whatever you've got on tap." Owen said. He turned to Blake. "What do you want, babe?"

The word 'babe' caught the attention of the same guy who had been staring at them earlier, who was now only a few feet away from Owen. He turned and looked at them again. He looked to be about forty years old, and his hairline was about as far back on his head as it could be. He had a rugged build, like he was a builder or a handyman of some sort, and was sporting a polo shirt with 'DOWNTOWN CITY FC' written in small letters on the left breast, where a pocket would often be.

"Rum and coke." Blake said, softly.

Owen caught the guy looking at him and turned and nodded to him.

"Alright, mate?" he asked.

"Alright." the guy said, forcing a smile back at him. "Don't see many of your sort in here!"

Owen frowned.

"What do you mean?" he asked, a genuine hint of confusion in his voice.

The man thought for a second, then seemed to save himself. "Young people." he said, smiling again. "Mostly old tossers like me."

Owen laughed, and pulled out his wallet to pay for the drinks. He tapped his card against the card reader, and the bartender slid across the two drinks. Blake returned hastily to the table.

"So, how was your day?" Owen asked, plopping himself down in his seat and taking a long sip from his pint of cider.

"It was alright." Blake shrugged. "I was surprised you wanted to see me again so soon."

Owen grinned.

"Of course! I really had fun at our last date!"

Blake smiled, starting to feel a little less awkward now that he wasn't alone.

"Me too." he said.

"You mentioned that you hadn't been dating much because of a bad break-up." Owen said. "What happened there, if you don't mind me asking?"

Blake sighed.

"It's a long story..." he said. "My ex, Alex... We had been together since college. He was the first guy I dated after I came out as trans. We'd been together for basically two years, then he just upped and left to join the army, without telling me."

"Jeez!" Owen exclaimed. "That's awful! Didn't even tell you he'd applied?"

"I knew he was thinking about it, but didn't know he had actually gone through with it." Blake said. "He left the day of my top surgery."

"Ooof!" Owen muttered. "I'm really sorry."

"It's okay, it's been a long time, I'm over it now." Blake replied. "Just made it hard to trust again."

"Did he ever explain why?" Owen asked.

"He wrote me a letter a little while later, said it had nothing to do with me, he was sorry about the timing, but he had to go. I never wrote back."

"Good on you." Owen replied. "Don't need toxic people like that in your life. Anyway, let's talk about something a bit happier."

Blake smiled, sipping his drink.

"You've got a dog, haven't you?" He picked a much more light-hearted topic.

Owen smiled and nodded.

"I do!" he said. "Archie. He's a staffy. Hopefully you'll get to meet him someday soon."

Blake blushed crimson, and hid behind his drink as he took another swig.

"I'd like that."

Owen met Blake's gaze, and slid his hand across the table to hold Blake's, running his thumb across Blake's hand. Blake suddenly became very aware that the man at the bar was staring at them again, and this time two of his friends were staring too. One of the friends was much younger, and the other had the look of someone who could be anywhere between the age of twenty-five and forty-five, but drugs and cigarettes had made it hard to tell.

"Do you mind if we get out of here?" Blake asked, softly. "I'm sorry, this place is setting off my anxiety. It's giving me weird vibes, can we go somewhere else?"

Owen shrugged and nodded.

"Whatever you want. Let's finish these drinks first."

He took a large gulp from his cider, taking it to half empty.

Blake downed his drink in one.

"Woah!" Owen laughed. "Nice one! Challenge accepted!"

He picked up the cider and, in four massive gulps, finished the rest of it.

"Come on handsome, let's get out of here!"

The two stood and walked, arm in arm, out of the pub. Owen was in a world of his own, happily chatting, but Blake saw the three men at the bar get up and follow them out.

"Hey! Hey!" one of the men called after them. It was the younger one, who couldn't have been much older than him and Owen.

Owen stopped and turned, confusion crossing his face.

"Just keep walking." Blake whispered.

"What?" Owen called back.

"Don't you know? Fags aren't welcome in our city!" the man shouted down the street, still walking towards them with purpose.

"Oh." Realisation crossed Owen's face, but he maintained his composure. "Sorry, I didn't realise this was homophobe city. I thought it was Downtown City."

"Owen, keep walking." Blake whispered.

The man was just a few feet away from them now, with his two friends behind.

"That's right, poof, keep walking." The man took the final few steps to be brought face to face with Owen. They were the same height, but the other man had his two friends behind him, who both looked much tougher.

"Why, are you afraid I'll seduce you?" Owen said.

"Kenny, leave it, it's not worth it!" the older man called forward. "Let them be!"

The man named Kenny didn't punch. He didn't kick. He simply tipped his head back, and brought his forehead crashing down into Owen's nose. Owen stumbled back clutching his face. Kenny stepped forwards, bringing a fist up into Owen's stomach.

"Wait, stop!" Blake grabbed hold of the man's arm to prevent him from hitting Owen again.

The attacker ripped his arm free and grabbed Blake by the shoulders, throwing him with force to the ground. Then, without a second of hesitation, he threw his foot with full force into Blake's stomach.

"You're even worse!" he spat. "You can't even decide what you are!"

"Get off him!" Owen roared, throwing himself at the man.

"Kenny, stop!" the older man rushed over and put a hand on Kenny's shoulder. Kenny shook him off and bent over Blake, grabbing him by the hair and pulling his face level to his.

"You make me sick." he hissed, and threw Blake back down to the ground. "This is why blacks and whites shouldn't mix. The kids will always be freaks."

Two old ladies rounded the corner just in time to see the man throw Blake back down. They were dressed in knitted coats and hats, both carrying handbags that looked as old as them, and the looks on their faces would have been almost comical shock, if it weren't for the horrific nature of the situation. The two other men grabbed the one called Kenny and pulled him away.

"Margaret, call the police." one of the old ladies said, rushing over to Blake.

"What was that about, Kenny?" one of them exclaimed as they ran. "I don't like 'em either but you crossed a line, mate!"

Owen rushed to Blake's side, who groaned and turned over.

"Are you okay?" the old lady asked.

Behind her, the other old lady had already called the police and was talking to them softly.

Blake shot to his feet and turned and ran the other way down the street, his heart racing.

"Blake, wait!" Owen exclaimed, running after him. "Where are you going!"

"Young man!" the old lady called, but Blake was gone.

Blake didn't stop running until he was outside his apartment building. Owen followed him the whole way. Every corner he turned, every person he passed, he panicked, his heart leaping and dropping in his chest until he felt like he was going to be sick.

"Blake, why did you run?" Owen asked, panting for breath as he leant against the wall.

"She was calling the police." Blake muttered. "I just… I panicked."

"Why?" Owen asked.

"My dad…. Well, my step-dad… I never knew my real dad..." Blake stumbled over his words, trying his best to catch his breath, slow his heart, and calm himself down. He started again."My dad was killed by a police officer when I was three. People like me… We don't call the police, we run from them. Even when we've done nothing wrong."

"Shit." Owen breathed. "I'm sorry. Look, let's get inside, I'll clean you up, I've got a friend who doesn't live far from here, we can go over to her place."

"It's okay." Blake said. "I live here. You can come in."

Rhiannon crouched in the doorway of the shopping centre, spanner in hand, pulling with all her strength to loosen one of the countless bolts that had been placed in the ground.

"Shouldn't we wait until the homeless outreach next week?" Louis said, as he looked up and down the street nervously.

"We'll have back-up then. A whole team of activists."

"I can't just stand by knowing people are sleeping rough." Rhiannon replied. "We've got to do something."

"Well the two of us alone can't do much, and we've got the protest tomorrow, we need rest." Louis pointed out.

"Everything we do, the council will have undone by the time we meet next week."

"So what?" Rhiannon said. "We shouldn't try?"

"No, that's not what I meant." Louis replied.

"I just can't, Louis." she said. "I can't rest, I can't sleep, all I can think about is that poor girl. If I stop for even a second, her face haunts me. She's fighting for her life because of those racist cops. I've got to do something... Something to make the world a better place. Even something as small as this. I just can't stop."

Louis sighed.

"You're right. As always. Here, let's swap. You keep guard." Rhiannon handed him the spanner, and her eyes caught sight of a hooded figure walking up the street, with massive, glowing gauntlets on each of his hands. The man stopped in front of a doorway, pointed a gauntlet at the ground, and a string of metal spikes and bolts screwed into the ground shot up and wrapped around his gauntlet, some floating in the air around it, some sticking to the metal glove. Opening a sack on his back, he poured the spikes and bolts into it.

"Is that... The Fist?" Louis asked.

He stopped as he saw Rhiannon and Louis, his eyes flicking down to the spanner, then to the bolts on the ground. He walked towards them and wordlessly indicated with a hand gesture for them to step aside. Once they were out of the way, he pointed a gauntlet at the bolts. The bolts shot out of the ground, hovering in the air in front of his hand, and he moved his gauntlet over the sack, releasing his fist and causing the bolts to drop into the sack.

"That's amazing." Louis muttered. "Respect, man."

The Fist nodded silently, and moved onto the next doorway.

"See, told you he wasn't just protecting his own." Louis muttered. "Maybe he really is doing this for the greater good."

"I hope so." Rhiannon replied. "Anyone who stands up for the homeless can't be all bad."

***

Big Tuna sat in his warehouse, a glass of brandy in one hand, a cigarette in the other. Across from him, Jeb entered and sat down, letting out a long sigh, his tie loose around his neck, several of the buttons undone. He ran his fingers through his short, dreadlocked hair, and there was a pool of sadness in his eyes that Big Tuna wasn't used to seeing in his usually stern, emotionless face.

"You wanted to talk?" Big Tuna asked, taking another sip of brandy.

"Yeah, it's about the girl who nearly got killed by those pigs." Jeb said. "I went to college with her, she was a good person."

"Shit, man." Big Tuna sighed. "I'm really sorry to hear that."

"There's a protest tomorrow against the police brutality and all that." Jeb said. "Word on the street is that the Bovver Boys want to turn up and cause some trouble."

"Well, they are a bunch of racist twats, that's no surprise." Big Tuna said.

"The protest will be going across the bridge, which is our territory." Jeb continued. "Boss, we gotta do something about it."

"What, protect our turf?" Big Tuna raised an eyebrow. "I don't think this is a move against us, mate."

"It's not about the turf, boss, it's about doing what's right. It's about standing up to racist pricks." Jeb said. "One of the reasons I keep working for you is 'cus you do the right thing. Standing up to racists is the right thing."

Big Tuna nodded, slowly.

"I'll have a think about it." he said. "Pour yourself a drink, Jeb, you look like you need it."

157

Jeb did as he was told, pouring himself a big glass of brandy, and the two gangsters sat back and drank together.

"Let's put some music on." Big Tuna said.

"I don't suppose it'll be Tupac or Snoop?" Jeb said, with a half-smile.

"I was thinking Sinatra and the Rap Pack."

"Shit, boss, again? What about some classic Bowie?"

"I could compromise on some Bowie."

"Let's do it."

CHAPTER TEN: ONE THOUSAND FISTS

Blake was awoken suddenly to the furious sound of someone pounding at the door. He jumped half out of his skin and he scrambled out of bed and walked into the living room and kitchen area of the apartment, where Owen was unconscious and snoring like a trucker on the sofa.

"Broooooo! Open up! It's me!" The voice outside was muffled, but familiar. Blake sighed and rolled his eyes, opening the door. Outside, a woman stood with her fist raised to pound on the door again, and behind her a giant of a man, at least over six and a half feet tall, broad shouldered, built like a tank, was leaning against the wall. Both of them were incredibly dark-skinned, the woman wearing a black hoodie with the letters BLM printed on it in giant yellow letters. The man was wearing a similar t-shirt, with a denim vest over the top decorated with an array of badges: the Antifa logo, the Extinction Rebellion logo, and a whole host of other social justice movements, covering the front and back of the denim vest. The woman fell silent as soon as she saw Blake, her expression dropping.

"Rhiannon." Blake sighed. "Who's your friend?"

"This is Louis, my boyfriend, I told you about him, right?" the woman said, pushing her way into the apartment. "What happened to your face? Are you okay?"

Blake caught sight of his reflection in a mirror hung near the door. There was a bruise on the side of his cheek from where his face hit the pavement, and another by the chin from where the attacker hit him.

The big man, Louis, smiled and gave a little wave as he

159

awkwardly stooped to get in through the door and hovered near the entrance.

"Hi." Blake said.

"He's just a bit quiet." Rhiannon said. "Well, what happened?"

"We were mugged last night." Blake said. "Some homophobic piece of trash. We were in the wrong part of town, I guess."

"We?" Rhiannon asked, and her eyes fell on Owen, who somehow hadn't been woken by all the commotion. A smile crept across her face. "Oh my god, has my step-brother finally got a new boyfriend?! Fan-friggin'-tastic! You sealed the deal yet? I guess not, since he's on the sofa."

"Not that it isn't great to see you, but why are you here?" Blake asked.

"The protest." Rhiannon said, as if it was obvious. "I'm helping to run it. I'm giving a talk. You're going to come, right?"

"I don't know, I'm so drained after last night." Blake said.

"Come on, bro, you need to be there!" Rhiannon exclaimed. "It's important. For dad."

"That's what you always say, but I'm just not cut out for the activism like you are." Blake replied, sitting on the arm of the sofa.

Rhiannon sighed.

"When you were attacked, what did you do?" she asked.

"I ran away." Blake replied.

"And then?" Rhiannon asked. "You called the police, and gave a statement, right?"

Blake hesitated.

"No…" he muttered.

"No, of course you didn't." Rhiannon butted in. "And why not?" She didn't wait for an answer. "Because of dad. Because of your skin. Because the other night, a girl who looked like us was nearly killed by the police, not because she took some chocolates or some sweets, but because the police saw her and immediately decided she was a dangerous threat that needed to be eliminated. You've got to come, Blake, because if we don't stand up now, things are never going to get better."

"I'm just not the 'change the world' type." Blake said.

"We went to Pride." Rhiannon pointed out.

"That was different, Pride is a celebration." Blake said.

"You know better than I do that Pride is a protest." Rhiannon replied, matter-of-factly. "I don't need to tell you the first ever Pride, Stonewall: gay black drag queens and transgender activists stood side-by-side. Don't tell me that you didn't have that in mind when you marched."

Blake sighed.

"Fine!" he exclaimed. "At least have a cup of tea with me first, I'm half awake. And quieten down a bit, my flatmate is asleep in the other room."

"No I'm not!" a tired voice carried through the wall. "Your sister is loud!"

"Sorry Kevin!" Blake called back.

He shook Owen awake and headed into the kitchen to make a cup of tea.

"What's going on?" Owen mumbled, slowly opening his eyes. "Ah! People!"

"Hey handsome!" Rhiannon grinned. "So, you're dating my step-brother?"

Owen looked from Blake, back to Rhiannon.

"Nice to meet you." Rhiannon said, extending a hand. "If you ever hurt my brother, the police will finally have a legitimate reason to arrest me."

"Noted." Owen said, shaking her hand. "Blake, your sister scares me."

"Is it because I'm black?" Rhiannon said.

"Uhhh…" Owen fumbled for an answer.

"I'm messing with you, white boy!" Rhiannon laughed. "Let's get some tea!"

***

The central police station was bustling with officers, but there was very little small talk. Everyone was tense and on edge, and no one was looking forward to the day ahead of them. A hush fell over the room as a white-haired man in his fifties strode into the centre of the main office where everyone congregated and cleared his throat. Everything about him was neat and tidy: his hair was neatly cropped, his moustache was trim and neat, his tie was straight, his clothes neatly ironed, every single one of his badges perfectly straight. Even the laces on his shoes were perfect.

The superintendent was back.

Everyone quietly gathered around.

"Good morning everyone." The superintendent had a well-spoken voice: soft but authoritative. "Tensions are high in the city right now, and it is our job to keep them from growing higher. The people are angry: they are angry with the council, over the defensive architecture measures carried out. They are angry with us: for the tragic accident the other night. They are angry with the government: over the refugee crisis. We have no idea how many people will be there: social media indicates it could be anywhere between fifty and five hundred. Maybe more. Officer Briggs."

Officer Briggs stepped forwards. He had bags under his eyes, and the colour never seemed to have returned to his face. He was older than most of the other officers already, but now it looked as though he had aged an extra decade in the past day.

"We have decided that it would be best if you take some leave, effective immediately." the superintendent said. "Initially it will be paid leave, until the investigation is completed."

Officer Briggs nodded silently, and went back into the changing rooms. He seemed to slump his shoulders in relief as he went.

"The rest of you: you will be divided into groups today. The other stations across the city have already been mobilised, and you will be aiding them. One squad will remain outside parliament, where the protest is due to start. The second will be stationed outside the Prime Minister's house, at Number 10, where we believe the protest will move to. Then finally, a squad will remain at the station, where the protest is scheduled to end up. Sergeant Burns will be stationed at parliament, and Inspector Warren will remain here. I will be stationed outside of the Prime Minister's house myself. The chief of police will be with me. He is already with the Prime Minister now.... Constable Parker."

Sabrina did a double-take, looking over to the superintendent. She had not been expecting to be called on, or even for the superintendent to know her name.

"Yes, sir?" she said.

"I am told that you have a skill for conflict de-escalation." the superintendent said. "I am also informed you were the one to step forward and administer first aid to Tamara Johnson. You may be seen as a more friendly face. I want you to pick five officers to follow the protest with you. You will go wherever they go, you will remain in constant contact with me over your radio. Any questions?"

"Yes, sir." Sabrina replied. "Will six of us be enough?"

"It will have to be." replied the superintendent. "We are stretched thin as it is. Once the protest has fully moved on from the houses of parliament, I may be able to redistribute some of the officers there, however we will have to play it by ear. Officer Parker, you and those following the parade are to remain in standard uniform, no riot gear. Everyone else, full riot gear, but absolutely NO conducted energy devices. *No tasers.* Be ready in ten minutes. Now remember. If anyone asks about the incident, you say two words: 'no comment.' If anyone asks for Officer Brigg's identity, or the identity of any of the officers at the scene, say 'no comment'. This is the thin blue line, people. Dismissed."

The officers all rushed to get their riot gear on, and Sabrina went to go pick five officers to join her.

"Constable Parker, may I ask who you will be picking?" the superintendent asked.

"I don't know." Sabrina replied. "I'm thinking Jones, Peters, Kumar, Ryans and… Harris…"

"Smart, Jones and Ryans are women, Kumar and Harris are people of colour." the superintendent nodded. "That'll be good for any publicity shots of the protest."

"I was more thinking they'd be better at keeping the peace." Sabrina replied.

"That too." the superintendent said. "But remember, if things *do* get violent, you radio for backup immediately."

Sabrina nodded silently, and the superintendent disappeared into the crowd of officers. Sabrina sat and waited for a moment, collecting her thoughts, before taking a deep breath and heading into the changing room to find her six officers.

This was going to be a long day.

***

Alex walked through the streets as the sun rose over a city in chaos. Strings of people headed across the bridge, towards the houses of parliament. Some held signs, some even carried banners. Alex walked with purpose towards Jason's place, near the train station.

Rounding a corner with speed, Alex walked directly into a giant of a man, looking up to see a startled guy, over six and a half feet tall, clad in a sleeveless denim jacket.

"Sorry, mate." Alex said, stepping out the way.

His eyes slowly trailed over the group of people the big man was with. A familiar woman, and two men: one who was very familiar. It hit him: it was the man and the woman he had seen the night before… But also...

"Blake!" Alex exclaimed. "Hi!"

"Hey Alex." Blake refused to make eye contact. "We're in a rush."

"Are you okay? What happened to your face?" Alex asked.

"He was mugged." the woman said, and as she spoke Alex recognised her as Blake's older step-sister. He couldn't believe he hadn't seen it the night before, but it was dark, and now that he saw her next to Blake, suddenly recognition settled in.

"Are you going to the protest?"

"Yeah, I'll be there." Alex said.

"Great." Rhiannon said, grabbing Blake's arm. "We'll see you there."

"What was that about?" Alex heard the big man ask as they rushed past.

"That's Blake's ex." Rhiannon hissed back. "Keep walking."

"There's something familiar about him." the big man said.

Alex's heart sunk, and he focused his mind back on the mission, walking with renewed purpose towards Jason's garage and pulling the door up. Jason was already in there, working, and he jumped as the door slid up.

"Jesus, Alex! Knock!" he exclaimed. "You r-ready?"

"I'm ready." Alex said. "What's the plan?"

164

Jason picked up a pile of clothes from the floor of the workshop.

"Bandanna, coat, armoured vest." he tossed the articles of clothing over, and then lifted a backpack, opening it to reveal the gauntlets and goggles.

"New and improved." Jason said. "I took apart a pair of smart glasses, built them into the goggles. You can now flick backwards and forwards between night vision, x-ray vision, and normal vision, you can zoom and enhance, you can even record. The gauntlets have a few extra functions too, but we don't really have much time to go over that. Put on the other stuff, but wait for the right moment to put on the goggles and gauntlets. Oh, and good work last night."

Alex and Jason looked over to the corner, where a big sack was filled with what looked like scrap metal.

"Here's an earpiece." Jason picked up what looked like a singular headphone with a hook that went around the back of the ear. "You can use that to communicate with me."

"What will you be doing?" Alex asked.

"Ah." Jason said. "I got this."

He tapped an object that was sitting on the desk. It took up most of the worktop: it had a bulky, black body, and four tiny propellers, protected by rings of black plastic.

"A drone?" Alex said.

"Yeah." Jason replied. "I'm g-g-going to be using it to track the movements of the p-police, look out for t-trouble, and find you an exit if you need one. Remember, you're there to make a statement, and to look out for the p-protesters."

Alex nodded, taking a deep breath, and extended his hand to Jason.

"We make a good team, Jason Fox." he said. "Good luck."

"Good luck to you." Jason took his hand and shook it. "Let's get to work."

***

Zakirah looked up at the sky, pulling her new green jacket tightly around her as she admired the Downtown City skyline.

In front of her, Asim and a cluster of other men and women

165

from the mosque walked towards the houses of parliament, carrying big bags filled with food parcels.

"I thought that England was supposed to be a wonderful place." Zakirah said, rushing to catch up with Asim and Saabira. "A paradise: Great Britain. But since I've arrived, the police have kidnapped innocent men, failed to arrest racist thugs, bullied the homeless, and now nearly beaten a girl to death."

"England is a complicated place." Asim replied. "Every country has its faults, and here is no different. All we can do is make an effort to help those in need, and to make the world a better place."

"You're a good man, Asim." Zakirah said.

As they got closer to the houses of parliament, they were greeted by another group of men, led by Naveed, the owner of the comic book shop.

"Greetings, uncle." he said to Asim. "And uncles." He greeted the other men. "I know we've had our differences in the past, but I'm here to help."

"You are always welcome, Naveed." Asim smiled. "Help me carry this bag."

***

Outside the houses of parliament, on the bank of the river running through Downtown City, there was a small area of greenery not quite large enough to be called a park. In that area, Rhiannon stood and watched as the grass and the path around it slowly filled with more and more people, first ten, then twenty, then fifty, then one hundred, then more and more. Her heart raced as she scanned the crowd. At the front stood her loyal cluster of civil rights protesters. Rhiannon had dedicated her life to fighting for human rights, and her team of young people was the most eager and dedicated team she could have ever asked for. Behind them, nearly two hundred black people and other people of colour had filtered into the crowd, and they were joined by another group: the homeless community of Downtown City. At the edge of the grass, a group of muslims from the local mosque, led by a bearded man in a Black Panther t-shirt and the imam, were handing out food

166

parcels to the homeless. The man in the Black Panther shirt caught Rhiannon looking at him and raised a single clenched fist. Rhiannon raised her own fist in response, then went back to scanning the crowd.

A black woman with the most spectacular dreadlocks Rhiannon had ever seen was forcing her way through the crowd, carrying a small step ladder under one arm and a megaphone under the other, leading the way for a much older man and woman. The woman with dreadlocks pushed her way to where Rhiannon was standing.

"You're Rhiannon?" she asked.

"Yeah." Rhiannon replied.

"I'm Marie, we've been speaking over text. Thanks for agreeing to come and help organise this at such short notice. We start in ten minutes, did you prepare a speech?" the woman said, speaking at a hundred miles an hour.

"Yeah, I can give a speech." Rhiannon replied. "It's a decent crowd we've got here."

"The people are angry." Marie replied. "It's fresh in their minds. It's keeping that passion alive long enough to ignite real change that's the challenge. This is Isaac and Delilah Johnson, they're Tamara's aunt and uncle. Her parents are at the hospital right now, but Isaac is going to speak on their behalf, after you. Could you introduce him?"

"Of course." Rhiannon said, and turned to the older couple. "I'm so sorry about what happened to Tamara. We will get justice."

The couple smiled warmly at her, though there was no light, no spark of joy in their eyes. They were empty smiles, born out of polite civilities and not emotion.

"You ready?" Maria asked.

"As ever." Rhiannon replied, a crooked smile crossing her face.

Marie set up the little step ladder and handed Rhiannon the megaphone.

Rhiannon stepped up onto the ladder, which had her towering above the crowd, and even slightly taller than Louis, who stood close by her side. Now that she was up high, she could see the line of police officers in high visibility jackets that had

167

lined up along the pavement, and the second line police officers in riot gear, holding shields, lined up in front of parliament.

"Yeah." Rhiannon snorted. "Like we're the violent threat here."

The crowd started to notice her standing on the step ladder and one by one began to turn their heads and quieten down to pay attention to her. Rhiannon held the megaphone to her face and pressed the button.

"People of Downtown." Her voice echoed into the distance. "We are here to protest the horrific injustices that we have suffered. We are here to say enough is enough." She paused, and the crowd murmured in agreement. "We are here to say that we will not stay quiet any longer. This is not just about the events of the last few days. This is not just about Tamara Johnson, who is fighting for her life in Downtown City Hospital right now. This is about how this government and the people who are supposed to protect us are constantly discriminating against us, and pushing us down. It's 2022, and the police still racially profile us, the government ignores our struggles, and the media stays silent. And overnight the council puts in spikes to stop people who are struggling to get by on the streets from getting a night of rest? They don't care about us! The people of Downtown are struggling, and what do they do? They put up barriers, they put up hurdles, they trip us up and they spit on us while we're down! Shame on them!" The crowd cheered in agreement again, their faces growing more lively and passionate. "Tamara Johnson was not the first, and she won't be the last unless we stand up and say enough is enough, we won't take it anymore!..." She scanned the crowd, meeting the eyes of some of the more lively crowd members. Applause broke out as she finished speaking, and once it had died down, she opened her mouth again. "This is Isaac Johnson, Tamara's uncle."

The crowd grew quiet again, and Rhiannon stepped down to let the old man take her place, handing over the megaphone. He fumbled awkwardly with the button, reading off a tiny piece of card.

"Tammie is a sweet girl." he said, his voice barely carrying.

"We can't hear you!" a voice shouted from the crowd.

Isaac fumbled with the megaphone again, and Rhiannon stepped forwards, taking hold of the megaphone and pressing the button, holding it in front of his face for him. He quietly thanked her, and looked back to the crowd.

"Tammie is a sweet girl." he said. "She wants to be a race car driver. She's passionate and smart and so, so funny. She has two brothers, who love her dearly. Two brothers that now, are scared they might lose their sister. The doctors say that she has internal bleeding. Currently, Tammie is in what they're calling an 'induced coma', that is supposed to raise her chances of survival. We don't know if she'll wake up. We don't know if she'll survive the surgery. Tammie is fighting for her life right now…" Isaac stopped, his voice cracking, as tears ran down his face. "Thank you all for fighting so that no one else ever has to suffer the way my family is suffering right now."

Isaac stepped down, and Marie placed a comforting hand on his shoulder.

Rhiannon took the megaphone and stepped onto the ladder. A solemn silence had fallen over the crowd.

"This is my brother!" Rhiannon said, indicating to where Blake stood. Blake looked up, startled. "Last night, my brother and his boyfriend were assaulted because of who they love! They were attacked just for being gay! But did he call the police? NO! Because he was just as afraid of the racist police as he was of the homophobic douchebags who attacked him!"

The crowd began to boo, a cloud of outrage settling over the people gathered there.

"The system is broken!" Rhiannon yelled. "We should be able to call the police on homophobes! We shouldn't have to fear the people there to protect us! We shouldn't have to struggle to find a place to sleep: we should always be able to find somewhere to rest our heads! We are so fed up with the system, some of us have even started putting on outfits and going out seeking justice for ourselves! The media is calling him the Fist of Justice. You know what I say? I say we are ALL the Fists of Justice!"

Rhiannon raised her fist to the sky, and in response she saw the crowd start to raise their fists in solidarity. Close to a thousand fists, all raised.

"Now!... What do we want?" Rhiannon yelled, at the top of her lungs.

"JUSTICE!" the crowd screamed back.

"When do we want it?"

"NOW!"

"What do we want?"

"JUSTICE!"

"WHEN DO WE WANT IT?"

"NOW!!!"

Rhiannon stepped down off the step ladder and beckoned the crowd, turning and walking towards the steps leading up to parliament. Louis joined her by one side, Marie by the other. Blake and Owen followed closely behind, Owen putting a comforting arm round Blake's shoulder. As they marched, Rhiannon held the megaphone high and continued to chant.

"NO JUSTICE, NO PEACE!" she cried.

"NO MORE RACIST POLICE!" the crowd chanted back.

"NO JUSTICE, NO PEACE!" she repeated.

"LET THE HOMELESS REST THEIR FEET!" the crowd chanted back.

As they passed the houses of parliament, the crowd booed, and reporters with cameras lined the steps, taking pictures. A news crew rushed forward with a film camera and a microphone on a stick, and Maria left the front of the crowd to go and talk to them.

Rhiannon turned her head to look back at the crowd marching behind her, snaking through the street. It was definitely over a thousand people now, with more and more joining every moment. Rhiannon's heart raced. This was the biggest protest she had ever helped to organise.

She continued to walk, leading the crowd along.

"One struggle, one fight!" she cried out.

"DAVID JONES, DO WHAT'S RIGHT!"

"One struggle, one fight!"

"LET THE HOMELESS SLEEP TONIGHT!"

They rounded the corner, joining the main road, where the road had been closed off and traffic police were redirecting traffic. Rhiannon wandered out into the middle of the road, and the protesters followed her, chanting as they marched towards the Prime Minister's house. It wasn't long before they were at the massive iron gates that blocked off the road to number 10. A line of police officers in riot gear lined up in front of the gate, and the crowd booed as they filled the road, coming to a halt near the gates.

"SHAME ON YOU, DAVID JONES!" Rhiannon chanted, and the crowd took up the cry.

"SHAME ON YOU, DAVID JONES! SHAME ON YOU, DAVID JONES!"

Rhiannon turned to face the crowd, continuing the chant as she did so. She caught sight of a figure pushing through the crowd. He was wearing a long coat and a bandanna with a red skull covering the bottom half of his face, with goggles covering the top half. He had a hood pulled over his head, and massive metal gauntlets on his hands, and was hunched over with the weight of a massive sack that he was hauling through the crowd. Around him, the people grew silent and parted as he made his way to the front.

"Is that… Oh my god…" Owen muttered.

The Fist made his way to the front of the crowd, peering at Rhiannon through his goggles. She cocked her head to one side, giving him a questioning stare. Awkwardly shifting the weight of his giant sack of metal into one hand, he raised the other hand with a clenched fist. Then, he stepped up to the line of police officers in front of the gate, and emptied the sack at their feet. A clutter of bolts and spikes and bench dividers clattered to the floor in a messy pile, and the officer closest jumped back with a yelp, dropping his shield. The other officers put their hands to their belts, where their batons were, unsure of what to do. The crowd cheered and whooped, some of them laughing and jeering at the police officers, and Rhiannon smiled.

The Fist turned back to her, and she smirked. Slowly, she offered him the megaphone…

Alex looked down at the megaphone, then over at the crowd. The crowd were waiting intently to see what he would do. Blake stood near the front, with the quiet giant he had nearly bumped into, and a younger man with his arm round Blake's shoulder. Alex cast his eyes around the rest of the crowd, and saw an array of different people: black people and other people of colour, and members of other minority groups. He saw members of the homeless community of Downtown City, he saw people carrying Antifa flags and BLM flags and all sorts of other banners and signs.

And it suddenly dawned on him: he didn't really understand their struggle. He was white. Technically he didn't have a home right now, he supposed, but he always had somewhere he could go. He was bisexual, but had never personally faced any discrimination because of it.

He turned back to Rhiannon, and shook his head. Turning back to the crowd, he beckoned a teenager holding a cardboard sign. On the front, the teenager had scrawled 'SAY HER NAME: TAMARA JOHNSON.' Alex pointed at the sign, and indicated with his hands for her to hand it over. She did so, and Alex did a writing motion. The teenager frowned, then said "oh!" and reached into her bag, pulling out a large marker pen. She handed it over to Alex, and he pulled off the lid, scribbling on the back of the sign.

"I'm not here to speak." Rhiannon read, as he wrote. "I'm here to make sure you're heard."

"I'm not here to speak, I'm here to make sure you're heard." Rhiannon read. She nodded approvingly, and the Fist held up the sign for all to see. The crowd cheered. Rhiannon leant in close to him, tapping him on the shoulder.

"I guess some white boys are alright." she said, with a wry smile. "Don't get too much of a hero complex, or I'll have to take those gauntlets off you."

She heard a chuckle from beneath the bandanna.

"March with us." she said.

She hadn't meant to say it with that inflection, but it came out sounding more like an instruction than a question. The Fist nodded.

Rhiannon turned and led the crowd away from the gates and down the road, towards the main bridge across the river. The roads were cleared leading up to the bridge, but something

172

ahead didn't look right.

Rhiannon frowned, squinting on approach.

"Heads up, trouble ahead." the Fist said, reaching up and touching his ear. "Fox, you seeing this?"

As they drew closer, Rhiannon finally saw what it was.

"Oh hell no." she exclaimed.

***

Sabrina walked with haste along the side of the pavement, just a few feet away from the protesters as they marched down the centre of the road.

"*The Fist is here.*" she heard over the radio. "*What should we do? Do we arrest him? He's the one who tore out all the spikes.*"

"*Negative.*" came the voice of the superintendent. "*Arresting him could anger the crowd, we don't want an angry mob.*"

Ahead, Sabrina noticed the crowd beginning to slow on approach to the bridge, and a murmur was passing along from the front of the protest.

"Something's happening up ahead." one of the officers called over to Sabrina, and she broke into a jog to get to the front of the crowd.

The front of the protest had reached the start of the bridge now, and the protest organisers had halted, and were engaged in a heated conversation. Sabrina noticed the Fist stood there, watching silently, his expression unreadable beneath the bandanna and goggles.

She turned and looked up the road, over the bridge, to see what all the fuss was about.

"Oh no." she muttered, as her eyes fell on the middle of the bridge, and the problem became suddenly very clear.

She reached up to press the button on her radio.

"We're going to need back-up at the bridge." she said. "There's a line of people blocking the path... It's the Bovver Boys."

As the protesters approached the line of counter protesters, the Bovver Boys unfurled a banner in front of their line which read 'ALL LIVES MATTER', and the group started up their own

173

chant. Although there were only around thirty of them, the chant was loud.

"BRITAIN FOR THE BRITISH! GET THE SCUM OFF OUR STREETS! BRITAIN FOR THE BRITISH! GET THE SCUM OFF OUR STREETS!"

The protesters booed as they heard the cheer, and a counter-chant began of:

"BLACK LIVES MATTER. GO HOME RACIST SCUM!"

"Come on." Rhiannon said, rage rising up inside her. "We're not going to let thirty racist knobheads stop us."

She marched forwards, and Louis joined her side, and the march continued, growing louder as they approached the centre of the bridge.

A string of about six police officers in high visibility jackets sprinted ahead of the march and formed the most pitiful line between the two groups, at least succeeding at keeping them thirty feet apart for the time being.

Alex's heart rate began to rise, now that he could see the faces of the hateful mob. One of the younger men stopped chanting and pointed over at Blake. Alex zoomed in with his goggles to look at the guy's lips. One of the only benefits of his hearing impairment: he could read lips with almost one hundred percent accuracy.

"Hey, look!" the guy said, nudging the man next to him. "Those are the little poofs I beat up last night!"

Alex's heart stopped for a moment, and then he felt anger bubbling in his stomach, his blood boiling. His fists clenched, and one single thought stained his mind: that man was going to pay.

The two groups got louder and louder, and the aggressions rose, and soon the fragile line of police officers dividing them wasn't enough any more.

"Why are you facing us?!" one of the protesters yelled at the police. "They're the dangerous ones! They're the racist bigots! Face them! Keep your eyes on them!"

Two or three of the protesters broke past the line of police and threw what looked like balloons at the line of white faces. Two of the balloons exploded harmlessly on the ground, but one of

174

them caught one of the men in the face, exploding and showering him with white liquid.

Milkshake. The protesters cheered. The one who had thrown the successful balloon (a young Chinese man) raised his fists triumphantly, and his friends patted him on the back.

"Enough of that!" one of the police officers pointed directly at the protesters who had thrown the balloons, his hand going to his handcuffs. "Stop right there!"

Officer Parker placed her hand on the police officer's shoulder, grabbing his attention, and shook her head.

"Leave it." she said. "There aren't enough of us here to be making arrests."

One of the Bovver Boys stepped forwards: a man in his fifties, with a clean-shaven head, and tattoos covering his arms. It was Johnny Johnson.

"Ent you gonna stop that?" he called to the police. "You're supposed to be here for protection!"

"Did you say protection?!"

The shout came from the other side of the bridge, behind the line of Bovver Boys.

Johnny turned his head to stare back at the speaker. On the other side of the bridge, a line of men and women in suits had formed, some holding bats, others brandishing knuckle-dusters. In front of them stood a man in a trilby hat and long, dark coat. He held a megaphone up to his face, and was walking with purpose across the bridge, the line of people in suits following him.

Big Tuna.

"Had you forgotten, Johnny?" Big Tuna yelled. "This Bridge is our territory! That's why they call us the Bridge Boys! That means you gotta get out of here! We don't welcome racist pricks in our part of the city!"

Officer Parker reached up and pressed the button on her radio. "There are gang members here. They're armed and dangerous. We need back-up on the main bridge NOW."

"Back off, Fishy!" Johnny roared. "This isn't about territory, this is about these snowflakes, faking tragedies so that they can make everyone walk on eggshells around them! A violent

175

robber gets what she deserves, and there's a march? Give me a break!"

"Violent robber? That's rich coming from you!"

The Bovver Boys turned their attention round on the Bridge Boys, dropping the banner. The insult to their leader was enough to get some of them riled up, and they pulled out knives and bats of their own.

The Bridge Boys broke into a run, led by their leader, sprinting towards the line of Bovver Boys. Some of the Bovver Boys thought better, and broke off from the group, turning tail and running away. The rest broke into a run to meet the Bridge Boys.

Behind Rhiannon, Isaac Johnson received a phone call. He put the phone to his ear, plugging the other ear with a finger as he struggled to hear. His face dropped.

"What is it?" Rhiannon asked.

"Tammie." he said. "She didn't make it."

A group of protesters nearby heard, and a cry went up amongst the crowd.

"Tamara is dead!"

The six police officers lost all control, and a cluster of more passionate protesters pushed past and ran to join the fight. They were joined by a few more, then a few more after that. Alex's eyes were fixed on the man who had attacked Blake. He was one of the few who had broken off from the group upon seeing the Bridge Boys, and was making a run for it. Alex rushed forwards, tripping the man as he tried to make his escape. He hit the concrete hard, groaning as he did so, and Alex leant over him.

"Stay down." he growled, kicking him hard in the ribs.

A cry went up from the back of the protest, and Alex turned to see a cloud of smoke rising over the bridge, and a shield wall of riot police pushed on forwards, yelling for the protesters to disperse and go home. Many of the protesters were doing as told, and the crowd was thinning, but some were simply enraged by the presence of riot police, and the news that Tamara was dead, and were throwing themselves against the shield wall, only to be slammed down with batons and arrested by a second line of police officers, marching along, batons in one hand, cuffs in the other.

A cluster of riot police pushed through to the front of the protest, and caught sight of Alex, standing over the man who had assaulted Blake. They rushed forwards and surrounded him, and one of them pulled out a canister of pepper spray, spraying Alex directly in the face. The goggles protected his eyes, but it took less than two seconds for the spray to seep through the bandanna, filling his mouth and lungs and causing him to choke. Alex dropped to his knees, coughing and spluttering, and the riot police surrounded him, pelting him with their batons. He threw up his gauntlets in front of him, and a wave of kinetic energy burst out, knocking two of the police officers backwards. Unfortunately, this just enraged the rest of them. Pain exploded through his back and head as a hail of baton blows pushed him hard into the ground.

A giant figure pushed through the cluster of riot police and threw himself protectively over Alex, taking the brunt of the baton blows. Alex struggled to catch his breath, retching and shuddering, the back of his throat on fire. He crawled out of the way as the towering black man freed him from the batons, and pulled himself up on the railings of the bridge. If he could just concentrate for one moment, he could help the man…

He felt something trickle down the back of his head. Reaching up, he pulled his hood down and placed his hand on the back of his own head. When he pulled it away, the gauntlet was covered in blood.

Alex's vision blurred, and he slumped back against the railings of the bridge. Darkness enveloped him.

Louis had acted purely out of protective instinct, but now he was on his knees, hands in the air, and the police were relentlessly beating him. He was numb, and the entire world seemed hazy.

He heard his girlfriend cry out.

"Stop it! He's surrendered! STOP IT!"

He lay on the ground, putting his hands behind his head, but the police didn't stop. One of them stooped over him, placing a knee on his back. Another placed a knee on his neck, and a third put handcuffs on his wrists.

177

Louis turned his head, gagging for air, and caught sight of the Fist, leaning against the railings, blood pouring down over his goggles.

The Bovver Boy that he had tripped was back on his feet now, and he stumbled over to the Fist, grabbing him by the collar...

And tossed him over the railings.

CHAPTER ELEVEN: DESPERATE MEASURES

Jason watched everything through the camera on his drone. He'd splashed out for a drone with a HD camera, and the drone transmitted perfectly to his laptop, forcing him to watch, helplessly, in high definition, as innocent protesters were assaulted by the police. He watched everything unfold in horror: the Bovver Boys marching up the bridge, the Bridge Boys coming to meet him, the riot police filling in behind the protest.

"Alex, get out of there!" he screamed down the earpiece. "Alex! Alex?!"

He watched from above as Alex was thrown from the bridge, tumbling down into the water, and disappeared beneath the waves.

"No!" he muttered. "No, no no no no!"

He pulled out his phone, his hands trembling, and called the only person he could think to call.

"Iona!" he stammered. "Iona, I need you! I've made a mistake! I've made a big mistake! Please, come quickly! I need help! I really need help!"

***

Zakirah stood on the bridge, watching as chaos unfolded around her. Protesters and police officers clashed around her. To one side, riot police were surrounding an angry protester, waving his banner and screaming at the top of his lungs. One of the officers smacked him in the side of the head with a baton and he dropped to the ground, and they were on him in seconds, slapping him in handcuffs. To the other side, a cluster of protesters cried out as tear gas canisters exploded amongst them, and rubber bullets and bean bags launched from canons

179

knocked them to the ground. Zakirah took a step forward, and as she did so, a brick that had been launched by one of the Bovver Boys landed in the spot where she had been standing. Zakirah gasped, turning to look round, turning just at the right second to see a member of the riot police who had just been tripped up by one of the protesters, stumbling towards her. She stepped out of the way and the officer fell into the spot where she had been standing.

"This is insane." she breathed. "How does this keep happening?"

A police officer sprayed pepper spray at an angry protester just a few feet ahead of her, and the spray missed. Zakirah flinched in anticipation of the spray catching her in the face, but it didn't. Time seemed to slow, and for just a second it seemed that everything around her was frozen. A bubble of light formed around Zakirah, and the pepper spray moved in a wave harmlessly around it, like a spray hitting a windshield moving at speed. Zakirah blinked, unable to believe her eyes, and time resumed again, and she was fine.

No time to dwell on it. Her eyes caught sight of the Bridge Boys and the Bovver Boys, unhindered by the police, who were preoccupied with the protesters, throwing each other this way and that.

And there was Johnny Johnson, blood-covered brass knuckles on each hand, grinning maniacally as he threw one punch after another at a Bridge Boy who was struggling to stay upright, his suit now stained red.

Hatred filled her heart as her eyes caught sight of the smug thug, and Zakirah looked to the ground, her eyes falling on a discarded baton. She picked it up and broke into a sprint, her eyes fixed on Johnny Johnson. It was time to use this luck of hers to do some good.

She cleared the distance between them in no time, and as she made the last few bounds towards him, Zakirah let out a wild cry, throwing all her weight behind the baton. And as she cried out, a stream of light burst up her arm, enveloping the baton. Johnny turned his head towards her, just a second too late, and the baton crashed into the side of his head, knocking him

180

backwards, and the light dispersed with a crack that sounded like thunder, burning the side of Johnny's face.

"Miracle Girl!" he said, spitting out a mouthful of blood, still somehow grinning. "Oh, I'm going to enjoy this!"

He took a swing at Zakirah, and she dodged, swinging the baton at him again. Johnny ducked, and brought his brass knuckles up into Zakirah's stomach. She winced, stumbling backwards, and Johnny raised his fists to strike her again.

"Guess your luck has run out, eh?" he grinned.

"Oh go jump off a bridge!" Zakirah hissed.

Johnny pulled his fist back to strike her, but suddenly, something stopped him. He frowned, his fists slowly dropping to his sides.

"What the hell?" he muttered, and his fists wobbled at his side, the veins starting to bulge as if he was trying to pull them back up, but some invisible force was holding them back. His face began to grow red with the strain, and one of his feet stepped forwards, then the next. He walked slowly, fighting back with each step, as if his arms and legs were literally being grabbed and dragged by an invisible force. Johnny resisted as long as he could, but ultimately it seemed that he had lost control of his body.

Zakirah watched, mouth agape, as Johnny was dragged to the side of the bridge, like a rigid puppet on invisible strings. Cursing wildly, he climbed slowly over the railings…

And jumped off the bridge.

Zakirah pulled herself upright, just in time to be surrounded by riot police. Without any time to process what had happened, she found herself being thrown in handcuffs and dragged away from the fighting.

***

Alex remembered hitting the water.

Then he remembered darkness. He couldn't breathe, he couldn't see, he couldn't hear.

He thrashed wildly, and his survival instinct kicked in. He felt himself swimming, though he couldn't see where. And then hands. Hands were grabbing him, pulling him to shore.

Above him, a hooded figure in a plain, white mask stared

down at him. The mysterious figure pulled him up the riverbank, towards a battered old Ford Fiesta.

Alex groaned, and his vision faded as the figure hauled him into the back seat of the car. The last thing he heard was the thud of the car door closing, and the tired old engine grumbling to life.

***

Iona knocked frantically on the door of Jason's bedsit, but there was no response. She pulled her phone out, dialling his number, and pushed it hastily up to her ear.

"Where are you?" she asked, her voice trembling.

"*Garage.*" was the one word reply.

She sprinted back outside and pulled the door up. Inside, she found Jason pacing backwards and forwards. His hair was a mess, and his eyes were puffy and red, his hands trembling as he walked unstably backwards and forwards.

"Well this can't be good." she said. "You never pace."

"It's me." Jason said, his voice cracking. "The Fist of Justice they keep talking about: it's my invention. M-m-my gauntlets."

"What are you talking about?" Iona frowned.

"I tweaked my invention after my fight with Dan. I turned them into a weapon. I thought I c-c-could use them to make the world a better p-place."

Iona's brow furrowed, and understanding finally hit her like a blow to the face.

"But… Who has been wearing the gauntlets?" she asked. "That can't have been you."

"A friend." Jason stammered, still pacing. "We t-thought we were d-doing a good thing!"

"Oh Jason!" Iona sighed. "You idiot."

"He's g-g-gone." Jason stammered. "He was at the p-p-protest! He fell off the bridge!"

Jason's phone was sat on the desk, and it started to vibrate. He lurched towards it, picking it up, frantically swiping at the screen to answer the call. Iona could hear the voice on the other end.

"*Jason, it's Alex, I'm at the hospital!*"

"Oh thank god." Jason breathed, his entire body relaxing. "You're okay!"

"*Jason, the gauntlets are gone.*" the voice said. "*Someone dropped me off here, but they took the outfit, the goggles, the gauntlets... Even the bandanna!*"

"What?" Jason exclaimed. "Okay... Okay. The important thing is you're okay. I'll be there as soon as possible."

He hung up and turned to Iona.

"Can you d-d-drive me to the hospital? I'll explain everything on the way."

Iona pulled up the car in the visitors' car park, as close to the hospital as possible, and rushed around to pull Jason's wheelchair out of the back of the car. After a few minutes of fumbling, the two of them rushed through to the A&E Waiting Room. The room was filled with injured protesters, some bruised and battered, others supporting broken bones. The staff were all so preoccupied treating patients that none of them noticed Iona and Jason going straight into the ward.

The ward was almost as busy as the waiting room, but Jason quickly spotted Alex, perched on a bed in the corner. His head was bandaged and he was covered in bruises, but otherwise he seemed fine. Jason rolled over, working his way delicately around the panicked doctors and nurses. Iona followed closely behind.

"What happened?" Jason asked.

Alex looked from Jason to Iona, and Jason raised a hand.

"It's alright." he said. "She knows e-everything, I t-t-told her."

"I didn't see their face. I don't really remember much at all." Alex said. "I remember falling off the bridge, or being thrown? I'm not sure. Then I remember coming to on the riverbank, and some guy in a mask pulling me to his car. And that's it. When I woke up here, the gauntlets, the coat... It was all gone. And since I'm not handcuffed, I have to assume the guy who saved me took them before dropping me off."

"It's okay." Jason said. "I p-put a GPS t-tracker in the gauntlets. Just in case."

Suddenly, commotion erupted and the ward was filled with noise as paramedics wheeled a bed in, yelling over to the

183

closest doctors. Jason turned his head to see a man who barely fit on the stretcher being wheeled into the ward, his face covered in blood.

"Jason." Alex hissed. "That's the guy who tried to save me from the riot police."

The paramedics were followed closely by a panicked woman, with tears streaming down her face. It was Rhiannon, the protest organiser, and her t-shirt was covered in her boyfriend's blood.

Alex forced himself up and off the bed, and limped over to listen to what the doctors were saying. One of the doctor's had just checked for a pulse and started chest compressions. A flurry of nurses were moving around the bed, and it was hard to make out what was being said, but the words "okay, he's stable" could be heard, as the doctor stopped chest compressions.

"For now." one of the other doctors said. "Quick, get him in for an MRI, we need to see if there's any internal damage."

They wheeled the bed down the hall.

"I owe him." Alex said. "He took a beating for me. We need to make sure he pulls through."

Rhiannon paced in the hallway, her mind a blur, waiting for one of the doctors to give her an update. In the next few minutes, which felt like hours, Blake and Owen arrived, rushing through the hallways.

"Sorry, we lost you in all the chaos." Blake said on approach. "Rhiannon, sit down. Owen, get her some water."

As Blake ushered Rhiannon over to some seats in an alcove in the hallway, one of the doctors stepped out of the room.

"You're the girlfriend?" she asked.

Rhiannon nodded.

"Would you be able to contact his parents or next of kin?" the doctor asked.

"I called his mum already." Rhiannon said. "Why? Is he okay?"

"When the officers knelt on his back and neck, they caused several fractures in his spine." the doctor said. "On top of that, it appears there may be some internal bleeding in his brain.

184

We're doing what we can, but there's a very large chance he won't wake up, and if he does… We don't know how much function will return. He may never walk again, he may even have some neurological difficulties."

Rhiannon's head dropped, and the tears began to fall again.

"Thank you, doctor." Blake said. "Please let us know if there's an update."

The doctor nodded, and headed back where she had come from.

"This is too much." Rhiannon said between sobs. "He's the kindest man I've ever known. He didn't deserve this."

"Is everything okay?"

Rhiannon and Blake looked up to see a man in a wheelchair hovering nearby. Behind him, Alex was staring through the window in the door into the room where Louis had been taken. A petite woman stood nearby, looking sympathetic.

"I'm J-Jason, these are my friends, Alex and Iona. We saw what your f-f-friend did on the bridge." the man in the wheelchair said. "He's a hero."

Alex didn't turn around. He was focused on the lips of the doctors, but all he could make out was "nothing we can do" and "walk again" followed by "wait for the parents."

"Those pigs, they broke his spine." Rhiannon said. "And he has bleeding in his brain. It doesn't sound good."

"My NanoVirus…" Iona mumbled, and Jason turned his head. "What?" he asked her, softly.

"My NanoVirus could fix all of that, no problem." she said. "But… It'd be very illegal. The serum isn't even approved for human trials yet."

"I didn't even realise it was that far along! Could it work?" Jason asked, his tone hushed.

"What's going on?" Rhiannon frowned. "Are you a doctor?"

"I'm a microbiologist and a nanotechnology expert." Iona said. "I've been working on an experimental serum, using microscopic robots to fix all sorts of medical problems. Fractures and breaks are easy, and it should be able to handle the internal bleeding too. It's been very successful in animal trials."

"If you think you can fix Louis, please, do it." Rhiannon said.

185

"I'll have to go back to my lab. It's a five minute drive, but traffic is gridlocked right now, I'll have to walk." she said.
"I'll be back in twenty minutes, half an hour tops... But you'll have to distract the doctors. They won't let me do it."
"I'll go with you." Alex said, eager not to be left waiting with his ex and his new boyfriend, who had just reappeared with two cups of water.
"With that wound on your head?" Iona exclaimed. "Like hell, you need rest."
"I'll go." Rhiannon said. "I can't sit here and wait, I'll go mad."
Iona nodded.
"Okay. Let's go." she said.
Iona and Rhiannon jogged towards the exit, and the others were left waiting in solemn silence.

The lab itself was empty when Iona and Rhiannon arrived, though there were a few weekend staff (mostly janitorial) wandering around the building.
"Stand guard at the door." Iona told Rhiannon. "I'm really not supposed to be taking this out of the lab."
Rhiannon stood at the door, watching as Iona entered the lab and opened a cupboard at the back. The cupboard was filled with vials of pale, blue liquid, stood up in plastic stands lit up with LED lights that illuminated the vials. Iona picked up one of the plastic stands and went over to the computer.
"What are you doing?" Rhiannon asked.
"The NanoVirus needs to be activated and actioned electronically." Iona replied. "They're still essentially machines. Basically, they need to be switched on and programmed. Keep watch."
She plugged the plastic stand into the computer via USB.
A young woman in a lab coat appeared at the end of the hallway, walking towards the lab. She frowned as she saw Rhiannon.
"I don't know you..." she said. "Are you one of the electricians brought in to set up the new computer lab?"
"Yea." Rhiannon said. "Yea, sorry, I... I got a little turned around looking for the canteen, could you show me?"

186

The woman smiled.

"Of course, it's this way." she said. "I knew I hadn't seen you before. I would have remembered you."

She smirked, looking Rhiannon up and down. Rhiannon smiled awkwardly back.

"It's just down the stairs here." the woman said. "Want to buy me a coffee?"

The two walked down the stairs and through a set of double doors into a mostly empty canteen with a single worker behind the till, already making coffee for another worker.

"I'm really supposed to be grabbing a drink and heading straight back, break is almost over." Rhiannon replied.

"Well, here's my number if you ever want to grab a drink." the woman pulled out a post-it and a pen and scribbled her number on it. "I better get back too."

She turned and left, turning to give Rhiannon another smile on the way out, and Rhiannon breathed a sigh of relief at not being caught out. She went the long way back to the lab in the hopes of avoiding being spotted by the same woman again, and Iona met her outside.

"Let's get out of here." she said.

When they arrived back at the hospital and found their way to the corridor where they had left the others, only Alex and Jason were left.

"Where have they gone?" Iona asked.

"They took him to a p-private room." Jason said. "He's not d-doing well. Follow me."

He took them down the corridor and off to a little room just off from one of the main wards, where Blake and Owen were all standing around a bed, with a much older woman sat in a bedside chair, holding Louis' hand. He had a tube down his throat now, and was hooked up to a heart monitor which was piercing the silence with a slow, but relatively steady beep. Alex opened the door so that Jason could roll in, and Iona and Rhiannon followed closely behind.

"Adah!" Rhiannon said to the woman. "You got my message! I'm so sorry. How is he?"

"The doctors say he's shutting down. They've had to put him on life support, but there's not much else they can do. If they don't operate, he'll die, but the stress of operating could kill him." Blake replied.

"Adah, this woman is a scientist. A microbiologist." Rhiannon said, leaning in to the old woman, who was gently sobbing and clasping her son's hand even tighter now. "She thinks she can help Louis."

"This treatment is really experimental." Iona said. "It's not been properly tested yet. I'll only do this if you tell me to, but none of you can ever tell anyone what I did, okay?"

"Just do it." the old woman said, through sobs. "Please. If it can help heal my son, please do it."

Iona nodded, opening her shoulder bag and pulling one of the vials out of the plastic stand. From underneath, she pulled out a syringe wrapped in plastic. She handed the vial to Rhiannon. "Take the stopper out of the top." she said, unwrapping the syringe.

Rhiannon opened up the vial, and Iona filled the syringe up with the pale blue liquid.

"Watch the door." she said to Alex.

Alex rushed over to the door, looking out into the corridor. "Coast is clear." he said.

"Here we go." Iona breathed.

And she pushed the syringe into Louis' arm, piercing the skin and injecting the NanoVirus.

There was a moment of silence. Everyone in the room held their breath.

"How long will it take?" Louis' mother asked.

Suddenly, before Iona could reply, Louis' heartbeat quickened, and his body began to convulse.

"Louis!" Rhiannon cried, and Adah jumped back in shock.

There was a crack, and then another crack, and Louis grunted, his body jerking from side to side.

"No, no no!" Iona breathed. "Come on, work, damn it!"

As quickly as they started, the convulsions stopped, and his heartbeat settled again.

"Oh my god...." Jason breathed, look.

He pointed to Louis' face. The bruises were shrinking away, disappearing as if by magic. Louis opened his eyes, peering around the room. He tried to speak, but there was a tube still in his mouth.

Iona lurched forwards and unstrapped the apparatus from his face, pulling the tube slowly out of his mouth. Louis gagged, but once the tube was out, he looked good as new, if not a little worn out.

"What happened?" he asked, his voice soft, and quiet for someone so big. "Where am I?"

"You're in the hospital, baby." Adah said. "You're okay, honey. You were hurt, but you're okay."

"Mum?" Louis said. "Mum, why are you crying?"

"I'm just happy you're okay!" Adah sobbed. She turned to Iona. "You're an angel, sent from god. You're an angel."

She threw her arms around Iona, not getting up from her chair, so she ended up hugging her belly. Iona patted the woman on the back.

"It's okay, really." Iona said. "I'm just glad it worked."

"Glad what worked?" Louis frowned.

"I injected you with an experimental serum: a blend of microscopic organisms that have been biologically engineered in a lab, and nanotechnology, programmed to aid the immune system and heal all injuries." Iona explained. "It's not approved yet, it hasn't even been tested… Well, except on you I suppose, so you can't tell anyone. You can't let the doctors take you in for any further scans or tests, I have no idea how the nanotechnology will respond to x-rays or MRIs… How do you feel?"

"I feel great." Louis shrugged. "Better than ever, really."

Iona put the syringe back in her bag, taking the vial from Alex and putting it away.

"Good." Iona said. "You contact me if you feel any weird side effects. Anything at all out of the ordinary, you tell me."

The door opened, and a nurse walked in, staring at her clipboard.

"The doctors have decided to-" she looked up, suddenly seeing Louis sat up and smiling.

The clipboard dropped from her hands.

"Impossible." she breathed. "Sir, you need to lay back down."

"I'm okay." Louis said. "I feel fine."

The nurse rushed behind him, placing her hands on his back

and working her fingers along his spine.

"Impossible…" she said. "It feels normal! Wait here, I'm going to get the doctor!"

She turned and rushed out the room.

"I think we should leave." Iona said. "Right now."

The group didn't need telling twice. Louis lifted himself out of the bed. As he placed his hands on the rail on the side of the bed, the metal bent from just the slightest pressure.

"Woah." Louis said. "I… Am I that heavy? Or am I stronger now?"

"No time." Iona said. "Let's go!"

One by one, they filed out of the room and towards the closest exit.

"Wait!" one of the doctors exclaimed, rushing down the hall. "Where are you going! We need to run some tests, you could still be hurt!"

"Keep walking." Iona hissed.

Together, the group turned the corner and headed out a set of double doors, into the parking area. A string of nurses and doctors were following them now, and one of the doctors rushed over to Louis.

"Sir, we really need to run some tests." he said. "I cannot advise that you go home until we have determined exactly what has happened here. Your spine was fractured. You had bleeding in your brain. You could still be hurt."

"A miracle is a miracle, doc." Louis replied.. "I'm going home."

***

Zakirah sat in the interrogation room of the police station, her hands cuffed in front of her. A short, round-faced man sat in a chair across the table from her, flicking through a file.

"It's interesting, you carry no ID on you, and we can find no record of you in the system. You say your name is Zakirah Bashir, but you have no passport, no driving licence, no social security number. You don't even have a registered address." the man said.

"Let me go." Zakirah growled, making direct eye contact with the man.

The man looked up at her, placing the file down on the table, and sighed.

"I'm afraid we can't do that..." he said. "We're going to have to hand you over to the Immigration Enforcement office."

"What?" Zakirah's eyes widened. She couldn't go. Not after all she had been through to get here. She couldn't bear the thought of being kicked out of the country now. "No, please, I can explain everything! I'm not an immigrant, I'm a refugee! Please, you have to listen to me!"

"I'm afraid my hands are tied." the man said, standing up. "This is not a police matter any more. Good luck."

He turned, straightened his tie, and left the room, leaving Zakirah in shocked silence. As soon as she was alone, her eyes began to well up, and she let out a loud sob. She didn't like this country at all. It was nothing like what she had expected. But she couldn't cope with the idea of having to move on again. It was too much. Zakirah felt her will to live fading away, and she tried to put her hands over her face to brush away the tears, but the cuffs restricted her reach. She lowered her head to her hands, resting it on the table, and cried.

CHAPTER TWELVE: THE GENTLE GIANT

There was a strange atmosphere across the city now, like the entire population had been drained of all energy. The streets were mostly empty, and everyone who was out walked slowly, dragging their feet as they went, staring at the ground. It was like the whole city was in mourning.

Jason, Iona and Alex stood in the reception area of the Railway Tavern, the cheery receptionist smiling across the counter at them, except this time her smile looked forced. The room smelled of potpourri, and there was a comforting quiet settled over the bar and restaurant, which offered a gentle respite from the horrific day they'd all had.

"Hey, how are you?" Jason said to the receptionist, wheeling as close to the counter as he could. "I was h-hoping we might be able to g-get a discounted room for my friend here. Just for one night, something b-basic."

"I'll see what I can do." The receptionist said.

"Jason, it's fine, I'll find somewhere else to stay, I'll call someone." Alex said.

"I'm checking you into the hotel, that's final." Jason said. "We'll find you somewhere more permanent to stay tomorrow."

Alex sighed.

"Fine." he said. "But I'm not letting you pay, I'll pay."

"So that's a single room for one night? That will be forty pounds." the receptionist said. "That's with our staff: friends and family discount, don't tell anyone."

Alex pulled out his wallet, offering a muttered thanks, his words made weak by the painkillers. He paid, and the receptionist handed over a room key.

"Check out is at 11AM." the woman said. "I'll be here all night, if you have any questions just call down. Have a nice night."

"Thanks." Alex said again.

"I'll see you tomorrow." Jason said. "We'll talk more then." He and Iona turned and left the hotel. As the door closed behind him, Iona breathed deep.

"What a day." she muttered.

"I'm sorry I didn't tell you what I'd been d-doing." Jason said. "It was just… I thought you might stop me."

"Only because I worry about you." Iona replied, her voice soft and full of warmth.

"Yeah, I know. Nobody thinks I can handle myself."

"It's not that, Jason." Iona said. "You're one of the most capable people I've ever known. But I care about you, a lot, and I don't want to ever see you get hurt. I only get angry and frustrated with you because I care."

Jason looked up at her, and for a brief moment their eyes met, before Jason's social awkwardness forced him to pull his gaze away.

"Jason." Iona said, softly.

"Yes?"

Iona leaned down to Jason's level and pressed her lips softly against his, just for a few seconds, before pulling away. Jason closed his eyes, the moment lingering in his mind for a few seconds.

"What you're doing is amazing, even if it's stupid." she said. "You're a good man. That's all anyone can ever ask of you." She pulled away, and an awkward silence settled over them, as neither of them knew what to say.

"Do you want to order takeout and pretend our lives aren't insane for a bit?" Iona asked.

"More than anything." Jason replied, with a smile.

They headed around to the back of the hotel to Jason's bedsit. As they went past, Jason noticed the door to his garage, open just a crack. He frowned.

"I left some stuff in my garage." he said, pulling the key to his bedsit out of his pocket. "You go let yourself in, I'll b-be there

193

in a m-minute."

"Okay." Iona said, taking the key.

Jason waited until Iona had gone in through the back door of the hotel and headed up to his garage, pulling the door tentatively open.

There was no one inside. It was dark and empty, but for the lights from his laptop, which he had left on when he rushed out in a panic earlier that day. And next to the laptop, on the table, were the battered gauntlets and goggles and armoured vest, soaked from the river, stripped off Alex by whoever had rescued him.

Jason frowned, wheeling into the workshop and flicking the lights on. Out of the corner of his eye, he noticed a little white dash, blinking at the top of his laptop screen. The screen was not off… It was simply blank.

'**I KNOW WHO YOU ARE.**'

The letters appeared on the screen as if someone was typing, but the keys did not move. No one was in the room.

"What the…" breathed Jason.

'**I KNOW WHAT YOU'VE BEEN DOING.**'

One by one, the newspaper articles and blog posts about 'the Fist of Justice' appeared on the black screen: when he had attacked Dan, when they had fought with the Bridge Boys at Covered Market, and the new 'Breaking News' segments about the protests.

"C-can you see me?" Jason said. "Can you hear me?"

'**YES.**'

"Who are you?" Jason asked.

'**I RESCUED YOUR FRIEND FROM THE RIVER. I WANT TO HELP YOU. YOU HAVE DONE SOME SMALL GOOD DEEDS. I CAN HELP YOU DO MORE. I CAN HELP YOU GO BIGGER. YOU CAN CALL ME GREY HAT.**'

"Why me?" Jason asked. "And why should I trust you?"

'**I TRUST YOU. YOU HAVE TO CHOOSE WHETHER TO TRUST ME. YOU CAN TAKE A LEAP OF FAITH. IF YOU WANT TO FIGHT THE CORRUPTION THAT IS RIFE IN THIS CITY, YOU NEED TO TRUST ME. THE CHOICE IS YOURS.**'

"Okay…" Jason said. "Show me what you've got."

'I AM COPYING SOME FILES ONTO YOUR COMPUTER. THE FILES CONTAIN INFORMATION INCRIMINATING SOME OF THE BIGGEST BUSINESS OWNERS AND POLITICIANS ACROSS YOUR CITY. I HAVE LOADED THE GUN. I NEED YOU TO PULL THE TRIGGER.'

"What?" Jason frowned. "I don't understand."

'I'M NOT SAFE. I NEED TO MOVE. I WILL CONTACT YOU SOON. LOOK AT THE FILES.'

Jason placed his head in his hands.

"What have I gotten myself into?" he muttered.

It didn't matter now. He was committed. There was no turning back.

***

Louis awoke to smells of baking filling the house. Louis and Rhiannon lived in a house-share with a small handful of friends, and their room was on the top floor, right at the back, as far away from the kitchen as physically possible. And yet, Louis could smell the warm, homely scent of fresh pastry baking as if he were in the room. He sat up, looking over to Rhiannon's side of the bed, but she wasn't there.

Slowly, Louis put his feet on the ground and stretched his arms high into the air. His back clicked, and he craned his neck round, clicking it in both directions with a satisfying grunt. On the floor, his clothes were strewn about. He reached down and picked up a green and black t-shirt with 'Portside Football Club' written across the back, and the number 13 in big, bold letters, sniffed it, and slipped it on, then grabbed a pair of shorts and did the same.

He left the room, his feet thudding loudly on the steps as he wandered down towards the kitchen, where Rhiannon was bent over, staring into the oven. Louis stopped in the doorway, taking a moment to admire his girlfriend's curves. Rhiannon turned and caught him looking at her.

"Creep." she grinned, pulling a tray out of the oven.

"Are those…" Louis stopped, taking a long, deep breath. The smell was even more powerful now… Intoxicating, even.

195

Raspberry, mixed with butter, and pastry cooked to perfection.
"Raspberry croissants, your favourite." Rhiannon said.
"Babe, you didn't have to." Louis said.
"It's the least I could do." Rhiannon said, smiling. "I'm just…
I'm really happy you're okay."
The smile wavered for a second, and her eyes began to water.
"Hey, hey!" Louis said, softly, wrapping his arms around her.
"I am okay."
"I nearly lost you." Rhiannon said, wiping her eyes. "You're
my rock, I don't know how I'd have kept going without
you…"
"Well, now you don't have to find out." He kissed her on the
forehead. "Now, let's have a lush breakfast."
Louis let go of Rhiannon and went to the cupboard to get
plates. As he did, Rhiannon's phone rang.
"Huh." she muttered. "Unknown number."
She answered.
"Rhiannon Paquet… Yes… Yeah he's with me now…"
She raised her eyebrows and offered the phone to Louis.
"It's a reporter from Downtown News Network." she said.
"They got my number from Marie. They want to interview
you… This morning, in two hours."
Louis halted, raising his eyebrows.
"Should I do it?" he asked. "They'll ask me about my injuries."
"It's a chance to talk about the cause, we've got to say yes."
Rhiannon said.
Louis took the phone.
"Hello…" he said. "Yeah… Yeah, I'll be there."
He put the phone down.
"I guess I'm going to be on TV."

***

Jason held the phone up to his ear, leaning against his garage
door as he took in some fresh air and forced himself to
exercise his legs.
"*Jason?*" the voice of his sister, Sarah, suddenly made him feel
like a child again, and he felt himself almost tearing up.
"*How's it going?*"

"Hey sis, I just wanted to check up on you." Jason said. "We haven't really spoken since you got to Edinburgh. How are you settling in?"

"I'm doing great. My friend Fiona introduced me to all her theatre buddies. She's doing a play, I've been helping out backstage. It's fantastic. They're going to be performing at the Fringe Festival soon."

"The Fringe? That's great. Maybe I'll have to come visit and see it."

"That'd be nice. How's it been back there? I heard it's been a bit crazy. I've been trying to avoid the news and just enjoy my summer, but it's impossible not to hear about the protests right now."

"Yeah, I saw you'd switched off from everything. You deactivated your social media?" Jason replied.

"I had to. Too much stuff about Dan on there. Chloe tried to call me to tell me about something that had happened to Dan but I made her stop and after that I just decided it was best to switch off. How are you getting on? Anything new in your life?"

Jason opened his mouth, then stopped himself. He wanted nothing more than to tell her everything he had been doing. He wanted to tell her all about the Fists of Justice. He'd never kept a secret from her before.

But he couldn't.

She seemed happy. Telling her would just make her worry about him. She might even come back. No, another time. When everything had calmed down.

He would tell her.

Eventually.

"It looks like things might be going somewhere with Iona." he said, instead.

"Finally!" came Sarah's reply. *"It's about damn time. You two were made for each other. She's much better for you than that girl you hung out with in first year. Hey, listen, I've got to go. They're doing a dress rehearsal and they need me to help sort out the costumes. I'll call you tomorrow, yeah?"*

"Okay, have fun. I'm glad you're doing okay. I love you, sis."

"*Love you too.*"

Click.

As the line went dead, Jason felt a pit forming in his stomach. He'd only ever lied to his sister about something this big once before. But how could he worry her? He knew she wouldn't cope well with all the danger he was putting himself in.

He put the thought aside.

"I w-w-will t-t-tell her." he muttered. "Eventually."

***

The morning was a rush, but within two hours Louis sat in the TV studio under the hot lights, sweating heavily and watching silently as the camera crew darted this way and that. He was sat on a long sofa, with Rhiannon next to him, and across from them the locally famous hosts of Dowtown News Network's morning show 'Good Morning Downtown', Ted Morris and Hayley Wilks, sat and made small talk. They were both overly smiley, stereotypical television hosts, with aesthetically pleasing faces and neat haircuts, him in a suit, her in a short dress, both with an overly enthusiastic energy surrounding them. It was all so fake, so scripted, even without the cameras on. It made Louis uneasy.

"Quiet on set!" the cameraman shouted. "We're on in three!..." He counted down with his fingers, then pointed over to the hosts. Louis and Rhiannon sat up straight, plastering fake smiles across their faces.

"Hello, and a very good morning Downtown!" Hayley said, addressing the camera with a cheery energy that seemed far more intense in the studio than it ever had to Louis and Rhiannon when they'd watched the show from home. "To those of you just tuning in after our ad break, we are now joined by Rhiannon Paquet, organiser of yesterday's eventful protest, and Louis Bishop, the miracle man who was reportedly carted into Downtown City Hospital on a stretcher yesterday after being seriously injured. The doctors told our reporter that Louis was admitted with several spinal fractures and internal bleeding within his brain, and yet mere hours later, Louis walked out of the hospital, seemingly without a scratch on him."

She turned her attention back to Louis and Rhiannon.

"Louis, could you tell us, in your own words, exactly what happened at the protest?"

"Well…" Louis said, stumbling over his words as he collected his thoughts. "Uh… We had gathered to protest the institutionalised racism and classism within the government and police force of this country. Everything fell apart when we reached the Central City Bridge. The bridge was blocked off by a line of counter-protesters: UKDL, BIP, that sort. They were chanting a bunch of racist… stuff…" Louis chose his words carefully. "They had concealed weapons, and they were threatening us, and everything just kicked off, I guess. A fight broke out, and the riot police came in and started arresting people."

"They were really throwing their weight around." Rhiannon interrupted, far more confident talking in front of cameras. "Beating down peaceful protesters, spraying people with tear gas. It wasn't arrests, it was police brutality. They didn't even go for the racist thugs with the weapons. They went straight for us: the unarmed, peaceful protesters."

"So what happened next, Louis?" Hayley asked. "How did you get injured?"

"It all happened really fast." Louis said. "My memory is really fuzzy. I saw riot police beating down that vigilante guy, the guy with the big fists. I went over there to try and calm everything down, but before I knew it the police were beating me with their batons and throwing me to the ground and kneeling on my back and my neck."

"And what do you think you did to provoke the police?" Ted asked.

"He didn't do anything to provoke them!" Rhiannon exclaimed, her words bursting out of her with fiery passion. "They just saw a big black man and they saw a threat! They saw the enemy."

"Do you remember anything else?" Hayley asked.

"Not really." Louis replied. "I remember being in the ambulance, and the paramedics talking to me, but I don't know what they said. I remember praying to god… And I remember

199

pain. A lot of pain. And then I remember waking up in a hospital bed, feeling fine."

"Some people are saying fake news, others are saying the doctors must have muddled up their test results. Others still are saying miracle. What do you have to say?" Hayley asked.

Louis shrugged.

"I don't know." he said. "Maybe the doctors got their scans muddled up, maybe they were wrong about my injuries. Maybe my prayers were answered. All I know is I was in a lot of pain. Those cops hurt me, a lot."

"It's all a little unbelievable." Ted said. "What do you say to the people who are crying fake news? There are some suggesting that you were paid to say you were injured, that doctors were paid off too. I must say, it does seem a little convenient that this would happen to the boyfriend of the woman who organised the protest."

"What are you saying?" Rhiannon said, her voice raising as her temper flared.

"I'm not saying anything, I'm asking what your response is." Ted replied, calmly.

"Listen, we're not the ones who said he had fractured his spine. We're not the ones who said he was in critical condition. We had the doctors scaring the life out of us saying he wasn't going to pull through, I had to call his mum all the way from Portside, and a few hours later he's walking away, right as rain." Rhiannon said. "We don't need to fake tragedies. What happened to Tamara Johnson was tragedy enough, and she's not the first. Countless black people have been harassed and killed by this country's police mob. We need to hold them accountable."

"I was lucky." Louis chimed in. "Tamara was not so lucky."

"What happened to Tamara Johnson was a tragedy." Ted said. "But she was shoplifting. Some would say the police were doing their job when they apprehended her."

Rhiannon snorted in derision, but Louis spoke up.

"Ted, do you know anyone who has shoplifted?" Louis said.

"I'm not sure." Ted said. "I've never asked."

"I've shoplifted." Hayley piped up, raising a hand as if she was in class. "When I was younger, I shoplifted. Just little things, like sweets. It was stupid really. I knew lots of kids who did."

"Shoplifting is a crime." Louis said. "But it's a crime with a punishment that fits it. Stealing a few chocolate bars would at most get you a slap on the wrist. For Tamara, it cost her life. Imagine if every person who ever shoplifted was killed because of it?"

"But the officers didn't mean to kill her." Ted said.

"They shot her with a taser." Louis said. "There are strict regulations controlling the use of weapons like that by the police force. Emergency situations only."

"The police officer interviewed by Metro City News said that the officer who fired the weapon did so in self-defence."

"He shot her in the back!" Rhiannon exclaimed. "In. The. Back. How do you shoot someone in the back, then say it's self-defence?"

The room fell silent for a moment, then Hayley took in a deep breath.

"I certainly can't argue with that." she said. "Powerful words, and powerful points. I'm afraid we're out of time, but thank you both for coming on the show and speaking with us."

There were a few seconds of silence, then a man behind the camera held up his hand.

"And we're in the ad break." he called.

"That went great." Ted said, leaning over to Rhiannon and Louis. "I hope you understand, I have to ask loaded questions like that, the audience wants to see more controversial and exciting conversations. Just playing devil's advocate, I'm sure you understand. I really do admire all the work you guys are doing."

Rhiannon and Louis didn't respond. They just fell into contemplation, and were ushered away as the camera crew prepared for the next segment. Rhiannon couldn't help but feel that they hadn't had enough time: that just a few minutes to talk about such a major issue wasn't enough. And yet, now it was over, and they had no choice but to leave.

The activist couple stepped out of the studio and into the city street. It was humid, and the sun was pelting down on the pavement, but it was a refreshing change from the cluttered filmset and the intense studio lights.

"Let's go home." Rhiannon said. "We've had enough drama, I want to collapse, eat junk food, and spend time with my wonderful, handsome man."

"Anything you want, babe." Louis said.

They walked away from the studio, and as they rounded the corner, a man called across the street.

"Hey!" he yelled. "It's you! It's him! That's the guy!"

The man was walking with his friend, both of whom were wearing cheap suits and carrying plain briefcases.

"What's up?" Louis asked, as the men crossed the street to approach them.

"You're the guy from the protest!" the man said. "Look, he's fine! I told you it was all faked!"

"Excuse me?" Louis frowned.

The guy poked him in the chest.

"An actor!" he said. "I knew it! How much did they pay you?"

"Don't touch me." Louis said.

"It's a shitty thing to do, lying to the country like that!" the man said. "Honestly, if you weren't so big, I'd teach you a lesson."

"Greg, come on, it's not worth it." the other man said.

"Yeah, listen to your friend, Greg." Louis said, his voice harsh. "Move along."

"What did you say to me?" the one called Greg said, shoving Louis. "Move along? Or what? You'll make me?"

Louis shoved him back with just a little more force.

Or so he thought. But the little shove sent the man flying eight feet backwards, landing with a thud against the pavement.

"Watch it!" the other man exclaimed, running to his friend's side. "Come on Greg, let's go!"

Louis looked at his hands, his eyes widening.

"Oof babe!" Rhiannon exclaimed. "Not that they didn't deserve it, but that was a bit hard!"

"I barely touched him." Louis muttered.

"Babe, you threw him like ten feet!" Rhiannon replied. "Come on, you big oaf, let's get home."

As they went to cross the road, Louis stopped in his tracks.

"Do you smell that?" he said, his brow furrowing.

"Smell what?" Rhiannon asked.

"Something's burning. Like, really intensely burning!"

"What are you talking about? I can't smell anything?"

Louis broke into a run, following his nose round the corner, and then another corner, and another.

"Babe, wait!" Rhiannon called, rushing after him. "Where are you going!"

The more Louis ran, the more intense the smell got, until it felt like he was being hit by a solid wall of smoke, and though he could still breathe his reflex was to gag, the odour surrounding him as he sought out the source.

Rhiannon caught up to Louis after a few minutes. She found him standing under an apartment building, staring up, a hand clasped over his mouth to block the smell: a smell Rhiannon could finally smell too.

"Oh my god…" she muttered, following his gaze.

There was smoke pouring out of a second storey window. A group of firefighters were rushing out of a nearby truck and into the building, but as they opened the door, a wall of smoke flooded out to meet them, and they retreated back to fetch the fire hose.

A string of people rushed out of the building, coughing and spluttering, and some of the firefighters beckoned them over, sitting them down on the curb.

"Is that a little boy up there?" Rhiannon said.

Louis scanned his eyes upwards. On a third floor balcony, a little boy was standing by the window, crying as the smoke billowed past him.

"Oh my god… Someone needs to help him." Louis said.

The firefighters were all preoccupied, trying to pull the hose into the building, where the fire seemed to be spreading.

Louis took off his denim jacket and handed it to Rhiannon.

"Hold this." he said, darting across the street.

"Louis, wait!" Rhiannon exclaimed.

Louis rushed over to the building, standing below where the boy was panicking two floors above.

"Here goes nothing." Louis muttered.

He bent his knees and leapt into the air. Louis was already over six and a half feet tall, but his legs propelled him higher than even he expected, and was able to easily catch hold of a first floor window ledge and pull himself up. He edged towards the end of the window ledge, reaching up to try and grab the window ledge above. One of his hands just managed to catch the next window ledge by the fingertips, and he gripped as tightly as he could, instinctively attempting to pull himself up...

And his body lifted, effortlessly.

"Oh my god!" Louis breathed, grabbing hold of the ledge with his other hand and pulling himself up.

The tiny balcony was just above him now: it was more of a window ledge than a full balcony. But in front of him, smoke was filling up the room and pouring out the cracks in the window. Louis felt the heat pouring out, and his skin began to ache. He held his breath, reaching up and grabbing hold of the metal bars around the window ledge above him, pulling himself up. The little boy stared at him as he lifted himself up, his eyes wide.

"Stand back, kid!" Louis yelled, and the boy backed away slowly.

In the street below, a small crowd had gathered, and the firefighters were shouting up at him.

"What are you doing! Get down, you're going to get yourself hurt!"

Louis ignored them, placing his hands on the window and pulling with all his might. The window frame cracked and splintered, and the window flew open, breaking off one of its hinges.

"Come here!" Louis said. "Don't be scared, I'm going to help you down. Hold onto me!"

The boy rushed forwards, wrapping his arms around Louis' neck. He was light as a feather, but holding the child left Louis with only one arm to climb.

"Close your eyes." Louis said, and he lowered himself back down onto the second storey window ledge.

This time the heat was overwhelming, and the smoke hit him in the face with force. Louis lost his balance, and then he was falling...

He bent his legs as he hit the floor, and he landed with a deafening crunch. The crowd gasped, and Louis toppled from his knees, onto his back, screaming out in pain.

The boy let go of him, running over the crowd of people, where a firefighter grabbed hold of him, checking to see if he was okay. A wall of smoke surrounded Louis, and the firefighters fought their way through, trying to make their way towards him. Louis looked down at his legs: one of them was obviously broken, bent out of shape, the other one with part of the skin torn away and bleeding from where it had scraped the wall on the way down.. It was almost as if seeing it made it real, and the pain hit him all at once as his eyes saw the bone, like a wave of intense pain, washing from his feet, up his entire body.

He watched, tears streaming down his face, as the bone twisted back into position with a horrible crunch. It was excruciating: the bones jerking back into place hurt more than the impact with the ground had. Louis screamed, his cries echoing through the city streets. But then his legs were back to normal, all signs of damage completely gone, leaving only the searing pain.

A firefighter rushed to Louis' side, and Rhiannon came close behind.

"Are you okay?" the firefighter said. "You could have killed yourself!"

"I'm fine." Louis said, pulling himself to his feet.

"You're a lucky bastard." The firefighter said. "You should have broken both your legs."

"I'm pretty big boned, I guess I got lucky." Louis said.

"Well, don't pull a stunt like that again." the firefighter said.

"Oh my god, Louis." Rhiannon exclaimed. "Stop scaring me like that!"

"Rhiannon." Louis pulled her close, wrapping his arms around her. Then, he whispered into her ear. "We've got to go, now."

The firefighter turned away to check on his colleagues, and Louis pulled Rhiannon away, disappearing into the smoke.

"Why are we running?" Rhiannon asked. "What's going on?"

"My legs." Louis said. "This one was broken, and the other one was bleeding. Look!"

205

He indicated down to his trousers. There was still a tear in the knee where it had been bleeding, blood sticking to the denim around the tear, but his skin had completely repaired, and the other leg had no signs of damage.

"Oh my god." Rhiannon muttered. "It must be that serum… It's made you invincible or something!"

"Or it just heals me, I don't know. I still felt it. I thought I was going to pass out from the pain alone. But that's not all. When I was climbing the building, my reflexes… Babe they were insane." Louis pulled Rhiannon away from the scene, walking with speed back towards their house. "I'm faster, I'm stronger, I'm like a superhero or something!"

"Babe, don't get ahead of yourself." Rhiannon said, rolling her eyes at the word 'superhero'. "We don't know what this is, or even how long it will last. Let's get you home, then we'll call that girl… Iona. Maybe she'll be able to help us figure out what's going on."

***

Jason sat in his wheelchair, tucked away in a corner in his little bedsit, scrolling through the files the mysterious hacker Grey Hat had sent him. Mere feet away, Iona lay in his tiny, single bed, sleeping soundly. Every so often, Jason stopped reading to look over at her, and smiled.

Iona's phone sat on the bookcase next to him, charging. It buzzed, and Jason quickly picked it up.

"Hey, this is Jason." he whispered. "Iona is sleeping."

"*Jason, this is Rhiannon, from yesterday. Look, we need to speak to Iona. A lot of weird stuff is happening to Louis, we're hoping she can help us.*"

Jason frowned.

"Weird stuff like what?" he asked. "Is he g-getting worse again?"

"*No, the opposite. He's stronger, he's faster, he's healing… He just hurt his legs. Like, really badly. And seconds later he was fine again.*"

"Oh my god." Jason said. "Iona always intended for the NanoVirus to keep aiding the body's immune system, but I

never imagined the results would be this g-good, this fast...
Okay, d-d-do you know where the Railway T-tavern is?"

"*Is that the little hotel near the train station?*"

"It is. M-meet us there this evening, in the carpark." Jason said.
"Don't panic. We'll t-talk. We'll figure it all out."

"*Okay. Thanks Jason.*"

She hung up, and Jason put down the phone. Iona opened her eyes, peering over at him.

"Who was that?" she mumbled.

"Rhiannon and Louis. The NanoVirus seems to still be working. It's m-making him stronger, and fitter, it's still healing him." he said. "I've told them to m-m-meet us here this evening."

"Oh my god." Iona breathed. "That means it works... It really works!"

She laughed.

"This is amazing, Jason! This could change the world!"
Jason smiled.

"I'm proud of you." he said, his voice filled with warmth and pride. She was right. This really could change the world. Jason had always known that Iona was brilliant, but it was nice to think that the world might get the chance to see her brilliance too.

Mere hours later, Jason sat in his wheelchair at the back of his garage, with Iona and Alex hovering behind him. Rhiannon was perched on the table, and on a bench in the middle of the workshop they had placed some planks of wood, which Louis was towering over.

"Okay, show us." Jason said.

Louis raised a fist above his head, hesitated, then slammed it down on the planks of wood. His fist cracked every single plank, passing straight through them, and cracked the bench in half.

He pulled his fist away, bloodied at the knuckles, and the group watched, jaws agape, as he pulled the splinters out of his fist and the cuts healed.

"Is this permanent?" he asked.

"I have no idea." Iona said. "It's likely there will be a period of

207

adjustment. You might notice some dramatic fluctuations… We'll just have to monitor you over time."

"In the meantime, I know you're both activists, and I hope you w-won't m-mind me being forward. I'd like to p-put those abilities to good use." Jason said. "We have something to show you. Alex."

Alex turned around, pulling his backpack from the corner of the workshop and opening it up. He pulled out the recently repaired gauntlets and held them up.

"Oh my god… You're the Fist." Rhiannon said.

"I suppose we both are." Alex said. "Jason built the gauntlets. I just do what I'm told."

"We're a t-t-team." Jason said. "And we'd like you to join or team… Both of you…"

"Both of us?" Rhiannon frowned. "What do you mean?"

"Listen, I've got the technical knowledge. And Iona, she's even smarter than me. And Alex… He's the toughest m-m-man I've ever known." Jason stammered. "But Louis' new abilities are above anything I've ever seen before, and you… Rhiannon, you are the most p-passionate and dedicated p-person I've ever known. Your speech was inspiring, and since I heard it I've b-been looking at your other work. Your civil rights group is fantastic. We joined together in this partnership because we wanted to do good. But we've n-n-never been activists before. We're new to all this. We need your experience and guidance."

"What he's trying to say is we want you to lead us." Alex said. "If you're willing."

"We can make this city a better place." Jason said. "If you're willing to join us."

Rhiannon looked at Louis, who shrugged.

"Looks like we're in." Rhiannon said.

Iona felt her phone buzz in her pocket, and pulled it out.

"It's Dr Wood." she said. "She's asking me to come into the office now… I've got to go."

"Is everything okay?" Jason asked.

"I'll fill you in later." Iona said, leaning in and kissing him on the forehead. "Stay safe."

Iona left a strange atmosphere in the air as she left, and Jason found himself wondering if she had been caught out: stealing the NanoVirus from the lab was a dangerous move that could get her fired. He knew they had made the right call, and that saving Louis was ultimately a good decision, but he hoped Iona wouldn't have to pay the price for it.

CHAPTER THIRTEEN: SMOKE AND MIRRORS

Johnny was sitting in the interrogation room at the police station when Huey arrived. His lawyers handled the paperwork, and Huey was allowed to go and sit with him. Johnny had bruises and grazes all over his face, and had been given some plain clothes to change into and a towel to wrap around himself, but was still dripping wet.

"What even happened?" Huey asked.

"I don't know mate. I blacked out during the fight. Woke up and they were pulling me from the river." He stared intently at Huey. "But that bitch from the mosque, she was there. There's something off about her, Huey. She can do things."

"Well, these riots solved nothing. I told you-"

"Don't."

"Johnny. You have potential, but you're throwing it away. You're capable of so much more. Have you seen the news? They're calling you a vicious, racist thug." Huey said, softly.

"Who cares what the media says?" Johnny scoffed.

"Grow up, Johnny." Huey firmly replied. "We tried doing things your way, and look how it turned out. It's time to do things my way."

Johnny fell into silent contemplation.

"Well?" Huey asked.

Johnny scowled.

"Johnny…"

"Fine!" Johnny exclaimed. "But not until we've dealt with Adkins. That fish is going to fry. Then we go legit, do it your way."

"Okay, but be careful. Wait until after the court case is done. Plan it all out properly." Huey said. "There can be no room for this to go wrong."

"You got it, little brother."

"I'm two two years older than you, Johnny."

***

The building was empty when Iona arrived, and she slunk through the hallways towards Dr Wood's office, staring into the darkened, deserted rooms.

Dr Wood was tapping away at her computer, the door slightly ajar, the light from her desk lamp spilling into the hallway.

Iona raised her fist to knock.

"Come in." Dr Wood said, before her fist made impact with the wood.

Iona walked in and hovered awkwardly in the doorway. In the back of her mind, she knew that she had been caught, but her instinct still had her playing it cool, acting as if she had done nothing wrong.

"Take a seat." Dr Wood said.

"What's this about?" Iona asked, pulling a chair up to the desk.

"You know we have security cameras, right?" Dr Wood said.

"I saw you enter the lab last night, take the NanoVirus, and leave, with the activist girl from the TV. And then, the next morning, I hear that her boyfriend has miraculously recovered from his injuries…"

"I can explain-" Iona said.

Dr Wood swivelled her chair around, fixing Iona with an intense stare.

"No." Dr Wood interrupted. "There is no explanation. It was a foolish mistake. If anyone found out, the project would be shut down. What you did was completely illegal and very much unethical. I have half a mind to fire you."

There was a look in her eye that Iona couldn't quite place. It wasn't anger, or even disappointment. Perhaps she would go as far to say that it was disgust. Dr Wood's lip was curled up into a subtle snarl, her brow furrowed so deeply that she had wrinkles climbing up her forehead to her hairline, and she was breathing heavily from her nose.

"You can't fire me, this is my project!" Iona exclaimed.

211

"*Your project* which *you* have compromised!" Dr Wood snapped. "Research that could save billions of lives, and you were willing to throw it all away! Do you have any idea-"

The sound of doors being thrown open and footsteps running down the corridor cut Dr Wood short. She frowned, the look in her eye suddenly replaced with confusion.

"No one is supposed to be here…" she said. "Stay here… I'm going to take a look."

She stood up and peered out of the room, then retracted, her face ghostly white.

"Call the police." she said, heading out into the corridor. "I think we're being robbed."

"What?!" Iona exclaimed.

She pulled out her phone, and Dr Wood disappeared into the hallway. Iona dialled the emergency number, her fingers trembling.

"Hello?" she said. "I need the police, I'm at Hera Laboratories, off Ditko Road. We're being robbed."

Suddenly, there was a loud scream, followed by a thud.

Iona poked her head out, into the hallway.

Dr Wood was gone from view, and there was no sign of whoever had been causing the commotion. As quietly as possible, Iona crept towards the lab where she and her research assistants carried out their research. A pit began to form in her stomach.

Through the window of the door, she saw four masked men grabbing all of their notes and equipment and shoving everything into black bags. They grabbed the vials of NanoVirus, even the cages of rats, and headed for the door. Iona rushed into the adjacent lab, tucking herself behind the door and peeking at them through the tiny window.

The masked figures headed out to the exit, returning without any of the stolen items.

"I think we've got everything." one of them said.

"Did you get the doctor?" another asked.

"Yeah, she's in the van." the first said.

"Great. Burn it down. Be thorough, we want them to think everything was lost in the fire. They can't know it was taken, or-"

He was cut short by the sounds of sirens.

"Are they coming here?" he said, in a panicked tone.

"It looks like it… They're pulling up outside."

"Who called them?"

"It must have been the doctor! She must have called them before we grabbed her!"

"Shit! Get out of here now! Run!"

There was a sudden flurry of movement, and then they were gone.

Iona took a deep breath, her hands trembling. The sound of tyres screeching echoed in the distance. She rushed down the stairs to the front of the building just in time to see a black van disappearing from view, flying straight through a red light as the robbers made their escape. As if by clockwork, the moment they were out of view, a police car came screeching round the corner from the other direction, the red and blue lights bouncing off of every window on the street. A police officer appeared at the entrance to the building, and Iona rushed over. It was Officer Parker. Iona opened the door, rushing over to Officer Parker. Her hands were still trembling, but now the shaking was spreading to the rest of her body.

"Did you make the call?" she asked.

Iona nodded, trying her best to steady her hands and her heartbeat.

"Did- did- did-" Iona couldn't get the words out, and her breathing grew more and more erratic, as if even her lungs were beginning to tremble. Her vision started to lose focus, not actually blurring, but struggling to stay fixed to one thing.

"Okay, okay." Officer Parker said, in a soothing tone. "I think you're having a panic attack. It's okay, they're gone now, and my partners are in pursuit. We're going to catch them, you're not in any danger. Have you had a panic attack before?"

Iona nodded, clutching her hands tightly around her body.

"Not - not this b-b-bad though…" she stammered. "I can't b-b-breathe."

"It's okay, you're going to be okay." Officer Parker repeated. "Come on, let's sit you down inside, I'll get you some water. Just breathe, okay?"

213

"They took - they - they took my boss." Iona stammered. "The men - they - they - took her…"

Officer Parker grabbed her radio.

"This is Officer Parker. Be advised: the suspects may have a hostage." she turned back to Iona. "Come on now, let's get you inside."

***

Zakirah was taken from the police station and driven approximately an hour away. It was night when she was taken, and it was hard to see where she was going. When asked, all the police officers had said was "Immigration Detention Facility." That seemed like a euphemism. The place they arrived at looked more like a prison. There were bars on all the windows, and massive metal fences topped with barbed wire around the outskirts of the building.

Inside, Zakirah was searched thoroughly, and once they were done all she had left were the clothes on her back and the shoes on her feet. She was led by a tired-looking guard into a massive room filled with cells... If you could call them cells. In actuality, it was just a large room with metal fences dividing it up into sections. Some of them had beds, some just mattresses, some even just roll-mats with pillows. The 'cells' opened up into a hall filled with metal tables and benches that looked like cheap copies of park benches.

Zakirah was handed a pillow and a foil blanket by the guard and led towards a 'cell' already occupied by three women. There was a bunk bed, as well as a mattress simply laid across the floor. Both the bed and the mattress were occupied. The other women looked just as sad and hopeless as Zakirah felt.

"Where will I sleep?" Zakirah asked the guard.

The guard rolled her eyes, walking over to a side room and coming back with a rolled up mat, like one would use for camping. She tossed it to Zakirah and walked away without a word.

"Don't worry," the woman on the mattress said. She had a thick African accent, and was about fifteen years older than Zakirah, with dark black skin, and beautiful long dreadlocks that flowed down her back. "We can take it in turns with the

214

mattress. Here, you look like you need it more than me tonight."

She shifted over and offered the mattress to Zakirah.

"Thank you." Zakirah said. "I'll be alright. I'm Zakirah."

"Chaya." the woman replied.

The other two women lifted their heads from their pillows to greet Zakirah. One of them was Indian, the other white.

"Fatima." the one on the bottom bunk said.

"Katerina." the woman on the top bunk said, in a strong, Russin accent.

Zakirah lay awake for most of the night, exhausted but also hungry, her stomach gurgling and moaning. When the sunlight finally started to shine through the distant windows, high up on the wall and blocked with bars, Zakirah was eager for breakfast. Their cells were opened one by one by the guards, and a hatch in the back of the hall opened, showing a kitchen where other women like themselves were busy preparing breakfast. Unlike most kitchens, there were no delicious scents of spices or fresh produce. Just the powerful aroma of cleaning products.

The first few cells of women were led down a hallway and into a bathroom, where there was a small row of showers on one side, and a small row of toilets on the other. On her way in, Zakirah was handed a wash bag, which contained a cloth, a bar of soap, a toothbrush, and the tiniest tube of toothpaste she had ever seen.

Once done in the washroom, they were brought through for the most disappointing breakfast Zakirah had ever seen. There was porridge, toast, cereal and fruit. The cereal all looked stale, the fruit all either over or under-ripe. The porridge was bland and flavourless, and the toast was already starting to grow cold. Zakirah sat with the women from her cell, wolfing down several pieces of toast spread with jam. She picked at her final piece, which was spread with the last bits of jam in a meagre, pitiful coating that barely covered the whole piece. She watched the guards intently as they wandered around the room, checking on the detainees.

A new girl was brought in, looking as bewildered and lost as Zakirah must have looked the night before. She couldn't have been more than eighteen years old, and she clutched her pillow with her, everywhere she went. She perched herself at the only available seat, at the crowded table where Zakirah was sat.

"What's your name?" Zakirah asked her.

"Priti." the girl replied. "Why are we here?"

"Deportation." Katerina replied, taking a spoonful of soup. "This is an immigration facility."

The girl's chin began to waver.

"But I'm legal." she said. "I don't understand, why didn't they tell me anything? They didn't even let me talk to a lawyer or anything!"

"Half the women here are legal." Chaya said. "I'm sorry, honey, but you can't expect justice in Great Britain."

Zakirah took hold of the younger girl's hand and smiled warmly at her.

"Don't worry." she said. "We'll look out for you, okay? It's not the end of the world, trust me."

The girl placed her head on Zakirah's shoulder and began to sob. Zakirah stroked her hair softly. Inside, she wondered what had happened to her string of good luck. Was it over? Or was she supposed to be here? Was Asim right? Was there some higher power, guiding her way?

All she knew is that not long ago she had told a man to jump off a bridge, and he had done it. That wasn't luck, that was something else... Something more powerful. And yet, on the way here, she had tried to harness that power again, to no avail. If only she could figure out how it worked, and do it again.

***

Iona arrived at the lab early the next morning, with bags under her eyes. She clasped a cup of coffee tightly in her hands, the warmth giving her some release. She hadn't had a cup of coffee in years, and the flavour was almost overbearing, but she needed the boost.

The entrance to the laboratories was closed, and crime scene tape formed a border around the building. Two men in suits were standing by the door, chatting. Iona ducked under the tape and wandered over to them.

216

"I'm Dr Page, I made the call last night." she said. "What's going on?"

"Dr Page, I'm Agent Bertie, this is Inspector Jones. We're shutting down the lab, and taking possession of any research left by the thieves." one of the men said. "We're shutting down all Hera Labs projects for the time being. If you have anything relevant to the project: any notes, any equipment, any computer files, we ask that you turn them over to us. Having possession of anything related to the NanoVirus project could put you in danger."

"What's going on?" Iona asked. "Did you not catch them?"

"We did not, and it seems the people were ghosts. They disappeared completely, and took Dr Wood with them. We have reason to believe that they may intend to weaponise your NanoVirus. Until we have caught the suspects and figured out what they intend to do with your research, we are suspending all research pertaining to nanotechnology."

Iona fell silent, staring up at the laboratory that for a short time had been her place of work. The building was meaningless to her now, all of her research and hard work was completely gone. She was left without a purpose, and with nothing to do and nowhere to go.

***

Jason sat, alone, in the garage outside his bedsit, his laptop switched on in front of him.

"Are you listening?" he said.

The laptop fan whirled. The screen came to life.

'**I AM HERE. HAVE YOU COME TO A DECISION ABOUT WORKING WITH ME?**'

"I h-have." Jason stammered. "But I need some things from you first."

'**WHAT?**'

"You are clearly an experienced and c-c-capable hacker." Jason said. "You want me to fire your gun for you. You want me to help with the d-dirty work. I'll do it. But I need you to help me. There's a lot of weird stuff going on around the city, and I need you to help me work out what's going on. People are going m-missing, and it's mostly people of colour. My

217

friend's lab was attacked and all her work taken. You help me find the missing people and find out who attacked the lab, and we have a deal."

There was a moment in which the screen remained blank. Then, one word.

'**DEAL.**'

ONE MONTH LATER…

Rhiannon sat alone on a park bench, her raincoat clasped tightly around her. Autumn had cast its spell across the city, and the ground of the park was covered with a layer of brown and orange as the trees shed their once green leaves.

"*All I'm saying is that you're not invincible.*" Alex's voice could be heard through the little earpiece in her right ear. "*Sure, you've got the strength and the speed, but I've got the experience. If you would just let me train you-*"

"*Look, mate, I've got on fine in my life without you and without my powers so far. Don't patronise me.*" Louis' voice replied.

"*I'm not trying to patronise you, I'm trying to help you. I've been doing this a little longer.*"

"*Like a week longer, man. Besides, I've been an activist since I was fifteen.*"

Rhiannon caught sight of a man walking towards her with purpose, entering the park from the nearest entrance. He was wearing jeans and a hooded jacket, and she couldn't quite make out his face, but the man was definitely heading for the bench where she sat. He had a suspicious walk: The way he would crane his head around to check no one was watching him, fidgeting with his hands, walking at an uneven pace as if trying to act natural, but completely overthinking it.

"Guys!" Rhiannon interrupted the argument, hissing into her earpiece. "The mark is here. Pipe down."

The trio fell into silence as the man approached Rhiannon. Now that he was closer, Rhiannon could see that the man was nearing forty, but looked like he was trying to dress younger.

"Sarah?" the man said, a look of confusion on his face. "You look different to your profile."

"That makes two of us." Rhiannon replied, a wry smile crossing her face.

218

The man took a step back, looking around nervously.

"What's the matter, Greg?" Rhiannon asked, standing up. "Am I too old for you?"

Without a word, the man turned and sprinted away through the park.

"*We've got a runner!*" Alex exclaimed.

"*I've got him.*" Louis replied.

Louis came out of the shadows, moving at speed to cut the man off. There were about a hundred metres between him and the man, but he closed that distance in ten seconds, barrelling into the man at full speed and knocking him to the ground. The man scrambled to his feet, trying to make a run for it again, but Alex appeared, blocking his way. The man instinctively took a swing for Alex, who dodged the punch with ease and sent his gauntlet smashing into the man's chin in an uppercut. The man fell backwards with a grunt, landing on the ground with a thud, and Alex gave him a swift kick to the stomach for good measure.

He leant in over the man.

"Not going to get up?" he muttered. "Shame, I was hoping for more of a fight."

The man let out a groan, and Alex grabbed him by the scruff of his collar.

"Next time you think about setting a fake profile to talk to young girls, I'll rip off your tiny tick tack." he growled.

"Who do you think you are?" the man spluttered. "The Fists of Justice?"

"That's exactly who we are." Alex replied, throwing the man back down to the ground.

"I had him." Louis said, stooping down to tie the man's hands up.

Alex shrugged.

"I know." he said. "But I suited up, didn't want to miss out on the fun."

Rhiannon approached.

"When you two are done measuring, how about we drop this pervert off at the police station?" she said. "It looks like it's going to rain."

Louis pulled the man to his feet, pushing him roughly in front of him.

"Do you guys ever feel weird about handing these creeps over to the police one day, and protesting the police the next?" Alex asked.

"The police are there to deal with people like this." Rhiannon said. "We can protest public servants when they step out of line and still expect them to do their jobs. It's not a double-standard, it's accountability. Now let's get a move on."

They marched the man out of the park, Louis holding him firmly to stop him from bolting, and Alex taking up the rear of the group, checking they weren't being watched or followed. As they left the park, no sign of them remained, and a minute or so later a couple passed through, and one commented to the other how serene the park felt at night.

***

Jason sat alone in his garage, tinkering with a set of massive, metal boots on his table. Next to him, his laptop was displaying the Downtown News Network's daily news update. The silver-haired news reporter sat in front of his desk, talking directly to the camera in that plain, regionless, well-spoken radio accent that all reporters seemed to speak with.

"*The Fists of Justice made another appearance this weekend, as the two new figures seen working with the Fist, who locals have dubbed the Gentle Giant and the Mystery Woman, were spotted preventing a mugging on Way's Approach. More on that later. In other news, the judge is set to reach a final verdict regarding Officer Briggs, the officer who shot Tamara Johnson last month. Theodore Briggs, who originally was set to face no punishment for his actions, lost his job and was made to stand trial after international protests. None of the other officers present are being charged. In related news, charges against the alleged ringleaders of the Central Bridge Riot that followed what was intended to be a peaceful protest on the day of Tamara Johnson's death are being dropped, since the police were unable to find any solid evidence tying the two men to the riots. Police originally believed that Antonio Adkins might be the gang leader known as Big Tuna, but were forced to drop the allegations due to insufficient* evidence tying Mr Adkins to any kind of organised crime. Mr Adkins claims that he is simply the co-owner of a delivery company operating across Downtown City. The other alleged ringleader was Josiah Wagner, otherwise known as Johnny Johnson. Johnny Johnson served a life sentence for a string of bank robberies in the 90s, and was released last year, claiming to have found a new passion: politics. Johnson wrote a book entitled 'GOD SAVE GREAT BRITAIN'. The book sold around a million copies and gained Johnson a significant following, and his second book 'PROUD BRIT: the struggles of a working class white man in an overly sensitive world.' is due to be released in early December. Since the release of his first book, Johnny Johnson has become a representative of the British Independence Party and has become a public speaker for right-wing clubs and events. Although Johnson was spotted at the protest, and multiple witnesses state that he was seen antagonising protesters and even fighting during the riot, the Crown Prosecution Service has decided not to press charges, claiming that there is no evidence Johnson instigated the riots, or that he was aggressor, and Johnson insists he only acted in self-defence, protecting himself after the riots broke out. Though the protests sparked controversy, they have found some success, in that Downtown Police will now be required to wear cameras at all times while on duty, and all officers will be required to take a course on proper safety and reasonable force. In addition, the Downtown City Police Department has committed to hiring two hundred new police officers, to ensure that officers are never overworked or made to feel they do not have adequate back-up, which one high-ranking official told reporters will make incidents like the death of Tamara Johnson less likely, though some have made the point that hiring more police officers in a time when people are so distrustful of the police is likely to make Downtown City locals feel less safe, not more safe. Many believe that the police specifically targeted black protesters, and until new anti-racism training measures are brought in, many feel they cannot trust the police."

There was a knock at the garage door, and Jason shut down his laptop and opened up the garage door. Alex, Louis and

Rhiannon slipped inside. Alex was wearing his bandanna, goggles and padded vest, underneath a long coat. Louis was sporting a similar bandanna, as well as a hoodie, with black bandages wrapped around his hands to protect his knuckles.

"How did it g-go?" Jason asked.

"Smoothly." Rhiannon replied. "We dropped the creep off outside the police station, tied all the evidence we had on him to his chest. Saw them pick him up, they looked uncertain but a guy like that… There's no way they'll be releasing him. Not with the evidence they have now. How's it going in here?"

"Slowly." Jason said. "Technical difficulties. I'll get there."

"Anyone want a drink?" Alex asked.

Louis rolled his eyes.

"You say that every night." he said. "You drink too much."

"I just like to celebrate a job well done." Alex said, taking off the gauntlets and goggles and pulling down his bandanna. "You got a problem with that?"

"Not tonight." Jason interrupted the conflict. "We all n-need rest tonight. I've heard from our m-mysterious hacker friend again."

"Grey Hat? Any clues as to who they are yet?" Rhiannon asked.

Jason shook his head.

"Not yet. But they sent me some worrying files from the Home Office. It's about the p-people who have gone missing around the city." he said. "It seems the government is secretly c-c-carrying out a massive involuntary deportation programme: the files imply they're illegal immigrants, but we cross-referenced all the names on the list and m-many of them are born UK citizens, children of immigrants and such."

"It's Windrush all over again…" muttered Rhiannon.

"Indeed." Jason said. "The information we've got is massively incriminating, and once in the hands of the press c-could cause them a lot of t-t-trouble, but that won't do much good for the first set of deportees. They're due to be deported from Portside Airport tomorrow night, unless someone stops them."

"We should get going then." Rhiannon said.

"We can't all go." Jason said. "Johnny Johnson and Big Tuna have had all charges d-dropped against them, and multiple of the instigators of the riot are due to be released. Both are out for blood. A gang war is basically inevitable at this p-point. I'm recommending that you and Louis go to Portside, and Alex and I will keep an eye on the t-tensions here between the Bridge Boys and the Bovver Boys."

"Surely forced deportation is our priority?" Rhiannon frowned. "Families will be torn apart. People's lives will be ruined."

"That's why I'm sending you to stop it." Jason said.

Rhiannon raised an eyebrow.

"You're sending me?" she repeated. "When you brought us onto the team, you said you wanted me to take charge, but so far you've been calling most of the shots."

"I'm sorry." Jason said. "I'm just trying to m-make sure we cover all our bases. We can't all leave Downtown City right now. People's lives could be at serious risk here too. And Alex knows B-b-big Tuna. He's an invaluable asset we need here."

"That's why we need more people." Rhiannon said. "I keep telling you we should expand our team. I have worked with some fantastic civil rights activists who could really be useful to us."

"I'm just not convinced now is the time to be bringing on new people we don't all know." Jason said. "It seems like a risk."

"You didn't know us." Rhiannon pointed out. "I've worked with these people for years. This is real life, not a comic book: you can't fix the world alone. Instigating change isn't done by individuals. It's done by groups. Harriet Tubman, Malcolm X, Martin Luther King Jr, Rosa Parks… These people had entire teams of dedicated activists around them. Figureheads may light the sparks but the masses… They're the flame."

"Rhiannon is right." Louis said. "At the end of the day, it's movements that instigate change, not individuals. We may remember individuals who were good at making speeches or igniting the passion of a crowd, but a movement needs to be able to stand strong, with or without those individuals at the helm."

"Okay." Jason conceded. "If you can find some trustworthy people to join you heading to Portside, do it. If it goes well, we'll talk about bringing them onto the team when you return."

"Finally." Rhiannon replied. "We should go. Portside is at least a two hour drive, we'll need to set off early tomorrow."

"M-m-meet us here at 6AM." Jason said. "I'm trying to put t-together some tech that might be helpful for you."

Rhiannon nodded.

"Later." she said, turning to leave.

"See you tomorrow, Jason." Louis gave Jason a friendly tap on the shoulder on his way out. "Oh, and good luck with your speech therapy session. I'm already noticing an improvement mate, I'm proud of you."

Jason smiled awkwardly.

"Thanks." he said. "That m-means a lot."

They slid the garage door closed behind them as they left, and Jason turned to Alex.

"How are they doing out there?" he asked.

"Rhiannon is great. She handles herself well under pressure." Alex said. "But Louis… The NanoVirus still heals him pretty quickly, and he's strong, and fast… I'm pretty sure he came close to beating the world record for one hundred metres today… But he has no finesse. He's clumsy, and he has no idea how to fight. If it wasn't for the super-strength and his size, he'd probably be a pretty gentle guy."

"Not necessarily a bad thing." Jason replied.

"I've taken martial arts classes since I was a kid, and I've been through the forces and even fought in battle scenarios. A team needs to be able to work together in the field. Just being strong and fast isn't enough." Alex said. "Sure, he might heal, but every blunder puts the rest of us in danger too."

"Well, his powers are useful." Jason said. "No one else can do what he can do."

"I could, if you let me take the NanoVirus." Alex suggested. "Iona still has a few vials left."

Jason rolled his eyes.

"We've talked about this. It's way too d-dangerous. We don't know the side-effects. Just because it worked for Louis, doesn't mean it will for you." Jason said. "This is why these things usually go through rigorous t-t-testing. The same drug can have no impact on one person and make someone else sick. And this is Nanotech. It's even less thoroughly researched."

"It's worth the risk, Jason." Alex said. "Imagine what I could do, with my training and his strength, speed and healing. Just let me test out the virus. I'm willing to take the risk."

"No, Alex." Jason said, sternly. "We only gave it to Louis because he was dying. This conversation is over."

The two fell into silence, and Alex sighed.

"Fine." he said, at last. "Look, I know you're just looking out for me, but I'm not worried about myself, I just want to do better."

"Well, if you won't worry about yourself, I'll worry about you for you. I'm your friend, Alex." Jason said.

"Thanks." Alex replied. "It means a lot."

"How are you settling into the new place?" Jason changed the topic swiftly, not wanting to argue any more.

"It's not too bad." Alex said. "I'm not sure how I feel about the day job, but it pays the bills."

"Working for a private security company seems like a good fit for you." Jason said.

"I'm a file clerk. I answer the phones and do the paperwork." Alex muttered. "Don't get me wrong, I'm grateful to Joe for the job, but office work isn't really me. Anyway, I should go get some sleep. I can't be late twice in my second week."

Alex turned and left, and Jason was left alone in the garage again. He turned back to his laptop, flipping it open again. He opened the terminal programme, and a big black window appeared on the screen.

'**Grey Hat. Are you there?**' he typed.

He waited for a few minutes, going back to tinkering with the metal boots on the table. Eventually, the reply appeared.

'**YES.**'

'**Any update on the NanoVirus theft?**' Jason typed.

'**STILL WORKING ON IT. THIS RABBIT HOLE IS DEEP. WHOEVER TOOK THE RESEARCH AND KIDNAPPED DR WOOD IS VERY POWERFUL, AND VERY GOOD AT COVERING THEIR TRACKS. BUT I WILL FIND THEM.**'

'**Ready to tell me who you are yet?**'

'**SOON. COMMUNICATION END.**'

CHAPTER FOURTEEN: THE CALM BEFORE

With summer's lease on Downtown city over and autumn creeping in, the mornings were becoming colder. Jason still sat in his garage at 5AM the next morning, and if it weren't for the portable heater he had installed and the blanket wrapped around his shoulders, he would be freezing. Bags had formed under his eyes, and still the boots sat on the desk in front of him. Outside, a grey canopy had formed overhead, and heavy rain pelted the roof of the garage. Distant thunder rumbled, and Jason went on with his tinkering.

"I still feel like it could do more…" he muttered to himself. Again, the rumbling of thunder. Jason rolled over to the garage door and slid it open, sitting in the entrance and watching the rain pour down. He found it cathartic, watching the raindrops bounce off the ground across the empty car park, seeing the rain drizzle down the shop windows across the street, and watching the lightning illuminate the skyline in the night. As thunder echoed in the distance, there was a flash of lightning, and suddenly an idea sparked in the back of Jason's mind. He pulled the garage door back down and went back to tinkering, pulling apart the boots and piecing them back together with new components. He pulled out an old pair of prototype gauntlets and started tinkering with them as well.

It was just over an hour later when he heard Louis and Rhiannon pull up in the car park outside. He pulled the door up just in time to see them getting out of their car, and at the other end of the car park, Alex appeared, a heavy army jacket wrapped around him.

"Good morning." Jason said as Rhiannon and Louis walked over to the garage. He waited until everyone was in the garage and Alex had closed the door, then pulled a folder out from the bag attached to his wheelchair.

"I have put together a file with all the information you will need on the deportations. They start loading up at 3PM. The flight will depart at 7PM."

He handed the folder to Louis.

"Any idea what your tactic is g-going to be?" he asked Rhiannon.

"I spent most of the night thinking about it." Rhiannon said. "We can't just rescue the deportees, as we'll be turning them into fugitives. But getting the press into the airport to expose the whole operation is just too risky. There will be armed police and airport security everywhere."

"Have you considered stopping the coach before it reaches the airport?" Jason asked.

"That's a good plan." Rhiannon said. "But we need to catch them red-handed, so there's no denying what they were doing."

Jason nodded, turning to his laptop and opening up a map.

"In that case, you need to stop them at the entrance to the airport here: before they're through airport security, but after the last available turn-off. There will be n-no d-d-denying where they are taking them. And you need as much press there as possible to witness it. I actually refashioned some of those anti-homeless spikes into traffic spikes to stop a car, they're in the back, you can t-take those, they'll help you stop them from making it to the airport."

"Great. Also, you might not be able to come with us, but you can help us contact all the news stations. This needs to be handled just right: the timing needs to be perfect, so that they all come to the airport, but the police don't get tipped off, or they'll simply change the deportation schedule." Rhiannon said.

"Okay." Jason said. "I'll g-get it done. These are for you." He indicated toward the gauntlets and boots. This set of gauntlets were far smaller than Alex's, but the boots were thick and heavy. "I spent all night working on them. There are some new features I think you'll really like."

Jason picked up the chunky goggles, which were now built

into an almost full headset, which covered the upper part of the wearer's face, and handed it to Rhiannon.

"I've m-made you a little instruction manual." he said.

Rhiannon looked at the bundle of tech.

"We'll have to test it on the road." she said. "I'll go load it up." She turned and headed out the garage, putting her equipment in her backpack and heading back to the car. Alex followed her.

"Rhiannon!" Alex called, jogging to catch up with her. "I wanted your advice."

"What's up?" Rhiannon asked.

"I've been arguing with Jason about the NanoVirus that Louis took." Alex said. "Iona still has several doses left. I think I should take it… having two super-powered people on our team could really help us in situations like this, when we have to split up."

"Isn't it dangerous?" Rhiannon asked. "We don't know if it will affect you in the same way it did Louis."

"I'm willing to take that risk." Alex said.

"Well, Jason isn't the boss of you." Rhiannon said. "It's your body, your choice. If you want to take that risk in the hopes that you might be able to help people, I can respect that. But be careful, Alex. You're a vital member of this team, with or without the abilities that Louis has. I'd rather have you as you are than not at all."

"Thanks." Alex said. "That means a lot. "

"I know you and Louis don't always see eye to eye, but when you've been doing activism as long as I have, you realise it helps to have some different viewpoints on your team, or you end up in an echo chamber. We still all really appreciate you, Alex."

Alex smiled.

"That really means a lot, especially with our history." he said.

Rhiannon sighed, placing a hand on Alex's shoulder.

"Look, I don't approve of how you left things with my brother. You really hurt him. But that was a long time ago, and you've proven over the past month that you are a good person who wants to do what's right. That's what matters most to me." she said. "Even if you were a dick, leaving Blake the way you did."

"I know. If I could go back and change it, I would. At the time, I thought I was doing the right thing for me, but I never thought about how it would impact him. I was selfish." Alex replied. He paused, taking a deep breath. "Good luck today. You'll do great."

Back inside the garage, Louis hovered awkwardly over Jason. With Jason sitting in his wheelchair, Louis towered over him, having to look down to meet his eyes. Louis did not like towering over people. He didn't like how they shifted awkwardly in his shadow. That being said, Jason acted that way with everyone, and that at least made Louis feel a little less singled out.

"Jason." Louis said. "I just thought I should say, you might want to keep an eye on Alex. His anger problems are getting worse."

"What do you mean?" Jason asked.

"Out in the field." Louis said. "He's always looking for a fight, it's like he's using our work as an outlet for his rage. He drinks to celebrate after every successful mission, he drinks to distract himself after every unsuccessful one. I just worry he'll snap."

"Noted." Jason said. "Alex has had a t-tough time since he was kicked out of the forces, but I trust him."

"He's a good man." Louis said. "But that's not always enough. Plenty of good men have had breakdowns."

"You're right." Jason sighed. "I'll k-keep an eye on him. Good luck today."

He extended his hand, and Louis took it and shook it.

"Keep our city safe while we're gone." he grinned. "Stay safe."

And with that, he turned and headed back towards the car.

Louis and Rhiannon drove away from the Railway Tavern, leaving Alex and Jason alone again. It had been a while since it had just been the two of them defending the city. It felt strange.

Louis and Rhiannon pulled up outside their house to the sight of a trio of activists standing on the doorstep. There was a white woman who looked around twenty, and a short Portuguese man with a neatly trimmed beard and a pair of plastic-framed glasses. Then there was a person with brightly

229

coloured hair sticking out from beneath their hood. All three were clutching their raincoats tightly around themselves and sheltering on the doorstep.

"You came!" Rhiannon exclaimed, beaming as she approached the house.

"We got your message. No one else could make it on short notice, I'm afraid." the woman said. "What's all this about?"

"Come on inside, we'll explain." Rhiannon said.

She unlocked the door and showed the team into the main room.

"Would anyone like a cup of tea?" Louis asked.

"Have you got coffee? Black, no sugar." the person with the bright hair said, pulling off their raincoat. Their hood came down, revealing hair that was partly coloured red, partly coloured blue, with a split down the middle of their head, and beneath the raincoat they wore a baggy, sleeveless t-shirt bearing the logo of a punk rock band. Their name was AJ, and they were non-binary, and they had been part of the group since they turned sixteen, which was only a few years ago. The woman was called Cindy, and was one of the first activists to join them. She was older than she looked, and was actually part of multiple groups, and even helped to run the local homeless outreach group. The man was called Ricardo. He had only moved to the UK two years ago, but had been part of an anti-fascist group back home and had quickly sought out a local group in Downtown to join after moving.

"I'll have a tea." Cindy said. "Two sugars."

Ricardo shook his head, and Louis disappeared into the kitchen. For a moment, it just felt like an ordinary meeting between friends: cups of tea, sharing pleasantries. But then the moment was over, and Rhiannon sighed, because it was time for things to get heavy.

"Before we get into details, I need to know I can trust you all." Rhiannon said. "This is not like the other activism we've done, and you three are among our most trusted activists… But today we're taking it to the next level. And it will be crossing the line of legality much further than any of you are used to."

The trio nodded.

"Pity Leon's not here." Ricardo muttered. "He'd be loving this."

"We're with you." Cindy said. "As long as we're helping people, I'm in."

"Okay." Rhiannon said. "Louis and I have been working with the Fist. He recruited us after the protest last month."

The three activists exchanged a look, their eyes widening. It took a second for Ricardo and Cindy to process the information, but AJ's mouth was flapping up and down immediately.

"What?!" they exclaimed.

"So, what, are you the new Fists of Justice?" Cindy asked. "The ones that have been on the news? The Gentle Giant and the Mystery Woman?"

"Is that what they've been calling us?" Rhiannon said. "I guess we are."

"That's amazing! I wondered why we hadn't seen so much of you two recently." AJ said.

"Anyway, one of our sources has sent through some government files referencing a large-scale deportation programme that is being carried out: today, a plane carrying around ninety people will leave Portside Airport. Some are refugees, some are the children of immigrants, some are illegal only by clerical errors or failure to submit the proper paperwork at the right time. Most of them have homes, jobs and families here, and nothing waiting for them on the other side. We are going to stop the deportation, and give these people a chance to be heard."

"How are we going to do that?" Ricardo asked.

"Can we trust the Fist?" AJ asked.

"We trust our sources. We have a plan." Rhiannon said. "However, if you choose to come with us, you will be in danger. We understand if you choose to sit this one out."

"Will the Fist be joining us?" Cindy asked.

"No." Rhiannon replied. "He needs to be here. Downtown is on the brink of a gang war, he says he can't leave now. This one is all on us."

The group fell into contemplation. Cindy was the first to speak up.

"I'm in." she said. "It's about time we stood up and did something major."

Ricardo and AJ nodded in agreement.

"We can take my partner's van." Cindy said. "She won't mind."

"Brilliant." Rhiannon said.

She dropped the folder on the coffee table.

"You will all need to take a look at this. This is all the information we have on the deportations. It's not much, but it'll have to be enough. There's something else we need. In this book, we have the information on every single person being deported tonight. Some of them have friends and family in the UK. If their family information is in the file, call them. If not, we need to search the phone books, search social media, search any way we can to find the contact details for these people. Let them know what is happening. Tell them to be at Portside International Airport at 3PM, with cameras, if they are able and willing, to try and expose what is happening here. Louis and I are going to head to the central offices of every national news network based in Downtown City with all the information we have, and make sure they are all there too. The more witnesses, the more chance we have of catching them red-handed. This needs to be timed perfectly: if they catch wind that they're about to be exposed, they will reschedule the deportation and our information will appear fake."

Cindy nodded, picking up the information pack, and Ricardo and AJ moved closer to peer in at it.

"This is big." Ricardo muttered. "We should call some of the activist groups in Portside."

"Call anyone you can." Rhiannon replied. "So long as we can trust them."

***

Zakirah sat, watching a group of the women in the facility playing cards together. They had invited her to play, but she preferred to just watch. She liked studying the expressions on people's faces when they received their cards, feeling the tension rise and fall at the climactic parts. She didn't know what game they were playing, but it didn't take her long to pick up how it worked. A month of being stuck in that facility had given her a lot of time to work out how all the different card games worked. This one seemed to be a game based around bluffing: players placed cards corresponding to the cards that were last placed down, and if they chose to, they could lie about the cards they placed. If they got caught lying, they had to pick up the whole pile. The objective was to get rid of all your cards.

Zakirah was so engrossed in the game that she did not notice the facility security open the locked, armoured door at the end of the hall, or the line of police officers who marched in. At the front of the line, a man in a shirt and tie, carrying a clipboard, clapped his hands to gain the attention of the room. The sound echoed through the hall, and everyone turned to look at him.

"Alright ladies!" he called out. "If I say your name, please come and stand in the empty space in front of me."

He cleared his throat, lifting the clipboard up so he could see it more clearly.

"Fatima Abbasi."

One of the women at the other end of the room stood up, wobbling with uncertainty, and wandered over to the empty space.

"Hessa Amir."

A much younger woman, from within the group of women around Zakirah, stood, dropping her cards, and marched over with her head held high. The man continued to read names, and one by one women from around the room started to walk over. It didn't take long for a pattern to emerge: the room was full or all sorts of different women, from a range of ethnic backgrounds, but the women being called forwards were Asian, and mostly from the same collection of countries: Syria, Lebanon, Iraq, Iran, Pakistan, and so on.

"Zakirah Bashir."

Zakirah's head shot up.

What did this mean? Was she being released?

Something told her it was unlikely.

All these women being from the same area of the world meant one, dark likelihood.

Deportation.

233

The man continued to read names as Zakirah stood and walked towards the front of the hall, her brain zoning out, her body on autopilot.

"Priti Chanda."

The young woman who had been brought in the day after Zakirah stood, shaking uncontrollably, and began to walk forwards. Her legs could barely carry her, she was so frightened. Zakirah rushed to her side and put an arm around her.

"It's okay." she whispered. "We're going to be alright."

Together, the two women walked to the front, and waited with dread to see what would happen.

***

Iona sat in the doctor's office, her mind a blur as the doctor placed the test results down on the desk and stared sympathetically across at her.

"I'm sorry it took us so long to process your results. We have been swamped recently, and our department is severely underfunded… Unfortunately it seems that the cancer is worse than before." Dr Patel said. "Your only real option at this stage is another round of chemotherapy, as soon as possible."

Iona sobbed, placing a hand on her forehead.

"I can't do it, doc." she said. "I can't go through that again. It's too much."

"If you don't go through another round of chemotherapy, the cancer will progress." Dr Patel said.

"How long?" Iona asked.

"Could be a few months or a few years, but I would expect your health to take a turn for the worse within the next month or so." Dr Patel leant forwards in her chair. "Listen, Iona, you're a bright young woman. And your lifestyle is healthy. I strongly advise you to take the chemotherapy treatments. You'll be more prepared for it this time. Trust me, you can do this."

"I don't know that I can." Iona replied, remembering the hell she had been through with her previous round of chemotherapy, and how weak and fragile she had felt. Every moment had been like a waking death: it was the most debilitating thing she had ever been through.

"Take some time to think about it." Dr Patel said. "I'm going to make you an appointment for Friday. We'll set up a treatment plan then."

Iona was not thinking about chemotherapy, though. Her mind was already on something else: the invention she had come up with so no one would ever have to go through what she went through ever again.

**

Rhiannon stood in the reception area of the UK Broadcasting Network. Around her, interns rushed to and fro, and reporters and journalists gathered in the lobby, but heads turned as the automatic doors slid open to reveal Rhiannon, clad in her balaclava and giant goggles, with the new prototype gauntlets and massive boots on, both lit up with a subtle, yellow glow.

"I need to talk to whoever is in charge." Rhiannon called out, and as she stepped towards the reception, two security guards rushed down the hall and placed themselves either side of her.

"Ma'am, we're going to need you to take off the gauntlets." one of them said.

"I'm not here to hurt anyone." Rhiannon said. "But something big is about to go down, and you guys are going to want someone there to report on it."

"Don't make me ask twice." the security guard warned her. "I will call the police."

Rhiannon slipped off the gauntlets and walked forward, placing them on the reception desk and ignoring the two guards.

"You have one of the Fists of Justice standing in your reception." she said to the receptionist. "Almost every news story for the last month has been about our group. What do you think your boss is going to say if he hears you ignored an opportunity to have your network get exclusive footage of the Fists of Justice in action?"

The receptionist indicated to the security guards to step back, and picked up the phone.

"Mrs Turner…" she said. "Yeah, you're going to want to come and see this."

***

Louis sat in the office for the CEO of Downtown News Networks TV studios, and in front of them, Richard Davies, the CEO, stared down at the folder, his brow furrowed. Louis had his bandanna over his face and was staring at the man, who seemed to be processing the information. In front of him, a duplicate of the information pack containing everything about the deportation scandal.

"So you're telling me that the government is illegally detaining and deporting people without following the proper process, snatching them up at random and just flying them out of the country?" the man said, his voice sounding very much unconvinced.

"It wouldn't be the first time. Governments all across the western world have done things like this countless times." Louis said. "You can choose to believe us or not, but the Fists of Justice are going to stop it. If you want to be the first news network to get exclusive footage of the situation, and the Fists of Justice in action, I'd recommend you send a camera crew with us."

The man sighed.

"I don't generally listen to people who climb in through my window and lock me in their office with them, but you make a good point." he said. "You can take a van, I'll send a small team to report. This better be good."

***

"Jason, I need to know where you put it."

"Iona, please, just st-stop and think about this."

Iona searched frantically through the garage, opening cupboards and tipping out drawers, growing increasingly more frustrated.

"Jason, this is my only hope." she exclaimed. "I can't go through chemo again. I just can't! This is what I made it for! And it works!"

"It worked once." Jason said. "We don't know if Louis was a fluke. The NanoVirus had so many unexpected side-effects.

236

Who knows if it will b-be the same for each p-person?"

"It's better than death." Iona replied, halting in her search to look at Jason.

Jason fell into silence, slumping back in his chair, defeated.

"I made the NanoVirus for people like us." Iona said. "And now it's gone and my research has been shut down, but I can still save myself, and if it works, we might even be able to use it to help you walk properly, without crutches."

"Not if it means risking our lives." Jason replied.

"We've *been* risking our lives trying to make the city a better place. If I don't do something, the cancer will spread and I will die. And I just can't take chemotherapy. This isn't me risking my life, it's me saving it."

Jason sighed, but eventually, he nodded. He reached beneath his work table and pulled out a small toolbox. Inside, the electronic stand holding the vials of NanoVirus was nestled, padded with some newspaper and ice packs. Jason plugged the stand into his laptop, tapping away at the keys. Next to the NanoVirus, in the case, was a syringe. Jason pulled it out, filling it up from one of the vials.

"You ready?" he said, holding up the syringe.

"No." Iona admitted. "But do it anyway."

Jason injected the pale blue liquid into Iona's arm. She winced as the needle pierced the skin, and Jason pulled out a little plaster to put over the hole.

"How do you feel?" he asked.

"I don't know." Iona replied. "Good, I think? I don't really feel different."

"Well, you should take it easy for the next couple of days. Maybe you should stay with me so I can keep an eye on you."

"I've already signed on as a research assistant for someone else's project. I need to keep busy." Iona replied. "Come over to mine this evening."

"Fine." Jason said. "But t-take it easy. If you notice anything strange, c-c-call me."

"I'm the one who invented the NanoVirus." Iona pointed out. "I know what I'm doing."

"I don't mean to patronise you, I'm just worried."

"I know, Jason." Iona said, kissing him on the forehead.

"Thank you for supporting me with this decision. I'll see you later."

She turned and left the garage, and as she did, she already felt different: not physically but mentally, like a huge weight had been lifted from her shoulders. The air felt fresher. The city seemed brighter. And suddenly, the world was full of possibilities, and nothing was holding her back.

***

Zakirah and the other women were led out of the building and towards a coach, and as she was led out, Zakirah got a look at the building she had been in for the first time: when she had been brought here initially it had been night, but now she could see the exterior of the building during the day. It was a great, brick building, completely surrounded by fences topped with barbed wire, in the middle of nowhere. The sign outside read 'DOWNTOWN CITY IMMIGRATION DETENTION AND REMOVAL CENTRE' but it didn't look to be anywhere near Downtown City. They were in an area of desolate countryside, surrounded by the most dreary and pitiful crop fields Zakirah had ever seen.

The coach was already partially occupied with a bunch of men who looked to be in the same situation as the women: handcuffed and looking a mixture of frightened and depressed.

The women had their cuffs checked one by one and were given a pat-down by a police officer as they were led onto the coach. As Zakirah stepped in for her turn, she made eye contact with the police officer, focusing all her concentration on the woman.

"Take off my cuffs." she said.

The woman looked back at her, cocked her head to one side, and smiled.

"Yeah, not going to happen I'm afraid." she said, and pat her down. "Clear, on the bus with you."

Zakirah cursed internally. Perhaps she had been imagining it. Perhaps it wasn't her who influenced Johnny Johnson to jump off the bridge. Perhaps she'd hallucinated it. Perhaps he'd just had a sudden mental breakdown. All she knew was that she

238

hadn't had any more good luck, nor had she been able to make anyone do anything, since the protest.

Once on board the coach, she saw the two men that had been taken at the attack on the mosque, over a month ago now. They looked exhausted, not just physically but mentally, and completely drained of any hope.

Zakirah knew she had to do something. She couldn't stand idle. She had gone through so much effort to get to this country. And yes, it wasn't perfect. It wasn't at all what she had imagined. But it was safe. And perhaps she hadn't built a real home here yet, but many of these people had, and they didn't deserve to be torn from those homes.

She just didn't know what to do.

CHAPTER FIFTEEN: PORTSIDE

Portside International Airport was a desolate, backwater airport with only one terminal and runway. It was obvious why the government had chosen it: it was in the middle of nowhere, and very few people chose to get flights in or out of there. It was called Portside Airport, but in reality it was over an hour from Portside City. It was surrounded by fields of crops, and the road that led to the airport barely classified as a motorway. Cindy's van arrived first, pulling off the main road and halting in a small layby that looked across the fields towards the airport. The activists could be seen inside, wearing various face coverings. Rhiannon pulled up in her car a minute or so later, with another car following close behind. Out of the second car stepped a reporter with a camera in his hands, immediately rushing to the fence to take a few quick photos of the airport, followed by a much bigger, bearded man, with a full film camera with a microphone mounted to the top sat on his shoulder. Behind him, a van with the Downtown News Network logo along the side pulled up, and Louis and Ricardo stepped out.

"They're going to see us coming from a mile away." Louis muttered.

"We'll have to go by foot from here." Rhiannon said. "Louis and I will go and check things out, see how much security there is, how busy the airport is. The rest of you, wait here for our call."

The activists nodded, and Rhiannon and Louis hopped the fence and started walking across the fields towards the airport. The big bearded man with a camera mounted on his shoulder was quick to follow, lurking behind and filming them as they

240

went.

It took them about fifteen minutes to make it to the outskirts of the airstrip. The airport was surrounded by high fences, and Rhiannon and Louis followed the perimeter round. As they got closer to the road again and reached the entrance to the airport, they started to see signs saying '**Airport closed for maintenance. All flights rerouted to Dockland City Airport. No admittance except employees.**'

A single plane could be seen on the runway, and two airport employees in hard hats and yellow high vis jackets were carrying out safety checks.

Louis and Rhiannon crouched down behind a bush, facing one another.

"This is where it gets real." she said. "We need to make sure that the coach never makes it into the airport, but if they do, we need to make sure those people are not deported. Louis, you need to get on board that plane. Stay hidden until you receive the signal. No matter what, it's your job to make sure that plane does not take off."

"What if there's too many police for us to handle?" Louis asked. "What if a fight breaks out and I'm not there to protect our team?"

"We only have one shot at this." Rhiannon replied. "We need this to work. You're the only one who can stop that plane from taking off alone."

"Okay." Louis sighed. "I trust your judgement."

Rhiannon turned and started heading towards the main road, beckoning the cameraman to follow.

"What's he doing?" the bearded man asked.

"Don't worry about him." Rhiannon said. "If you want to see the real action, follow me."

Louis waited until Rhiannon and the cameraman were out of view, and pulled a set of bolt cutters out of his backpack. A couple of snips with the bolt cutters and Louis was able to slip under the fence. His bandanna clung to his face as he breathed heavily in and out. His hood cast him in shadow. His dark clothes kept him from being spotted at a distance, but he was still incredibly tall, and getting all the way across the airstrip to the plane without being seen was going to be a challenge. Louis stayed low, his heart racing, sweat dripping down his body. Over a thousand metres between him and the plane. The two airport maintenance men had their backs turned to him. The plane was right up near the terminal, with only a few hundred metres between it and the entrance. Around it, there were a few other planes that were tucked idly into their bays, but this was the only one being prepared for takeoff. There were giant baggage trolleys and sets of steps on wheels scattered around. Louis sprinted, heading directly for a set of steps on wheels that were placed between him and the plane, hoping to use it for cover. He got there just in time, tucking away behind it as one of the airport employees turned around and started walking around the plane. Louis poked his head out, his heart racing so fast he could hear it in his ears. As the man disappeared out of view again, Louis made a dash for a giant, empty baggage trolley, and from there was able to tuck himself away behind one of those golf carts the airport staff used to get around quickly.

One of the men went back inside the airport, and the other walked up the steps and onto the plane. Louis took his chance, making the final dash up the ramp and into the cargo hold of the plane.

And he was out of view.

Louis tucked himself away in a corner and took a moment to catch his breath. It was more the excitement than the physical exertion that had him sweating and trembling. He was used to taking risks for the cause, but this was like nothing he had done before.

He slipped behind a shelf filled with bags and boxes with a generic airline logo on them. He leant back against the wall, closing his eyes, and tried his best to pretend he was anywhere else.

Back at the cars, Rhiannon gathered the activists and news crews around her. A few other cars had appeared, containing confused and worried looking relatives of deportees, and a few local activists with their cameras ready to livestream. Ricardo and Cindy had explained to the newcomers what was going on, and they stood nearby and listened to Rhiannon, some

242

muttering to each other under their breaths. All in all there were about thirty of them now, and one or two other cars were on approach. Ricardo went to flag them down. One of the cars contained Naveed, the comic store owner from Downtown City, and a few Muslims from the local mosque. The other car was driven by the imam himself.

"We have more coming." the imam said as he got out of the car. "I spread the word. Our community is sending as many people as can come."

Rhiannon nodded, and turned to the group of activists surrounding her.

"This junction is the only way into the airport." Rhiannon said. "And this road doesn't lead anywhere but the airport. We need to stop that coach before it reaches the airport, but after it's made the turning off towards the entranceway. The best place to stop them would be at the sign, just ahead, which says 'PORTSIDE INTERNATIONAL'. That way, all the camera crews will have the perfect backdrop of the airport: there won't be any way to deny where we are. We need to stop the coach and deal with the police entourage. They will be armed. We will create a blockade across the road, and I will deal with the police. Everyone else is to stay behind the line until the police are dealt with. I don't want anyone to get hurt. Is that understood?"

A series of nods. Some of the news crews looked a little concerned.

"Rhiannon." Ricardo pointed towards the road. Coming down the motorway, on approach to the junction, was a coach, with a police van in front and two police cars behind.

"That's them." Rhiannon muttered. "They're early. Alright everyone, in the bushes. It's go time."

Cindy went to the back of the van and pulled out a long, metal coil, filled with the same spikes that had been used to stop the homeless perching on walls, now fashioned into traffic spikes. Her and Rhiannon rushed to put it across the road at the narrowest point. The news crews quickly rushed to find the best spot at the side of the road, turning their cameras on Rhiannon and the activists. Rhiannon saw one of the reporters go for his phone, sneaking off behind one of the news vans.

243

"Hello, police?" she heard him say. She ignored it. It was too late now anyway.

***

Zakirah's eyes scanned the horizon as the coach made the turning off the motorway and towards the airport. There was no possible sign of escape, and her heart started to race as they drew closer to the airport. Through the window, she could see the entrance to the airport in the distance. There were police and airport security guards everywhere. The airport was deserted of all civilians and tourists, the car park empty. There was only one plane, waiting on the runway.

Zakirah closed her eyes and did something she hadn't done in a long time: She started to pray. She wasn't praying to any god in particular: not to Allah or Jesus, but instead just to any higher being that might be able to hear her.

Please, please, please, please. Give us some hope. Give us some chance for freedom. Please.

She was sure she felt something, but it wasn't external, but from within her: something stirring that she hadn't felt since the bridge.

Something mysterious. Something powerful. She wasn't sure how she knew, but suddenly she felt more certain than she had ever been of anything else in her life that the power she had came from within her: it was *her* power, she didn't owe it to anyone, and she was the one who controlled it. She didn't know how, or why her, but she was sure she could channel it again.

***

Louis stood at the top of a ladder in the middle of the cargo hold and slowly opened a hatch that led into the main section of the plane. When he poked his head through, he found himself in the staff only section, just beyond the passenger entrance, with the cockpit just ahead. The cockpit door was open, and the pilot and co-pilot had just entered.

Louis pulled himself out of the hatch and reached into his backpack, his hand clasping around the handle of a gun. He felt self-doubt niggling at the back of his mind, but there was no turning back now. He couldn't let Rhiannon down. Taking a deep breath, he lurched forward into the cockpit.

"Freeze!" he yelled. "This plane is not going anywhere!"

The co-pilot spun around, saw the gun, and screamed, throwing her hands in the air.

Louis closed the door to the cockpit and locked it from the inside. He pointed his gun at the pilot, jabbing it into his neck.

"What do you want?" the co-pilot whispered, her hands still in the air.

"To make sure those people you're deporting today are given the proper chance to challenge their deportation, and not just snatched up and flown away to another country with no notice." Louis replied.

"These people weren't informed they were being deported?" the captain frowned. "That can't be right!"

Louis pulled the folder full of information out of his backpack and handed it to them, gun still in his hands.

"See for yourselves. You don't have to believe it." Louis growled. "But this plane is not taking off. Now, either you're going to tell me how I can make sure this plane can't take off, or I'm going to stay here and make sure it doesn't."

***

The traffic spikes did not catch the police van off-guard: they saw them just in time, screeching to a halt. One of the officers stepped out of the van, frowning ahead, his hand on his taser. He held a hand up to the coach, indicating that they should stop, and several more officers got out the back of the van. As they were getting out of the van, AJ dashed into the middle of the road, a white plastic face mask covering their face, a paint grenade in their hands. They tossed the paint grenade into the centre of the cops and legged it down the road, into a section of trees.

The police officers panicked as the grenade landed at their feet, instinctively diving for cover, only to be showered with paint.

"Hey, you, stop!" one of the police officers yelled out, and a handful of the officers chased AJ into the trees.

Behind the coach, Rhiannon and Louis' car was the only one left in the layby, and it sprung into life, skidding onto the road, Ricardo in the driver's seat. He leant out the window, balaclava covering his face, paintball gun in his hands, and shot at the two police cars from behind, showering one of them with paint, then made a quick u-turn, the tyres screeching as he turned the car suddenly around and sped back towards the junction. The police car didn't hesitate in spinning around and following him away from the coach. Unfortunately for them, as soon as the car had gone past, Cindy had snuck in behind them and laid down a second line of traffic spikes. Ricardo had known exactly where they were and easily avoided them, but the police car went straight over them, the front tyres both popping, and the car skidded off the road. The two police officers inside were hit hard by the airbags, one of them knocked unconscious.

"No, no, no!" the one officer remaining in front of the van groaned. "They're picking us off! It's a trap!"

He went for his radio, pressing down the button, but before he could speak, Rhiannon appeared on the road in front of him, stamping her heavy booted foot down, hard, on the ground. The boot lit up with yellow light, and a wave of energy burst from it, directed down the road at the police car and van. As the energy wave touched the van, the lights went out. It did the same to the police car behind. The energy wave fizzled out, but it had done its job.

"Directional Electromagnetic Pulse!" Rhiannon called over to the police officer. "Fries all the electronic items it touches. Your radio won't be working now."

The officer went for his taser, and Rhiannon put her hands in the air. The two remaining officers in the van and the two officers in the police car behind had exited their vehicles and were heading towards her now, all pointing tasers at her.

"We're not here to hurt you." Rhiannon called over to them. "In fact, we're here to do your job for you: enforce the law. These deportations are illegal, and we're here to make sure these people are given the proper chance to challenge the deportation before being shipped away."

"Put down the gauntlets!" the lead officer shouted, unwavering as he stepped slowly towards her.

"I don't know if you want to shoot me in front of all these witnesses!" Rhiannon said, her voice calm. She indicated behind the coach. The empty police car behind was now quickly being approached by the line of witnesses and camera crews, as well as reporters frantically explaining to the cameras, which had just gone live, what was going on. Some of the family and friends of the deportees were holding cardboard signs, a few of which Rhiannon could now make out. One read 'PEOPLE ARE NOT ILLEGAL'. Another read 'ONE PEOPLE, ONE PLANET.'

The road was blocked by a line of vans from the news studios. The car that had crashed now had one conscious officer, who stood alone, watching the line of people appear from the trees and bushes at the side of the road and frantically calling for backup on the radio, being the only officer out of range of Rhiannon's EMP.

Some of the police officers turned to look at the line of approaching cameras, calling to them to stop, and Rhiannon took her chance. Bringing her gauntlets out in front of her, she clapped. The sound was like thunder, a clap no human could have generated, but that wasn't the most impressive part: a wave of kinetic energy burst from her gauntlets, larger than any Alex's gauntlets had ever generated, throwing the police officers several feet into the air and sending them sprawling across the road. Rhiannon rushed over to the commanding officer, placing a boot on his chest and pointing her gauntlet at him. One of the other officers clambered hurriedly to their feet, pointing their taser at her, and she pointed her other gauntlet quickly at them. A bolt of electricity shot from her fingertips, hitting the officer's taser and causing it to fizzle and spark. The officer yelped, dropping the device, and Rhiannon hit them with a blast of kinetic energy, knocking them down.

"Tell your men to stand down." Rhiannon growled. "No one has to get hurt here."

"I don't know what you've heard, but these deportations are all completely legal and in line with regulatory requirements." the man said, struggling under her boot.

"This isn't a negotiation." Rhiannon said. "Tell them to stand down. Now."

The officer looked over at his people, reluctantly waving his hand at them.

247

"Stand down." he called. "Stand down, too many civilians."
Rhiannon grinned.
"Stay where you are." she said. "I don't want to hurt you, but I will if you force my hand."

***

Inside the plane, the pilot and co-pilot flipped through the folder.
"This is insane." the co-pilot muttered. "I had no idea…"
The pilot turned to look at Louis.
"We have nothing to do with this, I swear, we didn't-" he stopped in his tracks, frowning, and suddenly a look of realisation crossed his face. There was a mix of confusion, realisation, relief, and then anger. "Hey, that gun isn't real!"
"Test me and find out!" Louis growled.
The pilot stood up.
"No, it really isn't!" he exclaimed. "It says Airsoft on the side!"
Louis cursed, lowering the gun. His deception now revealed, his confidence wavered.
"Does it matter?" he asked. "Now that you know, do you really want to be the pilot who carried this out? There's a line of reporters out there, filming everything."
The pilot was unconvinced, and he lurched towards the hatch. Louis grabbed him and threw him forcefully back into his seat, where he landed with a grunt.
"Don't test me, mate." Louis said. "I may not be armed but I'm far stronger than you."
"Stan, I don't want to be a part of this." the co-pilot said. "It's just wrong."
Louis' eyes searched the cockpit for some way of making sure the plane didn't take off. He was sure he didn't have much time before he was caught.

***

Zakirah watched in shock as the coach opened and the woman with the giant metal fists stepped on, grabbing the first security guard by the scruff of his jacket and tossing him off the coach. The other security guard rushed forwards, but the woman grabbed him with her gauntlet, and an electrical current flowed

248

into him, causing him to spasm and drop to the ground. The driver raised his hands into the air.

"They don't pay me enough for this." he said. "Do whatever you want, just don't hurt me."

The woman stood at the front of the coach and stared at the deportees.

"Don't be alarmed!" she called out. "We are sorry for everything you have gone through. Our government has wronged you: they were going to deport you without giving you the proper chance to challenge the deportation order. That's not how we do things here! We are here to make sure your voices are heard! Outside is a line of camera crews from various news networks around the country. They are here to hear your stories, so that we can expose what you've been through! I am asking for anyone who is willing to come out and talk to them to step forward now! Do not be afraid. We will make sure you are not deported today!"

Zakirah was on her feet without a moment's hesitation, while the others were still mumbling to one another.

"I'll do it." she said. "I'll talk to them."

"What's your name?" the mysterious woman asked.

"Zakirah Bashir." Zakirah replied.

"Come forward, Zakirah." Rhiannon said. "Anyone else?"

A man stood up.

"Hello, yes." he said. "I am Hussein. Hussein Isa. I will speak to the cameras."

One by one, a handful of other deportees stood up, and the woman led a cluster of about ten of them off the coach.

Outside, the police officers had been cuffed to the handles of their own cars by their own handcuffs, their hands behind their backs. Towards the airport, a line of airport security guards and police officers had started to realise something was up and were rushing up the road towards the halted vehicles.

The mysterious woman indicated towards the line of reporters, some of whom rushed forwards to interview the deportees.

"Don't worry about the police." she said. "I will deal with them."

One of the reporters was already talking to Hussein, a microphone shoved in his face, and he was giving his story.

"I assisted the British special forces in Syria as a translator, and in return I was told I would be allowed to come here and seek refuge. The application process took me two years. I have only been here for six months, living in Downtown City, but a month ago, when giving a statement to the police about an attack on our local mosque, the police told me that they had found an error in my paperwork, and that I was here illegally, and carted me away."

"Were you informed in writing of the deportation?" the reporter asked.

"No."

"Were you given a chance to challenge it?"

"No."

Rhiannon brought her radio to her face, pressing the button. "Alright guys, make yourselves scarce." she said. "This is the endgame now. You've done what you can do. I'll hold them off a little longer, then we have to trust that what we've exposed so far will be enough to shut this whole deportation project down."

In the distance, sirens blazed, as police thundered down the motorway, towards the commotion.

***

Back on the runway, Louis' eyes found what he was looking for: A fire extinguisher, and above it a case with a glass panel on the front that said 'BREAK IN CASE OF EMERGENCY'. Behind the glass: a fire axe.

Louis smashed the glass and pulled out the axe, swinging it with all his might into the control panel of the aeroplane. The pilot yelped, shrinking back in his chair, and Louis wrenched the axe out. Sparks flew from the massive, gaping wound in the control panel, and Louis swung again. With his increased strength, the axe buried itself deep into the panel.

Three or four more strikes, and the panel was in tatters.

Louis turned back to the exit to the cockpit, leaving the pilot and co-pilot shaking in their seats. He wrenched the door open and headed straight for the steps that led off the plane. On the runway, two airport security guards were walking towards the plane. As soon as they saw Louis, their hands went to their guns.

"Stop!" they called out. "Freeze!"

Louis threw himself over the railing on the steps, his knees bending as he landed on the runway with a thud. The officers went for their weapons, and Louis' eyes flickered between the fence at the end of the runway, and the two airport security guards, armed and heading towards him. He made a decision, sprinting towards the first of the guards and tackling him, wrenching the gun from his hands and sending him toppling to the ground. The other officer turned and aimed his own gun, but Louis was too quick, smashing his fist into the officer's chest. The officer groaned, keeling over, clutching his chest. Louis turned and sprinted towards the fence at the far end of the runway. From behind, there was another shout, then rapid-fire gunshots. Pain exploded through Louis' back and leg. He cried out, and suddenly he was on the ground.

Three bullets had hit him: one in the back, one in the side, one in the leg.

Louis groaned as airport security and police closed in on him. His vision blurred, fading in and out.

***

A line of police cars sped down the road, coming to a halt behind the lines of protesters and reporters, and within seconds officers were rushing out of the cars, batons in hand, screaming at the protesters and reporters to disperse.

Zakirah's eyes caught sight of the familiar face of Asim, amongst some of the others from the mosque, towards the back of the crowd. The police officers advanced through the crowd, pushing people to one side, targeting some of the more unruly protesters by grabbing them and handcuffing them.

"GET DOWN ON THE GROUND!" one of the police officers yelled.

"HANDS BEHIND YOUR HEAD!" another screamed.

"ON THE GROUND! HANDS BEHIND YOUR HEAD!"

"PUT YOUR HANDS IN THE AIR!"

"GET DOWN! GET DOWN OR WE WILL SHOOT!"

"STOP WHERE YOU ARE!"

251

Zakirah was hit by a wall of sound, their words pelting at her from every angle, and she felt utterly trapped, frozen in place. "Stop!" she whimpered. "Please stop!"

One of the police officers surged towards her, raising a baton above his head.

"STOP!" Zakirah screamed, flinching and throwing her arms up in front of her.

The blow never landed.

Zakirah lowered her arms, her heart still pounding. Around her, the semicircle of police officers had all just... stopped. They were frozen in place, silent and unmoving, some of them even half-way through a word, but now just standing still, doing nothing but breathing. Zakirah's eyes moved from one police officer to the other. One of them wobbled on the spot. Another blinked. Another's eyes flickered about to look at his colleagues.

But none of them moved. And it wasn't just them: the reporters, the protesters... Everyone had just stopped, and were frozen in place.

Above Zakirah's head was a blinding light, and when she cast her eyes up to see it, she found that it was coming from her: a stream of light bursting from her body and into the air, coming down in an umbrella that bathed the officers and the crowd around her in light, and the light held them in place.

Zakirah turned to look back at the mysterious woman, facing off against the line of advancing police and security guards. They were still moving.

"It worked." Zakirah breathed. "I do have power."

The sun was beginning to set now, and though lights lit up the airport and the many vehicle lights lit up the road, much of what Rhiannon could see in the distance was just silhouettes now.

There was the sudden sound of distant yelling, and then three loud bangs. Gunshots, across the runway. Rhiannon's head snapped round, and she saw airport security and police sprinting across the runway.

"Louis." she breathed. "No!"

There was nothing she could do for him. She had to trust his powers would protect him.

"ON THE GROUND, NOW!" The shout came from a police officer at the front of the advancing group. Behind, Rhiannon could hear distant sirens as countless police cars sped up the motorway, towards the chaos. Countless weapons were pointed at her now, and she wasn't sure if her gauntlets and boots were any match. She prepared to make a stand.

The officers were no more than twenty metres away now, and a line of handguns and tasers were pointed directly at Rhiannon. Behind her, there was chaos as more police cars arrived and started arresting people.

Rhiannon raised her gauntlets, and just as she prepared to clap, a figure shot past her, placing herself between Rhiannon and the police officers.

It was Zakirah, panting heavily, her heart racing. Her skin was shining, light escaping from every inch of her, even shining through her clothes. She took in a deep breath, raising her handcuffed hands in front of her, and screamed.

"**STOP!**"

The police officers and security guards halted in their tracks, frozen to the spot. One even had his foot raised into the air to take a step forward. The foot never landed. And then, in an instant, they all collapsed: and not just them but the ones behind, and the crowd of reporters, and everyone except for Zakirah and Rhiannon. And then the light was gone.

"Incredible!" Rhiannon breathed. "How did you do that?" Rhiannon turned to look at her. A trail of blood leaked from her nose. Her face was pale.

"I don't know." she muttered. "I don't... Feel so good." Rhiannon quickly wrapped an arm around her as she slumped, her legs wobbling.

"Quickly, let's get you out of here before they start moving again." she muttered.

She helped Zakirah rush away from the collapsed people, heading straight past the line of now unoccupied police cars. She pulled her radio up to her face again.

"Cindy, double back, pick me up, I need help."

Zakirah drifted from consciousness, as behind them everyone

started to move again, regaining consciousness and finding themselves all lying on the ground. At the end of the road, at the junction, Cindy's van sped into view, and Rhiannon rushed towards it, fully carrying Zakirah now. Behind them, everyone was slowly gaining the ability to move again, and they were all taking a moment to figure out what was going on, but Rhiannon knew they didn't have long. No time to ask questions. They needed to run.

***

In. Lights. Blurry shapes.
"Is he injured?"
One of the police officers bent over Louis, checking him over. His super-healing was all that kept him conscious, but the bullet-holes were still bleeding.
"He's hit! Get the medic!"
Out. Blackness.

In.
Louis lifted onto a stretcher, surrounded by police, and an ambulance sped onto the airstrip, the lights causing swirls in his vision.
Out. Darkness.

In. Flashes. Blinding light.
A line of police officers held back reporters as the ambulance headed through the gates. Their voices were muffled by the doors of the ambulance.
Out.

As the ambulance sprung to life, so did Louis. Two of the bullet wounds were through shots, where the bullets had entered one side of his body and exited the other, and the NanoVirus wasted no time healing up those holes, leaving only the slightest scars. But the bullet that hit his back was still lodged there, and as the bullet-hole closed in around the bullet, pain tore through Louis' back again and he screamed.
The driver of the ambulance yelped and swerved dramatically, and Louis sat up on the stretcher, the paramedic and two police

254

officers jumping back. One police officer instinctively went for his gun, and Louis ripped his hands free of the handcuffs, breaking the chain as if it was paper, and took the gun straight out of his hands.

"Pull over!" he yelled, pointing the gun at the driver.

The ambulance screeched to a halt just past the junction, and Louis threw the back doors open, sprinting out into the road. They had taken his backpack, but his phone was still in his pocket, and he dialled Rhiannon as he ran. He sprinted along the side of the road, but he was by a motorway now, and there was no path to run along. The occasional car or lorry sped past, the drivers staring at him, dumbfounded, as he sprinted past at the side of the motorway.

***

"Pull up all the cameras along the airstrip and outside the main entrance!"

The head of security at the airport stormed in the security office, his face red with rage, a cluster of police officers stood behind him, each on the phone to a different office: the local police departments, MI6, and all the different local authorities in the area. In front of him, a technician was typing frantically at his computer, a row of blank screens in front of him.

"All our cameras are down, sir." the technician said. "Even the traffic cameras. The feeds have been switched-"

"Switched?! What do you mean, switched?!" the man roared.

"Sir, it appears instead of transmitting a live security feed, they're now transmitting… Looney Tunes."

He flicked one of the screens on, and a string of cartoons appeared, flashing bright, comical images. The image spread across all the screens, until every security feed was filled with cartoons. Then, as quickly as they had appeared, they all disappeared, and a single textbox appeared.

'THANKS FOR PLAYING! BETTER LUCK NEXT TIME!

REGARDS, GREY HAT.'

***

The night was well underway when Rhiannon and her activist team, including their new companion, reached Downtown City again. They mostly drove in silence, attempting to process everything, and even once they were safe in Rhiannon and Louis' front room once again, they still sat and stared at each other, silent and wide-eyed. It was AJ who spoke first, standing and pacing up and down the room.

"That was insane." they said. "Absolutely insane!"

"I need food…" Zakirah muttered, underneath her breath. "I'm starving."

"I can't believe they didn't catch us or stop us." Ricardo muttered.

"It was insane!" Louis replied. "The police seemed to just miss us at every turn. It's as if someone was looking out for us, deliberately putting them off our scent."

"Wouldn't surprise me." Rhiannon said. "Louis, are you okay? You've been grimacing since we picked you up."

"I was shot." Louis replied. "But I think I'm fine."

"You were shot?!" Cindy exclaimed. "Let me see."

"I'm fine." Louis repeated.

"Louis, you know I'm a nurse, just let me take a look."

"Oh my god!" exclaimed AJ, turning to Zakirah. "I remember you now! From outside the mosque! They called you the Miracle Girl!"

Zakirah blushed and nodded.

"That's me… Has anyone got any food?"

Ricardo pulled out a couple of whole food protein bars and tossed them to Zakirah, who tore open the packets and hungrily devoured them one after the other, and as she did some of the colour seemed to return to her face.

Cindy walked over to where Louis was sitting, and he lifted up his shirt, showing the bullet wounds. The one in his leg and the one in his side had gone straight through, and now only scars remained. But the one in his back was still in there, and the bullet wound had closed around it, leaving a horrific, raised, purple bruise covering a large portion of his back.

"I don't… what?" she stammered.

"It's a long story." Louis said. "I was injected with an experimental serum… Now I heal really fast, but one of the bullet-holes has healed… with the bullet still in there."

256

"You're special, like me." Zakirah breathed.

"Like you?" Louis frowned. "What do you mean?"

"It looks like the bullet is still travelling slowly towards your spine. That's why it hurts so much. We need to take that out." Cindy said, pressing the area around the healed-up bullet hole. "It could do some real damage. Even with your healing, it's best taken out. How well do you heal?"

"I just healed from three bullet-wounds in under two hours, you tell me." Louis replied.

"Right. That's good, that means we can take it out immediately, and you'll likely heal without having to go to the hospital… Have you got a sharp knife, some pliers, some disinfectant, some thread and a needle? Oh and a cloth or some bandages or something, for the bleeding." she asked. "Louis, you might want a drink."

Rhiannon rushed off to get what Cindy had asked for.

"Lie down." Cindy instructed Louis. "This is going to hurt, a lot."

She took the knife, disinfected it, and cut into his back. Louis cried out as the cold blade cut his skin. Cindy made a second cut, and Louis gritted his teeth. Then, the pliers. They were almost worse than the knife, rooting around in his back for a few seconds then-

Pop. Louis grimaced, tears rolling down his face.

The bullet was out. Cindy slapped the cloth over the wound, applying pressure.

"I'll take that drink now." Louis said through gritted teeth.

"I'll need to sew up the wound - oh my god." Cindy lifted the cloth to peer at the wound, but it had already started to close, and the flesh seemed to be knitting itself back together.

AJ nearly fainted. Ricardo turned and puked into a bin by the sofa.

The only person who didn't reel back in shock was Zakirah. She stepped in closer, peering at the wound, and inside, her heart lifted.

She wasn't the only one with powers. She wasn't alone.

CHAPTER SIXTEEN: BROKEN PEOPLE

Alex stood outside the abandoned warehouse the Bridge Boys had claimed as their hangout, staring through his goggles at the aftermath of what looked to have been a terrible fight. To his left, a car was on fire, the windows smashed in. To his right, a Bridge Boy lay unconscious on the ground, his suit tattered and bloodstained. In front, the doors to the warehouse had been torn open, and Alex could see inside. The sofas had been overturned, the television smashed in, the chairs destroyed, the cupboards emptied. Even the portable toilet cubicle had been knocked over. One or two Bridge Boys were still on their feet, tending to the wounded. Some had stab wounds, many had broken bones. One or two lay in the middle of the warehouse, either unconscious or dead, Alex couldn't tell. Ash and blood lingered in the air, and Alex grimaced as the scent invaded his nostrils.

"What's going on?" Jason's voice came through his earpiece.

"We're too late." Alex replied. "The fight is over. Looks like the Bovver Boys won."

He walked into the warehouse, clenching and unclenching his fists within the gauntlets. One of the Bridge Boys, Jeb limped over to him. He was bleeding from a gash on his head, and it looked like he may have dislocated his arm.

"Not now." he pleaded. "Come on man, it's not worth it."

"I'm not here to fight you." Alex said. "Where is Big Tuna?"

"They took him to the riverfront." Jeb pointed out the back door. "Please, I know you don't have any reason to listen to me, but don't let them kill him. He's a good man, alright? He really is."

Alex broke into a jog, heading out the back of the warehouse.

Sure enough, a line of Bovver Boys, in hoodies and football shirts, carrying bats and switchblades, stood at an old, abandoned dock. The sunrise over the horizon turned the two figures on the end of the dock into silhouettes, but Alex knew who they were. The big, bulky form of Johnny Johnson, held the scraggly, struggling Antonio Adkins out over the water. Alex touched the side of his goggles, zooming in to get a better look at them. A line of snot rolled down Antonio's face. His hat floated in the water behind him, his suit crinkled and covered in his sweat.

"*Easy, Alex.*" Jason said. "*There are too many of them. You should retreat.*"

"They'll kill Antonio." Alex said. "I have to try and stop them."

He walked towards the dock, heading straight for the line of Bovver Boys.

"That's enough!" he called.

The line of Bovver Boys parted, some of them muttering quietly as Alex walked past.

Johnny Johnson, known to the Bovver Boys as 'The Gov' turned his attention away from Antonio, his intense gaze falling on Alex.

"The Fist of Justice!" he exclaimed, releasing his grip on Antonio. "This is the point where we're all supposed to run away, right?"

He released his grip on Antonio, and he fell down onto the wooden panelling of the dock, grunting in pain.

"You know, I always knew it was only a matter of time before social justice warriors like you got a little too carried away with their saviour complex and started trying to be actual superheroes." Johnny said, waving his brass knuckles about emphatically as he spoke. "I've got to hand it to you, at least you're not one of these snowflakes, just crying on the internet all day. At least you've got up and tried to do something, made a stand for what you believe. It's just a shame that what you believe is a load of old bollocks."

"What I believe is that people deserve protection from bullies like you." Alex replied, walking up the dock so that they were only a few feet away from each other.

"I am the protection!" Johnny roared. "We are the protection! We protect this country from outside threats! We protect proud, British traditions from corruption and degeneracy! You come along with your fancy outfit and your metal fists, trying to do what's right, and you side with the wrong bloody people! The looters and terrorists! Foreigners and illegals! You make me sick!"

"Enough talk." Alex growled. "Walk away, now. This is your last chance!"

"No, this is *your* last chance!" Johnny said. "You might have your special gloves, but you're massively outnumbered and, well, I've got this."

Johnny reached behind him and pulled out a handgun, tucked in the back of his trousers, pointing it at Alex.

"Now, because I'm a nice guy, I'll give you a chance here." Johnny said. "I'll put down the gun and tell my men to stand down, if you take off the gauntlets. We'll settle this like men. Winner gets to walk away with his life."

Alex turned around and looked at the line of Bovver Boys. There were at least twenty of them, and though some of them were injured, some of them looked ready for a fight. And unlike most of his previous escapades as the Fist, this time he didn't have the element of surprise. They knew what he could do.

"*Okay Alex. I believe in you. Kick his arse.*"

"You have a deal." Alex said, pulling off one of his gauntlets. Johnny grinned, dropping the gun.

"Good. I haven't had a decent one-on-one fight in ages." he said.

Alex placed both of his gauntlets down and pulled off his goggles, leaving only the bandanna covering his face.

"The brass knuckles too." Alex said.

"Only if you take off that armoured vest." Johnny replied. Neither moved.

"Well, let's do this then." Johnny said.

The Bovver Boys began to stamp, pounding their chests, softly chanting at first, then rising in volume as the two moved closer together, spreading their legs into a fighting stance, and began to circle each other, waiting to see who would throw the first punch.

"Ooh, aah, whoareya? Ooh aah, Bovver Boys. Ooh, aah, whoareya?! **OOH AAH, BOVVER BOYS!**"

The adrenaline got the better of Alex, and he moved in, taking a jab at Johnny's face. The bigger man dodged easily, bringing one of his fists up into Alex's stomach. The brass knuckles thudded hard against the kevlar vest, and Alex stumbled back. With an angry growl, he moved in for another punch. At the last second, he pulled away in a feint, and his other fist came quickly towards Johnny's jaw. He caught the man off balance, and Johnny had to take a second to steady himself. Alex took his opportunity, striking Johnny twice with one of his steel toecaps. Johnny curled over, dropping to one knee, and Alex brought his fist high into the air, ready to come crashing down on Johnny's head. But at the last second, Johnny burst up, his brass knuckles going straight into Alex's armpit. Alex stumbled backwards, and Johnny hit him again, and again, and again, first in the chest, then in the chin, then the side of the head. The blow to the head knocked his earpiece out and shattered his hearing aid. Another blow to the head had his ears ringing. One strike after another had Alex growing weaker and weaker. He was able to block some of them, but they just kept coming. Johnny had no finesse of technique, there was no particular form of martial arts he was using, it was just brute strength.

Alex stumbled back further, placing some distance between them, moving further up the dock towards Antonio. Johnny covered the distance quickly, going in for another attack, but this time Alex dodged, palming the blow to one side and striking Johnny in the side of the ribs. He quickly dodged behind Johnny, and from behind planted a boot into his back, kicking him hard. When Johnny spun round to face him again, he was ready for each punch, dodging this way and that. Johnny was stronger, but he was faster, perhaps he could wear the man out.

Johnny threw one punch after another and Alex continued to dodge and block, all his focus on Johnny's fists, until he'd completely lost count of the amount of punches the man had thrown, and then-

BAM!

Johnny's knee came up into Alex's stomach. A fatal flaw: the man had thrown so many punches, Alex had completely forgotten to watch out for his legs. As the knee hit him, he was caught off guard, and Johnny was able to strike him in the face, the brass knuckles making a sickly crunch as they hit his nose. Alex reached up to block the next punch, but he was too slow, and Johnny's fist crashed into his jaw.

He collapsed onto the dock, his bandanna shifting, and for a moment, his face was in full view.

"Alex?" Antonio muttered, his eyes widening.

Johnny knelt down and grabbed Alex by the collar.

"Looks like I win." he sneered.

There were sudden sirens, as a line of police cars pulled off the dirt road that led to the warehouse, and officers flooded into the warehouse and towards the riverfront. The Bovver Boys stopped chanting, a few of them breaking off from the main group and running away. All eyes were on the police cars for a second, so that no one saw Big Tuna rise to his feet and dart across the dock.

Johnny turned back to Alex, just in time for Big Tuna to press the cold barrel of the handgun into the side of his head.

"Leave him." Big Tuna growled. "Go."

Johnny backed away, his hands in the air.

"Alright boys!" he yelled. "Let's get out of here!"

The Bovver Boys turned tail and ran, leaving only Big Tuna and Alex, on the dock, alone. Big Tuna snatched up the gauntlets and goggles and handed them to Alex, who was still hunched over in pain.

"Let's get you out of here." Big Tuna said, grabbing Alex and helping him up. "I don't much fancy getting arrested again. I've got another hideout near here."

They disappeared along the riverfront, out of view underneath one of the minor bridges across the river, just in time as the police officers came within eyesight of the dock.

Antonio helped Alex to an empty, almost completely unfurnished house, half an hour's walk away, though it took longer with their injuries. It was a small house, with only one bedroom, a kitchen, a bathroom and a tiny front room.

"This is one of our safe-houses." Antonio said. "I better not find it's been raided by the police in a few days. I keep your secret, you keep mine."

"I don't work with the police." Alex replied, gruffly, fiddling with his hearing aid.

Big Tuna helped him into a chair and slumped against the wall. Both of them were battered and bruised, with very little energy left.

"So, you're the Fist. You're the one that's been causing us all this trouble." Antonio said. "Honestly, I should have seen that coming."

"We're just trying to improve our city." Alex replied.

"Well, I'm sure you've learned that's not as easy as you first thought." Antonio muttered. "The law doesn't work for the people any more. I'm not sure it ever really did. See, you never even stopped to consider that maybe the things I was doing WERE making things better for people."

"You're a bully with anger management problems." Alex replied. "Someone needed to hold you accountable."

"I admit, my anger has gotten the better of me." Antonio said. "But I used my resources to take on corrupt landlords and help people find legal loopholes to better themselves."

"And lined your own pockets in the process." Alex said.

"And so what?" Antonio exclaimed. "Soldiers get paid. Firefighters get paid. Doctors get paid. We've all got to earn a living. Besides, who are you to lecture me about anger management? We both know your history with anger, Alex. Or had you forgotten about the school forcing you into therapy for it? And what about those racists at the bridge? I dealt with them. Didn't gain anything from that."

He sighed, reaching up to touch his nose. A small trail of blood had begun to leak out of it.

"Come on, let's get cleaned up. Clearly we both have bigger issues than each other right now." Big Tuna said. "The enemy of my enemy and all that. I've got a first aid kit in the back."

As he stood and headed into the kitchen, Alex's phone rang. He pulled it out of his pocket. It was Jason.

"*Alex! Are you okay? What happened?!*"

"I'm fine. A little banged up but alive. Big Tuna saved me…"

"*Big Tuna? Does he know who you are now?*"

"Yes, he does." Alex replied. "You know, none of this would have happened if you had let me take the NanoVirus. I could have taken them all down."

"*Alex, we've talked about this, it's not worth the risk. Look, get home and get some rest. We'll talk later. Rhiannon and Louis should be back soon.*"

Jason hung up, and Alex was left alone, his mind lost amongst fantasies of what could have been, if he had Louis' strength and speed and healing.

***

Iona sat in the Dr Patel's office as she read the test results on her computer screen, her brow furrowed.

"What did you do?" she asked.

"What do you mean?" Iona replied.

The doctor sighed, turning away from her computer and fixing Iona with a concerned stare.

"I'm not an idiot, Iona." she said. "For months, you've been telling me about the advancements in your research, how it could be the next big medical breakthrough: cure cancer, fix genetic health issues, and then your research is shut down. And now, suddenly, out of the blue, after I tell you that your cancer has returned and that you need chemotherapy, you come back in and ask me to test you again, and the cancer is completely gone. What did you do?"

Iona remained silent, refusing to meet the doctor's gaze.

"Did you inject yourself with your NanoVirus?" Dr Patel asked.

"I didn't have a choice!" Iona exclaimed. "I couldn't go through chemotherapy again!"

"Iona!" Dr Patel said, her voice a mixture of disappointment and worry. "You know how dangerous that is! Not to mention illegal!"

"We'd made good progress with the animal trials, no negative

264

side-effects!" Iona said. "We only had to stop after Dr Wood went missing, but it was working!"

"You know as well as I do that animal trials are no substitute for human trials."

"I am the human trial!" Iona said, her voice growing increasingly filled with frustration.

"Human trials need to be carried out in controlled conditions, in a lab, where experts can properly monitor you!" Dr Patel replied. "You have no idea of the impacts this could have! Have you even considered the neurological impact the NanoVirus could have?"

"I'll take any side-effect over the cancer!" Iona yelled over the doctor.

"I'm just concerned for your safety, Iona." Dr Patel replied, calmly. "I insist that you go and see our neurologist."

She picked up the phone, pressing several buttons.

"I'll try and get you an appointment today."

The phone rang, and Iona could hear someone on the other end pick up.

"Dr Woolsey. I have a patient here who I would like you to see as soon as possible. She's taken an experimental treatment for her cancer, I am looking into the possible physiological side-effects but I could really do with your help making sure there are no unforeseen psychological or neurological side-effects... Could you fit her in today?.... Thank you so much. I will meet with you at lunch to go over the research."

Dr Patel put down the phone and turned back to Iona.

"I will need you to provide me with a copy of your research, if you have it." she said. "Iona, I am truly happy that your cancer is gone, but we really ought to make sure you really are healthy."

"I don't need it." Iona replied. "I'm fine."

"Please, just come back here at 4PM?" Dr Patel said. "For me?"

Iona sighed.

"Fine." she said. "But only so that I can reference any findings in my future research."

Without another word, she stood and exited the room.

The cancer was gone. The NanoVirus had worked.

She couldn't wait to tell Jason.

As she exited the hospital, she found herself walking faster and faster, until she was sprinting through the city. The faster she got, the more energy she felt, coursing through her body. A man jumped out of her way, cursing as she thundered past. She paid him no heed. The wind blew through her hair. She was moving faster than she had ever moved. The world was a blur around her as her feet pelted against the concrete.

This was amazing! She felt so alive! So strong! So fast! So full of energy! It was like she had been born again!

Taking the NanoVirus was the best decision she had ever made.

***

Big Tuna had picked out a suit for Alex to wear. Being that it was a Bridge Boys safe-house, shirts and suits seemed to be the main clothing in the cupboard, but at least it fit alright. The two shook hands and parted ways, agreeing to a temporary truce. The Bridge Boys were in no position to be facing anyone, but then neither was Alex.

He limped through the city streets, a sports bag containing the gauntlets and goggles, and his vest and bandanna, hung off one shoulder. He shifted the bag uncomfortably and wandered onward, heading for Jason's garage. If he had that NanoVirus, he could have won that fight, he could have beaten those racist thugs, and he could have wiped that smug grin off Johnny Johnson's face.

Whether Jason thought it was worth the risk or not, Alex had decided: this was his body, his life, his choice.

"*Fire your weapon private, that's an order!*"

The words echoed through his head again, piercing his thoughts. His hands began to shake, and he closed his eyes, shaking his head and willing away the images.

"Easy mate, you alright there?"

Lost in his thoughts, Alex had turned a corner and walked straight into a police officer. The voice sounded familiar, and Alex raised his head to meet the officer's gaze.

His heart stopped.

That face was etched into his mind.

266

It was the man who had assaulted Blake. The man who had thrown him from the bridge during the protest. And here he stood, in police uniform. He was young, probably around Alex's age, not the sort you would usually see with these racist groups, but there was definitely a harshness in his eyes.

Alex frowned.

"You're a police officer?" he muttered.

"You're observant, aren't you mate!" the man sniggered.

"I mean, uh.." Alex fumbled for words. "I'm a friend of Officer... uh... Parker. I've never seen you at the station before."

"Oh yeah!" the man grinned. "I'm a new recruit. Part of the government's initiative to clean up the police force, make sure no more nasty accidents happen. They're hiring new people, fast-tracking anyone with a military or security background through the exam process. It's my first day actually. I used to be a bouncer... Anyway, are you alright? You look a little banged up."

"I'm fine."

Alex walked around the officer and disappeared off into the street, his mind rushing, his heart pumping. How could they hire that guy? The homophobic, racist, Bovver Boy?

The police were utterly corrupt now. There was no one left to protect the people of Downtown City from the bigots and thugs. No one but him and his team.

That decided it.

Alex was going to inject himself with the NanoVirus.

At the same time as Alex hobbled into the car park behind the hotel, Iona appeared from out of the back entrance and walked up to the garage, knocking on the door.

"Iona!" Alex called out, limping up to her.

"Alex!" Iona exclaimed. "What happened to you? Are you okay?"

"Bovver Boys." Alex grunted. "Where's Jason?"

"I don't know, it doesn't look like he's here. I was about to call him." Iona said. "I just got out of the hospital. Alex, my NanoVirus worked!"

Alex frowned.

"What do you mean?" he asked.

"I took it." she said, beaming as she spoke. "I took it to cure my cancer, and it worked!"

"Oh my god, that's amazing!" Alex exclaimed. "That's proof then: your invention works!"

"Well, I'd need to do proper human trials, get some more test subjects, but it looks promising. As soon as we get our research up and running again, we may have a breakthrough."

"How about you use me as a test subject?" Alex suggested, as if the idea had just occurred to him.

Iona chuckled.

"Well, maybe." she said. "Once I have a lab and a team and funding, if you really wanted."

"No, I mean now." Alex said, his voice slightly more forceful than he intended. "You still have a few vials of the NanoVirus left. You can use me as another test subject, monitor my progress and all that."

"Alex, that's dangerous." Iona said, hesitantly. "We gave it to Louis because he was dying, and I took it because of my cancer, but you're healthy. It's not worth the risk."

"I'm risking my life out there every day trying to do good as the Fist." Alex replied. "I just had the crap beaten out of me because I was outnumbered and outmatched. The NanoVirus could give me the edge I need. It's worth the risk."

"Alex, I just can't." Iona said. "It's not ethical at all."

"Why not?" Alex asked. "Because it's not how things are usually done? We've already broken the correct procedure, what are the chances you'll even get funding again after everything that's happened? If I've learned anything these past few months, it's that sometimes you've got to take matters into your own hands."

Iona thought for a second, scrunching up her face and rubbing her forehead.

"Okay, okay." she said. "Let's do this."

She took out the spare key to the garage and opened it up, ushering Alex inside. The vials of NanoVirus and the plastic stand were already on the desk and plugged into the laptop from when Jason injected her. Iona booted up the laptop and primed the virus the way she had done before. She reached for a fresh syringe.

Her hand stopped.

"No, no I can't do this Alex." she said. "I'm sorry. I'm going in for some tests later today to check there are no negative side-effects. At least wait until after that. I would never forgive myself if I didn't at least wait for that."

"Iona, trust me." Alex said. "This is worth the risk. Louis is fantastic in a fight. Imagine how much good I could do with my training!"

"It's just a little while." Iona replied. "Just a little wait, just so I can be a little more certain I'm not putting you at risk."

She put down the syringe and turned to leave.

"I'm sorry. Clearly I'm not in the right mental state. Louis was a fluke but this is not what the NanoVirus is meant for." she said, casting her eyes at the ground. "This was a mistake, I'm going to go now."

And she rushed out of the garage.

As she left, Alex's eyes fell on the virus, and flickered over to the syringe. He turned around, watching and waiting until Iona had left the car park. When she was gone from view, he pulled out the fresh syringe, unwrapping it from its plastic packaging, and filled it up with the virus.

"If you want something done, do it yourself." he muttered.

And he injected himself.

For a second, nothing happened. Then, he felt his arm begin to grow cold, where he had injected the needle. He pulled the needle out and went to grab a plaster from the first aid kit. As he fiddled with the clasp, his hands began to shake. The cold sensation was spreading, not just up his arm but across his entire body. And then suddenly, it switched: not cold but hot now, like his skin was burning from the inside.

Alex let out a cry, falling to his knees.

The sensation stopped, but his heart was still racing, his hands still trembling.

He stumbled out of the garage, and though it had been a cloudy afternoon when he entered the garage, now it seemed like the sun was blinding. Everything was white, every sound overwhelming. He could hear a couple arguing, despite the fact that they were past the other side of the car park, on the other side of the street. He could hear people eating in the restaurant, despite the fact that they were the other side of a brick wall. His eyes finally adjusted to the light, but all the colours seemed so bright, so vivid. He stumbled to the edge of the car park, leaning against a bin. The scent of rotting garbage and half-smoked cigarettes filled the air, forming a cloud of odour that seemed to cling to him. He gagged, rushing away from the bin, and threw up in the corner of the car park. Alex pressed his back against the wall and groaned, waiting for everything to return to normal.

Surely this wasn't the same as what Iona and Louis went through? He thought to himself.

***

"Careful with that."

Jason leaned awkwardly against the wall in the hallway of Rhiannon and Louis' house as Louis carried his wheelchair into the living room. Inside, a small group of people sat on the sofa and on the floor around the coffee table. There was a petite person with red and blue hair, a fair-haired woman in her late twenties, a dark-haired woman who looked middle-eastern, and a man with a cropped beard and glasses. Louis carried the wheelchair in and put it in the corner by the door, and he and Rhiannon slipped past to perch on the sofa. The television was on, and the Downtown News Network had been talking about the deportation scandal all morning: they had dubbed it PortGate, partially after Portside airport, partially a contraction of deport. The presenter was sat in the studio, talking about the events of last night, with footage showing over his shoulder. Rhiannon picked up the remote and turned off the TV.

"This is AJ, Ricardo and Cindy, and this is Zakirah." Rhiannon said, indicating to each member of the group. "Guys, this is Jason."

"So, you're the Fist?" Cindy raised an eyebrow.

"Well, I guess, one of them." Jason replied. "I m-made the gauntlets."

"That's really cool!" Ricardo grinned. "Nice work!"

"Is anyone else home?" Jason peered back into the hallway, a worried look on his face.

"No, it's just us, we can speak openly." Louis said.

"The trip to Portside was a relative success." Rhiannon said. "We got the media talking about the deportations. It's been all over the news today. But our work isn't done. There are still plenty of people stuck in that deportation prison, and that's exactly where all those people are going to end up going back to."

"It's horrible in there." Zakirah said. "The living conditions are awful. It's cramped, it's overcrowded, there aren't even enough beds. Some of us were just given mattresses and tin foil blankets."

"Now that the media attention is on them, they'll likely clear up in there." Rhiannon said. "People will want to know what the facilities look like, so they'll straighten it all out quickly. We need to expose them before they do that."

"Even if the facilities are improved, there is still so much wrong with that place." Zakirah said. "People aren't allowed to make phone calls or contact legal advisors, no attorney visits or even family visits. It's worse than a prison, and many of the people in there are completely innocent."

"Okay." Jason said. "We obviously need to d-deal with this, but tensions are still high in the city as well. The B-b-bovver Boys attacked the B-bridge Boys late last night. Alex went down there to stop it but he was too late. He ended up getting the crap beaten out of him by Johnny Johnson."

"Damn." Louis said. "This is why we work better as a team. We need to be able to watch each other's backs."

"Rhiannon, you were right about bringing more people in." Jason said. "But we're st-still outmatched and spread too thin."

"I want to help you." Zakirah said.

"We appreciate that." Louis said. "But do you have any experience with this?"

"I stopped that gang from burning down the mosque." Zakirah pointed out. "Besides, I have powers too. Like you."

"You're super strong and can heal yourself?" Jason asked.

"No, not the same powers, different powers." Zakirah said. "I'm really lucky, and I can make people do things."

271

Jason raised an eyebrow.

"I'm not sure I understand." he said.

"She's telling the truth." Rhiannon said. "Outside Portside Airport, she told all of the police to stop and they just froze, in their tracks… Like she was controlling their minds or something."

"It was crazy." Cindy said. "We only saw it from a distance, but she stopped everyone."

Jason raised an eyebrow.

"How does it work?" he asked.

"I don't know." Zakirah admitted. "I can't fully control it yet. But I think it works best when I'm scared or angry, when my heart is really racing."

"Well, that's a useful power, but until you can learn to control it, it's too much of a risk to rely on it." Jason said. "If you w-w-want to join us, you're welcome, b-but I'm not comfortable creating any plans that rely on an ability you can only partially control."

Zakirah nodded, sinking back into silence. He made some good points. If she had been able to control her powers, she'd never have been put in the deportation prison in the first place. She needed to learn how her powers worked.

**

Iona sat in the doctor's office again, only this time it wasn't Dr Patel sitting across the table from her. Instead, a balding man with glasses and a long face sat, making notes on a print-out of Iona's research with a pen. It was a bulky document, in a bulky file, and watching him work through it was starting to get tiresome. The doctor, who had been introduced to her by Dr Patel as Dr Woolsey, wore a fine suit with a checkered tie, and looked more like a businessman than a doctor.

"Dr Page." he said, his voice formal and to-the-point, like he was interviewing her for a job. "Your research is fascinating, and this NanoVirus truly is a breakthrough. However, I note that not much consideration has been given to the psychological implications of this kind of treatment."

He looked Iona in the eye, putting down his pen.

"With any medication, whenever you look on the side of the

box or on the information leaflet that comes with it, there's always a list of possible side-effects that may occur on taking the drug." he said, his tone slightly informative, but also slightly condescending.

"You don't have to dumb this down, Dr Woolsey." Iona said. "I may be a patient but I'm also a doctor with a degree in microbiology and a PhD in nanotechnology."

"Indeed." Dr Woolsey said, seemingly unimpressed. "My point is that often, at least half of those possible side-effects are **psychological**. Your NanoVirus is specifically programmed to deal with **physiological** issues. It targets cancer, it mends damaged tissue. It's smart, and it learns, and it does what it can to aid the body in physiological recovery and betterment. The increased strength and speed and healing that come with it were, in all honesty, logical side-effects. But the nanotechnology within the serum has absolutely no understanding of how to deal with neurological issues, and no programming to tackle psychological disorders. Whether it will react positively or negatively is yet to be seen."

"Right." Iona said. "I had considered that, but decided it was worth the risks. I would rather deal with the possible psychological side-effects than have to deal with the cancer."

"And that is an entirely reasonable and logical decision." Dr Woolsey said. "I imagine that in your position, I would have done the same. But that does not mean that you are going to be completely fine. I have a theory. I believe that, while improving your physical health, this NanoVirus may have unexpected negative effects on your mental health. I believe that it could worsen conditions like anxiety and depression, or even paranoia and insomnia. Give this drug to someone with social anxiety, and would theorise that they could become a complete recluse, shying away from any social contact. Give it to someone with anger management problems, and I believe it would push them over the edge, making them more sensitive and erratic. I would like to carry out some tests on you in the coming months to see if we can track any possible negative impacts on your mental state."

"What has led you to this hypothesis, doctor?" Iona asked. Dr Woolsey leaned forwards.

273

"A lot of the time, psychological conditions can be caused by chemical imbalances in the brain. Every feeling, every emotion we have is just the outcome of a series of chemical reactions. But these reactions are in no way simple. It has taken doctors years to understand these conditions, and we still don't fully understand how they happen, and your nanotechnology isn't programmed with an understanding of these chemical reactions. I believe that there is a possibility that it will incorrectly perceive these to be appropriate and normal bodily functions and attempt to aid them. Imagine someone's brain is producing too much dopamine, leading to aggressive and impulsive behaviour, and your NanoVirus sees the overproduction of dopamine as a normal bodily function? It might try to increase the dopamine levels even higher: increasing productivity in a way only a machine would... This is just one example, but I believe that there is potential for some real psychological and neurological implications to this NanoVirus of yours. We would need to do more tests to know for sure."

Iona let out a deep sigh, and felt an internal pang of relief that she didn't inject Alex. As much as it pained her to admit it, Dr Woolsey could well be right.

"Okay." she said. "Schedule the tests."

"Brilliant." Dr Woolsey said. "I have a busy schedule, but this fascinates me and I will try and move some things around to schedule you in. And Dr Page, please do not take any of this as an insult to your work. I am taking special interest in this because I think your work is revolutionary and fascinating. But it's far from perfect, and I want to help you with that."

"Thank you, Dr Woolsey."

"Good day, Dr Page."

***

As the activists gathered around the table, trying to work out the best plan of approach at the deportation facility, Jason's phone began to ring, and he pulled it out.

"I'm sorry, it's Iona, I should take this." he said, pulling himself out of his chair and wandering into the hallway.

"*Jason! Hey! I tried to find you earlier. I had my scans today.*

274

The cancer is gone!"

"That's f-f-fantastic!" Jason exclaimed. "I'm so happy for you."

"*Yeah, thanks. Listen, Jason, that's not why I called. I told Dr Patel what I did and she set me up some appointments to speak with some specialists. I spoke to a neurologist today who thinks that there might be some psychological side-effects, like worsening things like anxiety and depression, anything like that.*"

"Right." Jason said. "Well I'm sure we can g-get through that, together. The c-cancer is gone, that's the main thing."

"*I'm just a little worried. I ran into Alex earlier, he looked really shaken up. He tried to convince me to give him the NanoVirus. I didn't do it but he was really pushing it. If Dr Woolsey is right and the virus could have psychological side-effects, Alex is the last person that should be taking it. We left the NanoVirus out in your garage, and we all have keys now. I wouldn't be able to forgive myself if he took matters into his own hands and took it.*"

"Crap." Jason sighed. "Okay, I'll make sure it's locked away. Where did you see Alex?"

"*At the garage.*" Iona hesitated. "*Jason, I'm really sorry, I almost gave him the NanoVirus. It was reckless at stupid. I didn't do it, but I can't guarantee that he won't have given it to himself. I should have taken it away, I just wasn't thinking straight.*"

"If Alex injects himself, that's on him, n-not you. I better go. Look after yourself."

"*I love you.*"

Jason hesitated, lingering in the moment. That was the first time she had said it.

"I love you too." he replied.

Jason hung up the phone and went back into the main room. "Iona is worried there might be psychological side-effects to the NanoVirus." he said. "Alex has been really pushing to take it, and with everything that happened last night, I think we should make sure it's locked away where he can't find it."

"I haven't noticed any side-effects." Louis said. "But if Iona's right, Alex definitely shouldn't take it. That man's a ball of

275

anger and alcoholism. I'll take you back to the garage now."

"What about the deportees?" Rhiannon asked.

"We'll be back here before you know it." Louis said, standing and heading to the door. "Besides, you're in charge, remember? You come up with the plan, we'll follow it."

Jason nodded.

"We trust you." he said. "We'll see you soon."

Louis lifted the wheelchair back outside and the two men climbed into the car and drove off towards the hotel.

Jason and Louis pulled up in the car park, both noticing the garage door left open almost immediately. Louis rushed over to it as Jason pulled himself slowly out of the car, limping over to the garage entrance. Moments later he came out, syringe in hand.

"He already injected himself." he said.

"Crap!" Jason hissed, pulling out his phone and dialling Alex's number. He put the phone up to his ear. "It's ringing."

Louis went over to the car and pulled out Jason's wheelchair.

***

Alex stumbled along the riverfront, carrying the sports bag, his senses finally starting to settle. His wounds had healed completely now, and he felt energy coursing through his body. He switched off his hearing aid, the sounds to overwhelming now. He supposed the NanoVirus must have fixed his hearing impairment, and found himself wondering if it was doing its job in other ways. He clenched his fist and threw a punch at a lamppost on the edge of the path. Pain shot through his arm, and he let out a cry.

But the lamppost was severely dented, bent out of shape. Alex put his hands on the lamppost and squeezed, bending it further, twisting the metal with his bare hands.

He had super-strength.

Alex grinned to himself, breaking out into a sprint along the path. The feeling was exhilarating. He could feel it now. He was faster. He was stronger. His energy levels were through the roof.

Just think of all the things he could do now!

Alex laughed, spinning around and throwing his arms out wildly.

"I'm invincible!" he screamed, shouting across the river. "I'm IN-VINCI-BLE!"

His phone rang, and he pulled it out of his pocket.

"*Alex! Where are you!*" Jason exclaimed.

"I took the NanoVirus, man!" Alex exclaimed, beaming with excitement. "It works, I feel so strong, I'm so fast! I feel like I could do anything!"

"*Alex, listen to me, the NanoVirus m-may have some unexpected side-effects. We n-n-need to get you to the hospital so that they can run some tests.*"

"What?" Alex frowned. "What do you mean? I feel fine. Look, there are more important things to deal with. The police are fucked, man. Like, really, truly messed up. That Bovver Boy who assaulted Blake? They hired him. He's a police officer now. There's no justice, Jason. No justice except the justice we make!"

He was practically frothing at the mouth by the time he got to the end of his speech, and though he didn't know where he was going when he started, he did now.

"We've got to take them down." he said. "I've got to take them down."

"*Alex, no, please. St-stop and think about what you're doing!*"

"You're either with me or you're not, Jason. I'm doing what needs to be done."

And he hung up, throwing his phone with force against the lamppost.

"Yeah!" he exclaimed. "Fists of Justice! Boo Yah!"

***

Jason put the phone down, turning to look at Louis.

"He's lost his mind," he said. "I think he's going to attack the police station."

"That nutter." Louis breathed. "Fine, I'm going to call Rhiannon, we need to stop him."

As Louis pulled his phone out and dialled Rhiannon, Jason's phone rang again. Unknown number.

"Hello?" he said, putting the phone up to his ear.

"*It's me.*" the distorted voice on the other end of the phone said. "*Grey Hat.*"

"Follow the white rabbit." Jason said: the first half of the password they had decided on to ensure they were not being duped.

"*There is no spoon.*" came the coded reply. So it was Grey Hat.

"What is it?" Jason asked. "We've got a lot going on right now."

"*I finally found out who took Dr Wood and the research on the NanoVirus.*"

"That's great, but can it wait?"

"*No. The people who took Dr Wood work for a series of corporate interests. Their power runs deep. They've got insiders within the US government, the EU, even within your government. Lots of friends in high places. Very powerful, very dangerous. They've got agents within the FBI, CIA, Interpol, MI6 and MI5. They've placed a recent order into some of their agents operating in the UK. They've worked out that Dr Wood didn't invent the NanoVirus, and they know it was your friend, Dr Page. Furthermore, it's just been placed on Dr Page's medical records that she injected herself with the NanoVirus. So now not only is she the person with the greatest understanding of what could be a potentially very dangerous weapon, she's also one only existing human test subject on record. They're going to be coming after her. She's not safe.*"

"No, no, no." Jason groaned. "Not Iona, not now. What can we do?"

"*Get her to safety. Somewhere away from the city. I'll try and figure out something we can do.*"

Grey Hat hung up. Jason turned back to Louis.

"Listen, I know, babe." Louis was saying, the phone pressed to his ear. "I know that's important, but this is important too… We're going to have to split up again. You and the others go to the facility, Jason and I will go after Alex. It's the only way. I love you."

He put down the phone and turned back to Jason. As soon as he saw the look on Jason's face, he took a deep breath.

"What?" he said. "What now?"

"Iona is in danger." Jason stammered. "I… I need to call her."

And he was back on the phone, his fingers trembling as he dialled Iona's number.

"*Jason? What's going on?*"

"Iona, babe. Listen, you're not safe!" Jason said. "Someone is coming after you. You can't go home. Where are you?"

"*I'm just getting home now.*" Iona said, and Jason heard the faint sound of a door opening. "*What's - that's weird, my door is open.... Hello? Oh my-*"

There was a loud thud, then a short, muffled scream, and the phone line went dead.

"They've got to her!" Jason muttered.

"Who has got to her?" Louis said.

"Some very dangerous people." Jason said. "They... I don't know, they work for the US government or something. They're going to take her, like they took Dr Wood."

"Okay, calm down." Louis said. "Iona's place isn't far from here. With my speed, I can run there in under five minutes. You go after Alex, I'll go rescue Iona."

Jason nodded, his hands shaking. Louis turned to head out of the car park.

"Louis?" Jason said. "Please, keep her safe. Get her out of the city, I don't care where, just make sure she's safe."

Louis nodded.

"Trust me, mate. I've got this. Go stop Alex. You're the only one who knows him well enough to talk him down without a fight."

CHAPTER SEVENTEEN: THE STORM

I

RHIANNON & ZAKIRAH

It felt strange to Rhiannon to be back in the van and on the road again, already, after everything they had gone through yesterday. And yet, she supposed, this was her life now. And in all honesty, she was happy with it. Proud of herself, even. If they could pull off this mission, then perhaps they really could make the world a better place.

Her gauntlets, boots and visor were fully charged again, and her team prepared themselves in the back of the van. Cindy sat next to Rhiannon, her hands on the steering wheel of the van. In the back, Ricardo had a balaclava on, and AJ had slipped on their white, plastic face mask again. AJ offered a spare mask to Zakirah. She shook her head.

"I am an illegal refugee in this country, who has already run away from deportation." she said. "There is no identity for me to protect. Let them add this to the list of things they want to arrest me for."

AJ shrugged and passed the mask forwards for Cindy.

Rhiannon's phone buzzed, and she looked down to check it. A text, from Blake.

'*Owen dumped me. Said my life was too crazy, the protest was too much, and he couldn't handle it. Can we talk? I need you.*'

Rhiannon hesitated, reading the text two or three times and cursing the timing.

"Are we sure we're going to have signal in there?" Ricardo asked.

280

Rhiannon put the phone away. Blake would have to wait. She needed to focus.

"Jason has contacted Grey Hat. The message will get out, so long as we follow the plan. Has everyone got everything they need?"

"I don't have a phone." Zakirah pointed out.

"Use mine. Rhiannon pulled out her phone and handed it to Zakirah. "Passcode is 1312."

It wasn't long before they exited the main road and found themselves going along backroads full of potholes, in the middle of nowhere. But soon enough, they found the facility. It was on the outskirts of the city, a few fields away from the signs that read 'YOU ARE NOW ENTERING DOWNTOWN CITY: PLEASE DRIVE CAREFULLY'. There was a dirt track that led up the side of a field that ran adjacent to the facility fence, and they parked the van in the corner of the field. The sun was just beginning its descent, and sunset would be beginning soon. By the time they left, it would likely be under cover of darkness.

"Let's move." Rhiannon said.

Together, they hopped the small wooden fence into the next field, and headed towards the massive, barbed wire fences surrounding the facility. Rhiannon pulled her bolt cutters out of her backpack and began cutting away at the fence. Ricardo did the same, and soon enough they had made a small hole.

"Give me ten minutes." Rhiannon said.

She pulled her balaclava on and placed on her goggles. She switched to night-vision mode, and kept low, running towards the facility. Luckily, the guards had little reason to be patrolling the courtyard, as none of the detainees would be out of the main hall or cells at this point. From the look of the courtyard, it didn't seem like the detainees got much time outside anyway.

The back door to the facility was locked, and next to it a set of stairs lowered into the ground, to another door below. The basement door was also locked, but Rhiannon's new gauntlets fried the electronic keypad and the lock sensor was tripped. Rhiannon pulled the door open and slipped inside. It was a basic basement: dark and damp, but behind all the boilers and machinery, a little metal box on the wall read 'FUSE BOX'. Rhiannon grinned, placing her gauntlets on the box. One strike with her fist, and the box broke open. Then it was a simple matter of flicking all of the switches to 'OFF'.

Through the open door, Rhiannon could see the lights up the stairs flicker and go out.

That was the signal for the others to move.

Zakirah allowed the other two to slip through the hole first, then followed, staying low to the ground as they rushed towards the back entrance. Rhiannon had already broken the lock with her gauntlets, and held the door open for them on their way in.

"AJ, with me. You two, good luck." she said, and they slipped off down the hall.

It took a moment to adjust to the darkness, but the emergency lights were just about enough for them to be able to find their way around. Once inside, Zakirah started to realise just how much bigger this facility was than the area they had been confined to. The thought made her sick: she went past corridor after corridor of storage rooms or empty rooms. But eventually, she came to a locked door which went into a familiar corridor: the area with the bathrooms and toilets.

Zakirah kicked the door. The electric locks had all been set to unlocked when the system went down, but this door had a manual lock as well. Luckily, it was just a latch, and since it was made to keep the prisoners on the other side, the latch was on Zakirah's side. She opened it, clicked the button to make it stay unlocked, and slipped into the familiar corridor.

At the end of the corridor there was a corner, and then she could see the double doors into the main hall in which the detainees were kept, in their cage-like cells.

On the other side of the door, Zakirah could see a security guard, pacing this way and that, a tired expression on her face. Zakirah slunk down the corridor, her heart racing, took a deep breath, and knocked on the door.

The security guard frowned, turning around to look through the little window, but Zakirah had tucked out of view.

The guard opened the door and stepped into the corridor.

"Who's there?" she said. "Harris, is that you?"

Zakirah came out of the shadows, holding a fire extinguisher aloft with both hands, and brought the metal canister tumbling down on the guard's head.

She dropped like a sack of potatoes, and Zakirah snatched the keys off her belt and slipped inside.

Inside, the detainees were all lying on the floor with their hands behind their heads. They would have been finishing up their dinner when the power was cut, and it seemed in the panic the guards had told them all to get on the ground while they sorted it out. Two more guards stood, flashlight in hand, and one of them shone the light over to Zakirah as she entered the room.

"Hey, you!" he called out. "Stop right there!"

He sprinted across the room towards her, but a steam of light burst from Zakirah and wrapped around his ankles, pulling him and causing him to trip. The light was subtle, and to anyone stood at a distance, the slip would have looked like dumb luck, but Zakirah was noticing more and more that her luck wasn't as simple as that. The guard came crashing to the ground. Zakirah leaned in close to him, her heart pounding.

"Stay down." she said.

The guard froze where he was, his eyes fixed on Zakirah, and she turned to the second guard, who was making his way across the room to her.

"Stop!" she said, her voice commanding and authoritative.

The man stopped in his tracks as if some invisible force had hit him in the face, and his legs flew out from underneath him as he fell backwards.

"Get out." Zakirah growled.

The guard scrambled to his feet, rushing out of the room in a panic. This time, she knew it wasn't her control that had done it: it was just fear.

Zakirah pulled out the phone and typed in the password. The live stream was already set up and ready. All she had to do was press the 'record' button.

"Hello ladies!" she called out. "I am here to expose the conditions in this place and get it shut down! However, if you would rather run, the door is open, but you will be on the run,

283

the police will come looking for you. I am here to fight for your freedom. It's your choice whether you go the legal route and stay, or take your chances out there."

Before she had even finished speaking, some of the women had already got up and sprinted for the door, but many still remained. Zakirah hit the record button on the phone.

"My name is Zakirah Bashir." Zakirah said, switching to the selfie camera, which just about lit up her face. "And I am standing in the Downtown Immigration Detention and Removal Centre. This is the place where I was kept for over a month, without being allowed to see a lawyer or legal advisor, or even have any visitors at all. There are many women being kept here, some of whom came here legally, many of whom were born here."

Zakirah switched to the front camera and cast the light around the room.

"This small hall holds almost three hundred women, kept in makeshift cells that look more like cages. There are proper cells across the facility, but they are all already occupied. This facility is meant to hold no more than eight hundred people: four hundred men and four hundred women. The women's section alone hosts close to a thousand women at any one time. Most of them do not have beds. Some of them are only provided tin foil blankets. And most of them will spend their time in this facility, whether it's weeks or months, almost entirely in this room."

She walked over to the first of the detainees, who were now on their feet and quietly talking to one another.

"Please, tell the camera who you are, why you were brought here, how long you've been here, and a bit about the facility." Zakirah said.

***

Rhiannon and AJ were standing outside the security room, where a single security guard sat, staring at the empty monitors, all now black because of the power failure.

Rhiannon listened at the door as he pressed the button on his radio.

"Any update on the power situation?" he said.

"Nope, seems to just be a power cut, someone's going to check the fuse box now."

Rhiannon burst into the room behind him, grabbing hold of him from behind and clasping a hand over his mouth.

"Scream, and I cut your throat." she growled.

She spun the chair around and ripped the man's radio away from his shirt.

"Where do you keep the security tapes?" she asked.

"We- we- we don't keep tapes." the man stammered, putting his hands in the air. "It's all saved on the electronic system."

Rhiannon pulled out a USB stick and handed it to the man.

"Put all the video files on there." she said.

"Are you kidding?" the man replied. "That's thousands of gigabytes of video for this month alone! It fills up the harddrive of this computer within two weeks and has to be moved."

"So two weeks worth of security files are on this computer?" Rhiannon asked.

"Well, yeah." the man said.

"Change of plan. AJ, unplug the computer, we're taking it with us."

***

Ricardo burst through the double doors, into the main section where the male detainees were being held, bat in one hand, pepper spray in the other. The guards were marching the men into their cells when they saw Ricardo enter. There were four of them, and one of them was only feet away from the door. Ricardo swung his bat at the man, knocking him into the wall. The other three men rushed him all at once.

"Stop!" one of them yelled.

"Put down the bat!" another yelled.

Ricardo sprayed the first with pepper spray, but the second barrelled into him, tackling him at the waist, and he came crashing to the ground. In seconds, he was in handcuffs, being marched out of the hall.

"Crap." Ricardo muttered to himself, as the guards ripped off his face covering and marched him down the corridor.

"We have intruders in the facility." one said into their radio. "This is not a power cut, it's a break-in. Call the police."

***

AJ and Rhiannon were on their way out of the building when the lights came back on, and as they reached the hall to the back exit, the two guards who had been sent to check the fuse box came back in.

"Stop right there!" one of them yelled, pulling out a baton. Rhiannon broke into a run towards the two men. The first was ready, and the baton raced towards Rhiannon's head and she ducked past it, grabbing hold of the first guard. Electricity travelled through the gauntlet and caused the man to go into immediate convulsions, dropping to the ground. The second guard made a grab for Rhiannon, grasping her tightly from behind. Rhiannon kicked him hard in the shin, and his grip loosened just enough for her to pull free, spinning around to smack him hard in the face with her gauntlet. He stumbled backwards, dazed, and Rhiannon hit him with an electric shock too.

AJ watched, mouth agape, stood just a few feet away.

"Come on!" Rhiannon exclaimed. "Let's get out of here!"

AJ and Rhiannon made it back to the van first. A few minutes later, Zakirah followed.

"Any sign of Ricardo in there?" Rhiannon asked.

"No." Zakirah said. "But I think I heard something on one of their radios. I think someone was caught."

Rhiannon cursed, pulling out her radio.

"Ricardo, do you copy?" she said. "Ricardo, are you there?" She turned to AJ.

"Try phoning him."

AJ nodded, pulling out their phone and dialling, but was simply met with Ricardo's answerphone.

"Okay." Rhiannon said. "Priority is that we get you guys to safety. I'll stay here, watch out for Ricardo. You go home."

"We're not leaving without you." Cindy said.

"We all stay." AJ agreed.

II

JASON & ALEX

Alex's mind was a mess by the time he reached the police station. The adrenaline coursing through his body had sent his heart into overdrive, and his heartbeat was beginning to feel like the rapid pounding of a bass drum in a speed metal band. His senses were so heightened now that it was, ironically, becoming hard to process all the information: he heard every tiny sound around him, from the shuffling of the bugs at his feet, to the honking of a car horn several miles away, but together the sounds just became a horrific, overbearing soundscape. His eyes could pick out and read the menu placed on the table at a pub through the window on the other side of the street, but it was impossible for him to know what to focus on, and his eyes were becoming red and sore. Every time he passed a bin or a busy road, he had to clamp his hand over his nose to block out the horrific stench of pollution and rotting food.

Alex marched up to the door of the police station, bandanna over his face, goggles over his eyes, gauntlets back on his hands where they belonged. He didn't open the door so much as destroy it, striking it with his gauntlet. Just one punch, and the door flew off its hinges, landing with a thud in the reception area. The receptionist screamed and slammed on the emergency alarm, and Alex could see every cop in the building scrambling for their weapons. Two near the door were on him in seconds. Alex processed everything so much quicker than usual: the weapons at their hips, just batons. The badges on their uniform: Andrews and Weston. Their fists, clenching as they moved. Every movement, every detail: he missed nothing. The fault in Andrew's step. The uncertainty in the swing of Weston's fist. Alex dodged their attacks with ease, hitting them both with a wave of kinetic energy from his gauntlets. "Who's next!" he roared.

All at once, the other officers surged towards him.

Jason arrived at the police station what must have been minutes too late. Not only was the door forced open and on its hinges, but the alarms were blaring, echoing through the surrounding streets. Jason rolled with haste towards the entrance, the electronic motor in his wheelchair going at full power.

At the entrance to the station, Officer Parker stood, baton in hand, staring in through the open door, alert and ready. She saw Jason rolling across the car park and put the baton away, walking towards him.

"You can't come in here." she said. "We have a situation."

"I know." Jason replied. "I know the m-man who is in there."

"Jason, I'm sorry, but I can't let you in there." Officer Parker said. "I've been ordered to stand watch until reinforcements arrive from the next station."

"The man in there is sick and n-needs help." Jason said. "I can talk him down, no one n-needs to get hurt."

"I appreciate your bravery, but leave this to the professionals." Sabrina said, blocking his way.

"The professionals who killed Tamara Johnson?" Jason asked. "Or the professionals who broke up a peaceful protest with riot gear and tear gas, while failing to arrest the violent racists who attacked the protest? Or perhaps the professionals who have been snatching people off the street and deporting them without cause or due process?"

Sabrina shifted uncomfortably.

"Did you see what happened when the Fist attacked?" Jason asked.

"From a distance, yes." Sabrina replied.

"And do you really think those professionals you're talking about can take him down without any casualties?" he added.

The police officer hesitated, casting her eyes at the ground.

"Just let me try." Jason said. "What harm could it do?"

Sabrina let out a long sigh.

"I don't know." she said, looking back at the door.

"Well, I'm going in." Jason said. "Arrest me if you like, but you'll have to physically restrain me."

Sabrina stepped aside.

Jason took a deep breath, steadying his heartbeat, and rolled into the police station. His wheelchair struggled to get over the lip in the doorway, and then the broken door lying awkwardly on the ground was blocking his way. With a sigh, he pulled himself out of the wheelchair. His legs were already weak, buckling under his weight: he'd done more walking today than he would have liked. But, gritting his teeth and ignoring the pain, he pulled himself upright, leaning on the reception, and walked through to the main section of the police station, where all the constables had their many shared desks.

The station was a tip. Tables were overturned, papers were everywhere. Two unconscious officers lay in the entrance. More wounded officers were strewn about the room, some nursing broken bones, others bleeding and bruised. But at the far end of the room, Alex stood, kevlar vest, gauntlets and all, holding a police officer into the air. His goggles lay on the ground next to him, and though the bandanna still covered his face, Jason could see the passion in his eyes. His eyes were red and his face pale, his veins bulging and prominent all across his face. The officer was a typical Downtown local: a tough, white, working-class-looking man, at least six feet tall, and yet Alex held him in the air with one hand like he was made of cardboard, and he thrashed his legs and struggled for breath.

"Alex, that's enough." Jason said, leaning against each desk he went past as he hobbled across the room.

"Do you know who this is?" Alex shouted, his voice only slightly muffled by the bandanna. "He assaulted Blake! For no reason! And he threw me off the bridge! He's a racist, homophobic, transphobic piece of shit!"

"He is, but what you're doing isn't going to help." Jason said. "If you kill him, you t-turn him into a martyr for everything we are against. You sully all the good work we've d-done."

"The good work we've done is for nothing if men like him continue to have power over us!" Alex yelled, his eyes beginning to water.

"Then we need to change the system and confront its flaws." Jason said. "Taking down one man isn't going to help. Y-you know this. Alex, you're sick. This isn't you."

Alex turned to look at Jason, then looked back at the cop dangling at the end of his arm. With a wordless cry, he threw the police officer against a wall, and he slumped down with a grunt.

Alex turned his attention to Jason.

"How would you know whether this is me or not?" he growled. "You don't know me! You just use me because I can do the things you can't!"

"That's not true, Alex, you're my friend." Jason said.

"I'm not your friend, I'm your weapon!" Alex pulled down his bandanna, towering above Jason. The veins in his neck were bulging and blue, forming sickly lines across his pale skin that ran down, under the kevlar vest.

Alex grabbed hold of Jason's collar with both hands and hoisted him up.

"You don't know me!" he exclaimed, showering Jason with spit. "You don't know me at all!"

"I know you're a g-g-good man!" Jason stammered. "I know you want to do good. I know y-you joined the army to make the world a better place!"

"And I was kicked out!" Alex exclaimed. "You don't even know why! Not really! You weren't there! I'm not a hero, and neither are you. We're just broken people who don't know what we're doing!"

"Alex, please, put me down!" Jason pleaded, his back and legs burning as he struggled to break free of Alex's hold. "You're hurting me!"

Alex pinned him up against the wall, moving his face in close to Jason's.

"We don't live in a comic book, Jason. We can't fix the world just because we believe we can! You have a hero complex, and it's just going to get everyone around you hurt!"

"I don't want you hurt, Alex, I love you." Jason stammered, the pain spreading through his body. "You're my best friend! I want to help you, but I can't unless you help yourself! If we don't leave now, they're going to arrest you, or maybe even kill you. I don't want to lose my b-b-best friend, p-please p-put me down!"

Alex looked around the room, as if he was suddenly noticing all the havoc he had caused for the first time. As his eyes fell on the injured police officers, his hands began to shake, and in his mind, he saw the pictures again. Only this time they were so much more real, and Alex didn't feel as though he was remembering, he felt as though he was there.

"Fire your weapon, private, that's an order!"

"I can't. I can't! I can't! I can't do it!"

A hail of gunfire. Panicking civilians. Soldiers ducking for cover.

Alex stared over at his opponents. A young boy, no more than fourteen, held an AK-47, his hands shaking, his eyes wide.

"They're just kids! Stop! They're just innocent kids!"

"They are enemy soldiers, private, and they are firing on your brothers! You are disobeying a direct order! Fire your weapon NOW!"

"NO!" Alex screamed, throwing down his gun. "This is wrong!"

"Alex?" Jason shook his friend. "Alex, are you okay?"

Alex suddenly came to, and he was back in the real world, and the memories were just memories once more.

"It's too late for me, Jason." he said, his breath heavy, the images fading. "I've gone too far to turn back now."

He released his grip on his friend and stumbled backwards, leaning against a desk. He was broken, and only now, far too late, was it occurring to him just how broken he was.

Physically, he was stronger than he had ever been. But mentally, he'd never felt weaker, never more unstable.

"I'm sorry for what I said, I didn't mean it. I'm just... I don't know, I feel so lost, so broken." he sobbed. "You need to get out of here, Jason."

"Not without you." Jason replied. "Come on, if we move quickly, we can get out the back entrance before reinforcements arrive."

Alex lifted his head and nodded, wiping the tears away from his eyes.

"Come on, let's get out of here." he said.

He wrapped his arm around Jason's waist, and Jason draped his arm around Alex's shoulder, and they rushed through the hallways, to the back exit. A set of fire doors led out into a parking lot, where all of the police vans and cars were kept. Alex threw the door open, stepping out into the night.

"FREEZE!"

Neither of them had any time to take in their surroundings, because the word was closely followed by a string of tasers, fired directly at the two men. Alex's reflexes kicked in, and he turned and threw Jason back through the door, out of harm's way. Jason landed on the ground with a thud, and once again pain burst through his back, spreading quickly through his arms and legs.

Three tasers struck Alex, and he let out a howl of pain as god knows how many volts ripped through his body. One by one, he tore the wires from the CEDs off his body, and raised his gauntlets, ready for attack.

"Alex, no!" Jason cried out, and Alex turned his gaze back to his friend, lying on the ground, his arm outstretched towards him.

Alex stopped in his tracks, looking at the semicircle of police officers surrounding him, some hid behind cars, others holding riot shields, others ready with tasers and batons.

Slowly, Alex sunk to his knees, pulled off the gauntlets, and placed his hands behind his head.

The next few moments seemed to be in slow-motion, and Jason watched as a swarm of police officers ran towards Alex, batons in hands, striking him again and again. Alex simply remained, hands behind his head, as the batons smashed into his skull, his back, his shoulders, his chest. Within moments he was on the ground, the cops furiously pounding away at him until his body lay limp.

Tears rolled down Jason's face, and two of the officers ran over to him, grabbing his arms and pinning them behind his back. The cold metal of the handcuffs pressed against his skin, and Jason cried out as he was pulled roughly to his feet and marched past the limp body of his friend. His legs went limp, no longer able to support his weight, and the police officers simply dragged him away. Alex lay on the ground in a pool of his own blood, his eyes closed, no movement.

One of the officers knelt down to check his pulse as another officer put him in handcuffs.

"He's alive." the officer called out. "He's breathing, barely." Jason was loaded into the back of a police van, and as the doors were slammed shut behind him, he lost sight of his friend and partner.

And he was alone.

III

LOUIS & IONA

Louis took every side-street and shortcut he could think of, sprinting faster than even he knew he was capable of, towards Iona's apartment building. As he ran along the main road, he could have sworn he was outrunning some of the cars. He ducked into an alley, catapulting himself right over a parked car, and within minutes he was outside the apartment building. He ripped the door open, the lock flimsy and weak compared to his superhuman strength, and barreled up the stairs. The door to Iona's room was open, and inside there were signs of struggle. A man with a balaclava over his face and black overalls over his body was slumped in the corner, unconscious, but there was no one else there. Louis cursed under his breath, heading back out into the hall. From the stairwell, he heard sounds of commotion. Rushing back to the stairs, he heard loud footsteps above.

Louis sprinted up the stairs, taking them three or four at a time, following the sounds to the roof. Two men stood at the door onto the roof, pistols in their hands, preparing to go through. They were dressed the same as the unconscious one in Iona's room, and when they saw Louis, they immediately turned their guns on him, but Louis kept moving, leaping up the final set of stairs and grabbing the first man, throwing him over the bannister. The second man shot at him twice, but Louis ducked out of the way, grabbing the gun from the man's hands, ripping it from his grip and tossing it down the stairs. The man launched himself at Louis, who didn't even bother dodging. One hard punch to the side of the head, and the man dropped, his head slamming against the bannister on his way down, and he fell limp to the ground.

Alex tore the door to the roof open and rushed out. Iona was backed up against the edge of the roof, struggling with a much larger man, and two other figures, armed with guns, but not

293

firing: They wanted Iona alive. Iona had two tranquiliser darts in her arm, but the NanoVirus kept her upright, the sedative in the darts not quite enough to take her down. Louis grabbed the first of the two and threw him into the second figure. The second, though much slimmer and smaller, pushed the first aside without even fumbling, pointing the gun at Louis and firing several shots. It was a dart gun, and one dart landed in Louis' arm, the other in his chest. He stumbled in his step, pulling the darts out and growling. The figure moved in close, dropping the dart gun and pulling a pistol from his side, aiming at his face, but Louis wasn't going to be taken out like this. Not without saving Iona first.

Iona, hands still shaking, grabbed the bigger man and threw him to one side, taking a step towards Louis. As she stepped forwards, the shaking spread from her arms, and up through her body, and she let out a cry. The figure pointing the gun at Louis turned their attention towards Iona, and Louis took his chance, grabbing the gun and wrenching it away from them. The figure let out a cry turning back to Louis, who made a grab for them. The figure dodged out of the way, but Louis managed to grab hold of the balaclava and wrench it from their head.

It was a woman, early thirties, with short black hair. She let out a roar and threw herself at Louis, spinning around and raising her leg up quickly in a roundhouse kick, aiming for his face. She caught Louis in the chin and he stumbled backwards, and she immediately moved in again, dodging each of Louis' attacks and planting another punch or kick into him. Louis was far stronger, but she was trained, and it didn't matter how strong Louis was if he couldn't land a punch. The drug from the darts coursing through his system slowed his reflexes, and for a moment it seemed as though she had the upper hand.

Iona backed away, leaning against the wall sliding to the ground, her hands still shaking. Her head spun around in jarring movements, and she brought her knees up to her chest, scratching at her arms.

Louis roared in frustration, switching tactics and throwing his entire body-weight at his attacker. The dramatic change in attack caught her off-guard, and the two of them tumbled to the ground. Louis landed on top, and quickly pulled himself upright, smashing his fist into the woman's face. She fell back, bleeding from the nose, and completely unconscious, and Louis rushed over to where Iona was sitting, shaking violently.

"What's happening?" Louis asked. "What can I do?"

"It's an anxiety attack." Iona managed to force the words out through clenched teeth. "The NanoVirus - the - the NanoVirus.. It's making it worse."

"Okay, it's alright." Louis said, his voice soothing. "Don't worry. I used to get anxiety attacks when I was a kid. Do you have any coping mechanisms?"

Iona nodded emphatically through the shaking.

"I- I breathe, and I count my- I count my- I count my fingers." she stammered.

"Okay, well let's do that together." Louis said, sitting down on the ground in front of her and holding up his hands.

Iona struggled to mimic the movement, her hands still shaking, her head still jerking this way and that.

"Breathe in..." he said. "And hold... Now release... Count, 1, 2, 3, 4, 5, 6, 7, 8."

As he counted, he touched his thumb to each finger on his left hand, then each finger on his right hand, releasing his breath slowly as he spoke.

Iona took in a deep breath, held it, and then released it, counting her fingers in unison with Louis.

"And repeat." Louis said.

"B-b-but the people. Those people." Iona stammered. "They're going to come b-b-back."

"Don't worry about them." Louis said. "We can handle them. You know we're like the strongest people in the world now, right?"

Iona smirked a little, just for a second, and Louis smiled warmly back.

"See?" he said. "Was that a smile? We're okay, see. Now, again, breathe in…. Hold, release, and count: 1, 2, 3, 4, 5, 6, 7, 8…"

Behind them, one of the attackers was getting to his feet.

"Now, close your eyes and keep doing that." Louis said.

Iona nodded, closing her eyes and taking in another deep

breath.

Louis stood up and walked over to the attacker, grabbing him by the collar.

"In." he said, punching the attacker in the face. "Hold." Through the door to the stairwell, three more men rushed in, guns in their hands.

"Release." Louis threw the man he was holding at them, and he flew through the air, knocking them backwards. "One" Louis rushed forwards "two" picking up one of the guns from the ground "three" he aimed the gun, shooting two of the men in the kneecaps. "Four" the gun ran out of bullets and he tossed it to one side. "Five. He rushed at the final man, "six" pushing the gun and his arms to one side with his left hand "seven" and brought his right hand up, his fist crashing into the man's side, his shoulder, and as he keeled over, the back of his head. "Eight."

Iona opened her eyes, looking over to where Louis was now standing, over the bodies of their attackers, some unconscious, some groaning and clutching their wounds.

Louis rushed over to Iona.

"I think I'm okay." she said.

"Good." Louis replied. "Let's get out of here."

He helped her up, and they walked arm in arm towards the door. Just as Louis reached for the door, he felt something hold and hard press into the back of his neck.

"Impressive." came a voice, which sounded distinctly kiwi. "I've seen a lot of people fight, but no one quite like you: no style, no technique, but more raw power than I've ever seen. I was told to take her in alive, but something tells me they'll want you alive too."

"You're cocky for someone who just watched me take out all his men, alone." Louis said, craning his head round to look at his attacker. The man was tall and lean, and definitely Maori, with short black hair and pale brown skin. He definitely didn't look like the others that Louis had fought: for starters, he wasn't wearing a mask: he wore only a bulletproof vest, dark trousers, and high top boots, and on his belt hung two knives and a handgun. There was an air of confidence surrounding him: fearsome, bold, and scarily calm.

"Oh, they're not my men… They were just the appetiser."
Louis took a deep breath, then, harnessing his speed, he pushed Iona out of the way and spun around, kicking his attacker in the chest. The man stumbled, landing on his back, but within a split second was on his feet again, a long, black stick in each hand. He spun the sticks round, and the ends of them sparked with electricity.

"Alright, let's do this." he said, raising one of the sticks and charging towards Louis.

Louis blocked the first stick, coming in from above, and was jabbed in the side with the second, and pain tearing through his side as sparks flew off the stick. He threw a wild punch at his attacker, but the man easily dodged and struck him twice in the back, shocking him again. Louis let out a growl, throwing himself at the man full force, but again he managed to dodge. This time Louis was able to grab one of the sticks, tearing it from his grasp and tossing it away. The attacker shrugged and drew a knife from his belt. Even with Louis' speed and strength, the man ran rings around him, dancing this way and that, dodging each of Louis' attacks, only to slash him with the knife or jab him with the electrified stick. Every blow Louis landed had the potential to be lethal, so the attacker didn't let him land any. Within minutes, Louis was on his knees, and though each wound healed rapidly, he still felt the pain, and that alone was enough to be completely overwhelming.

"You fought well." the man said. "Most people don't last thirty seconds against me."

He jabbed Louis in the chest with the stick, keeping it there as the electric current flowed through Louis. With a sudden cry, Iona threw herself at the man, her fist catching him hard on the jaw. Normally, a punch from her wouldn't have done much to a man of his size, but with the NanoVirus now coursing through her veins as well, her strength was amplified, and the man was sent flying, his head cracking against the ground and leaving him unconscious.

"Quick, let's get out of here!" she said, and this time it was her turn to help Louis up.

"Yes please." Louis breathed, still panting from the extreme pain. They headed out the door and rushed down the stairs, leaving the roof littered with unconscious bodies.

CHAPTER EIGHTEEN: THE MISSING GIRL

Rhiannon stood by the side of the road and watched as the police van exited the prison-like immigration facility. As it reached the edge of the back road, ready to head out onto the main road, Rhiannon stepped out, blocking its path. She brought her hands out in front of her and clapped.
The sound wave that rippled through the air caused the van to swerve, and the driver slammed on the brakes, bringing them skidding to a halt. Out of the back of the van rushed four police officers, in riot gear, running towards Rhiannon and full speed. Zakirah stepped out beside her, taking a deep breath.
"FREEZE!" she yelled.
The officers stopped in their tracks, frozen in place.
"I'll watch them, you go get your friend." Zakirah said.
Rhiannon rushed to the back of the van, where one final police officer sat, guarding Ricardo. He jumped out of the van and attempted to spray Rhiannon with pepper spray, but she dodged the canister and grasped his shoulder with her gauntlet, sending electricity flowing through his body.
"What are you doing?!" Ricardo exclaimed.
"Saving you." Rhiannon said. "Come on."
"No." Ricardo replied, staying put. "Rhi, they've seen my face. I'll be on the run."
"If you stay, you'll be prosecuted and sent to prison." Rhiannon said. "Maybe even deported back to Portugal."
"That's a risk we all take." Ricardo said. "I'd rather do this the right way. Fight my case in court. Besides, if I get sent back to Portugal, that's not so bad. My family is all there. I'll be better off than most of these people. Go. I'll be fine. I would rather

do it this way."

Rhiannon let out a long sigh, then extended her hand.

"Good luck, Ricardo. You're a good man, and a fantastic activist."

Ricardo took her hand and shook it, smiling warmly.

"Go." he said.

Rhiannon turned and fled back to the others, indicating to them to retreat. As soon as they were out of view, the police officers began to move again, rushing back to the van to check the prisoner was still there. Several of them rushed after Rhiannon and her team, but they were long gone.

***

Louis and Iona sat in Iona's car, driving mindlessly through the city. Louis sat behind the wheel, and Iona sat next to him, quietly counting her fingers. Just when they thought they were a safe distance from Iona's apartment building, a motorcycle appeared in the rear-view mirror, and though he was now wearing a helmet and leather biker's jacket, it was clearly the same man from the rooftop.

"For the love of god!" Louis groaned. "How did he follow us?" He sped up, trying his best to overtake the few cars on the road, but it was hopeless. The motorcycle could weave in and out of the traffic, and Louis couldn't. As Louis tried his best to lose their stalker, his phone started ringing. Number withheld. He handed it to Iona.

"Answer it." he said.

"Who is this?" Iona said, putting the phone up to her ear.

"*A friend. You can call me Grey Hat.*" The voice was distorted, like something out of a movie. It was low and almost robotic. "*The people coming after you can track your phones, your tablets, any piece of smart technology you have. You need to ditch it all. I have a safe place you can go to, but they may be listening in, so all I can do is give you clues.*"

"Okay." Iona said, her voice shaking. She put the phone on speaker. "What are the clues?"

"*Go to where Jason was when he got the call that started all of this.*" Grey Hat said. "*Continue straight until you see a sight that might make the Gentle Giant and the Mysterious Woman*

300

angry. I will be waiting for you there. Do you understand?"
"I… I think so? Where Jason was when all this started? And a sight that… No I'm lost…" Iona said.

"*You'll have to figure it out. Ditch your phones. Stay ahead of the motorcycle. I'll deal with him. Good luck.*"

"The place where Jason was when he got the call that started all this?" Louis frowned. "What does that mean? The call from Grey Hat telling us you were going to be attacked?"

Iona's eyes widened.

"No!" she exclaimed. "I know what he means! Ditch the phones!"

Louis handed Iona his phone, and Iona threw them both out of the window. Louis winced.

"That was an expensive phone." he muttered.

"The place where Jason got the call! The National Science and Engineering Convention, at the Downtown Arena! That's where he got the call that his sister had been assaulted. That's when he decided to take the law into his own hands, which resulted in him meeting Alex and them becoming the first Fists of Justice!"

"Brilliant!" Louis said. "We're not far from there!"

He took a sharp left-hand turn at the next corner, and the motorcycle nearly toppled over attempting to make the maneuver. The next set of traffic lights turned amber as they approached, and Louis sped through, the lights conveniently turning red for the motorcycle, who sped through anyway, to the furious honks from the cars attempting to cross the junction. Louis managed to put a few hundred metres between them and the motorcycle, and just as the motorcycle sped up to catch them up, two police cars appeared, one from behind, one from in front, sirens blaring, cutting the motorcycle off. There was no doubt this was Grey Hats work, though Louis was impressed at how quickly he had managed to dispatch the police. It didn't matter whether their stalker was arrested: the distraction gave them enough time to fully lose him.

It took them ten minutes to reach the turn-off for the arena, and Louis indicated to come off the main road.

"No, keep going!" Iona said. "Grey Hat said to continue straight until we see a sight that would make you and

Rhiannon angry… What does that mean?"

"I have no idea." Louis continued on down the road. The main road led down and along the riverfront now, and they could see a massive courtyard that ran along outside the arena and along the riverbank, with steps that formed seats, and a big concrete square of flat ground, used for outside performances.

At the end of this area, there was a small, botanical garden, through which several statues could be seen, with intricate flowers and plants woven around their feet.

"Oh, there!" Louis exclaimed. "There's a statue of Robert Milligan on the other side of that garden! He was a major slave plantation owner in the 1800s, Rhiannon has been petitioning online to get it torn down for ages!"

"Well, let's go down there then!" Iona said.

Louis pulled off the main road and parked up in a side-road that led up to the riverfront. It was dark now, but the silhouette of a single figure, waiting by the statue, could be seen.

Iona and Louis got out of the car and wandered slowly over, both squinting to try and see the face of the person. They were wearing a white mask, and a hood that went over their head. Quite short, not at all the imposing figure that Louis had pictured.

"Are you Grey Hat?" Louis called.

The figure didn't answer. They just raised their arm and beckoned for Louis and Iona to approach.

***

Jason sat in the interrogation room of a police station on the other side of the city. Across the table from him, a man and a woman, both dressed in plain suits, with plain white shirts, and plain black ties, sat and stared at him. A file sat, unopened, in front of them.

"Mr Fox." the woman said. "It seems you've created quite a stir recently. I must admit, your gauntlets are quite impressive, and you and your team seem to have caused a lot of bother. Now, we know that Alex Axton is the one the media has been calling 'the Fist', but who are the other two vigilantes you've been working with? The Gentle Giant and the Mysterious Woman. Did you know they attacked an airport last night?"

302

Jason remained silent, forcing himself to make eye contact with the two people. He could not show weakness. He could not show emotion. He would not be broken.

"Mr Axton is clearly the muscle behind your little operation, so I guess that makes you the brains." the woman continued.

"You know, it won't take us long to get through the security on your smartphone, and then we'll have all the information we need, so you might as well talk, take this chance to make some sort of deal."

Jason glared intensely at the woman.

"We b-both know that if you t-try and get past the encryption on my phone, the failsafe will erase all the d-d-data and fry the phone and you'll be left with nothing." Jason said. "Besides, you need my consent or a warrant to access m-my phone."

The woman leant forwards and cocked her head to one side. Her colleague looked up from the file at Jason.

"Nervous, Mr Fox?" he said, with a smirk.

"I have a speech impediment, you j-jackass." Jason replied.

"Do you really think that after everything you've done, you'll be subject to the same standard procedure as any common crook?" the woman said, raising her eyebrows. "Do you think we are police?"

Jason fell silent, glancing down at his hands.

"You're likely to be prosecuted as a political terrorist." the woman said, leaning back in her seat. "I'd be surprised if the prosecution pushes for anything less than a life sentence for your friend, and as his co-conspirator, I imagine you'll receive similar. Luckily for you, you have something we want."

Jason looked up, his brow furrowing into a frown.

"I do?" he said.

"Indeed." the woman replied. "We have reason to believe that you've been in contact with a cyber-terrorist who goes by the name Grey Hat. Do you know who he is?"

Jason shook his head.

"I haven't g-got a clue what you're t-talking about." he said, though his expression betrayed him, and even he knew the lie wasn't convincing.

"Grey Hat is a cyber-terrorist that we've been tracking for some time now." the woman continued. "He's wanted by the

303

FBI, CIA, Interpol, MI6, and Europol. Almost three months ago, he killed Senator Andy Sanders, previously known as Andreas Sarkissan, the Armenian-American politician. You may have seen him on the news. He was involved in a scandal with several major international corporations, covering up some major breaches in international environmental law. Grey Hat tried to blackmail him into exposing the business owners and companies he was involved with, but ended up killing him. The only witness to the murder was Senator Sanders' daughter, Anna Sarkissan, who immediately went on the run to escape Grey Hat. A month ago she was spotted entering the UK, and she hasn't been seen since. We believe Grey Hat entered the UK trying to track her down so that he could get rid of the only witness to the murder. We do not have any pictures of Grey Hat, but this is Anna Sarkissan."

The man opened the file and pulled out a photo, sliding it across the table. The photo was of a young woman, probably a similar age to Jason, maybe a bit younger, with long, frizzy black hair. He couldn't believe it. It was her. She was even wearing the same leather jacket.

"That doesn't make any sense." Jason muttered.

It was the girl he and Alex had rescued in the alleyway, the night they had met. But that must mean that those men that were coming after her… They were sent by Grey Hat. Suddenly it all fell into place. Who else would have the resources that Grey Hat had, but a cyber-terrorist?

"Why would you think I would be working with a cyber t-terrorist?" Jason asked. "And why would a cyber-terrorist want to w-work with me?"

"Grey Hat doesn't usually kill." the woman said. "That's not his M.O. He leaks government secrets and blackmails people. Think Edward Snowden and Julian Assang, but much more ruthless. Opposing the system? Challenging the status quo? All the things you've been doing are exactly the kinds of causes Grey Hat likes to align himself with. But he takes it too far. If you were to help us catch him, we could make it so that you didn't serve any time… Scrub the records, make it look like you were never here."

"You really want to catch this guy, huh?" Jason said.

The two people stayed silent.

"So if, hypothetically, I were able to help you." Jason said. "I think we both know it would be worth a lot more than my freedom."

"You're not in a position to bargain, Mr Fox." the man said.

"I think I am." Jason said. "The police force in Downtown City? It needs some serious changes."

"That's not really the kind of deal we're authorised to make." the woman said. "We-"

Jason held up a hand to stop her.

"And Alex." he said. "The reason he attacked the police station is that he's been injected with an experimental drug that messed with his mental state."

"Yes, we are aware of the NanoVirus." the woman said. "Mr Axton is in Downtown Hospital right now. It appears the NanoVirus has healed some of his injuries, but his body is rejecting the serum and fighting back against it. His condition is unstable."

"You make sure he ends up in a hospital where he can receive the care he n-n-needs, not in a prison, and that he never has to appear in front of a court, then m-maybe we can talk about Grey Hat."

"That's not the offer on the table, Mr Fox." the woman said, starting to grow impatient. "Mr Axton hurt a lot of police officers."

"That wasn't him." Jason said. "He wasn't in control."

"Neither is any meth head or drug addict but they still have to stand trial for their actions." the woman pointed out. "So will he. We are offering you your freedom, in exchange for Grey Hat."

"Then the answer is no." Jason said. "I care more about Alex's safety than I do my own."

The woman sighed, and the man leant over to whisper something in her ear.

"Give us a minute." she said.

The two of them stood and exited the room. Jason sat back, his heart pounding, and waited. The seconds felt like hours, but in reality it was only a minute or so before they re-entered the room. The woman was holding Jason's phone. She slid it

305

across the table to him.

"You contact Grey Hat." she said. "Arrange a meeting. If we have Grey Hat in custody within twenty-four hours, your friend will not be charged, on the condition that he undergoes a psychiatric evaluation upon completion of his treatment. And another thing… Your release and freedom, and your friend not being charged, are contingent on one thing."

"What is it?" Jason asked.

"Your technology. We want it. If you agree to work with us, creating weapons like the ones you and your friends have been using, we will make sure your friend never has to stand trial." Jason thought for a second, rubbing his chin in contemplation.

"Who even are you?" he asked. "Who would I be providing my weapons to? The police? MI5? MI6?"

"We work for the government." the woman said. "That's all you need to know."

"I'll need to know a lot more if I'll be working with you." Jason said. "Do you have names?"

"You can call me Agent Sparrow. This is my partner, Agent Stoat." the woman said. "So, do we have a deal, Mr Fox?" Jason shrugged.

"I guess so." he said.

***

Zakirah stood on the doorstep of Amir's house, her heart racing. It had been a month since she had been taken. Did they know what had happened? Would they even welcome her back?

It didn't matter. She had nowhere else to go, and her heart had felt empty ever since she left their home.

She knocked on the door.

It took a minute or two, but eventually the door slid slowly open, and Zakirah was greeted with the bewildered face of Saabira. The old woman had her coat on, and was carrying a bag. Her eyes widened, and she threw her hands up over her mouth.

"Zakirah?" she exclaimed. "We thought you were gone forever! We never stopped looking for you! When we saw you at the Airport, in front of all those cameras, we feared the

306

worst!"

"The police dragged me away after the protest." Zakirah said, her eyes tearing up. "They tried to deport me but I got away. I've missed you so much. Where is Amir?"

"Oh." Saabira's expression darkened. "I'm sorry, my dear. Of course, you don't know yet."

Zakirah's heart missed a beat.

"Know what?" she asked.

"Last night, when we got back to the city, Amir wanted to pray. We went to the mosque. Someone was inside, there was smoke pouring out. I tried to talk him out of it, but Amir went inside, alone. He tried to stop them. He tried to put the fire out all by himself." Saabira choked, struggling to force the words out.

"He's not…" Zakirah couldn't bring herself to say it.

Saabira shook her head.

"No." she said. "He's alive, the firefighters got there just in time. But he's in a coma. I just got back from the hospital a minute ago. I haven't even had the chance to put my bag down yet."

Zakirah's heart felt like it had just had a hole punched right through it.

"I'm sorry." she sobbed, grabbing Saabira and pulling her into an embrace. "I should have been here. I should have been here to help him."

"There's nothing you could have done. Come inside, let's get you a drink and something to eat. You must be so tired."

Saabira ushered Zakirah into the house, and the two women headed through to the kitchen, drying their tears. Internally, Zakirah made a vow to get revenge.

She didn't know how, or when, but she was going to make sure Johnny Johnson paid. When she was done, he would never hurt anyone, ever again.

***

Jason rolled into the car park behind the hotel, uncertain of what he was about to do. At the entrance to his garage, Rhiannon was standing, frantically texting on her phone. She saw him approach, and rushed over to him.

"*Stay on task, Mr Fox.*" The earpiece in Jason's ear sent the voice of Agent Sparrow ringing through his head. "*We're watching you.*"

"Jason!" she exclaimed. "I've been texting and calling like crazy! Louis isn't answering his phone, and he hasn't come home yet. What's going on?"

"Louis didn't come home?" Jason's heart started to race. If Louis didn't come home, perhaps he failed in rescuing Iona. *No, calm down.* He told himself. *You told him to go somewhere safe. He probably just got rid of his phone so he couldn't be tracked.*

"I thought he was with you, what happened?" Rhiannon asked.

"It's okay, Rhiannon, calm down." Jason said, in the most soothing tone he could manage. "Iona was in danger so he went to help her. You should just g-g-go home, I'll find them."

"Like hell!" Rhiannon snorted. "If you're going to find my boyfriend, I'm coming with you."

"*Take her along. Just get back on task.*"

"Right, okay." Jason said.

He headed to his garage.

"They're with Grey Hat." he said. "I'm just going to contact Grey Hat to meet us here."

Jason unlocked the garage door and slid it upwards. Inside, his laptop screen lay dark. Rhiannon walked in behind him, and Jason reached to switch the laptop on. Before he could even reach the power button, the screen lit up. Slowly, as had happened before, words began to appear on the screen, as if some invisible person were typing.

'**JASON. I KNOW WHAT THEY TOLD YOU. IT IS A LIE. MEET ME, AND I WILL EXPLAIN.**'

Jason winced as the earpiece buzzed with static.

"Mr Fox …. Is happening…. We….. interference…." The voice of Agent Sparrow was distorted and disrupted with static. And then, she was gone.

'**I HAVE TEMPORARILY DISRUPTED THEIR COMMUNICATIONS. IN THE TOP DRAWER OF YOUR DESK YOU WILL FIND A PHONE. TAKE IT, AND GO TO THE COORDINATES PROGRAMMED INTO THE MAP. LEAVE YOUR PHONES HERE. I**

WILL DEAL WITH THE AGENTS. TRUST ME.'

"What's he talking about?" Rhiannon frowned. "What agents?"

"I'll explain later, we have to go now." Jason said, opening the drawer and pulling out the phone. "Have you got your car?" He took his phone out of his pocket and left it in the drawer. Then, he pulled out the earpiece he was wearing, and the wire that the agents had taped to his chest, and put them down too.

"No, Louis had -" Rhiannon stopped, spotting her and Louis' car parked in the car park, right next to the garage.

"Right, let's go." Jason said. "Quickly. Leave your phone." Rhiannon put her phone with Jason's and took out her keys, unlocking the car as Jason locked the garage. She then helped Jason fold his wheelchair and lift it into the back.

They hit the road as quickly as possible, and it seemed like every traffic light was working with them, turning green at just the right second. Jason typed the coordinates in on the new burner phone, and they led them to the outskirts of the city, soon heading out onto the motorway. They passed a massive electronic billboard with an advertisement for coffee on it, but as the car drew closer the advertisement flickered and disappeared, and a message appeared on the screen, only for about fifteen seconds.

'DITCH THE PHONE. TAKE THE NEXT EXIT, THEN TURN RIGHT.'

"Did you see that?" Jason asked.

"Yeah." Rhiannon said, handing Jason the phone that had been directing them so far.

Jason opened the window and threw out the phone, and Rhiannon turned the car off at the next junction. They were led off the motorway, onto a main road which circled round the outskirts of the city. Rhiannon took the next turning right, which took them down a back road, through a much more green and empty area. At the end of the road was a petrol station, with an electronic sign outside displaying the prices. The sign flickered, and for a moment was just replaced with the words '**TURN LEFT**'.

"There's another one!" Jason said. "Turn left."

Rhiannon turned the car off down a single track road littered with potholes. The road didn't go on for long, and eventually they hit a dead end, where the car was blocked by a locked fence, and the road turned into a footpath, through the woods.

"What now?" Rhiannon asked.

Jason shrugged.

"Maybe we took a wrong turn." Rhiannon said.

"Let's have a look around." Jason replied.

Rhiannon parked up the car just off the side of the road, in a tiny layby next to the fence, and they got out. Jason limped over to the little gate onto the footpath. There was a sign on the gate 'public footpath' and an arrow pointing down the forest path. Underneath the sign, someone had written with a marker pen 'Jason'.

"Look, here!" Jason exclaimed, beckoning Rhiannon over. "This way!"

Rhiannon sighed.

"Can your wheelchair manage that path?" she asked.

Jason peered over the gate at the unsteady path, filled with roots and rocks jutting out of the soil.

"Unlikely." he said. "I'll have to walk."

Rhiannon opened the back of the car and pulled out her gauntlets and goggles. She put the goggles on her head, and clicked her fingers, and a light shone out the front of one of the gauntlets. She locked up the car and opened the gate, and Jason hobbled through. His eyes scanned the forest floor for a stick, and he found one about walking stick length and bent over to pick it up, groaning as his back and knees bent.

The stick supported his weight somewhat, and he followed Rhiannon off down the forest path. They walked for a good fifteen minutes, and even though Rhiannon's gauntlet lit up the path, the darkness of night had still settled in and every so often they tripped or stumbled, cursing the darkness.

Eventually they hit a point where the path split in two. Signs on a post denoted the different footpaths. One led back towards the city, one led out across the countryside. The one that led back to the city went through the forest. The other one led across a field. Again, the word 'Jason' was scrawled across one of the signs, this time the one heading across the fields.

"We better be close, I'm getting tired of this cat and mouse game." Rhiannon grumbled.

"At least you can walk." Jason replied, leaning heavily against his stick.

The duo headed out across the field, eventually coming to a fence surrounding the back garden of a mansion. There was no gate in the fence, and the footpath actually led away from the mansion, but Rhiannon's gauntlet illuminated a figure standing in the garden, waiting.

"Rhiannon!" the figure called out. "Jason!"

"Oh my god, it's Louis!" Rhiannon exclaimed.

She scrambled over the low fence and ran over to Louis, grabbing him in a tight embrace and planting her lips on his.

"I was so worried about you!" she exclaimed.

"I was worried about you too, babe!" Louis replied. "Come on, Grey Hat and Iona are inside."

"A little help here!" Jason called, trying his best to clamber over the fence.

Louis rushed over and lifted Jason over with ease.

"Put your arm around me, I'll help you." Louis said.

Jason draped an arm around the gentle giant, and together they walked towards the mansion. On closer inspection, the great house looked to be completely abandoned. All of the windows were boarded up, there was graffiti all over the outer walls, rubbish strewn all across the garden, and there were 'KEEP OUT' signs everywhere. Louis led them to the back door, which had been forced open, and they stepped into the house. The door led into a kitchen, which was in total darkness and disrepair. The doors hung off the cupboards, which were bare, and most of the furniture was missing. Rats could be heard scuttering about behind the walls and beneath the floors.

Louis led them through into a corridor, and immediately they could see one room that was lit up. The front room. Unlike the other rooms, this room was partially furnished, with an old sofa covered in blankets, and shelves filled with canned food. There was a camping stove where you would expect a TV to be, and a portable heater, and a row of car batteries like in Jason's garage. There was a desk, with a laptop, and wireless network router, and a wire that led up to the light which lit up the room.

Iona was lying on the sofa, clutching the blankets around

311

herself, deeply asleep. But at the laptop sat a short figure, a hood over their head, facing away.

"Grey Hat?" Jason said. "We've g-got a lot to t-talk about."

"Yes, we do." the person said.

Their voice wasn't that of a man, it was a woman: American, with a twist of Armenian. Grey Hat turned around, and immediately everything Agent Sparrow had told Jason was flipped on its head.

Grey Hat wasn't trying to kill Anna Sarkissan. Grey Hat *was* Anna Sarkissan.

"I… I don't understand." Jason stammered.

"Let me guess? They told you I was an evil cyber-terrorist? That I killed my father and was on the run?" she said.

"Yeah." Jason replied.

"Well, that's half right." she said. "I am on the run. But I didn't kill my dad. Take a seat, and I'll explain everything."

Jason breathed a sigh of relief, and sat on the massive sofa at Iona's feet. Anna turned her chair around to face him.

"When my father became a politician, he made it his duty to take on corrupt corporations and hold them accountable for their actions, and to try and stop them from destroying the planet with fracking, overfarming, reckless oil spills in the ocean, to stop the exploitation of workers in the third world, sweatshops and child labour, and to hold them accountable for their tax evasion and constant twisting of the media to lie to people. But he got on the wrong side of the wrong people, and he uncovered some dirt on some very powerful politicians. He threatened to expose them, and they had him killed for it. I saw the whole thing, and they would have killed me too if I hadn't run. Luckily for me, I'm a computer programmer who has studied hacking all my life. They concocted this lie of a terrorist blackmailing and killing my dad so they could cover their own asses. The only thing I don't know is which of the people my dad was trying to take on had him killed. And every time I try to settle down long enough to find the information I need to identify and expose them, they find me and I have to go on the run again." She let out a tired sigh, putting her head in her hands. "I kept an eye on you and Alex after you saved me from their bounty hunters in that alleyway. It didn't take

312

me long to figure out that I needed help, and I didn't know where else to go but you guys. I hoped if I helped you for long enough, maybe you would help me."

Jason took a moment to process everything. The person he thought was a dangerous, powerful cyber-terrorist and murderer, was actually just a scared young girl, barely out of her teen years yet.

"Well." Jason said. "I suppose this is what I got into this for. To stand up to villains, and make the world a better place."

Anna lifted her head up and fixed Jason with a long stare. "Really?" she said.

"I'm in too." Rhiannon said. "If we don't take a stand against corruption, what even is the point?"

"Well, they don't call us the Fists of Justice for nothing." Louis grinned.

***

"What were you thinking, Johnny?!" "Huey-" "I thought we talked about this, I thought we agreed!" "Huey, listen-" "and to then go and burn down the mosque, after everything-" "HUEY!"

Johnny grabbed hold of both of his brother's shoulders and shook him.

"It wasn't me."

Huey frowned.

"But I thought… When I saw the news, that the mosque was burned down, I assumed…"

Johnny shrugged.

"I don't know who it was, perhaps some of my boys, hyped up after beating the Bridge Boys. But it wasn't me, the order didn't come from me. I've been thinking, and you were right. What with these vigilantes running round, those Fists of Justice… The way to take them down is not with violence. Knock one down, two more show up, and the public love them. We've got to change that. Make the people hate them. This is a political fight, like you were saying all along."

"Huh." Huey took off his glasses and started to rub them clean with his shirt. "Well, I'm glad you're coming over to my way of thinking."

313

"I need your help, bruv. I need you by my side for this. I got big plans for next year, but I can't do it without you."

"Okay…" Huey said, hesitantly. "Let's grab a beer and you can talk me through it."

"You not got the kids?" Johnny asked.

"Nah, they're with Linda, it's all good." Huey said. "I'm all yours. Tell me what you're thinking."

**

It was the early hours of the morning by the time Jason rolled back into the car park behind the hotel, and though the street lights lit up the street, night still formed a blanket over the city. Agents Sparrow and Stoat were on him in seconds, appearing out of nowhere as Jason approached the back door to the hotel.

"What the hell happened?" Agent Sparrow exclaimed, red in the face, her voice full of frustration. "You were supposed to lead us to Grey Hat."

Jason wheeled his chair around to face them, scowling at the two agents.

"Our deal was that I help you track down the cyber-terrorist that killed a US senator and was hunting down his daughter. NOT, that I help you hunt down an innocent girl!" he exclaimed, staring daggers at the two agents.

Agent Sparrow frowned.

"What are you talking about?" she said. "We told you who Grey Hat was. We've been on his trail for months-"

"Don't treat me like a moron!" Jason interrupted. "Don't act like you don't know that Grey Hat *is* Anna Sarkissan! You tried to trick me!"

The two agents shared a look, and their eyes widened.

"If Grey Hat is the girl, that means we've been manipulated." Agent Stoat muttered to Agent Sparrow, just loud enough that Jason could make out the words.

"That means our agency is compromised." Agent Sparrow replied. "We need to get out of here."

The two agents turned and ran across the car park without another word.

"Hey!" Jason called after them. "What about our deal?!"

But they were gone, and Jason didn't feel like he was going to get anything more out of them.

He sighed and headed back into his bedsit.

After everything that had happened the past few days, going to bed just felt… Weird.

After a night of much needed sleep, Jason headed into the hospital and found his way to the room where Alex was being kept. Two police officers stood, guarding the door. One of them was Officer Parker.

"Jason!" she exclaimed, as he approached. "I heard you made some sort of deal for your release. Between you and me, I don't think they'd have been able to charge you with anything."

"Is he allowed visitors?" Jason asked.

"You can go in, but I'll have to stay in the room with you." Sabrina said. "Sorry."

Jason nodded, and Sabrina opened the door and let him roll in, following him and hovering in the doorway.

Alex was lying in the hospital bed, his hands cuffed to the metal bars running down the length of either side of the bed. Some of his wounds had healed, but he was still slightly battered and bruised, and looking incredibly pale. He turned his head as Jason entered and forced a weak smile.

"Jason, is that you?" he croaked. "I'm very high on painkillers right now."

"Yeah, it's me buddy." Jason said, rolling up to the side of the bed. "How are you doing?"

"Not so great, mate." Alex replied, his voice weak. "My body seems to be rejecting the NanoVirus. The doctors are trying to work out some way to extract it from my system, but it'll take some time." He took in a deep, raspy breath. "I'm really sorry, Jason. I thought I was doing the right thing."

"I g-get it." Jason muttered. "It's okay."

"I don't think I'm cut out for this hero business." Alex said. "After I was kicked out of the army, I felt so lost. And then you came along, and I felt like I had a second chance to help people, but I just messed it up again… I think maybe I need to find some other way to help the world. Something that doesn't

315

involve getting into fights and beating people up."

Jason nodded.

"Whatever you think is best." he said. "I'll be here for you, whatever you decide, and whatever happens. We don't have to be partners to be friends."

"Well, I suppose it doesn't matter now." Alex replied. "I imagine I'm going to be locked up for a while now."

Jason placed his hand on top of Alex's and squeezed it, comfortingly.

"Don't give up just yet." Jason said. "You've got a g-g-good defence. Now that the d-doctors have confirmed that your behaviour was down to the NanoVirus, we should be able to get you a reduced sentence."

"I'm not just going to blame it on the NanoVirus, Jason." Alex said. "I was angry. I wanted to make those cops pay for everything they'd done. Sure, the NanoVirus might have given me the push I needed to act, but I'd been angry for a long time. It was always going to come out eventually. There is one plus side."

"What's that?" Jason asked.

"I think the NanoVirus cured my hearing impairment." Alex grinned. "Every cloud, eh."

Jason let out a tiny chuckle.

"That's the spirit." he muttered.

***

Far away, in a meeting room in the back of an unassuming office, where normal officer clerks and administrative assistants would usually be working, though now the entire office was empty, a woman sat, clicking her pen and staring across the table with an intense look in her eyes. A soldier, of Maori descent, dressed in black kevlar, sat across the table, silently waiting for a response.

"Mrs Crawford? Do you want me to go after the doctor again? I'll need more men." he said, repeating what he had already asked.

"No." the woman finally said. "No... If she's got Grey Hat and these Fists of Justice on her side, it's not worth the risk. Grey Hat has eluded us for a long time now, and that was when she was working alone. These Fists of Justice are an enemy we don't know. Especially the Gentle Giant… He's definitely been injected with the NanoVirus. No. If we are going to face this foe, we need to learn more about them. Besides, their weapons and technology are impressive. They may be of more use to us alive."

"You want me to surveil them, then?" the man asked. "That's not really… my skill set."

"No, I have someone for that kind of job." Mrs Crawford said. "But the agents we sent to interrogate Jason Fox have gone AWOL. Track them down. Find out what happened to them. Find out why they ran."

"My pleasure." the man replied, turning to leave. He stopped, halting in the doorway. "If you're going to be experimenting with that NanoVirus, I would like to put myself forwards as a test subject. If it can give me even half of the strength that black guy has, I could be unstoppable."

"I will take that under advisement. You are dismissed." the woman said.

The man nodded and exited, leaving the woman alone. She clicked her pen again, letting out a long sigh. As soon as the man was out of sight, she slumped into her chair, her rigid demeanour fading and exhaustion setting in over her.

"This business is going to be the death of me." she muttered. And then she gathered up her things to leave, and the office became just another unassuming, entirely usual office once more.

***

When Jason arrived back at his bedsit, he found himself texting Anna. There was something he wished he had done a long time ago.

'Grey Hat, can you access a file from the British Armed Forces?'

It took a minute, but by the time Jason was settled by his desk, next to his bed, his laptop open, he had his reply.

'WHAT'S THE FILE?'

'Alex Axton's military service record and discharge papers.'

'GIVE ME A MINUTE.'

317

It was a good couple of minutes later, but Jason's phone eventually buzzed with the response.

'**THIS FILE IS HEAVILY REDACTED. IT WILL TAKE A LITTLE WHILE FOR ME TO ACCESS THE REDACTED INFORMATION**'.

Ten minutes later, a file opened on Jason's computer. Jason found himself scrolling through until he found the final few reports and the discharge papers.

'*Reason for dismissal from service: Private Axton ignored a direct order in a combat situation. Axton refused to fire on enemy combatants during a firefight, which resulted in several soldiers being wounded, and the unit was forced to retreat. When questioned on why he had disobeyed orders and laid down his arms, Private Axton's only response was to cite the age of the enemy combatants. Axton went on the record saying "they were just kids. They didn't look older than fourteen. I couldn't do it. I just couldn't. I'd rather turn my gun on myself than shoot a bunch of kids." Discharge effective immediately.*'

Jason sat back in his chair, letting out a deep sigh. He knew that certain terror groups were known for using child soldiers, but this just made it so much more real. No wonder Alex was so broken.

As well as the horror over what he had read, Jason felt another feeling rising up inside: Pride.

He didn't care what Alex said. That man was still a hero to him.

On the desk, Jason's phone rang. It was Sarah.

Taking in a deep breath, Jason picked up the phone. It was time.

"Hey sis... Listen, there's something I need to tell you."

END OF BOOK ONE.

CALL TO ACTION

We all like to think that if we got superpowers, we would become superheroes: that we would do the right thing and make the world a better place, and stand up against injustice, and that the only thing holding us back is, well, that we don't have superpowers. Our own mortality and vulnerability keeps us at bay.

But that's not the case. Not if we're honest with ourselves. Every comic book and every superhero film or TV show out there tells us that it's not the powers that make the hero. Iron Man still fights for what's right, with or without the suit. Steve Rogers stood up against bullies and did his best to protect people before he became Captain America. Superman still fights back even when Kryptonite weakens him, the Flash still makes a stand even when he loses his speed. These heroes don't only make a stand when there is no risk.

We are presented with opportunities to be heroes every single day, and unfortunately although *most* of us are physically and mentally able, most of us still don't. So this is a call to action: If you were inspired by the characters in this book, then take a stand for what you believe in too. I guarantee that your area will have homeless outreach groups, Black Lives Matter protests, Extinction Rebellion or other climate action groups, PRIDE events, Animal Rights organisations like the Hunt Saboteurs or outreach groups. Nationally, you'll be able to find refugee action groups, or charities that help struggling people in the third world.

One of the most famous quotes about activism is "stand for something, or you'll fall for anything", but for a lot of us that's not the case. For those of us that are privileged, in the western world, with a job and the means to get by, if we don't stand for something, the likelihood is that we'll be fine. We won't fall if we don't stand. But every day we have the chance to make a difference, even in a little way. And it's so saddening that we will rush to the cinemas to watch rich celebrities pretend to be heroes when we could go and and **BE** heroes. It's not all about fighting villains and exciting action. It's about always doing what you can to make the world a better place. We all have causes we care about, but do we all stand up for them, even when we're not forced to by circumstance?

I know so many people who like to think if they saw a woman being assaulted, or a homeless person being bullied, or a dog being tortured, they would step in and do something. But day by day, we all watch people walk by the homeless person on the street, or file into McDonalds for a cheap burger, and social media is filled with people ignoring the cries for help from everyone who has ever said "#metoo", or scoffing when someone shares actual proof that a product that they don't need, or an action they are needlessly contributing to, is having a profound and significant negative impact on the climate. We can all do better. We need to do better.

And to those of you who **DO** take part in protests, or in outreach programmes, or any other form of activism, thank you, from the bottom of my heart. You are all my heroes. And you are the reason this book exists.

CHAPTER ONE: ANIMAL LIBERATOR

Louis and Rhiannon stood outside a giant stone building, five storeys high. They were on the outskirts of Oxbridge City, looking up at the gates to one of the biggest laboratories in the country. Oxbridge was located in the Midlands of England, two hours away from Downtown, and was a much more rural city. In the centre of the city there was a castle, and the walls of the castle stretched out through various portions of the city centre. Rather than brick, the majority of the city was hewn out of stone, and a lot of the buildings were the same buildings that had been there for centuries.

It was a lovely summer evening, one year since they had started working with Grey Hat, and they had finally tracked down the laboratory that had taken over Iona's work. It had taken them weeks to come up with a plan for getting in that they were all comfortable with, but finally they stood outside, ready and waiting. Louis wore his simple black bandanna over the lower part of his face, and around each of his knuckles he had wrapped a red piece of cloth. He wore an unassuming hoodie and jeans, doing his best not to stand out. Rhiannon, on the other hand, was clad in a kevlar vest, her metal boots and gauntlets glowing with a pale yellow light, with a balaclava and her massive goggles covering her face, with not a single item of clothing giving any clue as to who she really was. She looked like something dragged out of a steampunk novel.

"The gate is open." Louis pointed out. "Have you already cut the power?"

"*Someone else already cut the power.*" Anna's voice came through his earpiece. "*It seems someone else is breaking in.*"

"Well, we've been planning this for weeks, can't turn back now." Rhiannon said, and she walked through the gate and up towards the front entrance.

Just in front of the door, there was a big plastic sign with a map of the labs. At the top, it had a logo showing a blue butterfly, with 'MBN INC.' in big letters underneath it.

"What's MBN Inc.?" Louis asked.

"*Microbiology and Nanotechnology Incorporated. They're a research corporation owned by Illumination Industries, which in turn is owned by the Freeman Group.*" Anna replied.

"*They're one of the companies my dad was trying to expose. They've got significant political lobbying power, and seem to have more resources than any other corporation in the world. Head up to the third floor.*"

Louis and Rhiannon headed for the stairs and climbed up to the third floor. They met surprisingly little resistance: not a single locked door or security guard. It was almost as if someone had already cleared the way for them.

The third floor opened up into a long corridor of different laboratories, each with long windows that allowed you to look inside. Each room was filled with cages containing various different animals: first rats and mice, and guinea pigs, then dogs, then birds, then monkeys, even reptiles and insects, and one room filled with tanks of various different fish. Each species was crammed into cages that only just seemed to fit them, each animal looked malnourished and exhausted, each with a sad look in their eyes.

"This is horrible." Rhiannon breathed. "Why would they do this?"

"*Animal testing. Oxbridge is infamous for their animal testing facilities. That must be why they've chosen to set up here.*" Anna said.

"Look, Rhi, there's someone in this one!" Louis whispered, pointing over to a room with an open door.

Rhiannon crept over and peered in the door. Inside, a woman dressed in black, wearing a scarf around her face, was knelt down by one of the cages. The cages in this room contained small primates, with a mixture of white, grey and brown fur. On the door, there was a sign that read 'LAB 3.07: COMMON SQUIRREL MONKEYS'.

"Don't worry little fellas, it's going to be okay." the woman was saying, taking pictures of the monkeys. "I'm going to get as many of you out of here as I can, but first I need to take some pictures, so we can show the world the disgusting things they're doing to you, okay? Okay."

As the woman continued to take pictures, a door at the other end of the room opened, and several security guards rushed in.

"Retreat!" Rhiannon hissed, pushing Louis into one of the rooms across the hall.

"You there!" one of the guards yelled, pulling out his sidearm and aiming it at the woman.

It was a handgun. What were security guards at a lab doing with handguns?

Rhiannon and Louis watched through the window as the woman pushed a table across the room and into the security guards, knocking them off balance, and sprinted for the door that Rhiannon and Louis had been behind moments before. The guards followed her as she rushed into the corridor and threw herself into another room, slamming the door shut behind her. The security guards followed, smashing through the door.

Rhiannon and Louis rushed back into the corridor and crept towards the room they had all rushed into, hoping for a better look.

The woman was backed into the corner of a large room filled with tall, cylindrical tanks, the security guards all aiming their guns at her. The tanks weren't full of fish, but instead full of a pale blue liquid. Rhiannon recognised it immediately: it was the same colour as the NanoVirus serum that Louis had been injected with.

"Freeze!" one of the security guards yelled, and the woman dived behind one of the cylindrical tanks. The security guards opened fire, but instead of hitting the woman, they hit one of the tanks. The bullet went straight through, cracking the glass, and the entire tank shattered, sending the NanoVirus serum everywhere. It soaked the activist and poured across the floor.

The activist woman clambered to her feet and broke into a run, ducking behind the other tanks as cover, and one of the security guards shot at her again and again, shattering one of the other tanks.

"Derek, stop!" one of the other guards yelled, forcing him to lower the gun. "You're damaging the tanks!"

It didn't matter. One of the bullets had already hit the woman, and she slumped against the wall, letting out an agonising moan.

"They're going to kill her!" Rhiannon whispered to Louis. "We've got to stop them!"

"We don't even know who she is!" Louis pointed out.

"It doesn't matter!"

Rhiannon ran to the entrance of the room bringing her gauntlets together and clapping them hard in front of her. There was a mighty sonic boom, and a sound wave rippled from her body, throwing the security guards across the room. That's not all it did though: the sonic blast also cracked the remaining six or seven giant cylindrical tanks.

"Crap." Rhiannon muttered.

"Get out of here!" one of the security guards yelled, scrambling to his feet and pulling one of his colleagues out of the room. The other followed quickly.

The tanks all shattered, and the liquid serum containing the NanoVirus flooded across the floor. Rhiannon jumped back out of the doorway, but the woman who had been shot was now thoroughly bathed in the stuff, and it had soaked through all her clothes and left her completely drenched

"*Guys, get out of there!*" It was Iona's voice this time. "*You've been made, it's not worth the risk!*"

"Louis, carry her." Rhiannon said, pointing to the injured woman, lying on the ground.

Louis rushed forward and did what he was told, lifting the woman up in his arms. Rhiannon led the way, and they rushed down the stairs and out of the front of the building.

A white van pulled up in front of the laboratories, and the back opened, revealing Anna in the back. Louis and Rhiannon sprinted up to the vehicle, loading the woman into the back and jumping in after her.

"Iona, drive!" Rhiannon yelled, and Anna pulled the doors closed.

The van sped away, and Louis and Rhiannon leaned in to check the woman, who was lying on the floor of the van, not moving. Rhiannon checked for a pulse, but there wasn't one. "Starting CPR." she said, pumping down on the woman's chest, then going to give her mouth to mouth. One breath into the woman's mouth, and she came spluttering back to life, coughing up a lungful of the NanoVirus serum. As soon as she was breathing again, her body started to spasm, and Louis had to hold her to keep her from throwing herself around the floor of the van. Not only was her body shaking, but her skin seemed to be shifting, as if countless tiny creatures were moving beneath the surface, and changing shade: one minute blue, the next green, then brown. Bits of fur started to burst up on her arms and neck, then scales, then fur again, her body constantly shifting.

"What's happening to her?" Anna asked.

"They had these massive tanks full of what looked like the NanoVirus." Louis said. "The tanks all cracked and she got absolutely soaked in it, looks like she swallowed a lot of it."

"Oh crap." Iona muttered. "What animals did they have in those labs?"

"All sorts." Rhiannon replied. "Mice, dogs, lizards, fish, monkeys. And that was just one corridor."

"That's not good." Iona said, turning the corner and driving the van towards the motorway.

"What?" Louis asked.

"The nanotechnology within the serum is basically a whole load of microscopic robots designed to function like microscopic life-forms, except specifically programmed to aid the body." Iona said. "They have some degree of artificial intelligence, but the reason that I had to prime them before injecting Louis and myself and Alex with the NanoVirus, is because they need a starting point: they need basic information about the subject they're being injected into: be it their species, their gender, their blood type. The more information they have, the better they can aid that person's healing and enhance their physiological attributes."

"What are you saying?" Rhiannon asked.

"If that was the NanoVirus, and it was primed to be injected into specific different species, there's no telling what it will do when it gets into a human host." Iona said. "We need to get her back to our lab, as soon as possible, otherwise the NanoVirus could cause permanent mutations, and even I can't predict what it will do to her."

...

Chapter continued in book two

THE NIGHTLIGHT NOVELLAS

The Fists of Justice is the second in a series of novels, novellas and short stories that I have been working on called 'the Nightlight Novellas'. The Nightlight Novellas are all separate texts existing in separate universes, which share common themes: promoting social justice, striving for diversity within their naratives (including more people of colour and LGBTQ+ characters) and pushing myself as a writer to break free of the cliches and stereotpes of any given genre.

The first book in 'the Nightlight Novellas' was called *The Slope* and is available on the Amazon Bookstore as an e-book. The Slope is a fantasy fiction novel suitable for all ages (though realistically at a reading age of 11+). Tonally, it's very different to Fists of Justice, but I hope you will enjoy it none-the-less.

Fists of Justice 2 will hopefully be released some time next year (we will see). Follow my social media pages for more updates about that. I really hope you enjoyed, and thank you so much for choosing to read my work!

FISTS OF JUSTICE ROLEPLAYING GAME

Feel like you need more? Think you'd enjoy getting wrapped up in the world of 'Fists of Justice'? Well, you're in luck! As it so happens, I created a roleplaying game set in the future of the Fists of Justice world, with the help of my friend Peter Hamilton, a talented artist who worked tirelessly to design the characters and artwork for the RPG.

The Fists of Justice RPG is designed to help people learn how to take a stand for the causes they believe in, but it doesn't have to be used that way: You can just use it to have a bit of fun with your mates! It's a very basic Roleplay game, so if you've never played an RPG before, this is a great one to start with, as it doesn't have as many intricate details to get your head around as games like Dungeons & Dragons. At the time of writing this, the 'Fists of Justice' game is still in it's BETA form, and is not completed, but it is available completely for free online! So check out my social media pages for more information about that!

That's all from me folks, all the best

Zachary Coleman

www.facebook.com/ZacharyDavidColeman
www.instagram.com/ZacharyDavidColeman
www.twitter.com/ZacharyDColeman
www.youtube.com/c/ZacharyDavidColeman